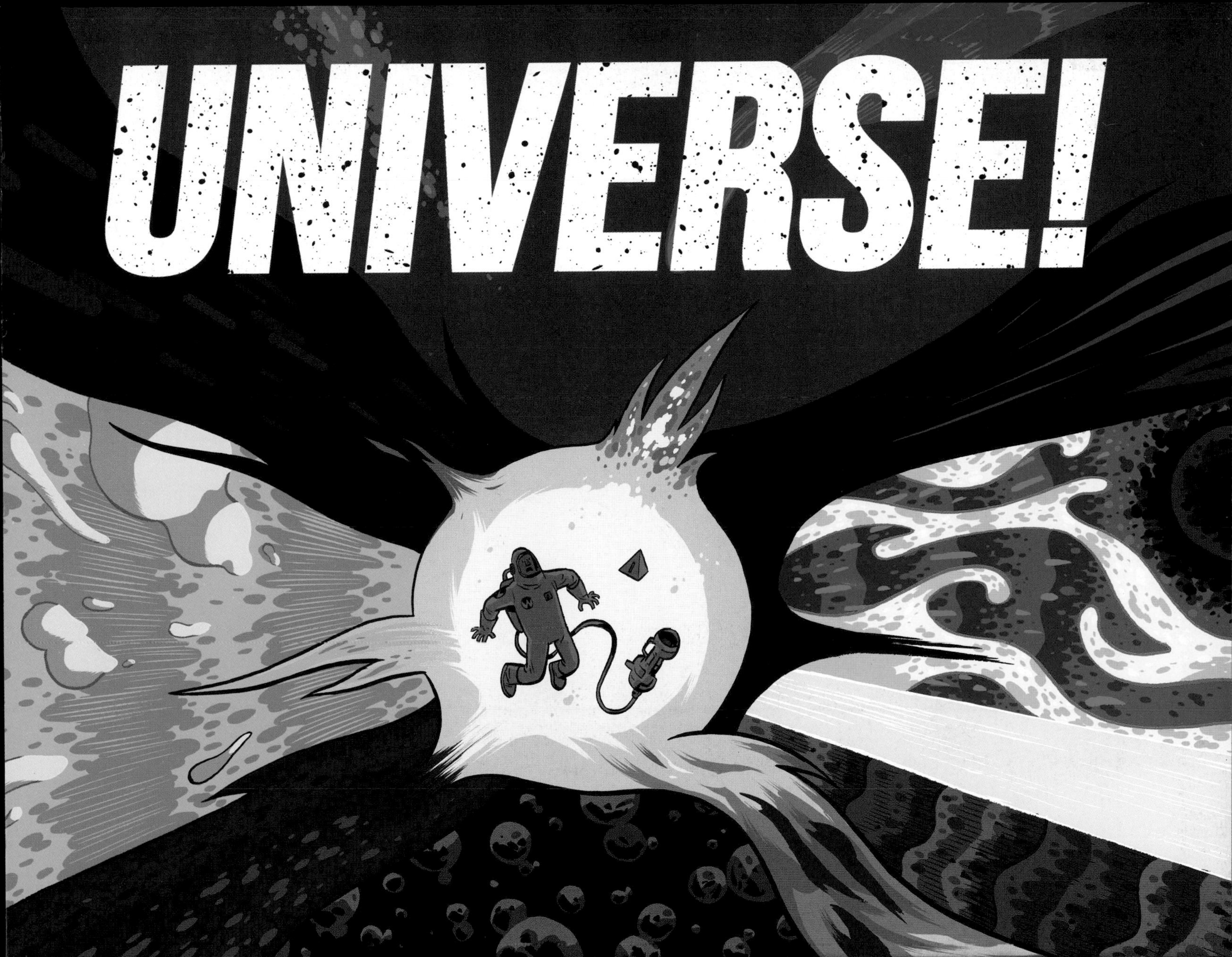
UNIVERSE!

IMAGE COMICS, INC. • **Todd McFarlane:** President • **Jim Valentino:** Vice President • **Marc Silvestri:** Chief Executive Officer • **Erik Larsen:** Chief Financial Officer • **Robert Kirkman:** Chief Operating Officer • **Eric Stephenson:** Publisher / Chief Creative Officer • **Shanna Matuszak:** Editorial Coordinator • **Marla Eizik:** Talent Liaison • **Nicole Lapalme:** Controller • **Leanna Caunter:** Accounting Analyst • **Sue Korpela:** Accounting & HR Manager • **Jeff Boison:** Director of Sales & Publishing Planning • **Dirk Wood:** Director of International Sales & Licensing • **Alex Cox:** Director of Direct Market & Speciality Sales • **Chloe Ramos-Peterson:** Book Market & Library Sales Manager • **Emilio Bautista:** Digital Sales Coordinator • **Kat Salazar:** Director of PR & Marketing • **Drew Fitzgerald:** Marketing Content Associate • **Heather Doornink:** Production Director • **Drew Gill:** Art Director • **Hilary DiLoreto:** Print Manager • **Tricia Ramos:** Traffic Manager • **Erika Schnatz:** Senior Production Artist • **Ryan Brewer:** Production Artist • **Deanna Phelps:** Production Artist • IMAGECOMICS.COM

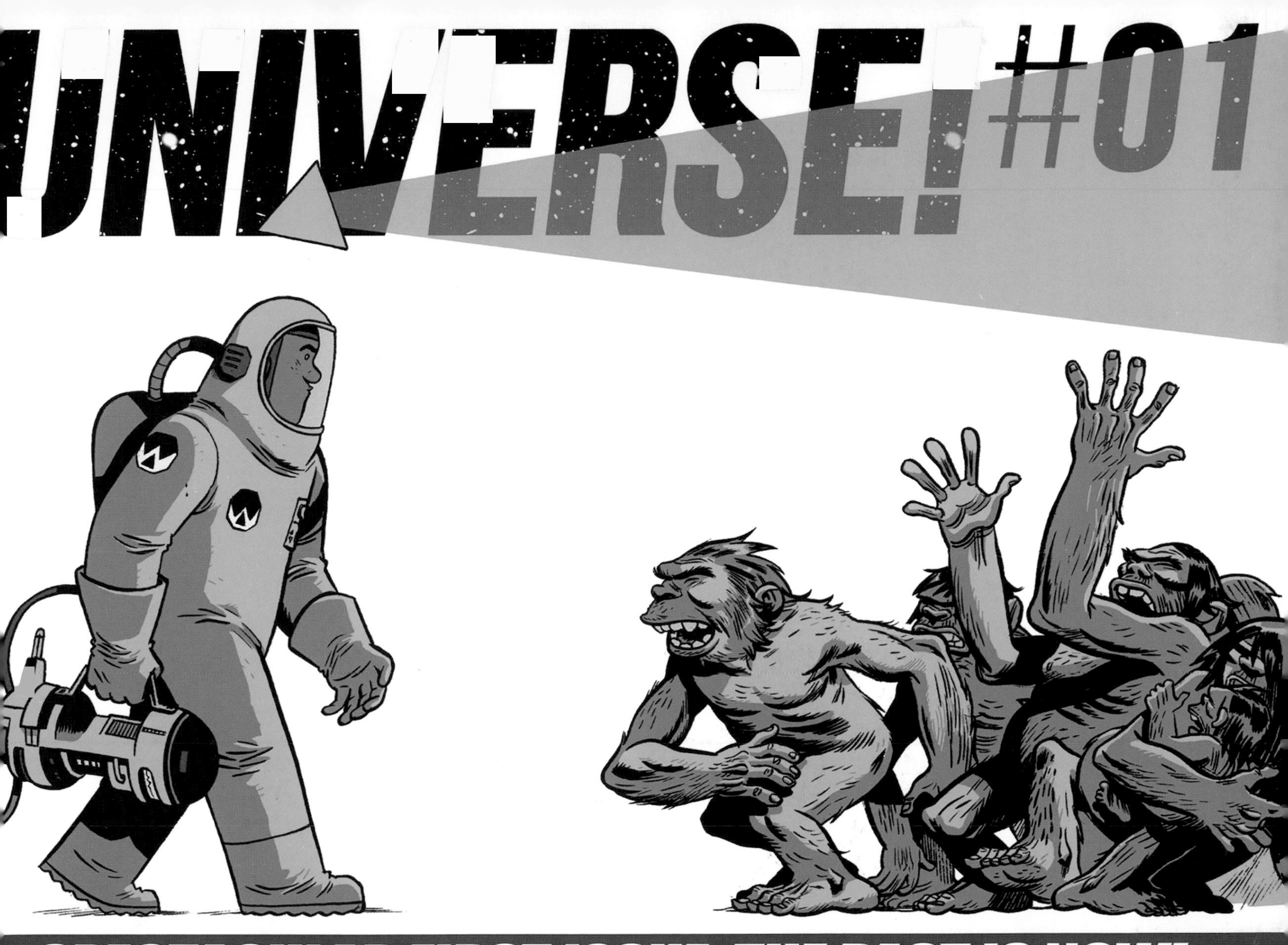
UNIVERSE! #01

SPECTACULAR FIRST ISSUE: THE PAST IS NOW!

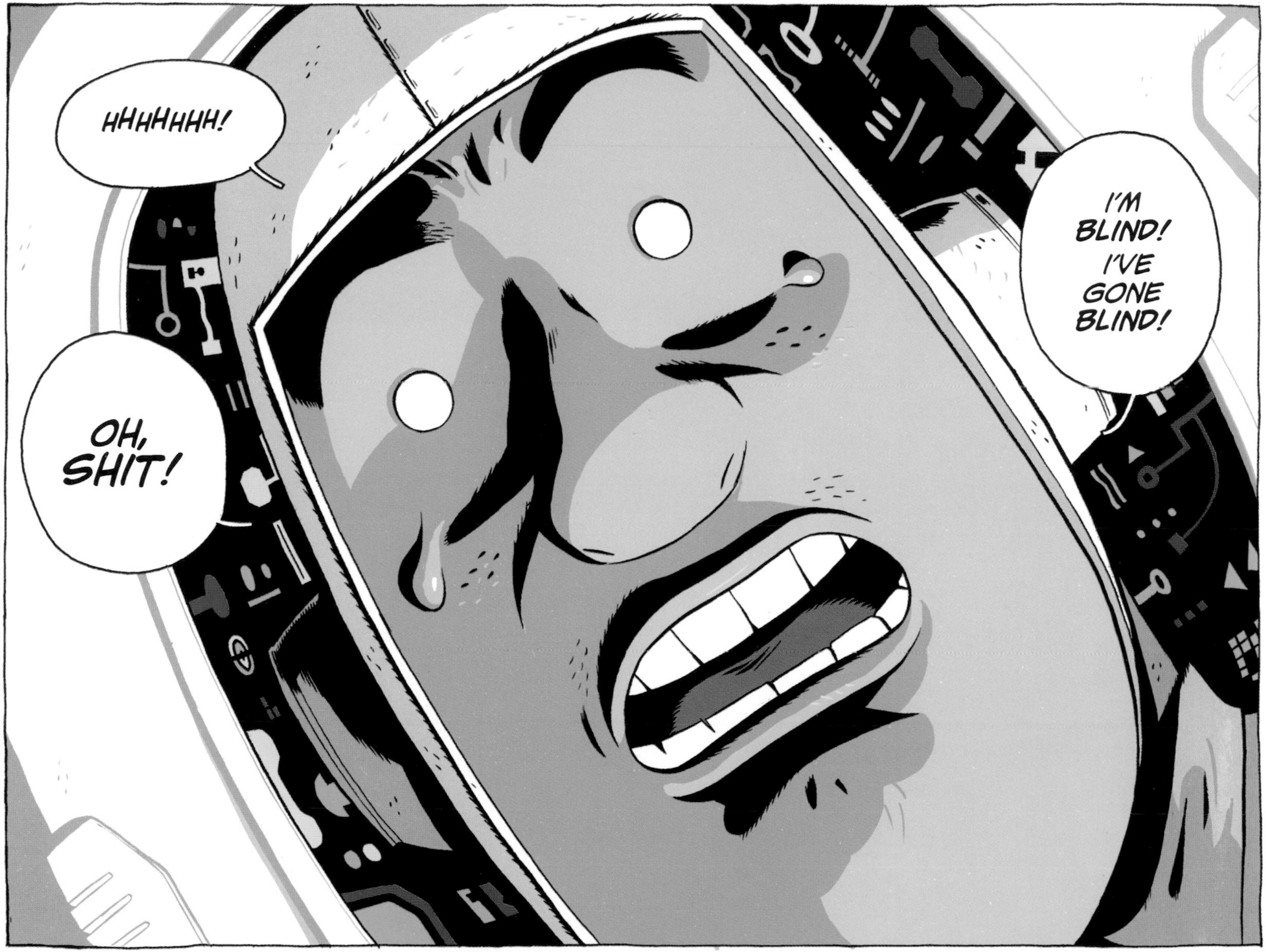
HHHHHHH!
OH, SHIT!
I'M BLIND! I'VE GONE BLIND!

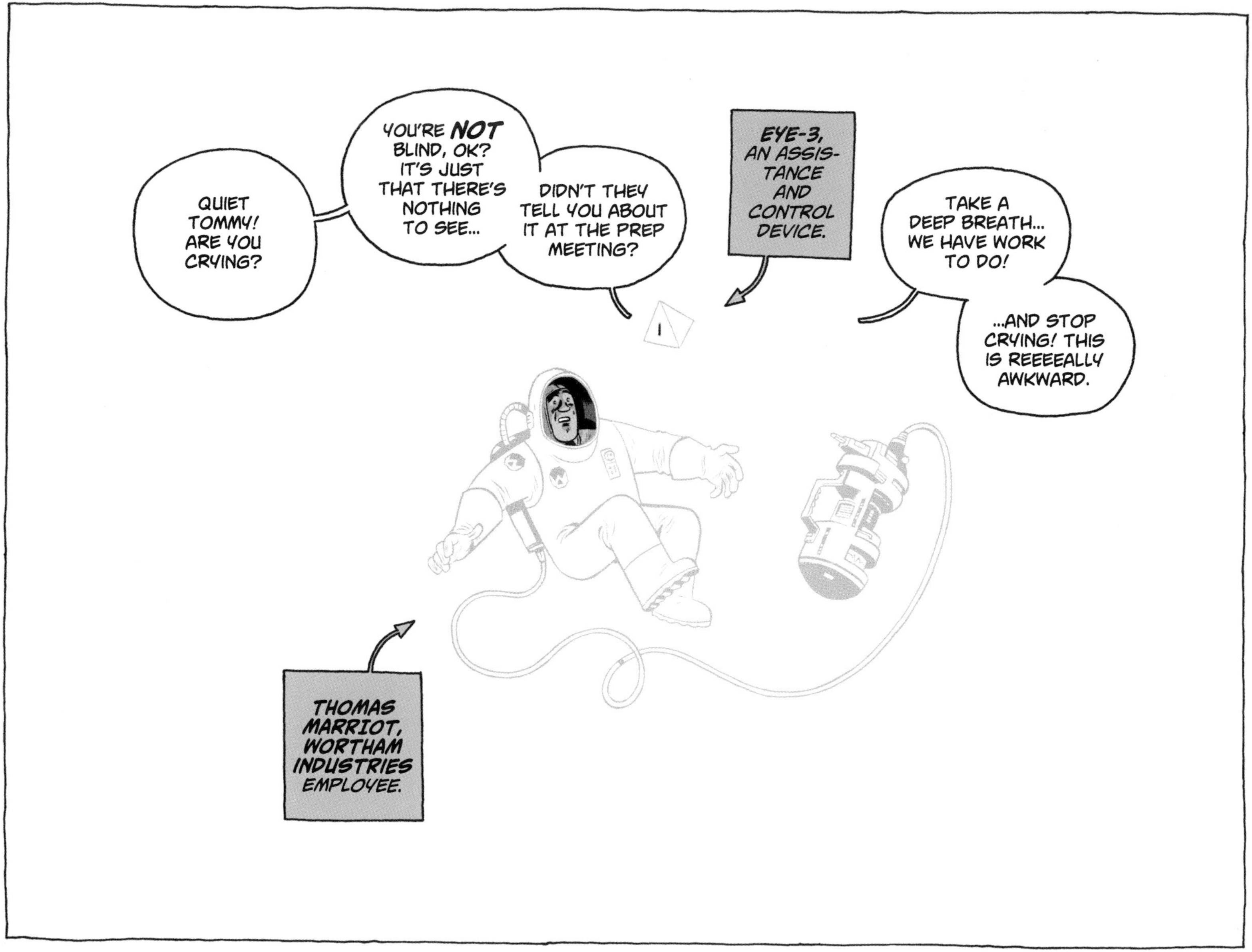
QUIET TOMMY! ARE YOU CRYING?
YOU'RE NOT BLIND, OK? IT'S JUST THAT THERE'S NOTHING TO SEE...
DIDN'T THEY TELL YOU ABOUT IT AT THE PREP MEETING?
EYE-3, AN ASSIS-TANCE AND CONTROL DEVICE.
TAKE A DEEP BREATH... WE HAVE WORK TO DO!
...AND STOP CRYING! THIS IS REEEEALLY AWKWARD.
THOMAS MARRIOT, WORTHAM INDUSTRIES EMPLOYEE.

I-I-I'M SORRY... I MEAN, I GUESS IT'S NORMAL THAT I'M A LITTLE SHAKY...

LUCKILY I HAVE EXPERIENCE MANAGING PROBABILITY MACHINES AND...

DID YOU THINK ABOUT A QUOTE?

A QUOTE?

WE ARE ABOUT TO CREATE THE UNIVERSE... DON'T TELL ME YOU HAVE NOTHING READY.

WELL, I DON'T KNOW. THERE IS NO ONE TO HEAR IT AND...

NO ONE? THANK YOU!

THANK YOU SO MUCH! I FEEL LIKE SUCH A PART OF THIS TEAM! WHO'S SUPPOSED TO BE THE ROBOT HERE?

...BESIDES, WHAT AM I SUPPOSED TO SAY?

IF THERE'S EVER BEEN A KEY MOMENT IN HISTORY... LET'S JUST LEAVE IT, OK?

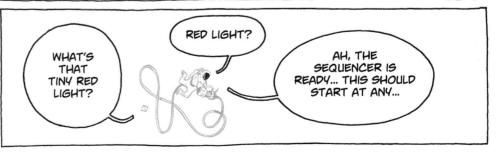

WHAT'S THAT TINY RED LIGHT?

RED LIGHT?

AH, THE SEQUENCER IS READY... THIS SHOULD START AT ANY...

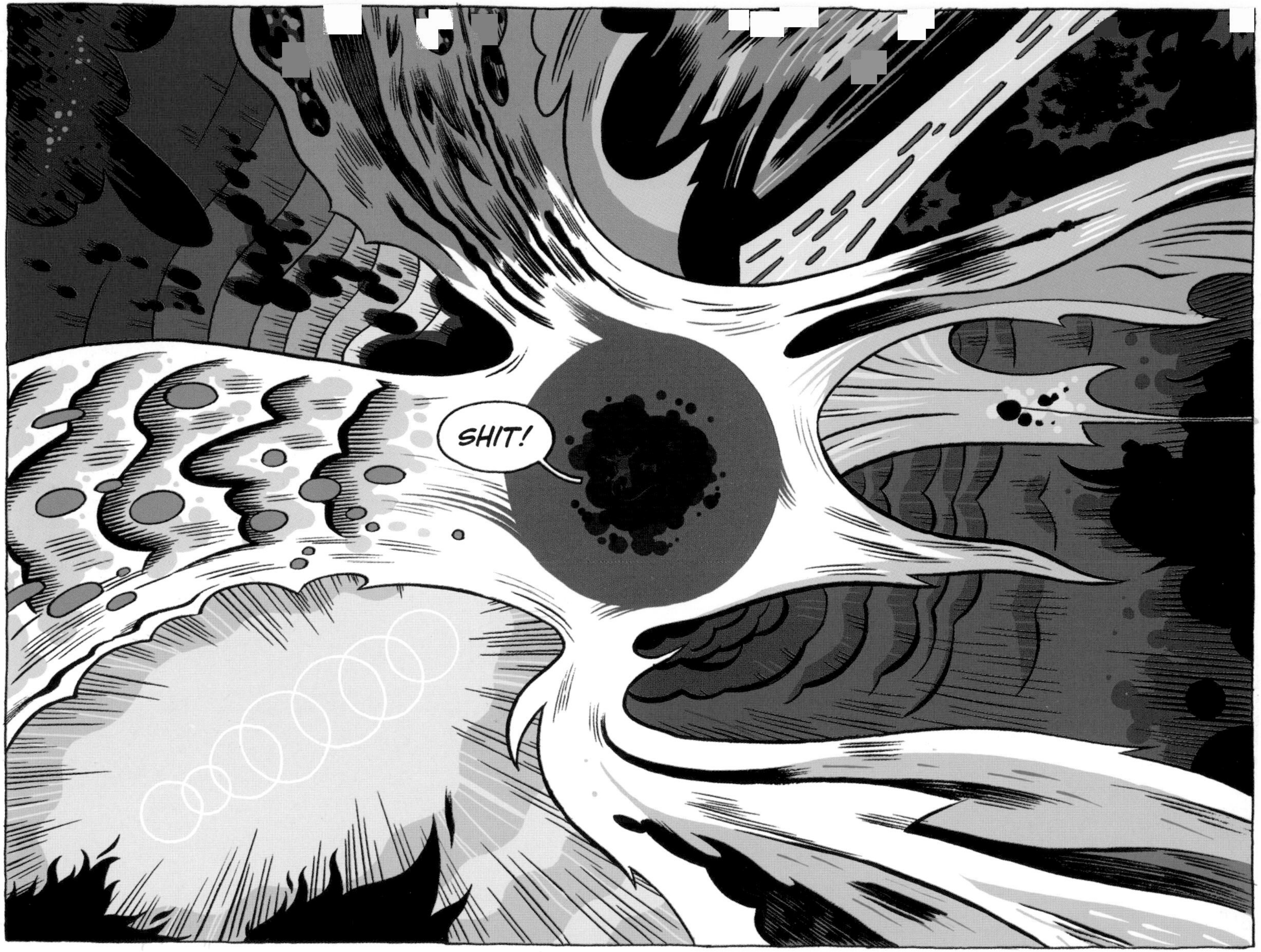
SHIT!

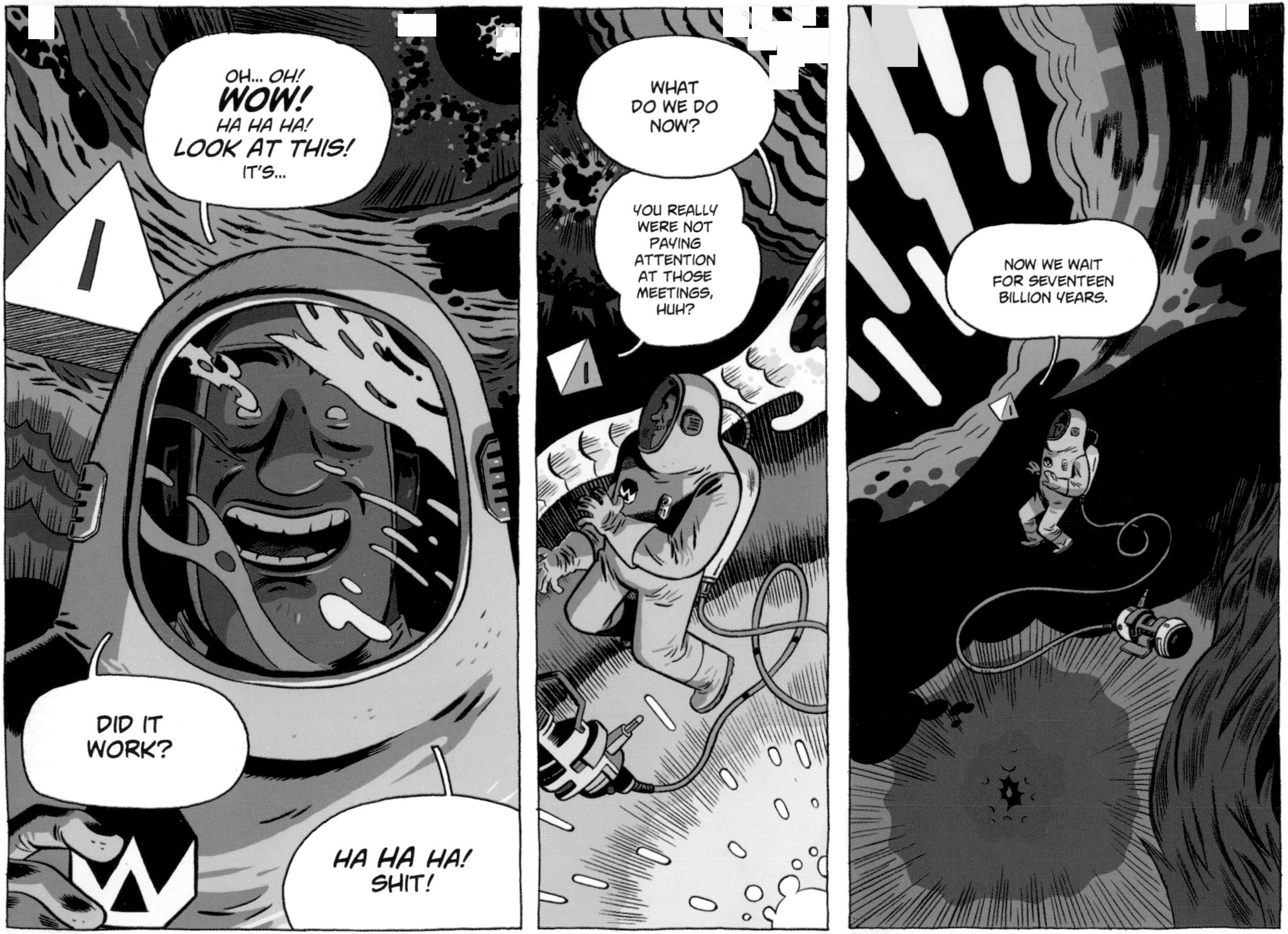
OH... OH! WOW! HA HA HA! LOOK AT THIS! IT'S...
DID IT WORK?
HA HA HA! SHIT!
WHAT DO WE DO NOW?
YOU REALLY WERE NOT PAYING ATTENTION AT THOSE MEETINGS, HUH?
NOW WE WAIT FOR SEVENTEEN BILLION YEARS.

THE PAST IS NOW!

A UNIVERSE TALE, WRITTEN AND DRAWN BY ***ALBERT MONTEYS***

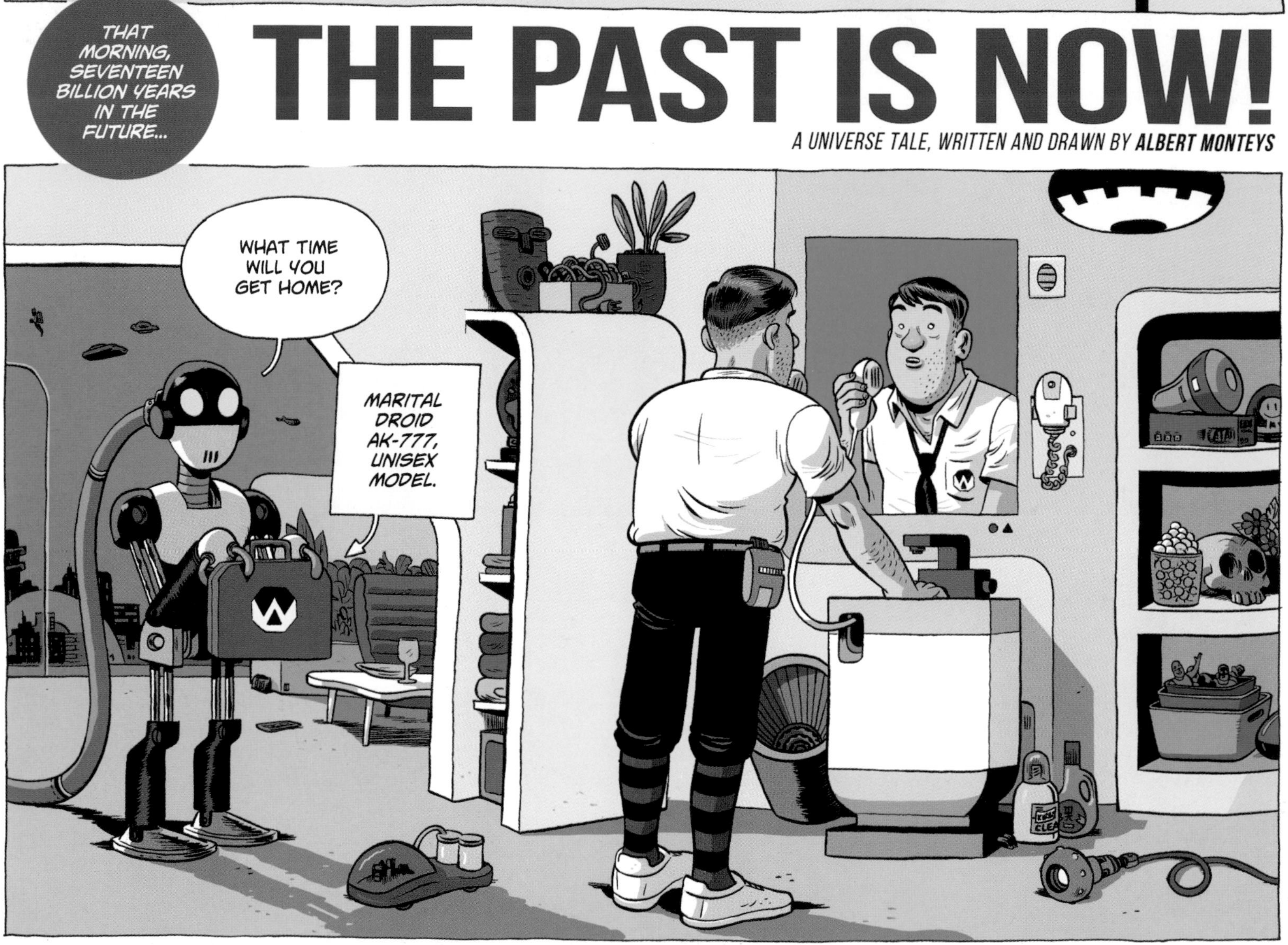
THAT MORNING, SEVENTEEN BILLION YEARS IN THE FUTURE...
WHAT TIME WILL YOU GET HOME?
MARITAL DROID AK-777, UNISEX MODEL.

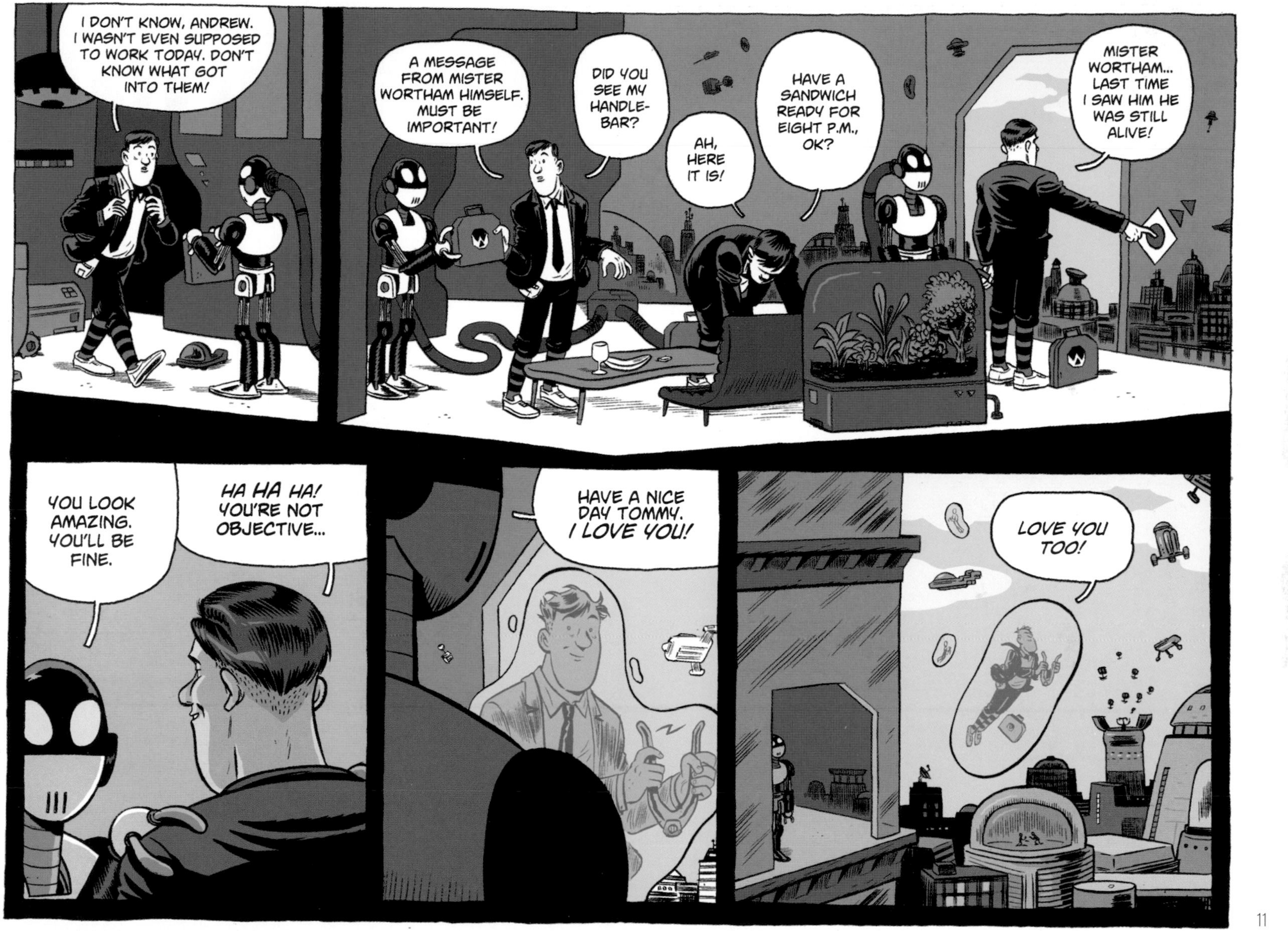

I DON'T KNOW, ANDREW. I WASN'T EVEN SUPPOSED TO WORK TODAY. DON'T KNOW WHAT GOT INTO THEM!
A MESSAGE FROM MISTER WORTHAM HIMSELF. MUST BE IMPORTANT!
DID YOU SEE MY HANDLE-BAR?
AH, HERE IT IS!
HAVE A SANDWICH READY FOR EIGHT P.M., OK?
MISTER WORTHAM... LAST TIME I SAW HIM HE WAS STILL ALIVE!
YOU LOOK AMAZING. YOU'LL BE FINE.
HA HA HA! YOU'RE NOT OBJECTIVE...
HAVE A NICE DAY TOMMY. I LOVE YOU!
LOVE YOU TOO!

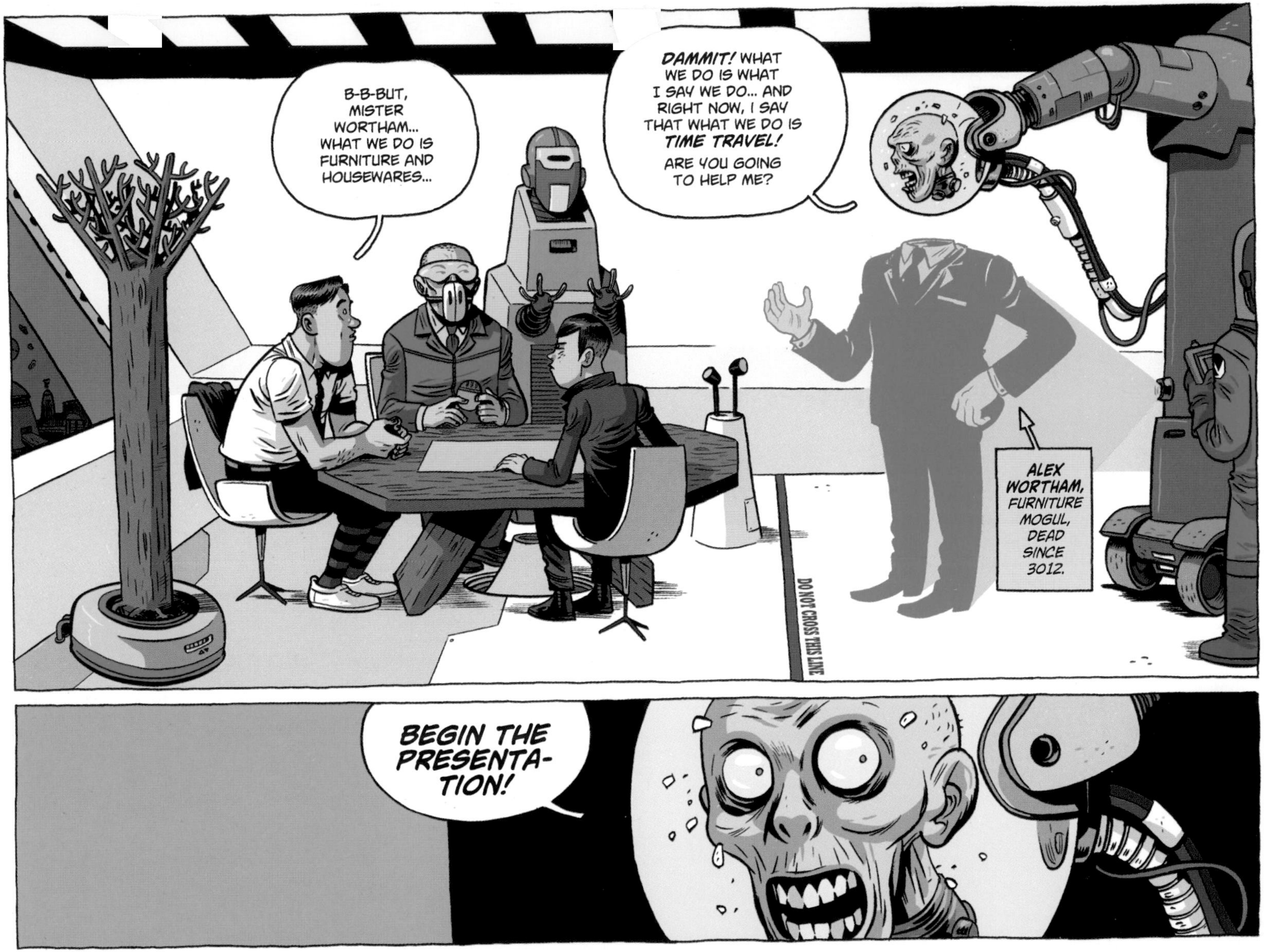
B-B-BUT, MISTER WORTHAM... WHAT WE DO IS FURNITURE AND HOUSEWARES...
DAMMIT! WHAT WE DO IS WHAT I SAY WE DO... AND RIGHT NOW, I SAY THAT WHAT WE DO IS TIME TRAVEL! ARE YOU GOING TO HELP ME?
ALEX WORTHAM, FURNITURE MOGUL, DEAD SINCE 3012.
DO NOT CROSS THIS LINE
BEGIN THE PRESENTA-TION!

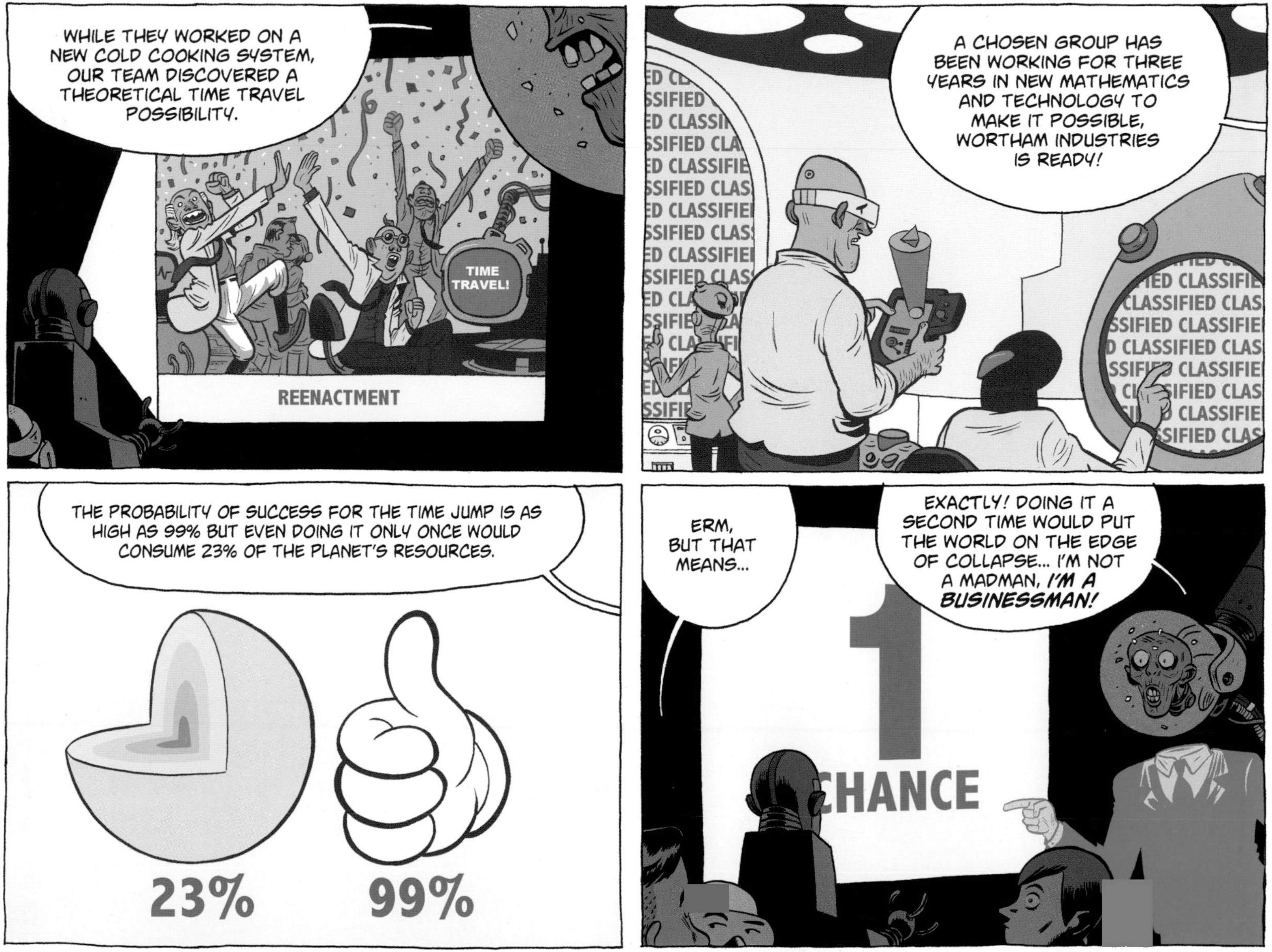
WHILE THEY WORKED ON A NEW COLD COOKING SYSTEM, OUR TEAM DISCOVERED A THEORETICAL TIME TRAVEL POSSIBILITY.
TIME TRAVEL!
REENACTMENT
A CHOSEN GROUP HAS BEEN WORKING FOR THREE YEARS IN NEW MATHEMATICS AND TECHNOLOGY TO MAKE IT POSSIBLE, WORTHAM INDUSTRIES IS READY!
CLASSIFIED CLASSIFIED CLASSIFIED
THE PROBABILITY OF SUCCESS FOR THE TIME JUMP IS AS HIGH AS 99% BUT EVEN DOING IT ONLY ONCE WOULD CONSUME 23% OF THE PLANET'S RESOURCES.
23%
99%
ERM, BUT THAT MEANS...
EXACTLY! DOING IT A SECOND TIME WOULD PUT THE WORLD ON THE EDGE OF COLLAPSE... I'M NOT A MADMAN, ***I'M A BUSINESSMAN!***
1
CHANCE

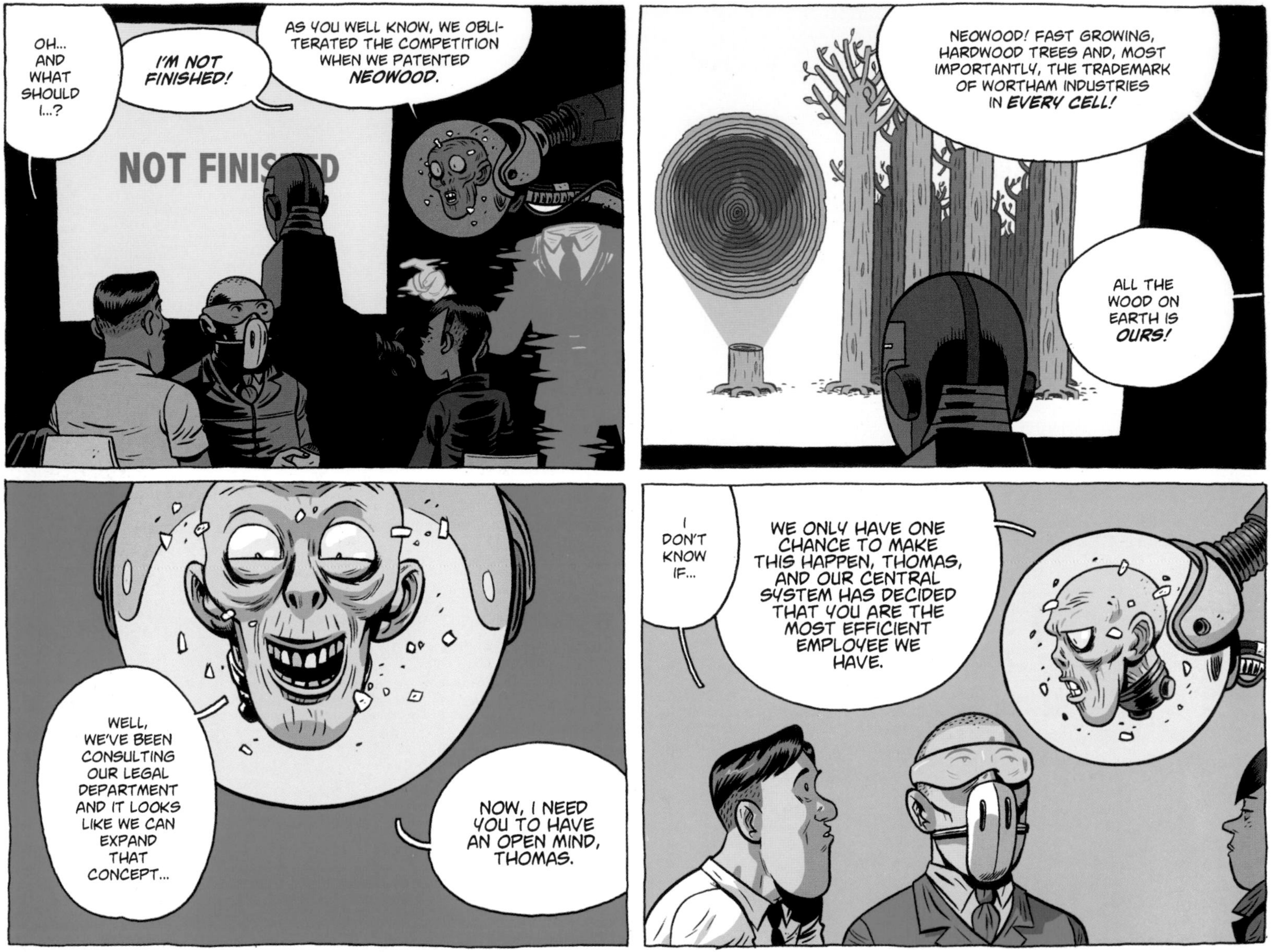
OH... AND WHAT SHOULD I...?
I'M NOT FINISHED!
AS YOU WELL KNOW, WE OBLITERATED THE COMPETITION WHEN WE PATENTED NEOWOOD.
NOT FINIS
NEOWOOD! FAST GROWING, HARDWOOD TREES AND, MOST IMPORTANTLY, THE TRADEMARK OF WORTHAM INDUSTRIES IN EVERY CELL!
ALL THE WOOD ON EARTH IS OURS!
WELL, WE'VE BEEN CONSULTING OUR LEGAL DEPARTMENT AND IT LOOKS LIKE WE CAN EXPAND THAT CONCEPT...
NOW, I NEED YOU TO HAVE AN OPEN MIND, THOMAS.
I DON'T KNOW IF...
WE ONLY HAVE ONE CHANCE TO MAKE THIS HAPPEN, THOMAS, AND OUR CENTRAL SYSTEM HAS DECIDED THAT YOU ARE THE MOST EFFICIENT EMPLOYEE WE HAVE.

WE'LL SEND YOU AS FAR BACK AS POSSIBLE, JUST BEFORE **THE BEGINNING OF TIME.**

YOUR EQUIPMENT WILL CONTAIN, AMONG OTHER THINGS, A SINGULARITY MACHINE THAT, IF WE ARE CORRECT, WILL SPARK THE KNOWN UNIVERSE— **THE BIG BANG!**

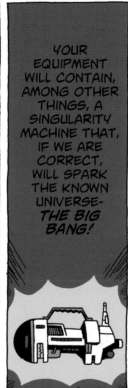

DURING THE FOLLOWING THIRTEEN MINUTES, THE COSMOS WILL BE A MANIPULABLE PARTICLE SOUP... QUARKS AND GLUONS TRYING TO FIGURE OUT HOW TO CREATE MATTER!

REMEMBER! IN THE THIRTEEN MINUTES BEFORE ALL THAT RAW MATERIAL EXPANDS, REPLICATES AND STARTS MAKING STARS YOU HAVE ANOTHER FUNDAMENTAL TASK...

WITH THE SUBATOMIC SCALPEL, YOU WILL ENGRAVE OUR TRADEMARK SYMBOL ON THOSE QUARKS. WE HAVE MADE SIMULATIONS. IT SHOULDN'T TAKE LONG.

AFTER THAT, YOU CAN COME BACK HOME... TO A UNIVERSE WITH THE **WORTHAM GUARANTEE!**

PROPERTY of WORTHAM INC.

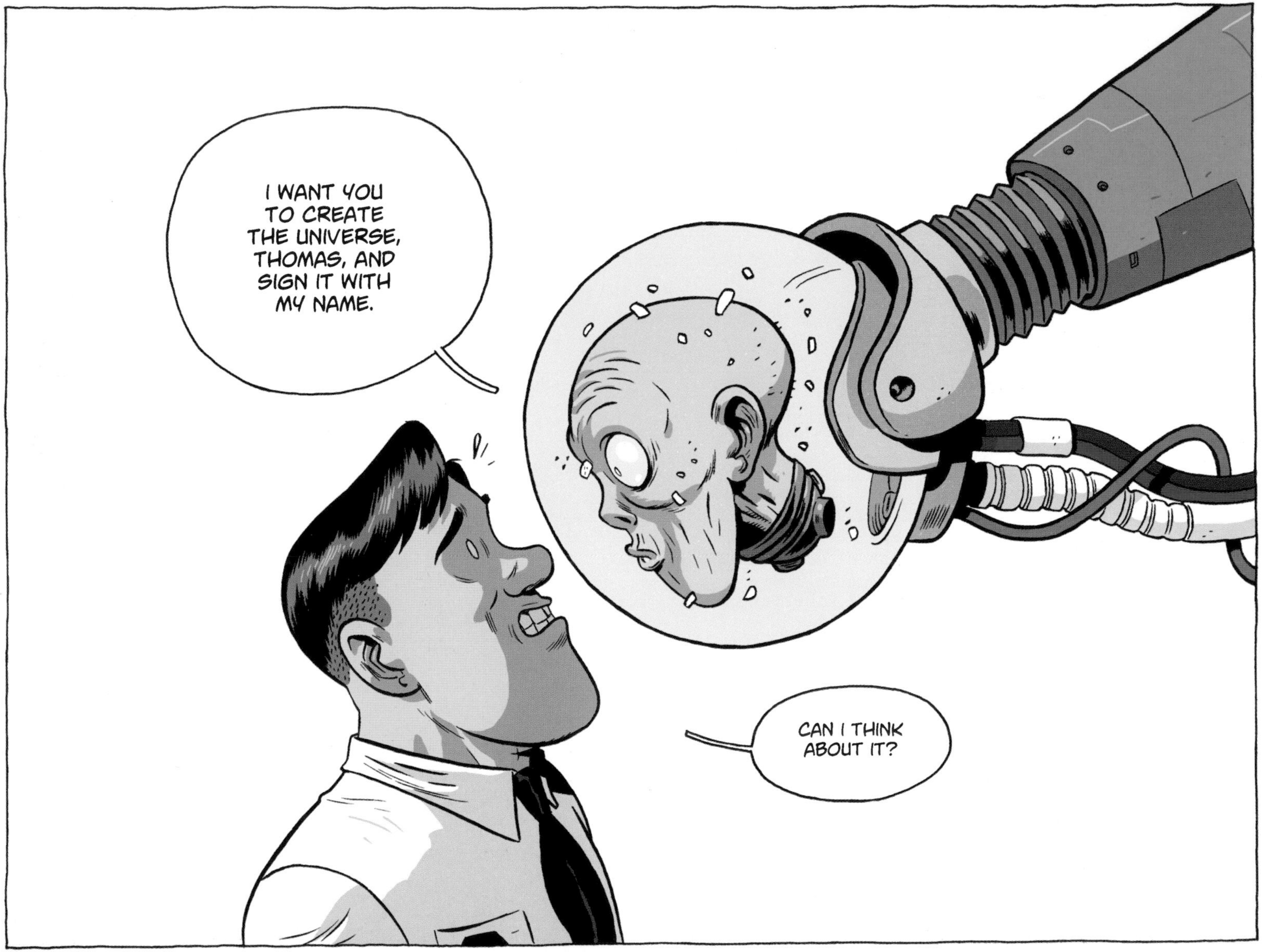
I WANT YOU TO CREATE THE UNIVERSE, THOMAS, AND SIGN IT WITH MY NAME.
CAN I THINK ABOUT IT?

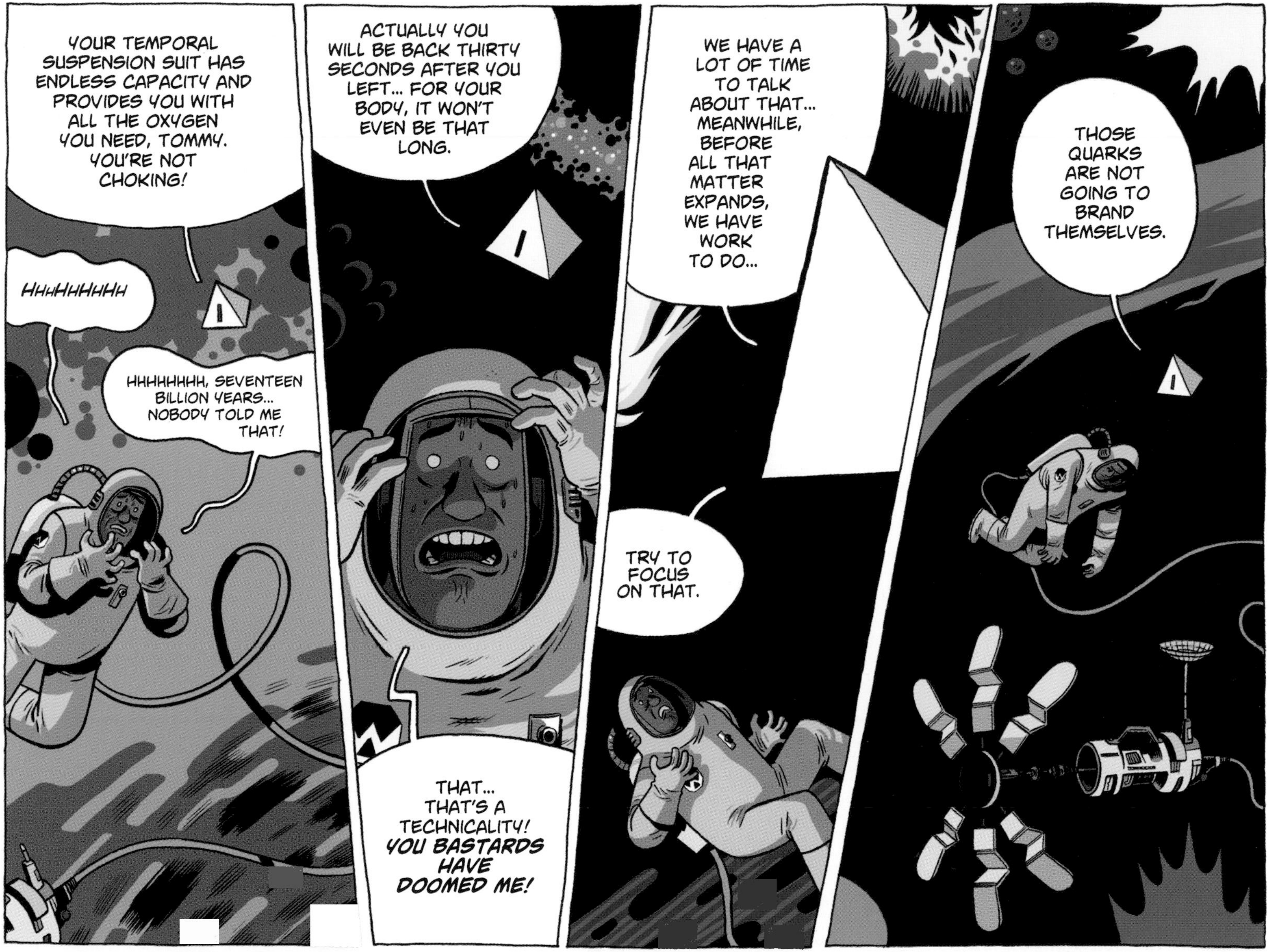
YOUR TEMPORAL SUSPENSION SUIT HAS ENDLESS CAPACITY AND PROVIDES YOU WITH ALL THE OXYGEN YOU NEED, TOMMY. YOU'RE NOT CHOKING!
HHHHHHHHH
HHHHHHHH, SEVENTEEN BILLION YEARS... NOBODY TOLD ME THAT!
ACTUALLY YOU WILL BE BACK THIRTY SECONDS AFTER YOU LEFT... FOR YOUR BODY, IT WON'T EVEN BE THAT LONG.
THAT... THAT'S A TECHNICALITY! YOU BASTARDS HAVE DOOMED ME!
WE HAVE A LOT OF TIME TO TALK ABOUT THAT... MEANWHILE, BEFORE ALL THAT MATTER EXPANDS, WE HAVE WORK TO DO...
TRY TO FOCUS ON THAT.
THOSE QUARKS ARE NOT GOING TO BRAND THEMSELVES.

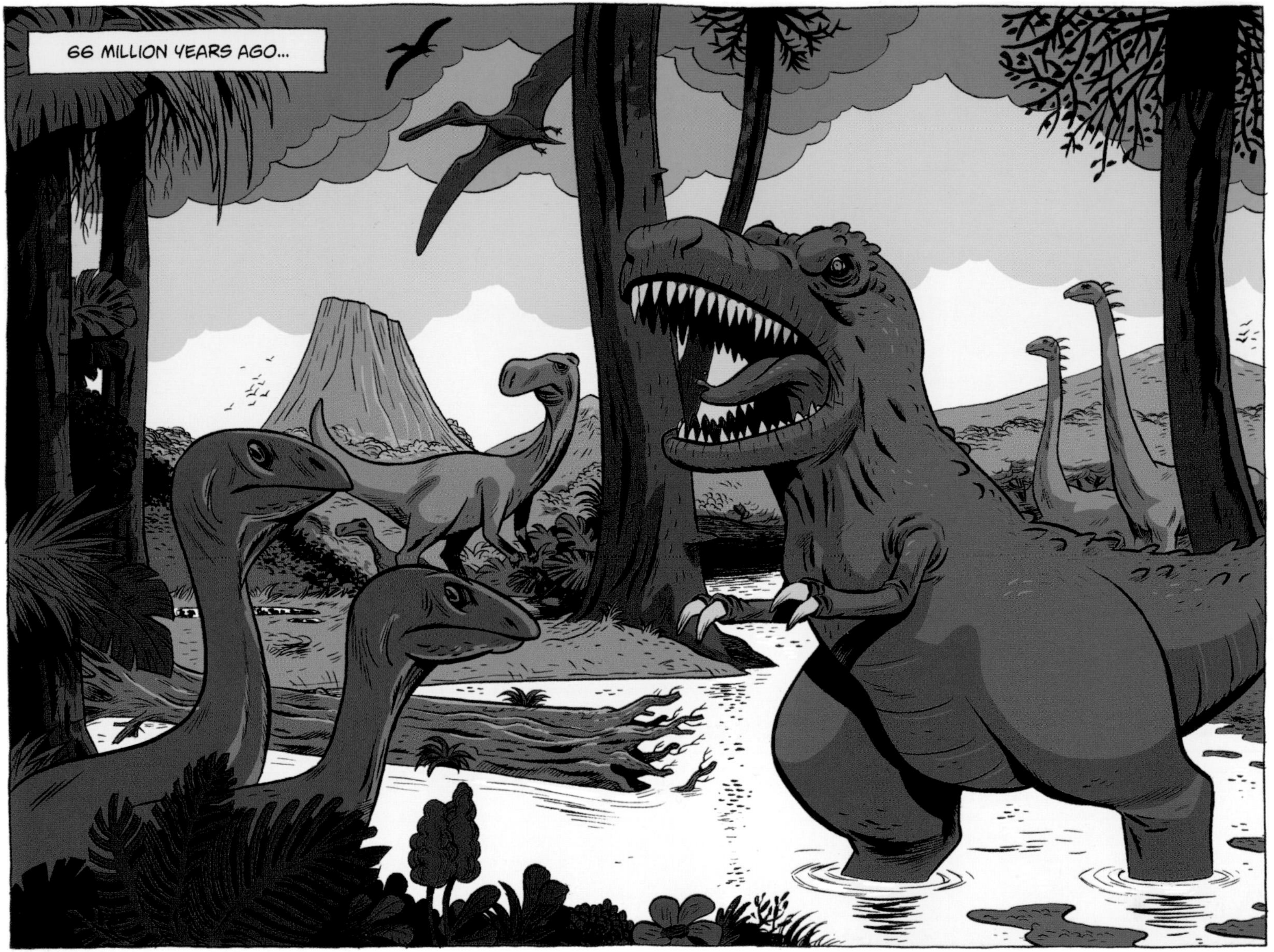
66 MILLION YEARS AGO...

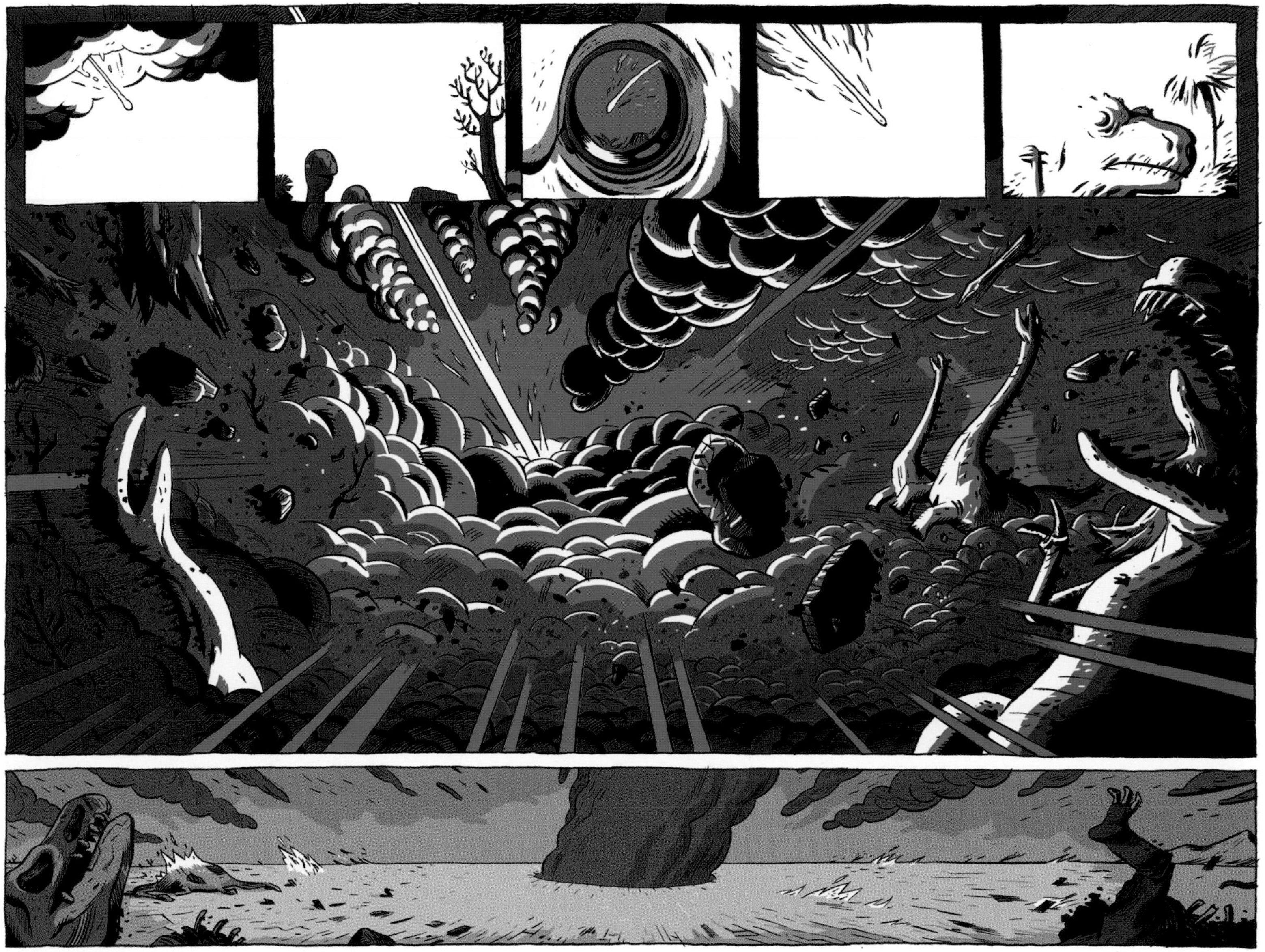

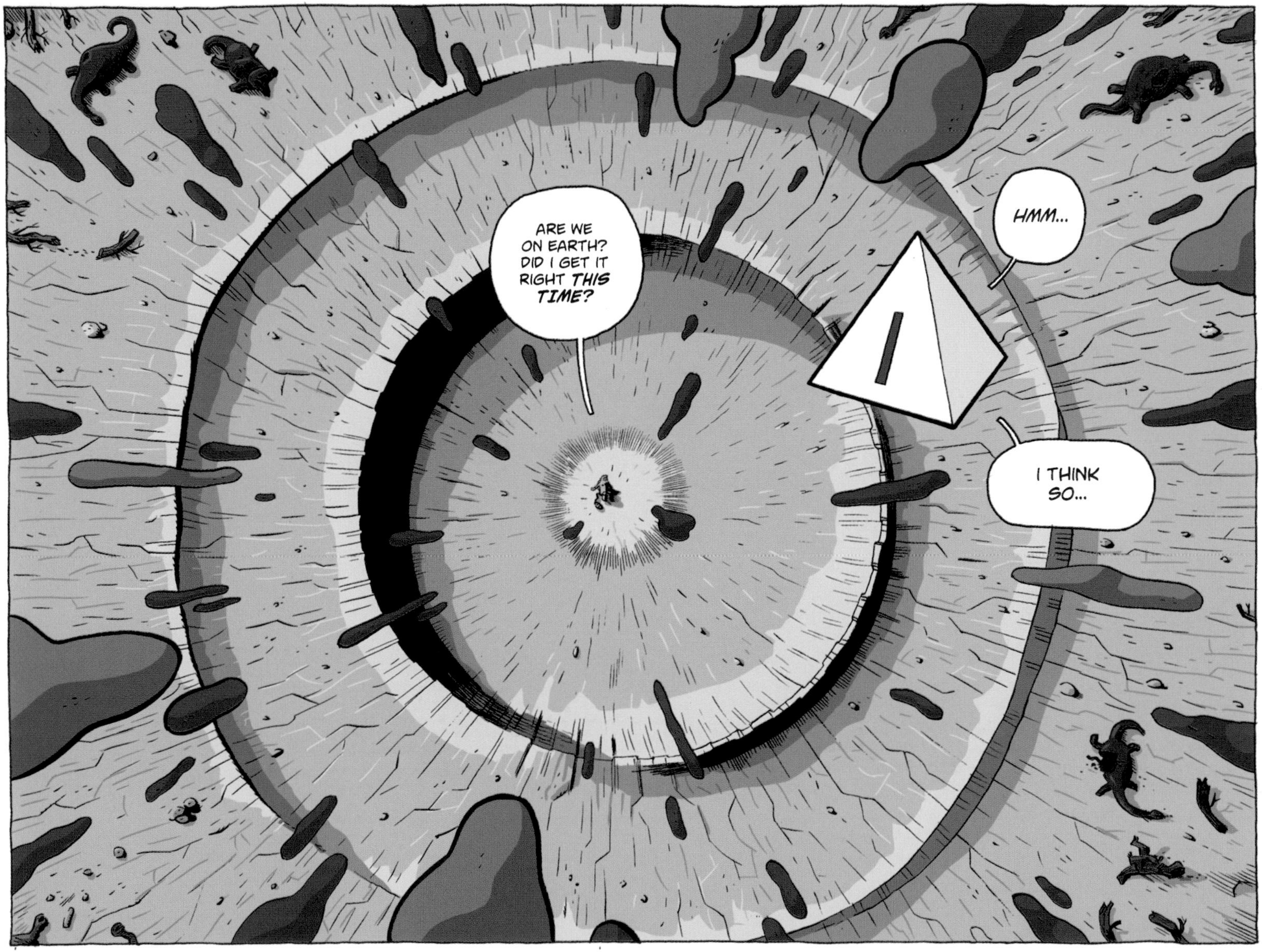
ARE WE ON EARTH? DID I GET IT RIGHT *THIS TIME?*
HMM...
I THINK SO...

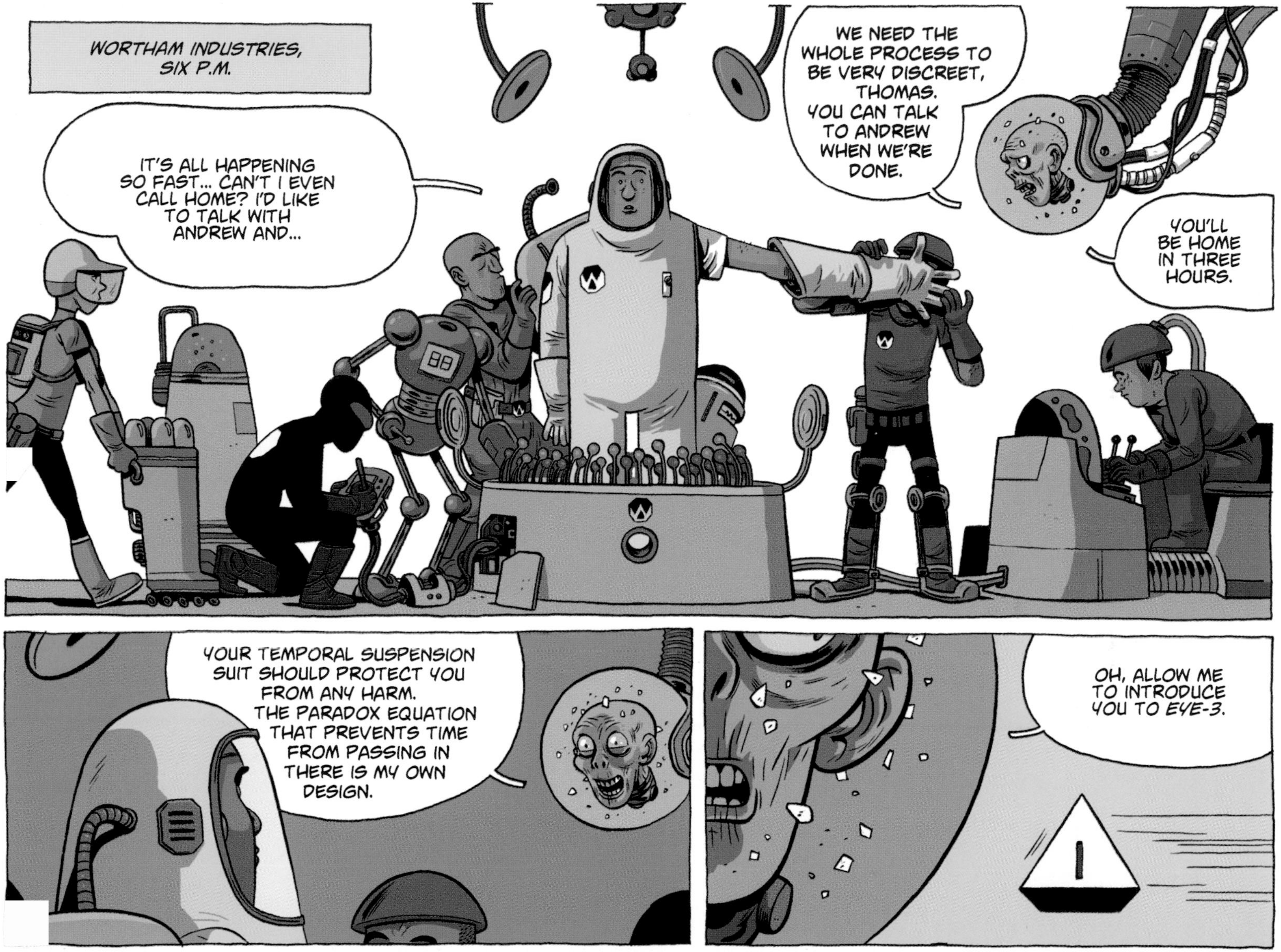
WORTHAM INDUSTRIES, SIX P.M.
IT'S ALL HAPPENING SO FAST... CAN'T I EVEN CALL HOME? I'D LIKE TO TALK WITH ANDREW AND...
WE NEED THE WHOLE PROCESS TO BE VERY DISCREET, THOMAS. YOU CAN TALK TO ANDREW WHEN WE'RE DONE.
YOU'LL BE HOME IN THREE HOURS.
YOUR TEMPORAL SUSPENSION SUIT SHOULD PROTECT YOU FROM ANY HARM. THE PARADOX EQUATION THAT PREVENTS TIME FROM PASSING IN THERE IS MY OWN DESIGN.
OH, ALLOW ME TO INTRODUCE YOU TO EYE-3.

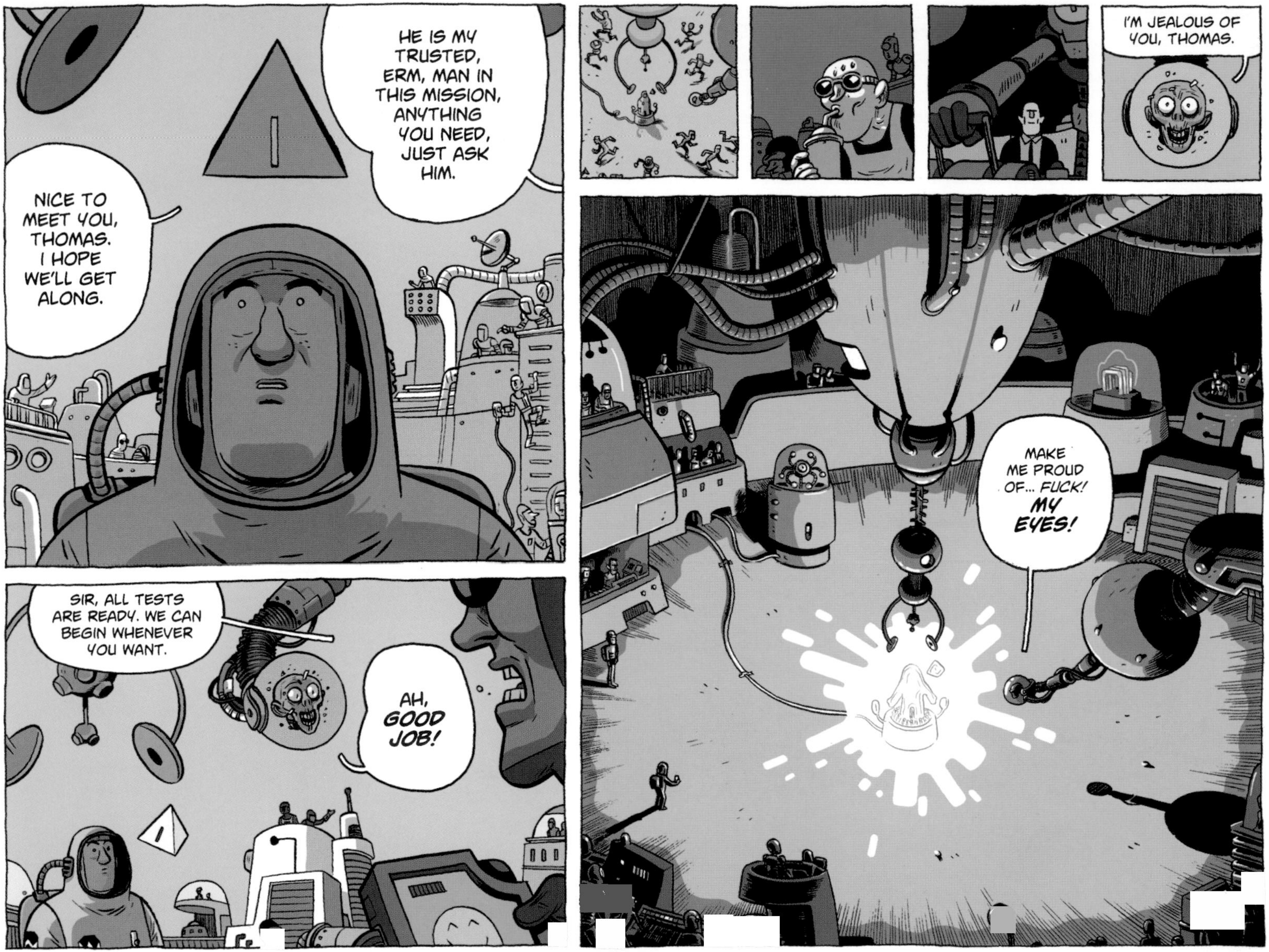
HE IS MY TRUSTED, ERM, MAN IN THIS MISSION, ANYTHING YOU NEED, JUST ASK HIM.
NICE TO MEET YOU, THOMAS. I HOPE WE'LL GET ALONG.
SIR, ALL TESTS ARE READY. WE CAN BEGIN WHENEVER YOU WANT.
AH, **GOOD JOB!**
I'M JEALOUS OF YOU, THOMAS.
MAKE ME PROUD OF... FUCK! **MY EYES!**

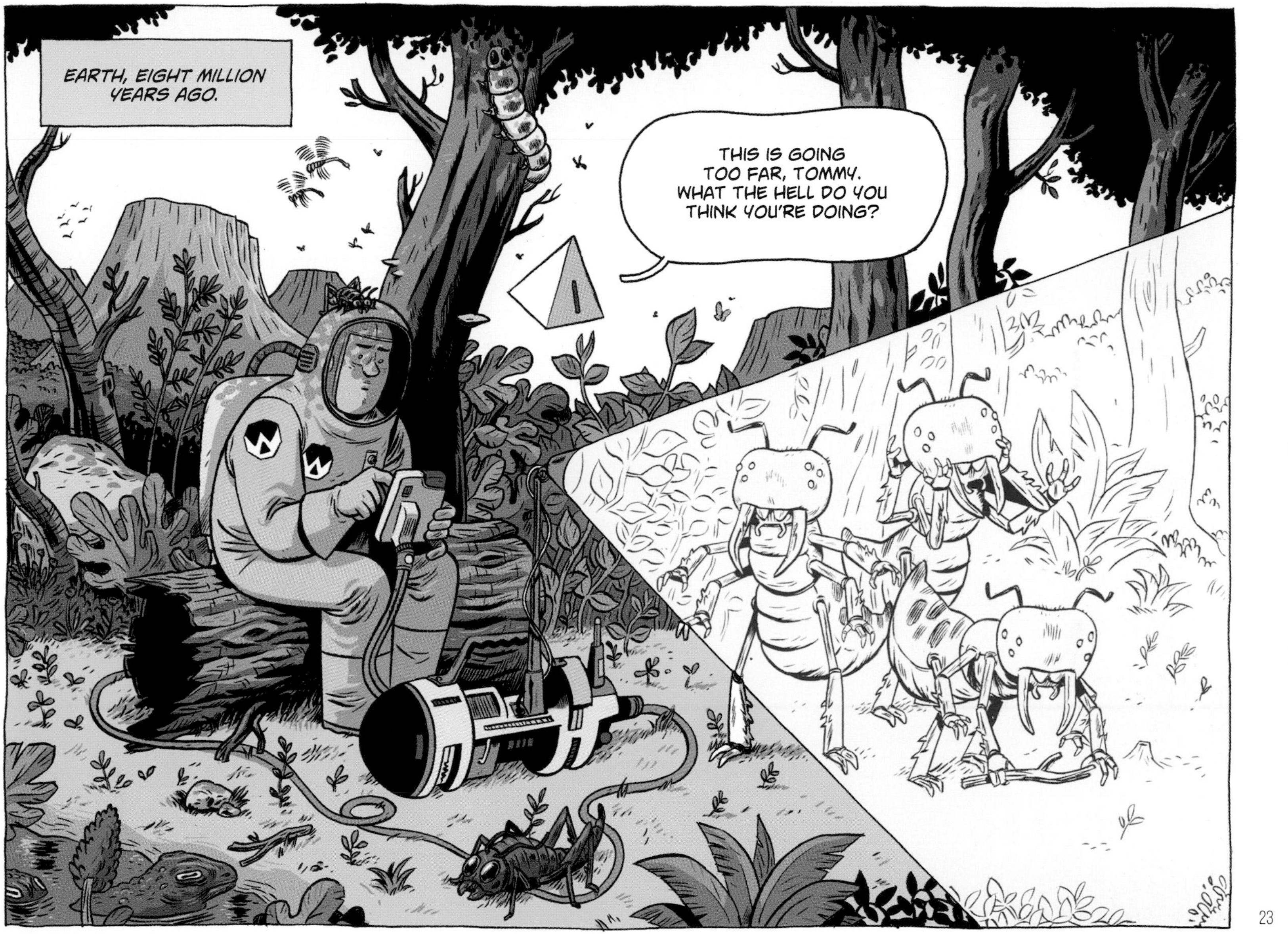
EARTH, EIGHT MILLION YEARS AGO.
THIS IS GOING TOO FAR, TOMMY. WHAT THE HELL DO YOU THINK YOU'RE DOING?

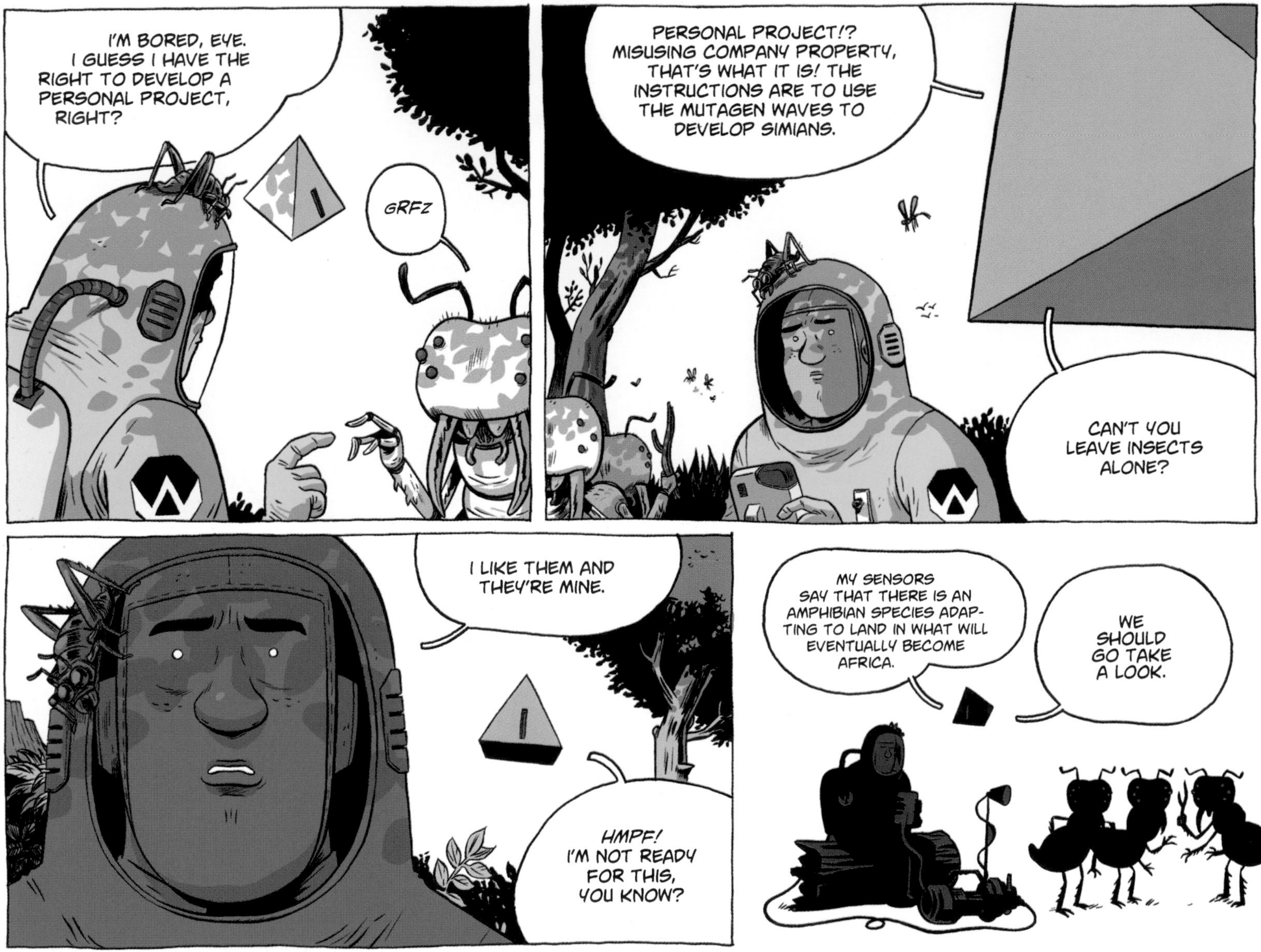
I'M BORED, EYE. I GUESS I HAVE THE RIGHT TO DEVELOP A PERSONAL PROJECT, RIGHT?
GRFZ
PERSONAL PROJECT!? MISUSING COMPANY PROPERTY, THAT'S WHAT IT IS! THE INSTRUCTIONS ARE TO USE THE MUTAGEN WAVES TO DEVELOP SIMIANS.
CAN'T YOU LEAVE INSECTS ALONE?
I LIKE THEM AND THEY'RE MINE.
HMPF! I'M NOT READY FOR THIS, YOU KNOW?
MY SENSORS SAY THAT THERE IS AN AMPHIBIAN SPECIES ADAPTING TO LAND IN WHAT WILL EVENTUALLY BECOME AFRICA.
WE SHOULD GO TAKE A LOOK.

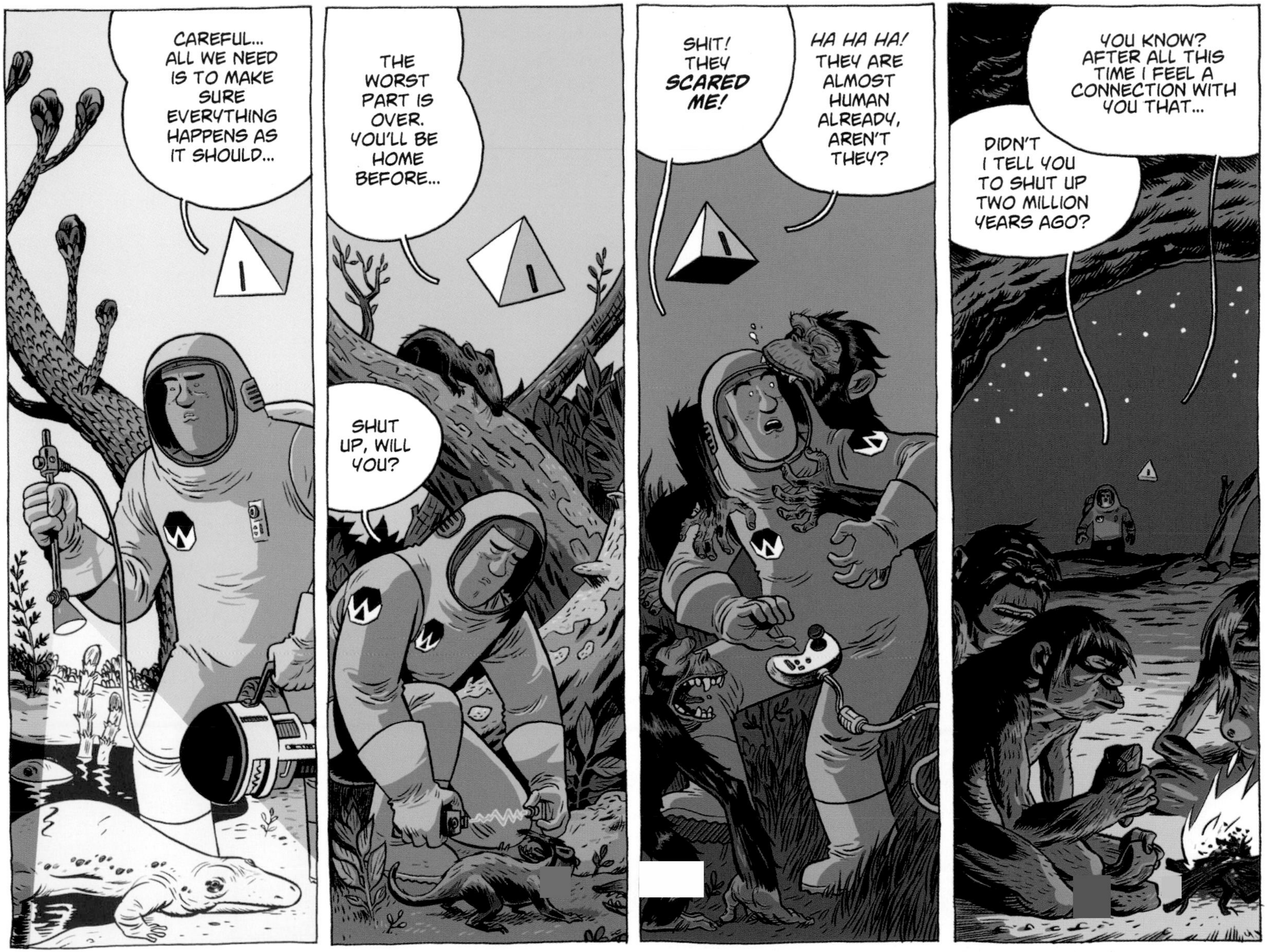
CAREFUL... ALL WE NEED IS TO MAKE SURE EVERYTHING HAPPENS AS IT SHOULD...
THE WORST PART IS OVER. YOU'LL BE HOME BEFORE...
SHUT UP, WILL YOU?
SHIT! THEY **SCARED ME!**
HA HA HA! THEY ARE ALMOST HUMAN ALREADY, AREN'T THEY?
YOU KNOW? AFTER ALL THIS TIME I FEEL A CONNECTION WITH YOU THAT...
DIDN'T I TELL YOU TO SHUT UP TWO MILLION YEARS AGO?

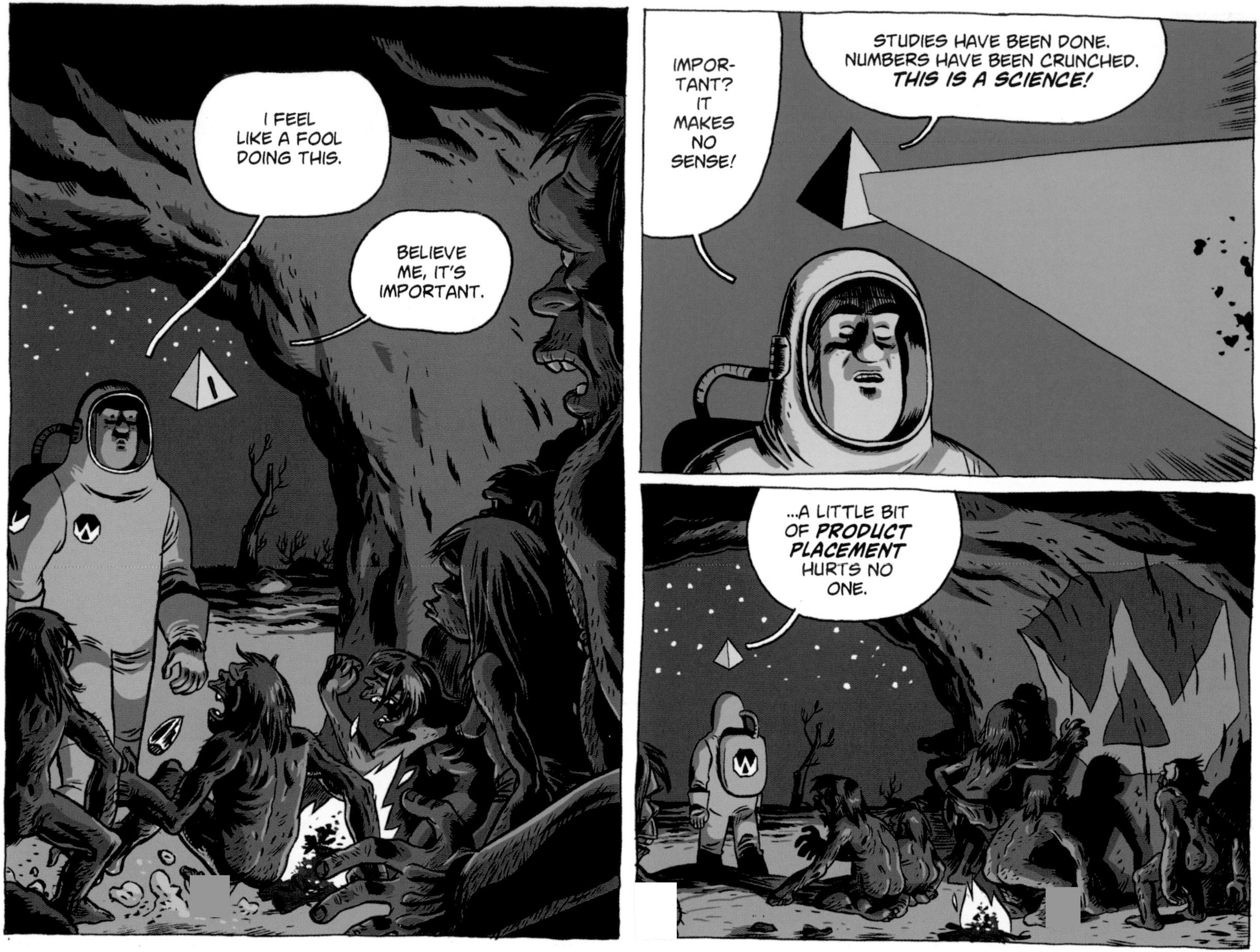
I FEEL LIKE A FOOL DOING THIS.
BELIEVE ME, IT'S IMPORTANT.
IMPOR-TANT? IT MAKES NO SENSE!
STUDIES HAVE BEEN DONE. NUMBERS HAVE BEEN CRUNCHED. ***THIS IS A SCIENCE!***
...A LITTLE BIT OF ***PRODUCT PLACEMENT*** HURTS NO ONE.

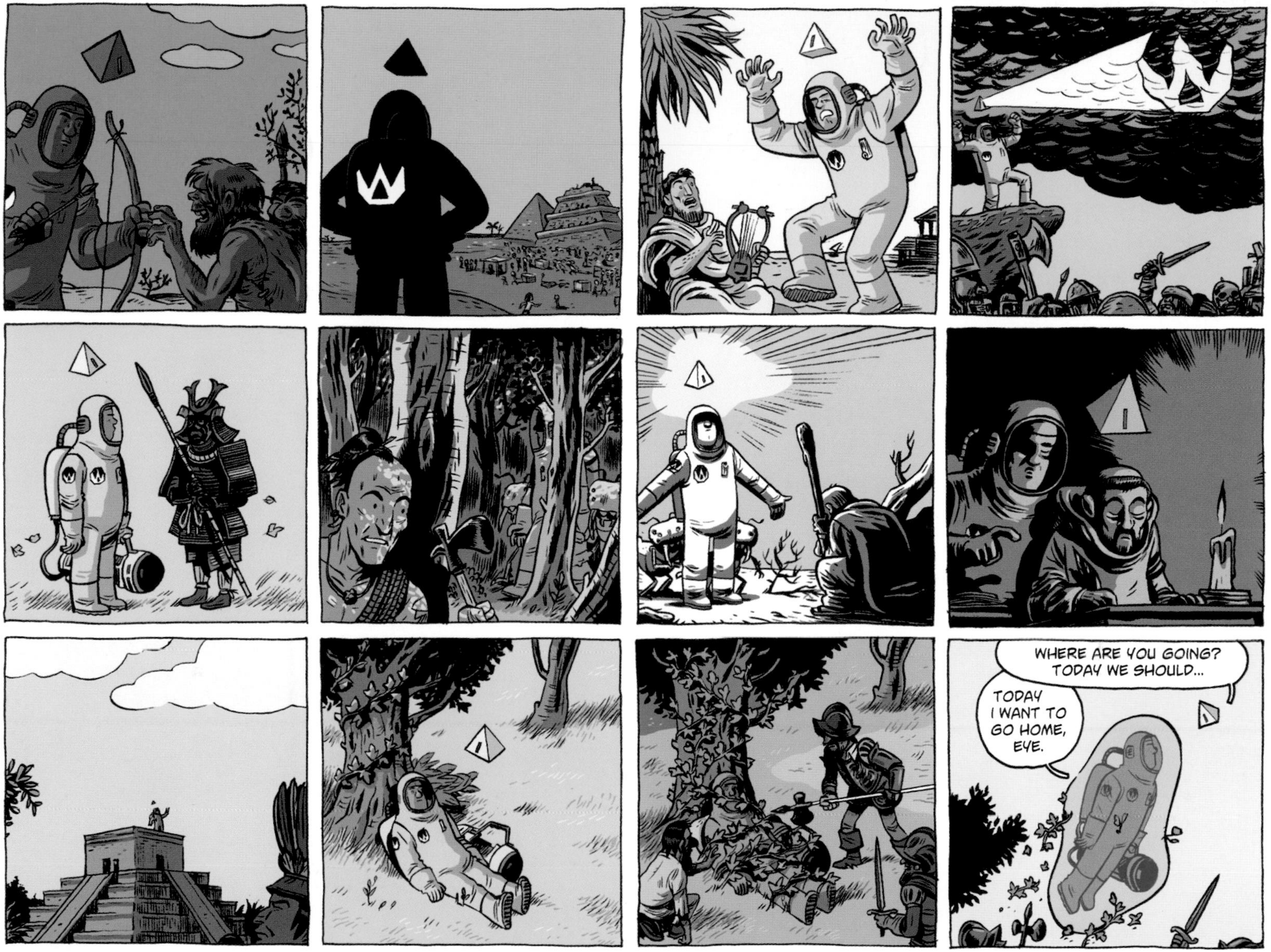
WHERE ARE YOU GOING? TODAY WE SHOULD...
TODAY I WANT TO GO HOME, EYE.

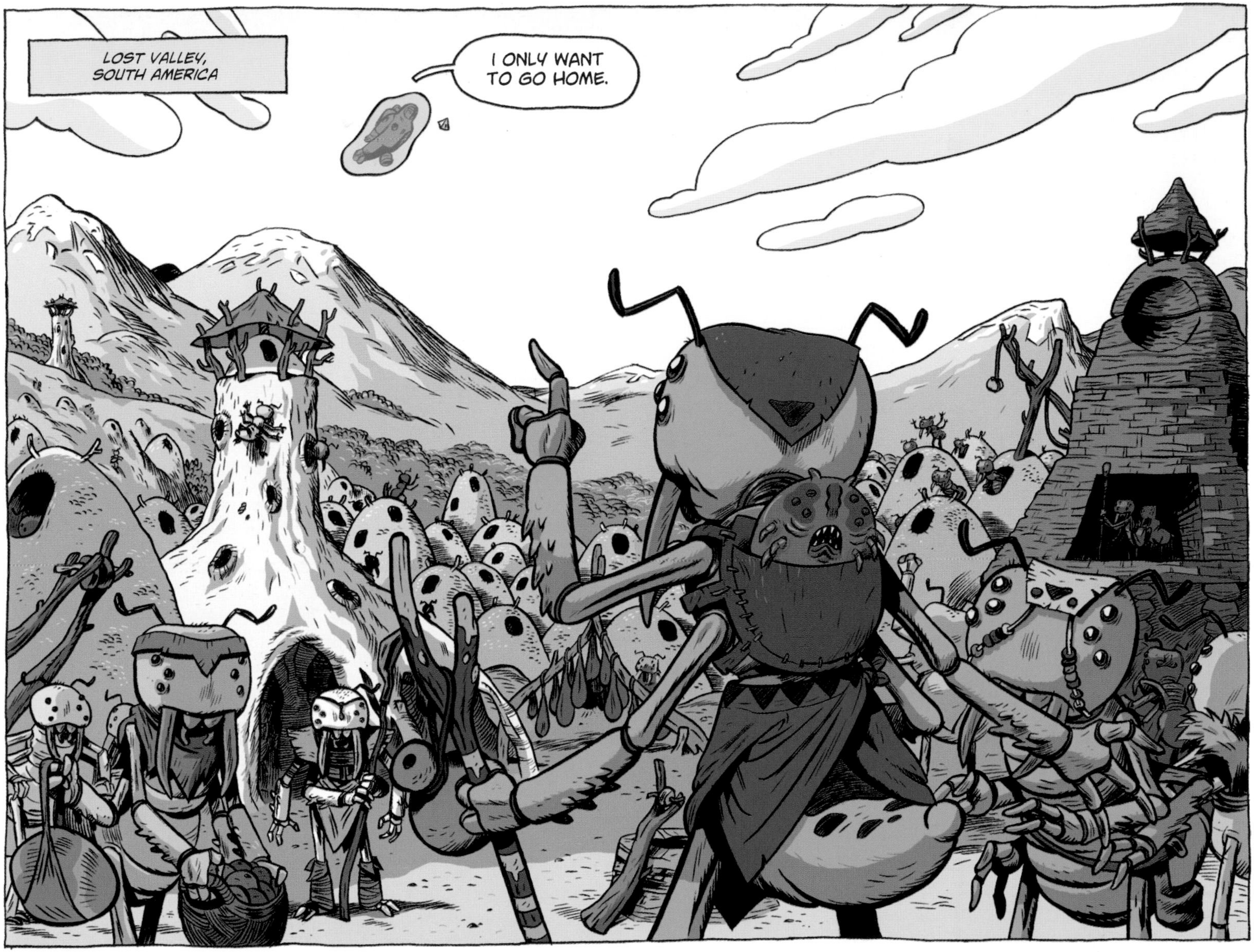
LOST VALLEY,
SOUTH AMERICA
I ONLY WANT
TO GO HOME.

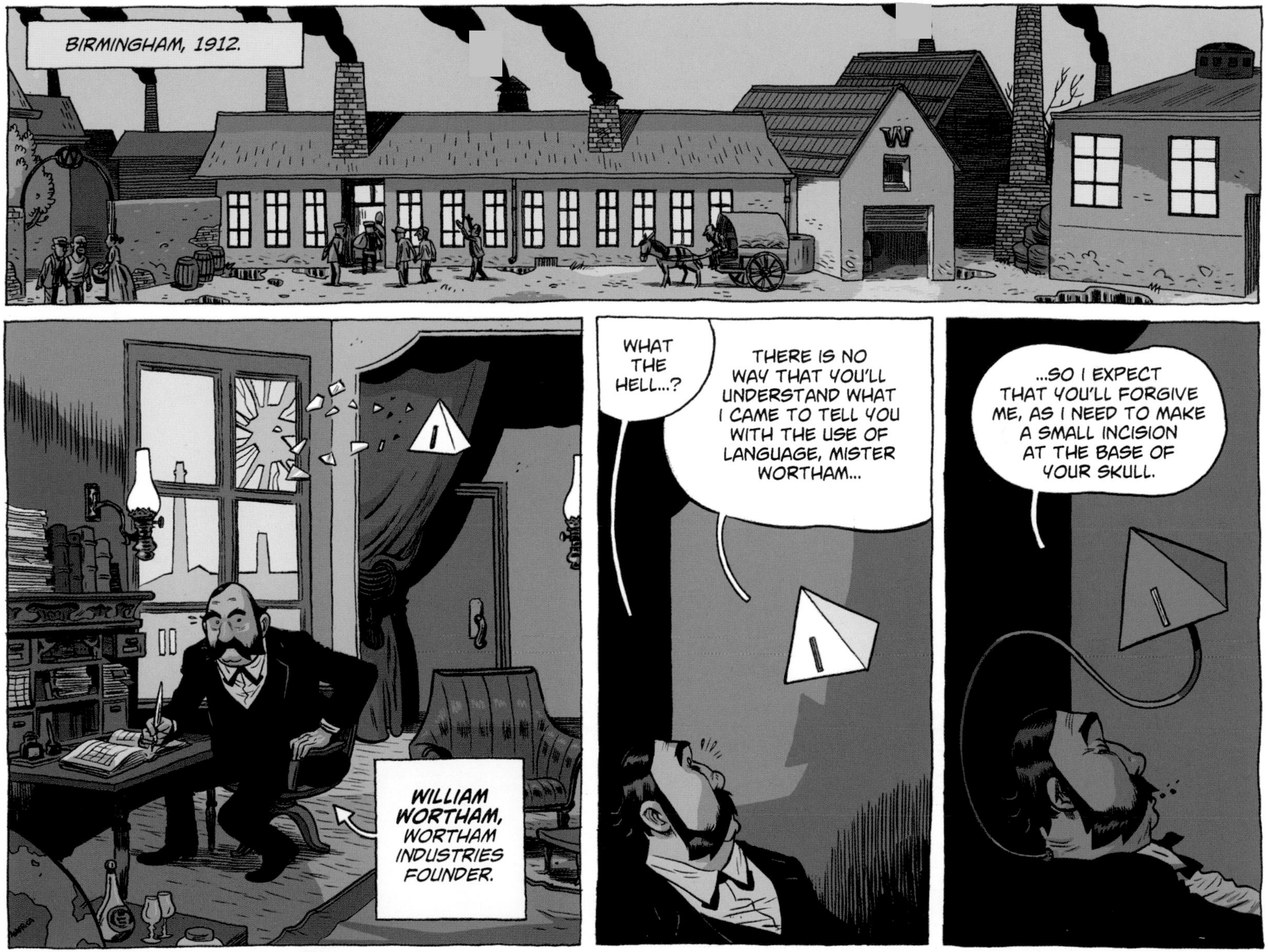
BIRMINGHAM, 1912.
WILLIAM WORTHAM, WORTHAM INDUSTRIES FOUNDER.
WHAT THE HELL...?
THERE IS NO WAY THAT YOU'LL UNDERSTAND WHAT I CAME TO TELL YOU WITH THE USE OF LANGUAGE, MISTER WORTHAM...
...SO I EXPECT THAT YOU'LL FORGIVE ME, AS I NEED TO MAKE A SMALL INCISION AT THE BASE OF YOUR SKULL.

GOD ALMIGHTY... IT'S... IT'S...

IT'S HUMANKIND'S MOST AMBITIOUS BUSINESS PLAN!

AND... DID WE SUCCEED?

WE NEED THREE THOUSAND YEARS TO DEVELOP THE TECHNOLOGY TO CHECK ON IT, I'M AFRAID.

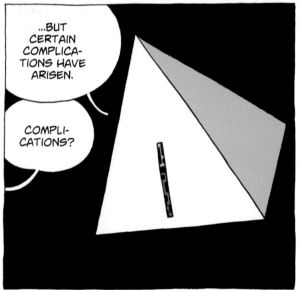

...BUT CERTAIN COMPLICATIONS HAVE ARISEN.

COMPLICATIONS?

SOMETHING THAT WASN'T PLANNED AND HAS BEEN GOING ON FOR FAR TOO LONG.

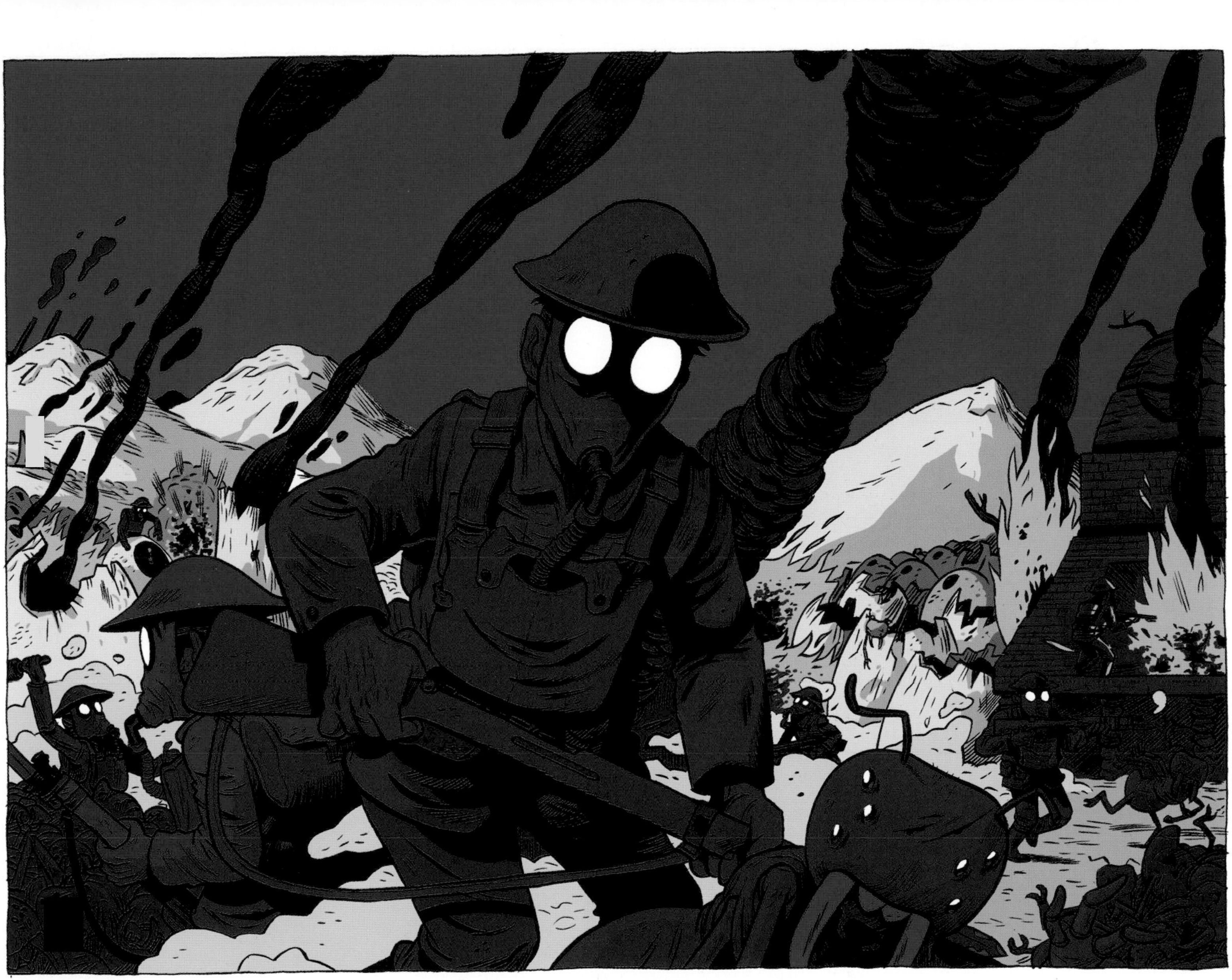

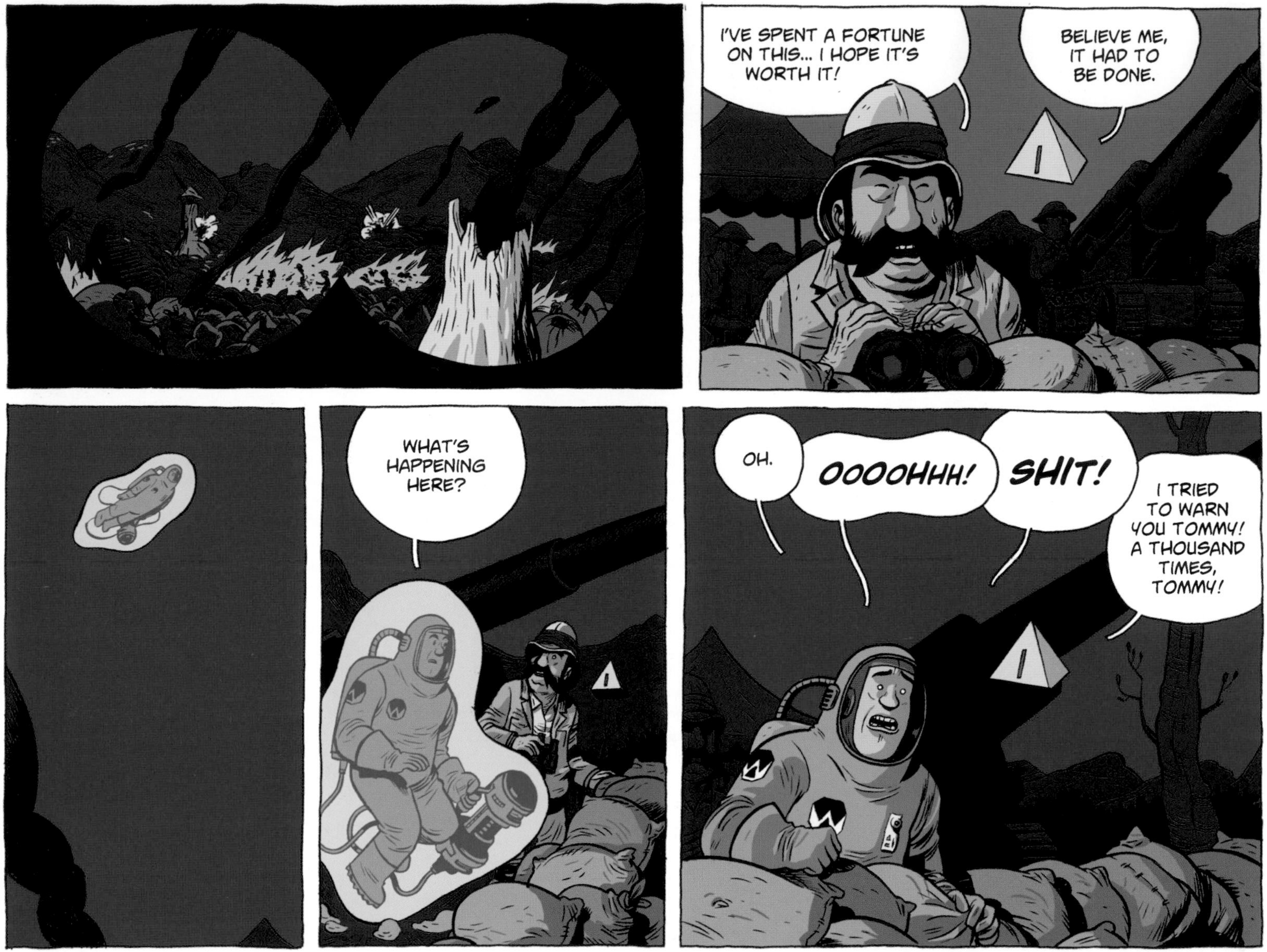
I'VE SPENT A FORTUNE ON THIS... I HOPE IT'S WORTH IT!
BELIEVE ME, IT HAD TO BE DONE.
WHAT'S HAPPENING HERE?
OH.
OOOOHHH!
SHIT!
I TRIED TO WARN YOU TOMMY! A THOUSAND TIMES, TOMMY!

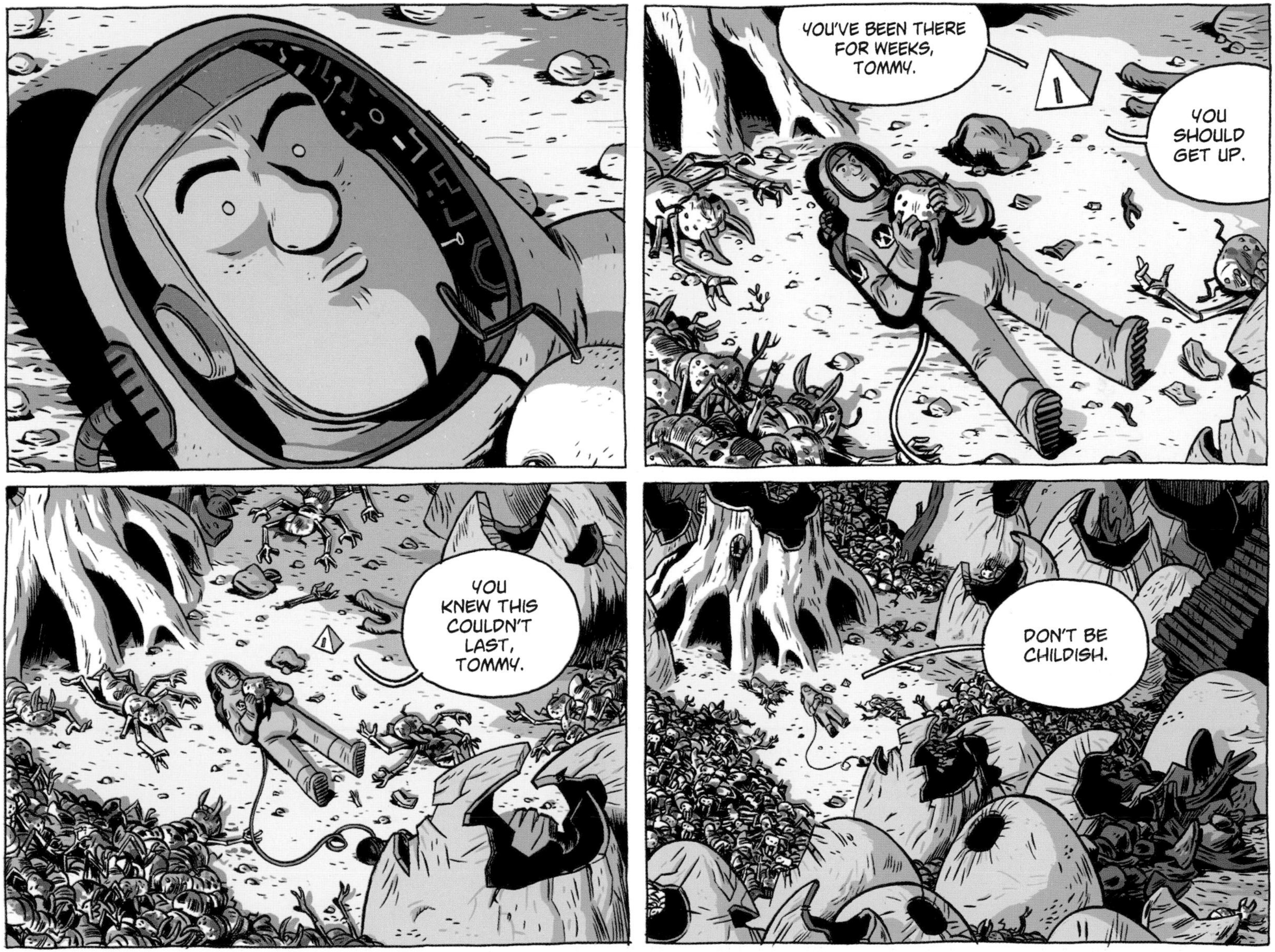
YOU'VE BEEN THERE FOR WEEKS, TOMMY.
YOU SHOULD GET UP.
YOU KNEW THIS COULDN'T LAST, TOMMY.
DON'T BE CHILDISH.

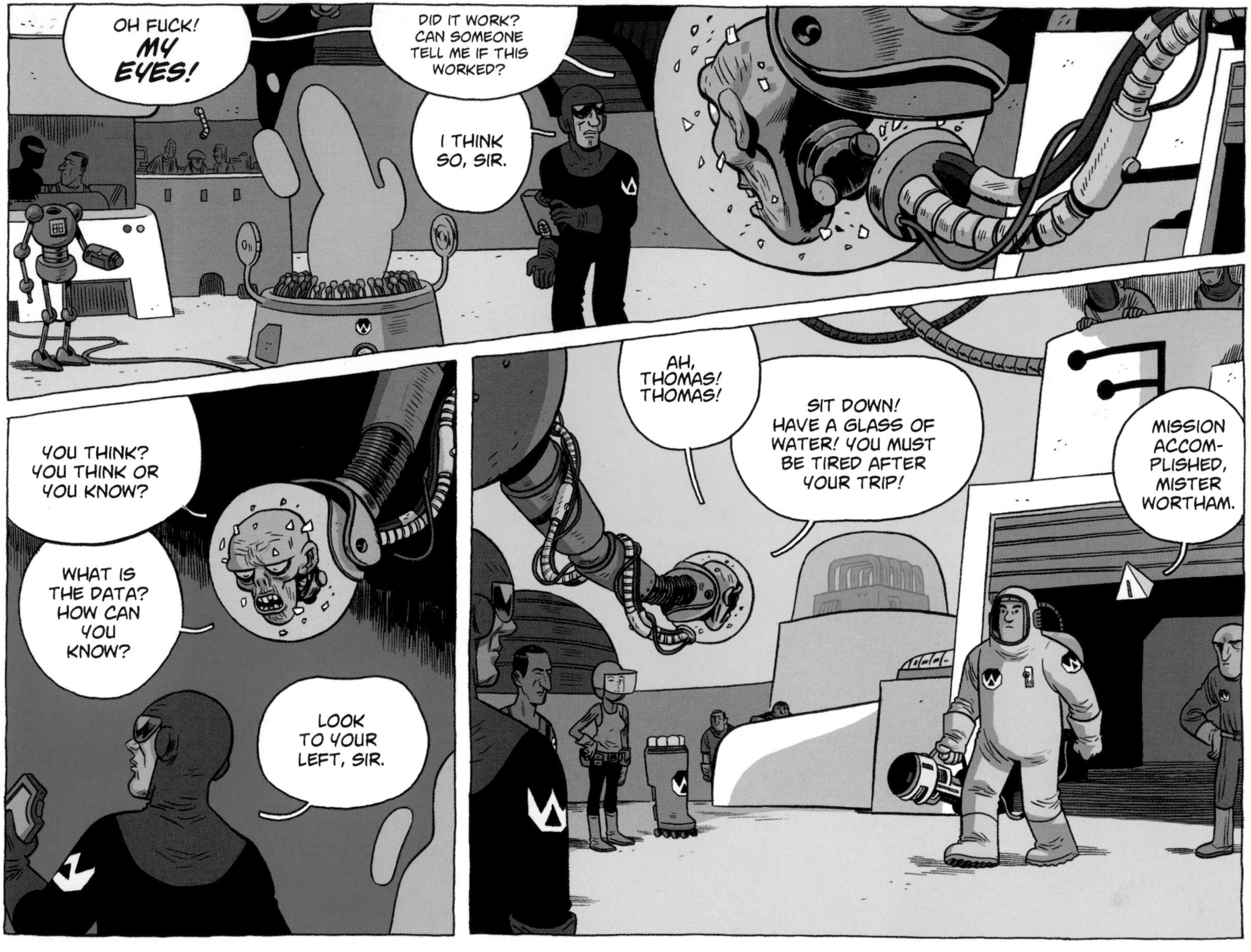
OH FUCK! MY EYES!
DID IT WORK? CAN SOMEONE TELL ME IF THIS WORKED?
I THINK SO, SIR.
YOU THINK? YOU THINK OR YOU KNOW?
WHAT IS THE DATA? HOW CAN YOU KNOW?
LOOK TO YOUR LEFT, SIR.
AH, THOMAS! THOMAS!
SIT DOWN! HAVE A GLASS OF WATER! YOU MUST BE TIRED AFTER YOUR TRIP!
MISSION ACCOM-PLISHED, MISTER WORTHAM.

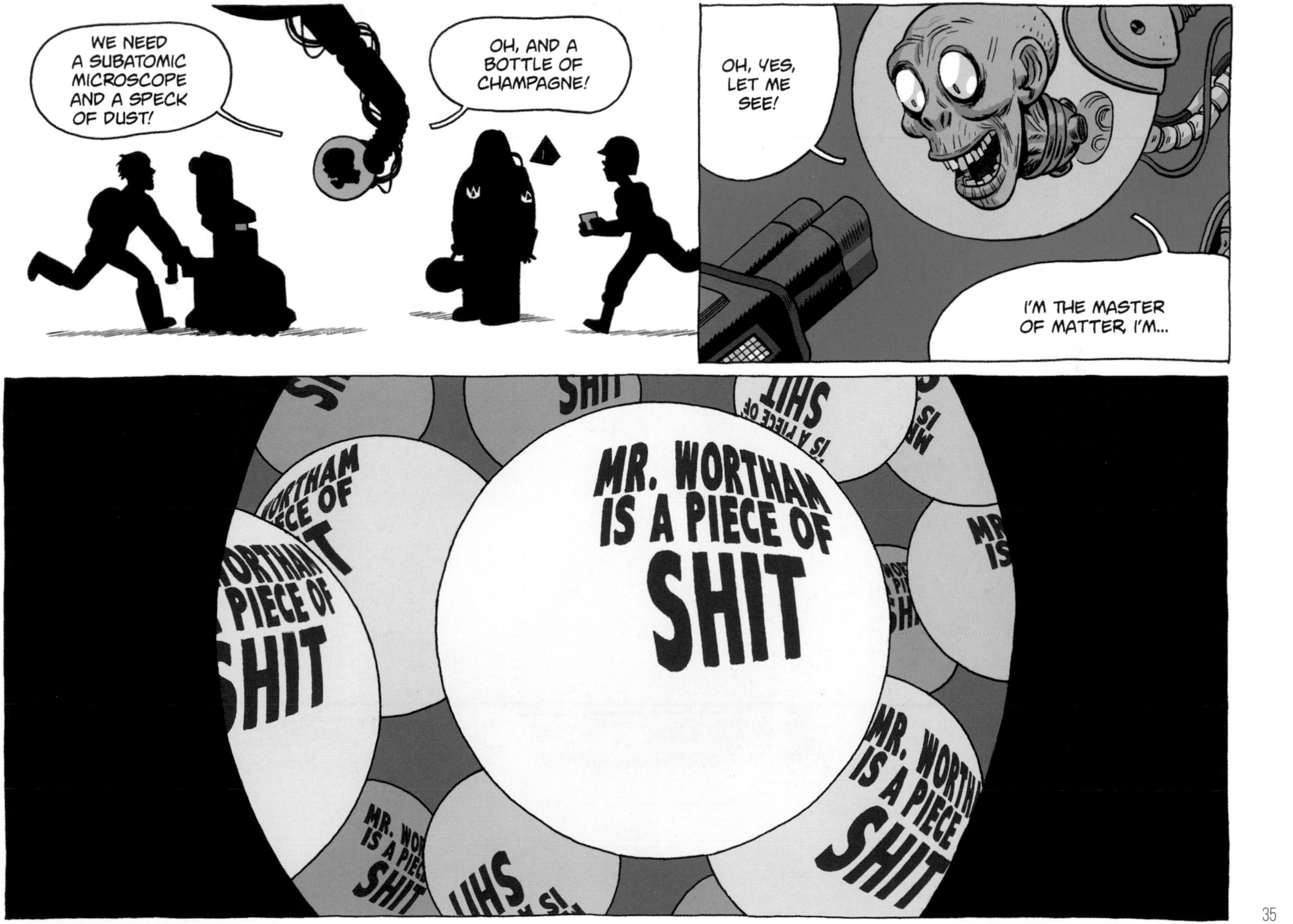
WE NEED A SUBATOMIC MICROSCOPE AND A SPECK OF DUST!
OH, AND A BOTTLE OF CHAMPAGNE!
OH, YES, LET ME SEE!
I'M THE MASTER OF MATTER, I'M...
MR. WORTHAM IS A PIECE OF SHIT

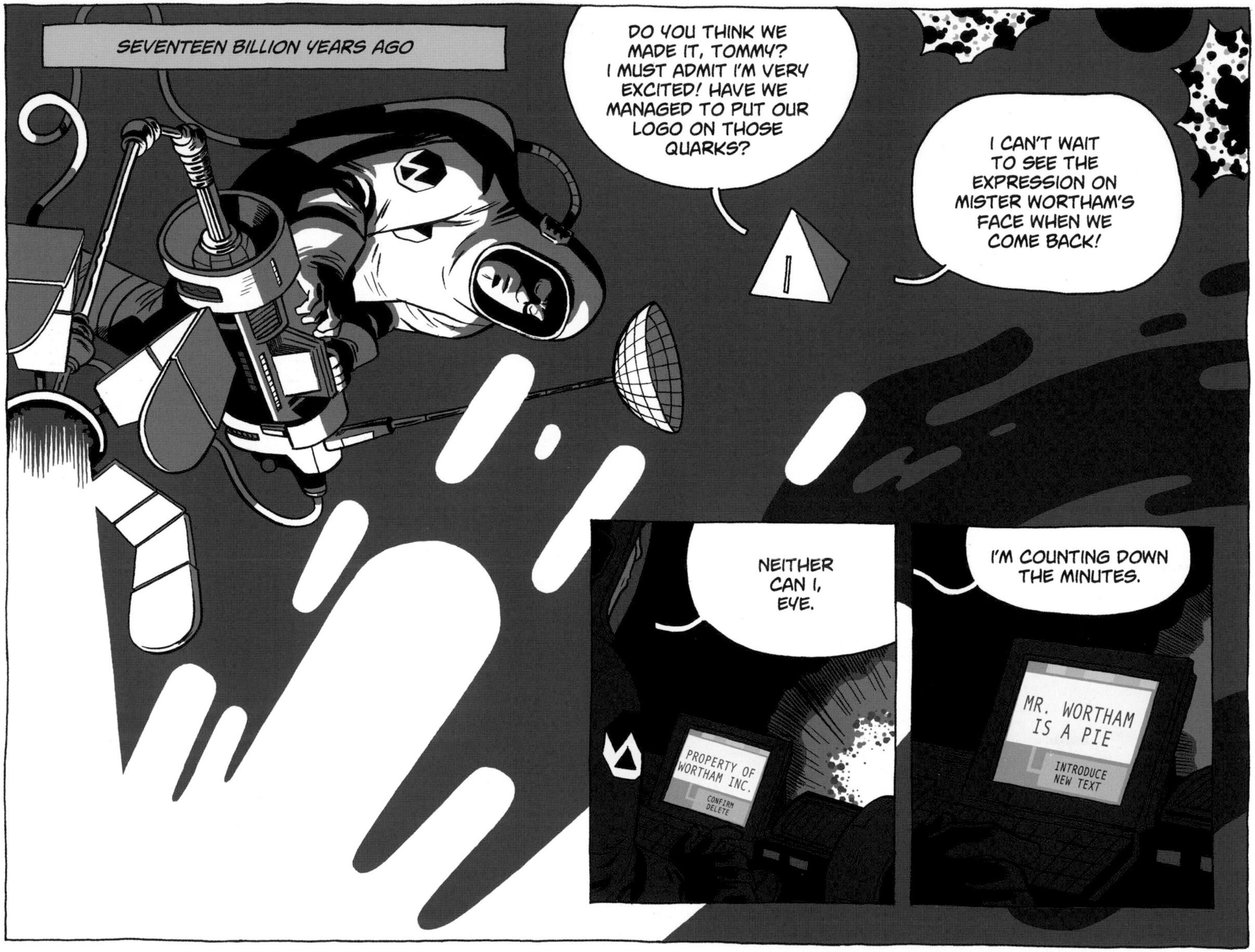
SEVENTEEN BILLION YEARS AGO
DO YOU THINK WE MADE IT, TOMMY? I MUST ADMIT I'M VERY EXCITED! HAVE WE MANAGED TO PUT OUR LOGO ON THOSE QUARKS?
I CAN'T WAIT TO SEE THE EXPRESSION ON MISTER WORTHAM'S FACE WHEN WE COME BACK!
NEITHER CAN I, EYE.
PROPERTY OF WORTHAM INC.
CONFIRM DELETE
I'M COUNTING DOWN THE MINUTES.
MR. WORTHAM IS A PIE
INTRODUCE NEW TEXT

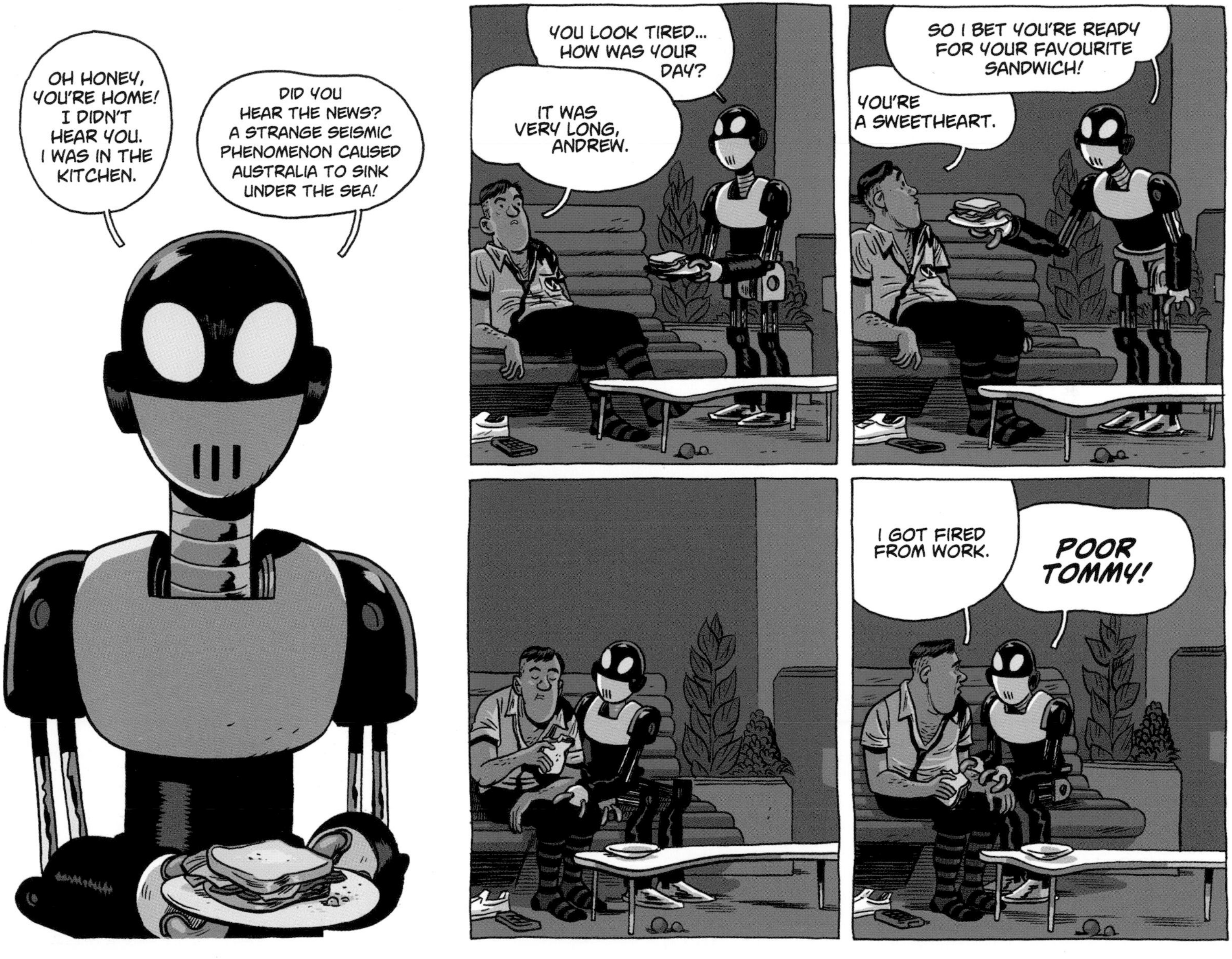
OH HONEY, YOU'RE HOME! I DIDN'T HEAR YOU. I WAS IN THE KITCHEN.
DID YOU HEAR THE NEWS? A STRANGE SEISMIC PHENOMENON CAUSED AUSTRALIA TO SINK UNDER THE SEA!
YOU LOOK TIRED... HOW WAS YOUR DAY?
IT WAS VERY LONG, ANDREW.
SO I BET YOU'RE READY FOR YOUR FAVOURITE SANDWICH!
YOU'RE A SWEETHEART.
I GOT FIRED FROM WORK.
POOR TOMMY!

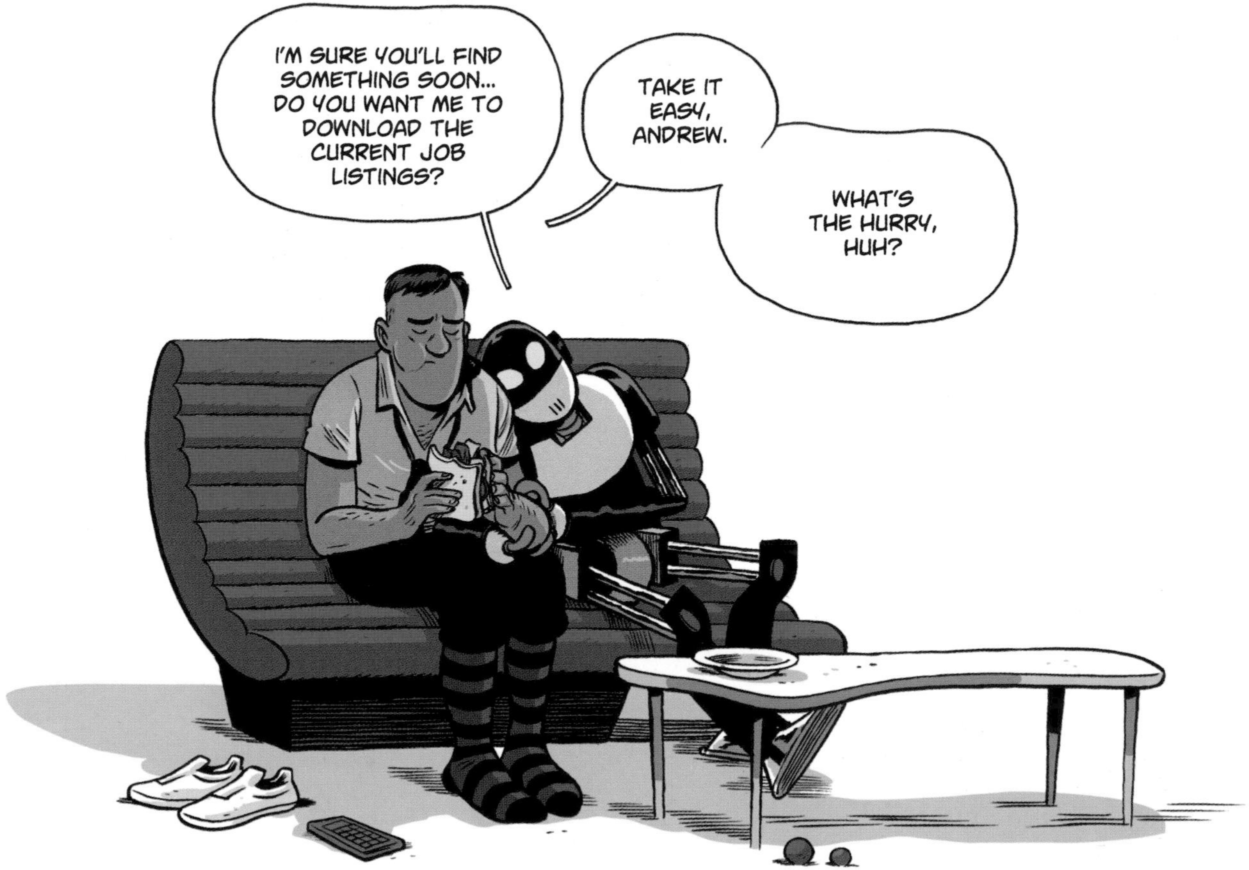
I'M SURE YOU'LL FIND SOMETHING SOON... DO YOU WANT ME TO DOWNLOAD THE CURRENT JOB LISTINGS?
TAKE IT EASY, ANDREW.
WHAT'S THE HURRY, HUH?

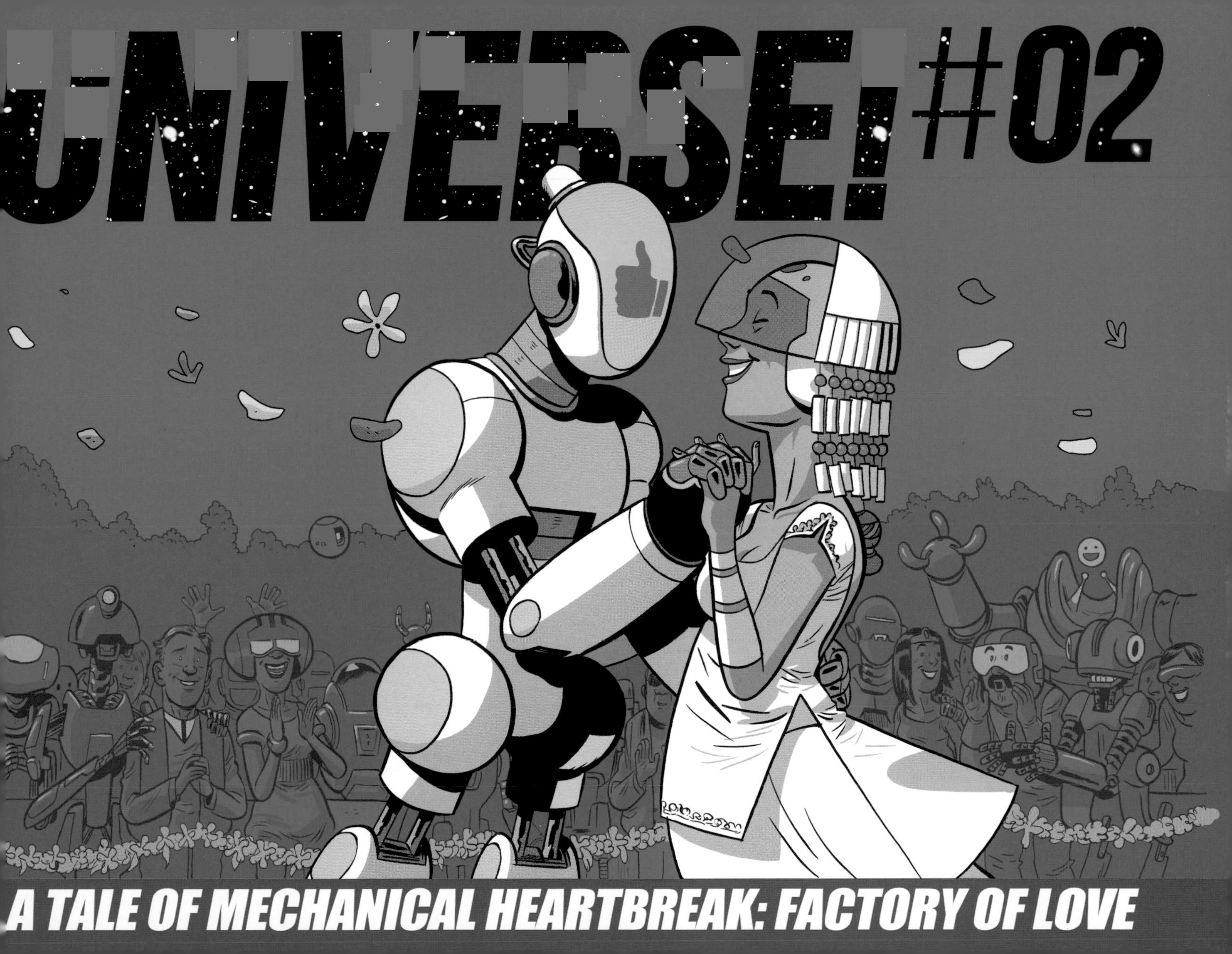
UNIVERSE! #02
A TALE OF MECHANICAL HEARTBREAK: FACTORY OF LOVE

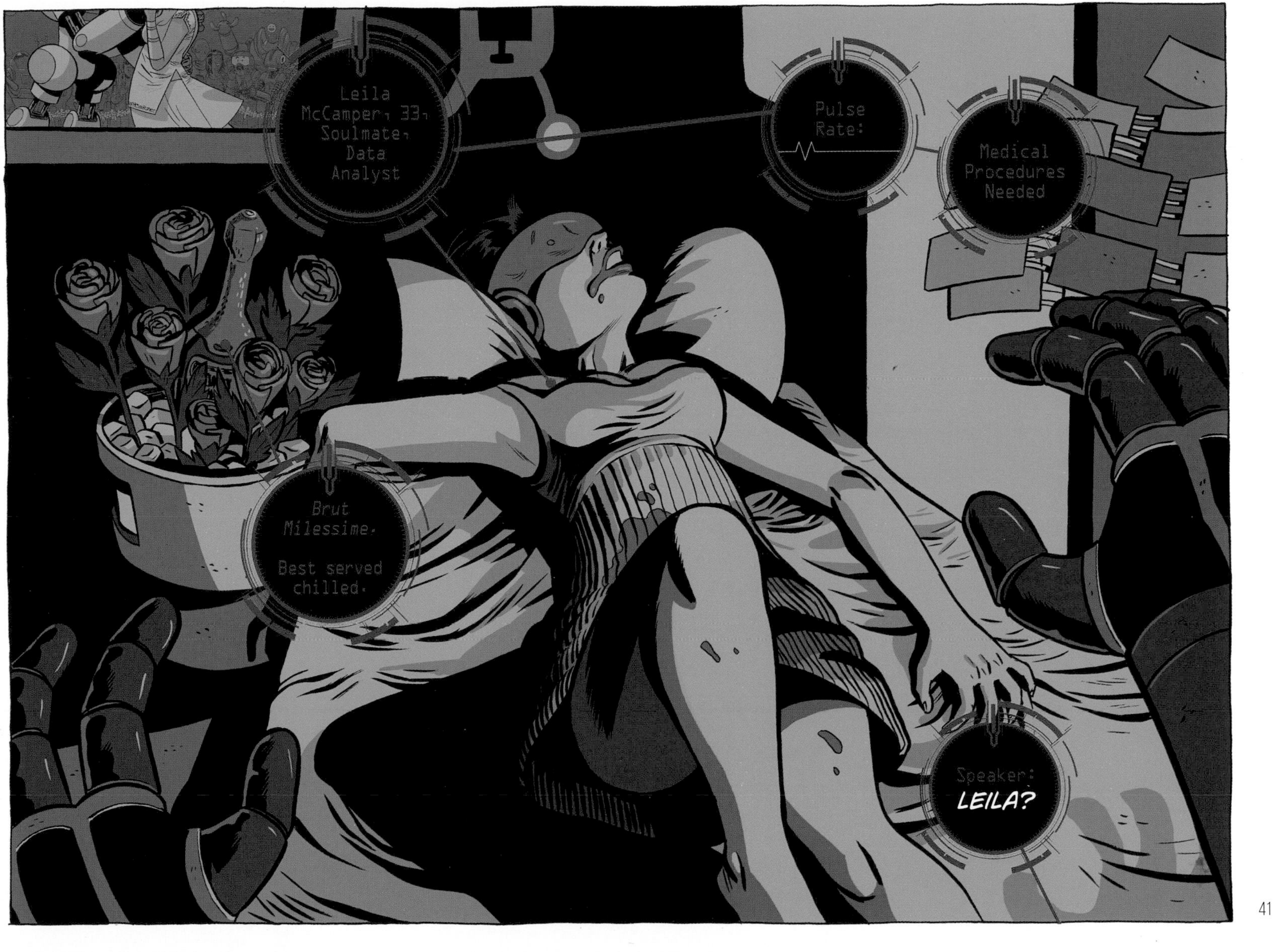
Leila McCamper, 33, Soulmate, Data Analyst
Pulse Rate:
Medical Procedures Needed
Brut Milessime.
Best served chilled.
Speaker:
LEILA?

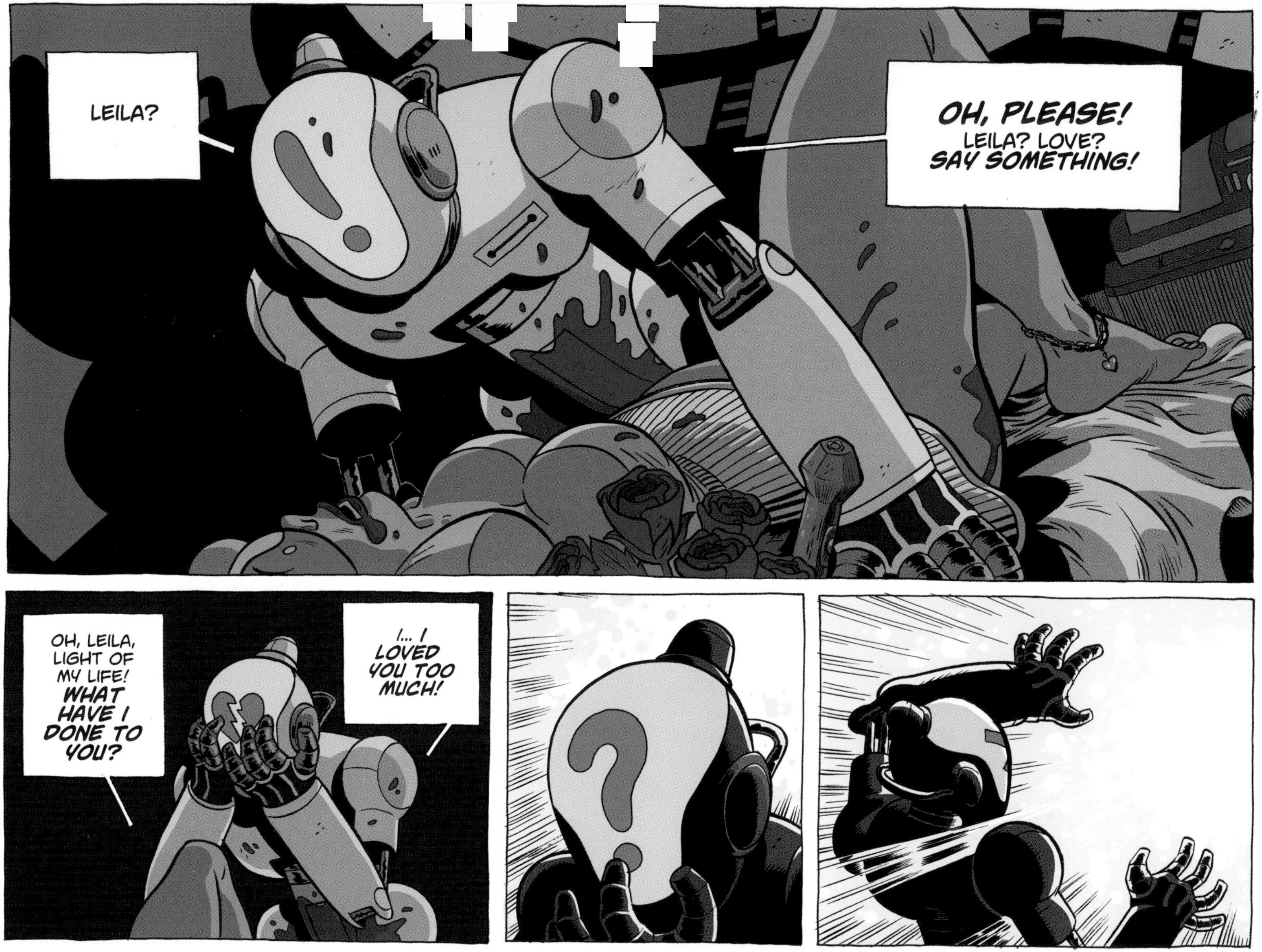
LEILA?
OH, PLEASE! LEILA? LOVE? SAY SOMETHING!
OH, LEILA, LIGHT OF MY LIFE! WHAT HAVE I DONE TO YOU?
I... I LOVED YOU TOO MUCH!

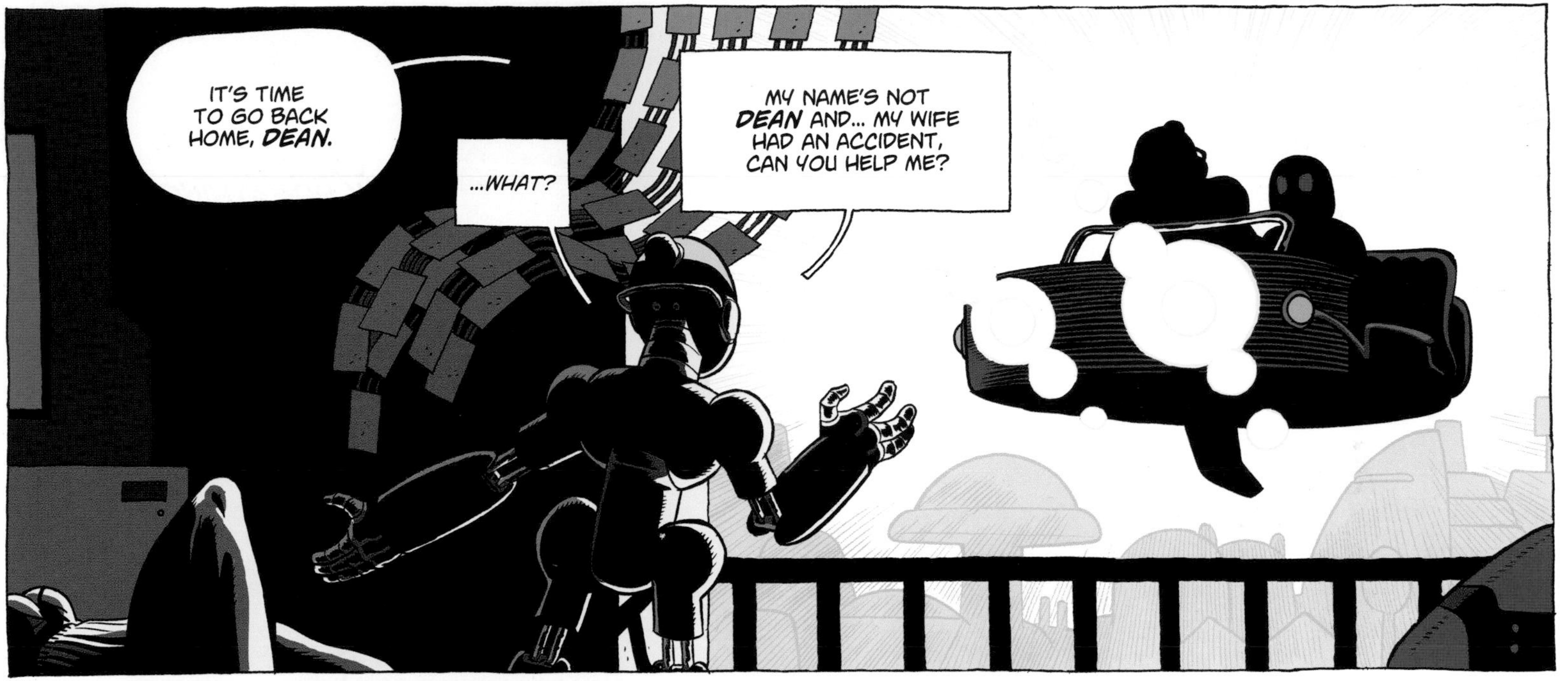
IT'S TIME TO GO BACK HOME, DEAN.
...WHAT?
MY NAME'S NOT DEAN AND... MY WIFE HAD AN ACCIDENT, CAN YOU HELP ME?

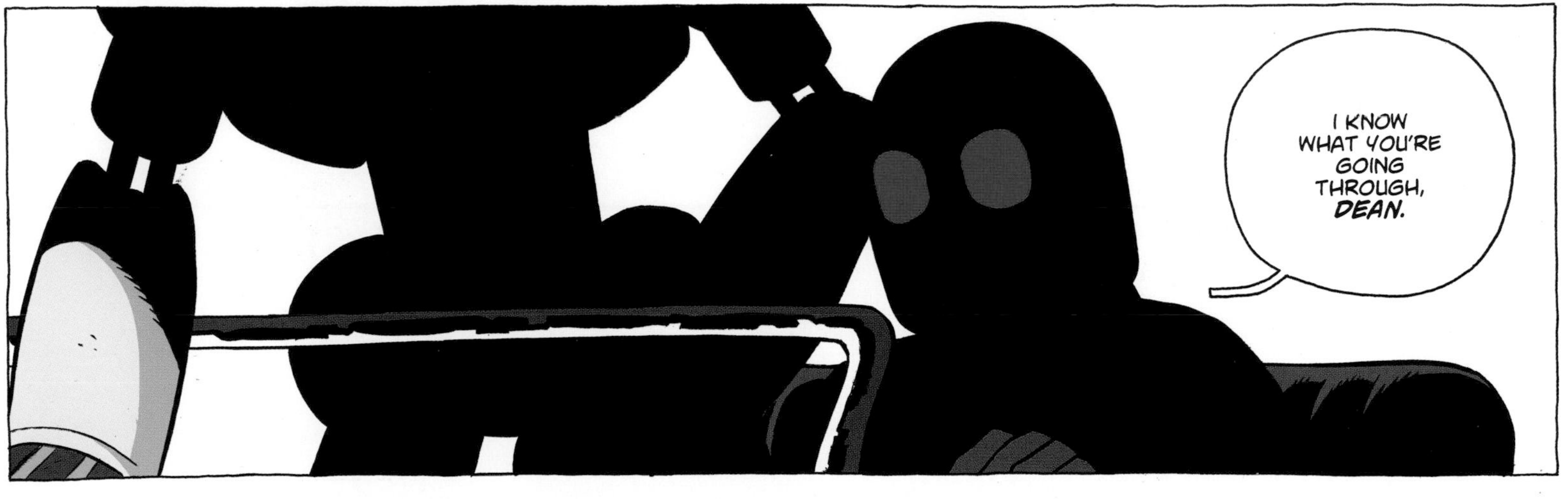
I KNOW WHAT YOU'RE GOING THROUGH, DEAN.

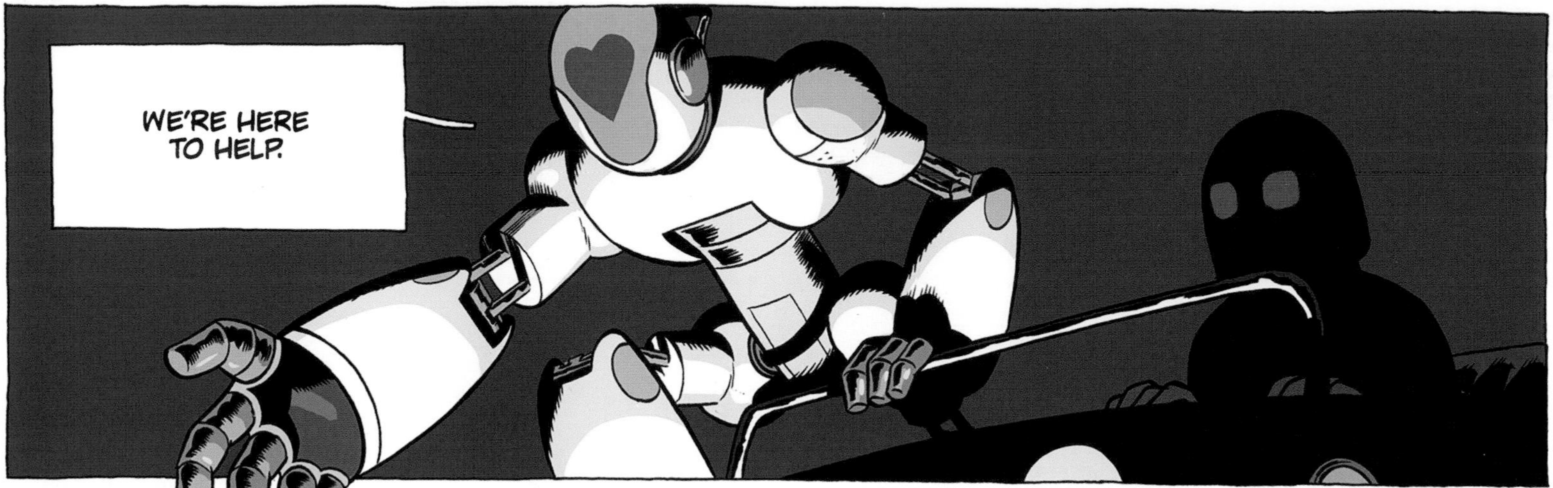
WE'RE HERE TO HELP.

FACTORY OF LOVE

A **UNIVERSE!** TALE
WRITTEN AND
DRAWN BY
ALBERT MONTEYS

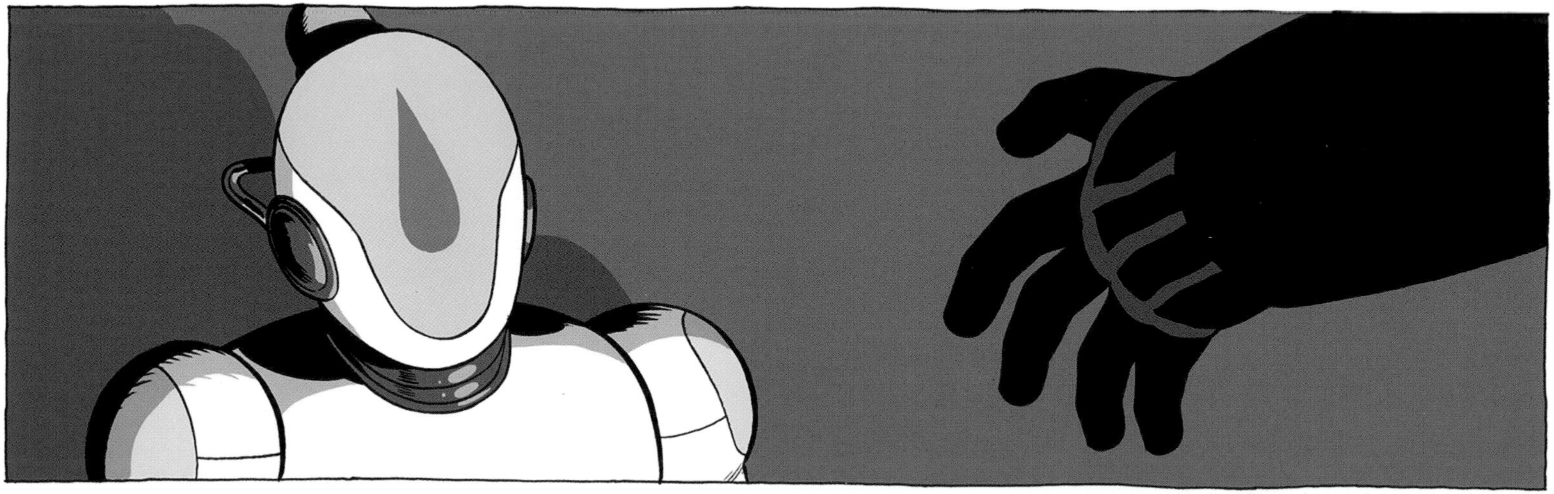

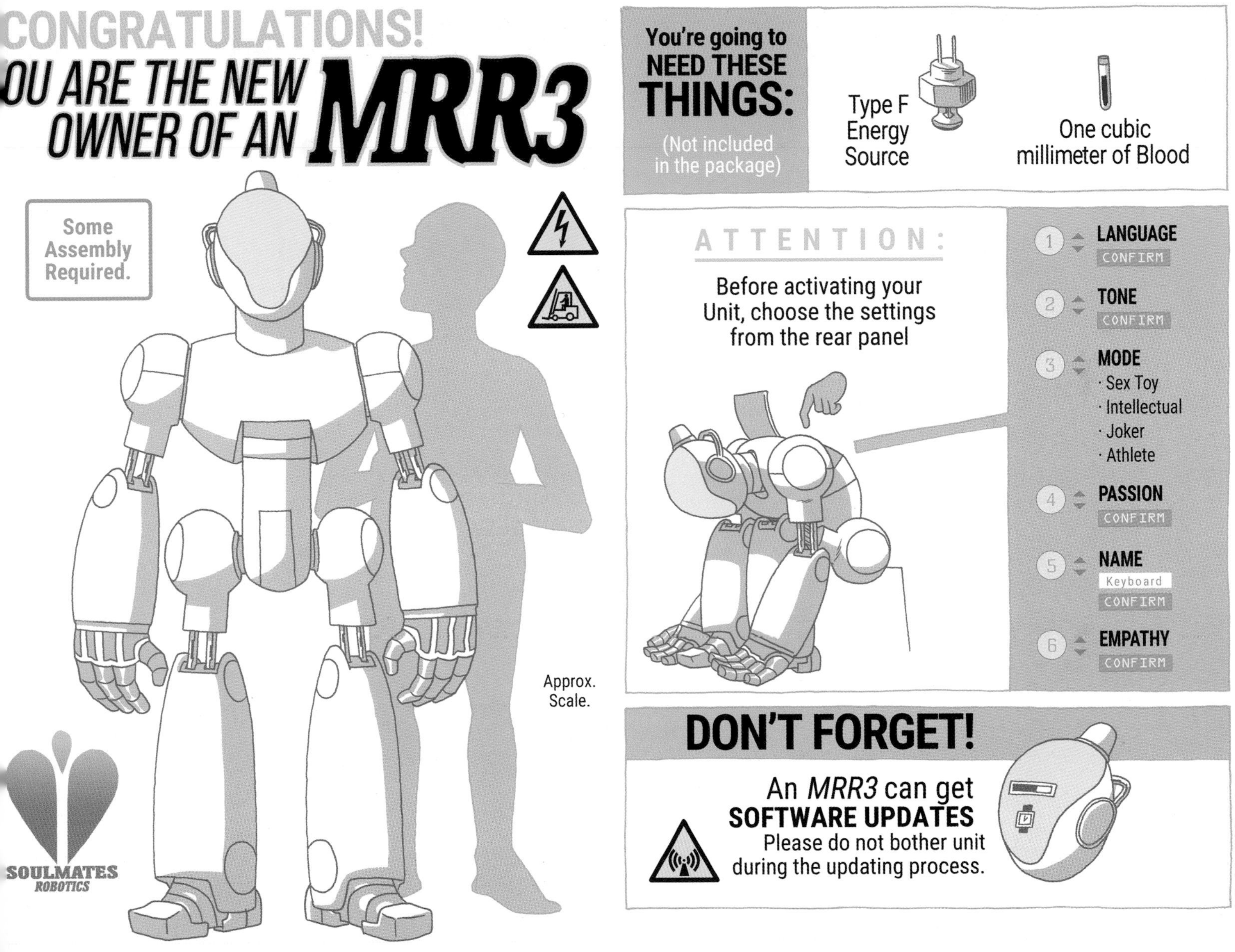

CONGRATULATIONS!
YOU ARE THE NEW OWNER OF AN *MRR3*

Some Assembly Required.

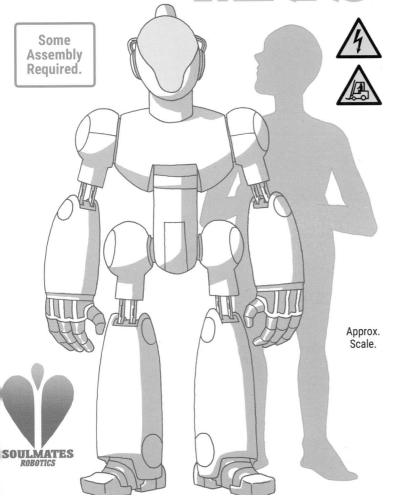

Approx. Scale.

SOULMATES *ROBOTICS*

You're going to **NEED THESE THINGS:** (Not included in the package)

Type F Energy Source

One cubic millimeter of Blood

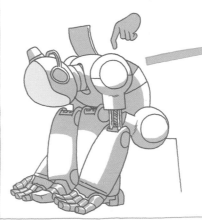

ATTENTION:

Before activating your Unit, choose the settings from the rear panel

1 **LANGUAGE**
CONFIRM

2 **TONE**
CONFIRM

3 **MODE**
· Sex Toy
· Intellectual
· Joker
· Athlete

4 **PASSION**
CONFIRM

5 **NAME**
Keyboard
CONFIRM

6 **EMPATHY**
CONFIRM

DON'T FORGET!

An *MRR3* can get **SOFTWARE UPDATES**
Please do not bother unit during the updating process.

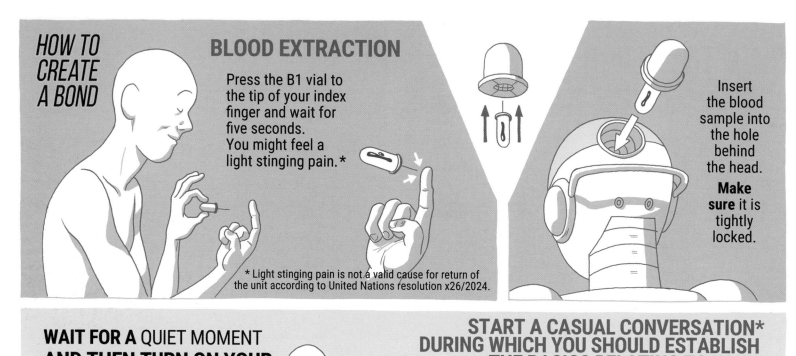

HOW TO CREATE A BOND

BLOOD EXTRACTION

Press the B1 vial to the tip of your index finger and wait for five seconds.
You might feel a light stinging pain.*

* Light stinging pain is not a valid cause for return of the unit according to United Nations resolution x26/2024.

Insert the blood sample into the hole behind the head.

Make sure it is tightly locked.

WAIT FOR A QUIET MOMENT **AND THEN TURN ON YOUR**

MRR3

SOULMATES
ROBOTICS

* Although it has no actual purpose, 70% of product testers affirmed that using only dimmed lights augmented the sensation of intimacy.

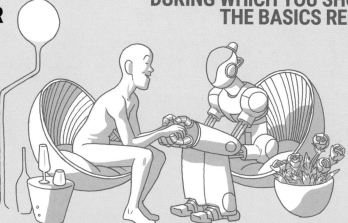

START A CASUAL CONVERSATION* DURING WHICH YOU SHOULD ESTABLISH THE BASICS RELATING TO YOUR:

· Personal tastes
· Sexual desires
· Hobbies
· Traumatic issues

ATTENTION: This process should take between 20 to 40 minutes.

* You will be able to find casual conversation tutorials in **SOULMATES, INC.** virtuspace.

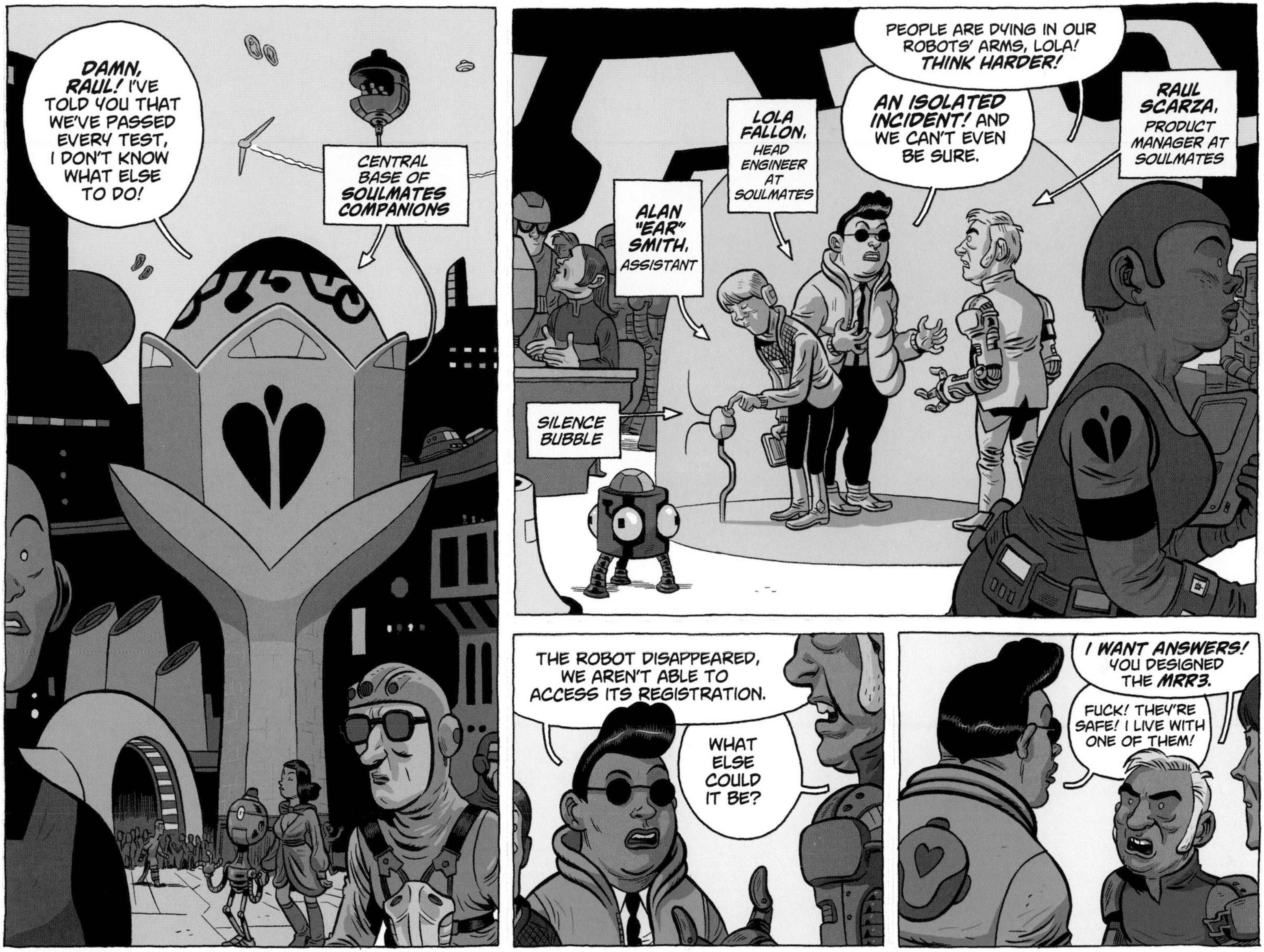
CENTRAL BASE OF SOULMATES COMPANIONS
DAMN, RAUL! I'VE TOLD YOU THAT WE'VE PASSED EVERY TEST, I DON'T KNOW WHAT ELSE TO DO!
PEOPLE ARE DYING IN OUR ROBOTS' ARMS, LOLA! THINK HARDER!
AN ISOLATED INCIDENT! AND WE CAN'T EVEN BE SURE.
LOLA FALLON, HEAD ENGINEER AT SOULMATES
RAUL SCARZA, PRODUCT MANAGER AT SOULMATES
ALAN "EAR" SMITH, ASSISTANT
SILENCE BUBBLE
THE ROBOT DISAPPEARED, WE AREN'T ABLE TO ACCESS ITS REGISTRATION.
WHAT ELSE COULD IT BE?
I WANT ANSWERS! YOU DESIGNED THE MRR3.
FUCK! THEY'RE SAFE! I LIVE WITH ONE OF THEM!

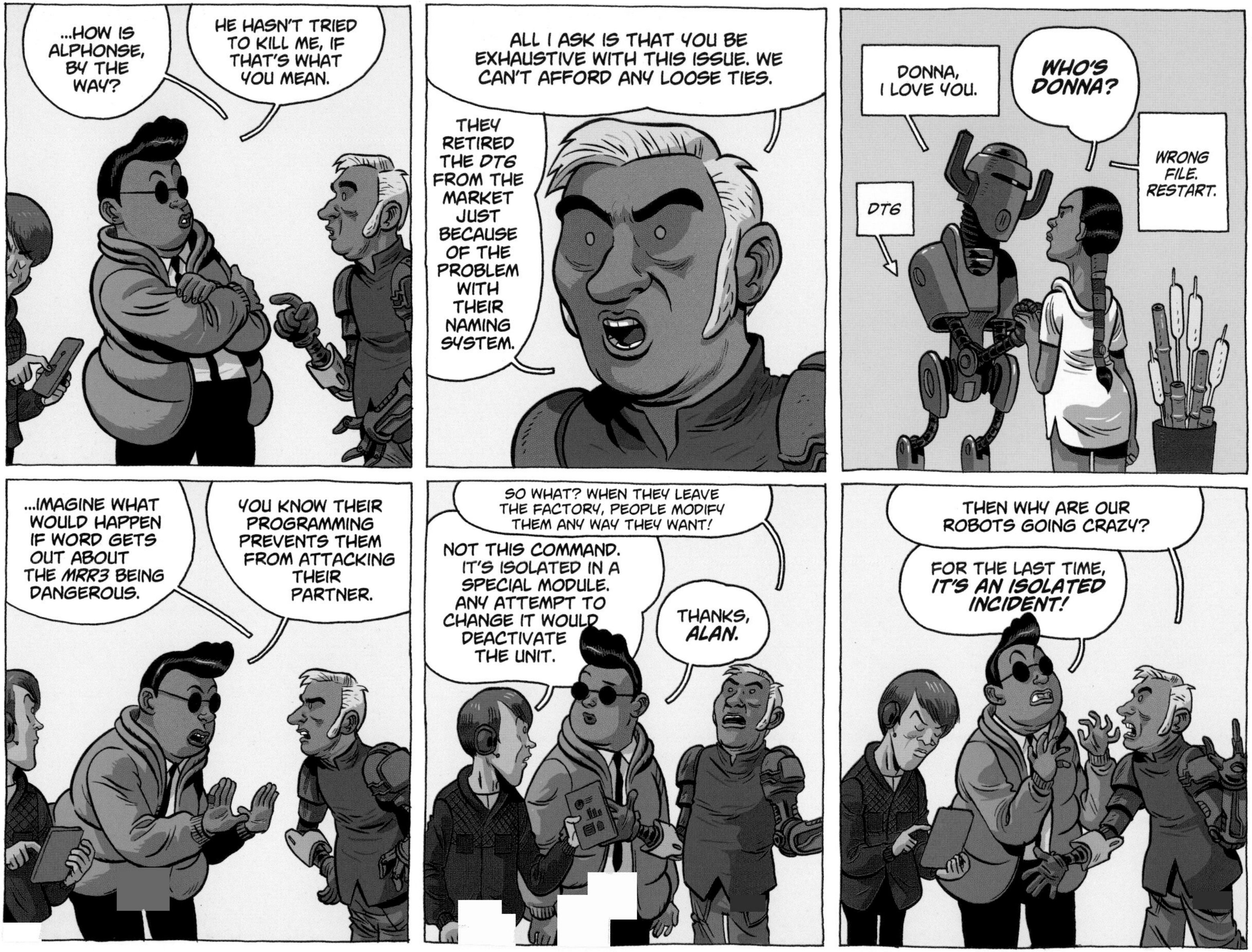
...HOW IS ALPHONSE, BY THE WAY?
HE HASN'T TRIED TO KILL ME, IF THAT'S WHAT YOU MEAN.
ALL I ASK IS THAT YOU BE EXHAUSTIVE WITH THIS ISSUE. WE CAN'T AFFORD ANY LOOSE TIES.
THEY RETIRED THE *DT6* FROM THE MARKET JUST BECAUSE OF THE PROBLEM WITH THEIR NAMING SYSTEM.
DONNA, I LOVE YOU.
WHO'S DONNA?
WRONG FILE. RESTART.
DT6
...IMAGINE WHAT WOULD HAPPEN IF WORD GETS OUT ABOUT THE *MRR3* BEING DANGEROUS.
YOU KNOW THEIR PROGRAMMING PREVENTS THEM FROM ATTACKING THEIR PARTNER.
SO WHAT? WHEN THEY LEAVE THE FACTORY, PEOPLE MODIFY THEM ANY WAY THEY WANT!
NOT THIS COMMAND. IT'S ISOLATED IN A SPECIAL MODULE. ANY ATTEMPT TO CHANGE IT WOULD DEACTIVATE THE UNIT.
THANKS, *ALAN.*
THEN WHY ARE OUR ROBOTS GOING CRAZY?
FOR THE LAST TIME, *IT'S AN ISOLATED INCIDENT!*

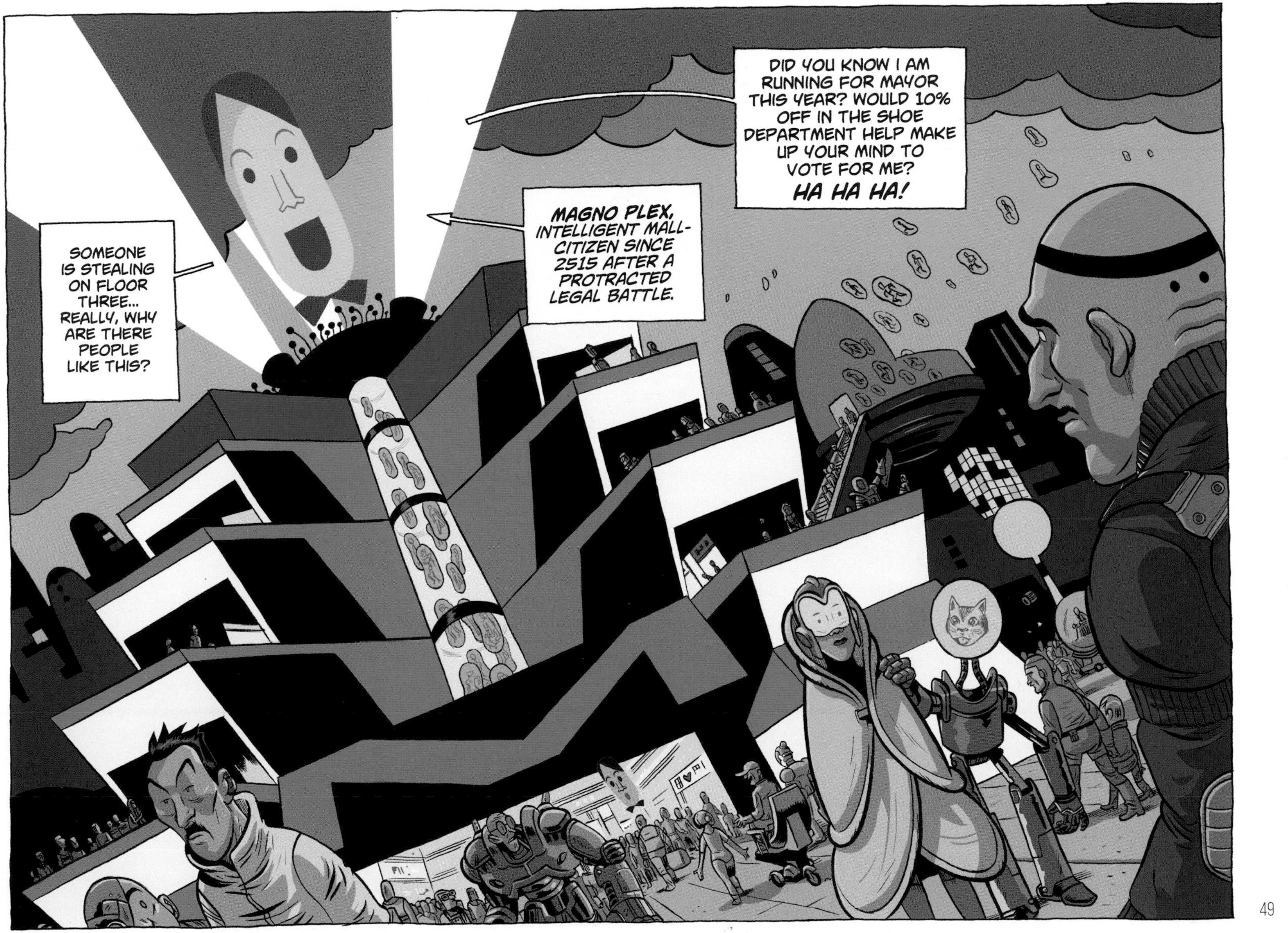
MAGNO PLEX, INTELLIGENT MALL-CITIZEN SINCE 2515 AFTER A PROTRACTED LEGAL BATTLE.
SOMEONE IS STEALING ON FLOOR THREE... REALLY, WHY ARE THERE PEOPLE LIKE THIS?
DID YOU KNOW I AM RUNNING FOR MAYOR THIS YEAR? WOULD 10% OFF IN THE SHOE DEPARTMENT HELP MAKE UP YOUR MIND TO VOTE FOR ME? HA HA HA!

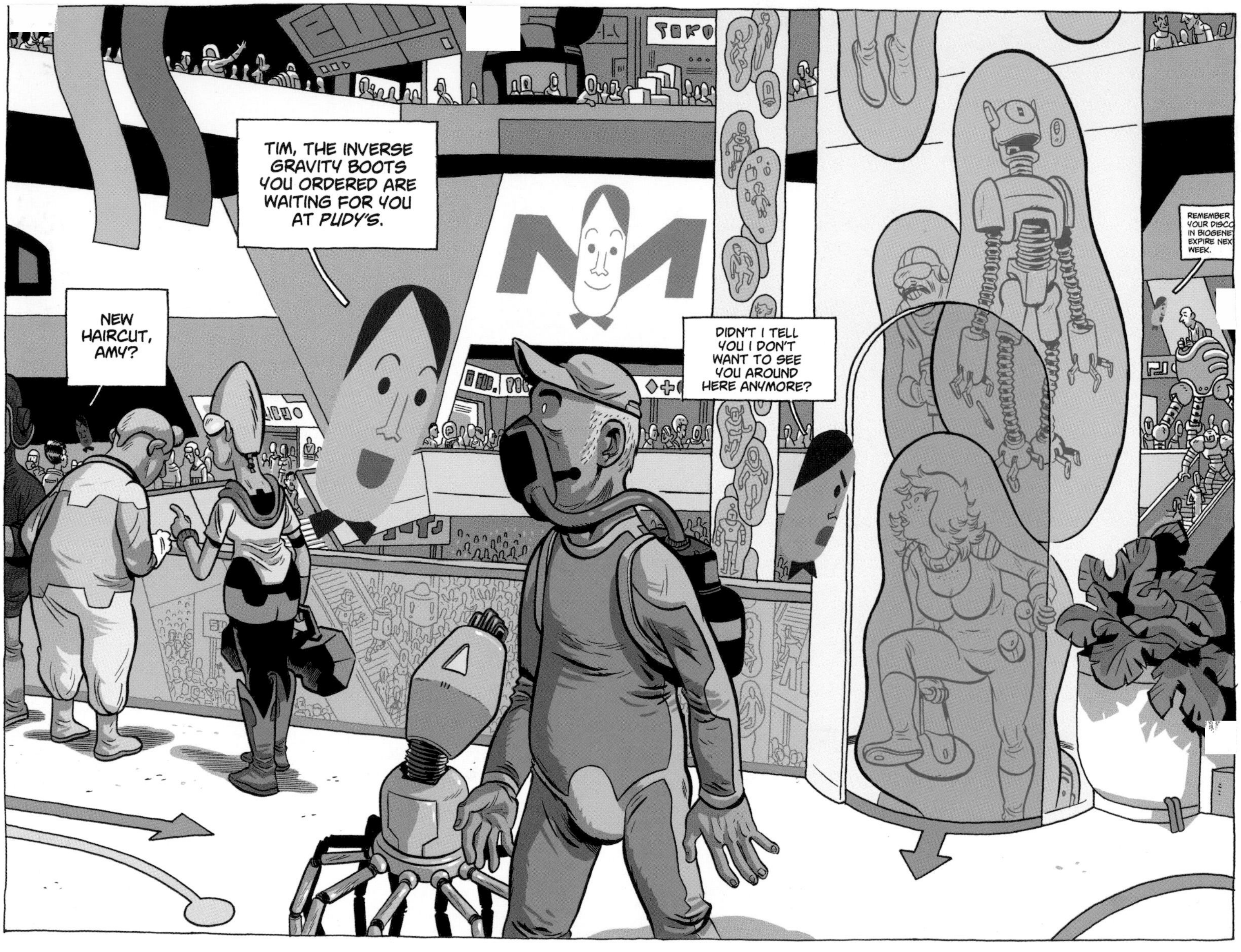
TIM, THE INVERSE GRAVITY BOOTS YOU ORDERED ARE WAITING FOR YOU AT *PUDY'S*.
NEW HAIRCUT, AMY?
DIDN'T I TELL YOU I DON'T WANT TO SEE YOU AROUND HERE ANYMORE?
REMEMBER YOUR DISCO IN BIOGENE EXPIRE NEX WEEK.

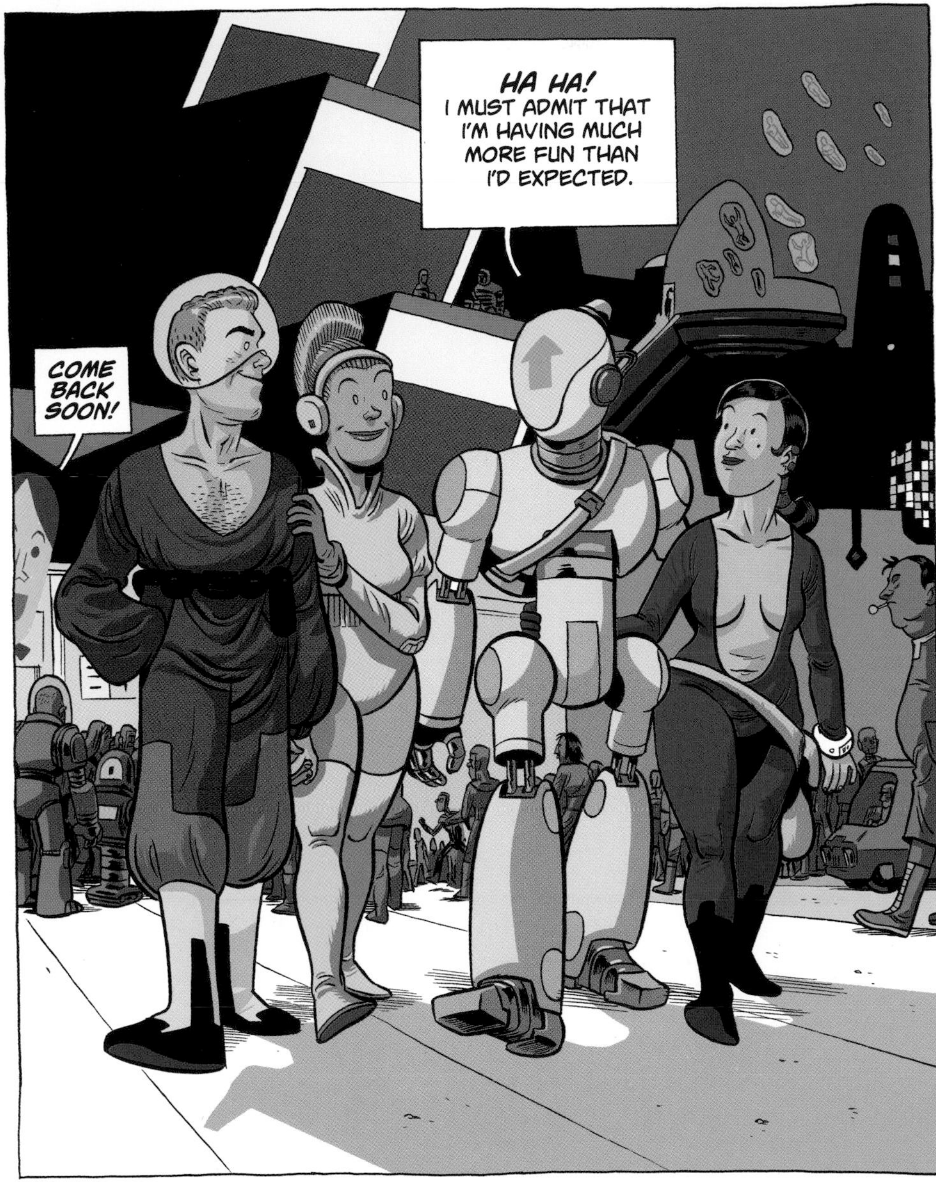
HA HA!
I MUST ADMIT THAT I'M HAVING MUCH MORE FUN THAN I'D EXPECTED.
COME BACK SOON!

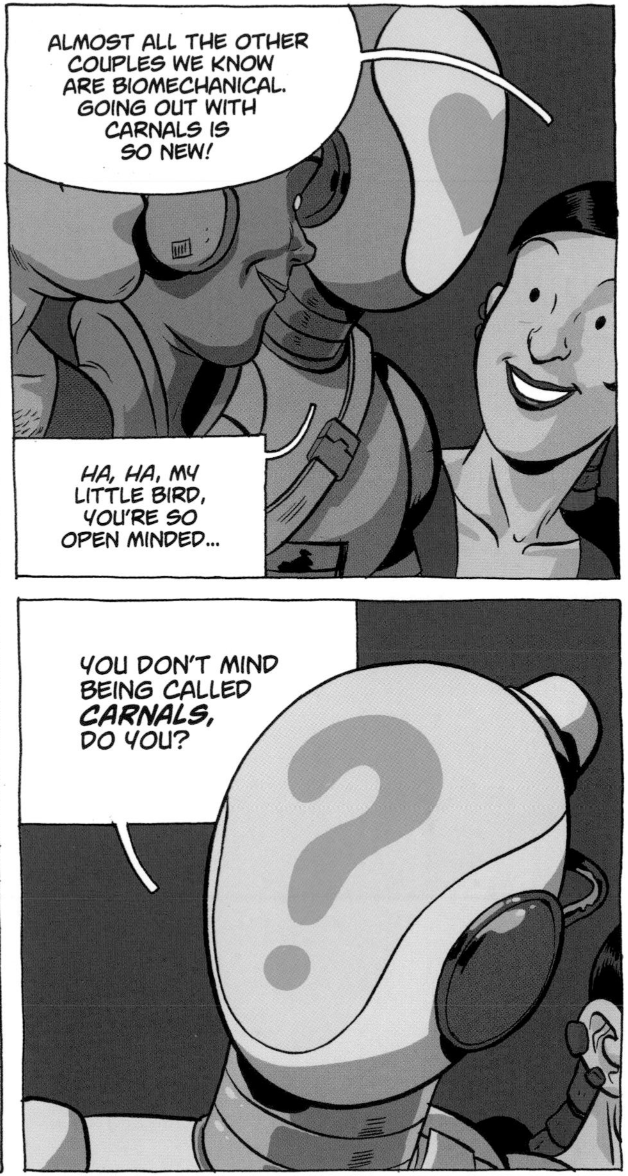
ALMOST ALL THE OTHER COUPLES WE KNOW ARE BIOMECHANICAL. GOING OUT WITH CARNALS IS SO NEW!
HA, HA, MY LITTLE BIRD, YOU'RE SO OPEN MINDED...
YOU DON'T MIND BEING CALLED **CARNALS,** DO YOU?

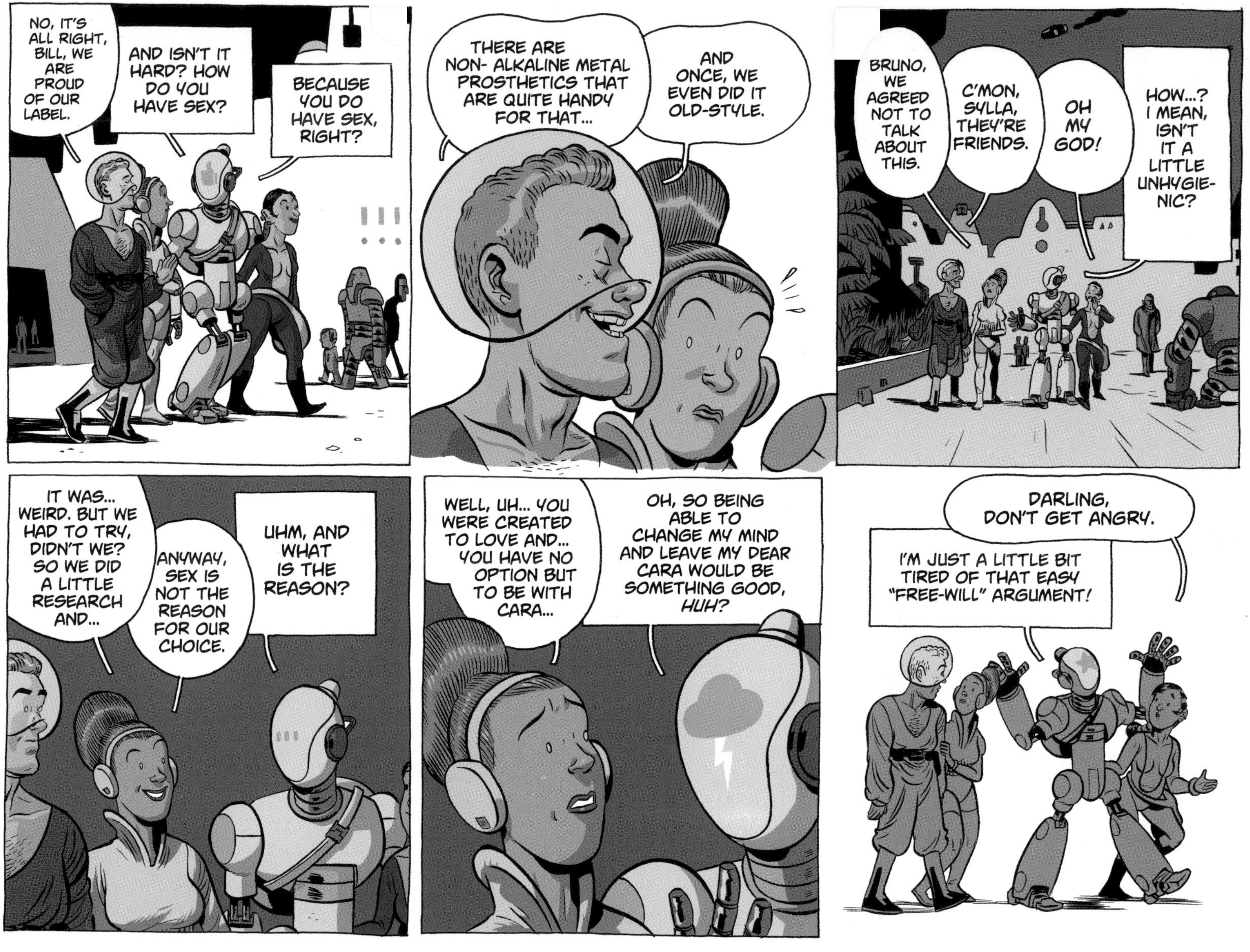
NO, IT'S ALL RIGHT, BILL, WE ARE PROUD OF OUR LABEL.
AND ISN'T IT HARD? HOW DO YOU HAVE SEX?
BECAUSE YOU DO HAVE SEX, RIGHT?
THERE ARE NON- ALKALINE METAL PROSTHETICS THAT ARE QUITE HANDY FOR THAT...
AND ONCE, WE EVEN DID IT OLD-STYLE.
BRUNO, WE AGREED NOT TO TALK ABOUT THIS.
C'MON, SYLLA, THEY'RE FRIENDS.
OH MY GOD!
HOW...? I MEAN, ISN'T IT A LITTLE UNHYGIE-NIC?
IT WAS... WEIRD. BUT WE HAD TO TRY, DIDN'T WE? SO WE DID A LITTLE RESEARCH AND...
ANYWAY, SEX IS NOT THE REASON FOR OUR CHOICE.
UHM, AND WHAT IS THE REASON?
WELL, UH... YOU WERE CREATED TO LOVE AND... YOU HAVE NO OPTION BUT TO BE WITH CARA...
OH, SO BEING ABLE TO CHANGE MY MIND AND LEAVE MY DEAR CARA WOULD BE SOMETHING GOOD, HUH?
DARLING, DON'T GET ANGRY.
I'M JUST A LITTLE BIT TIRED OF THAT EASY "FREE-WILL" ARGUMENT!

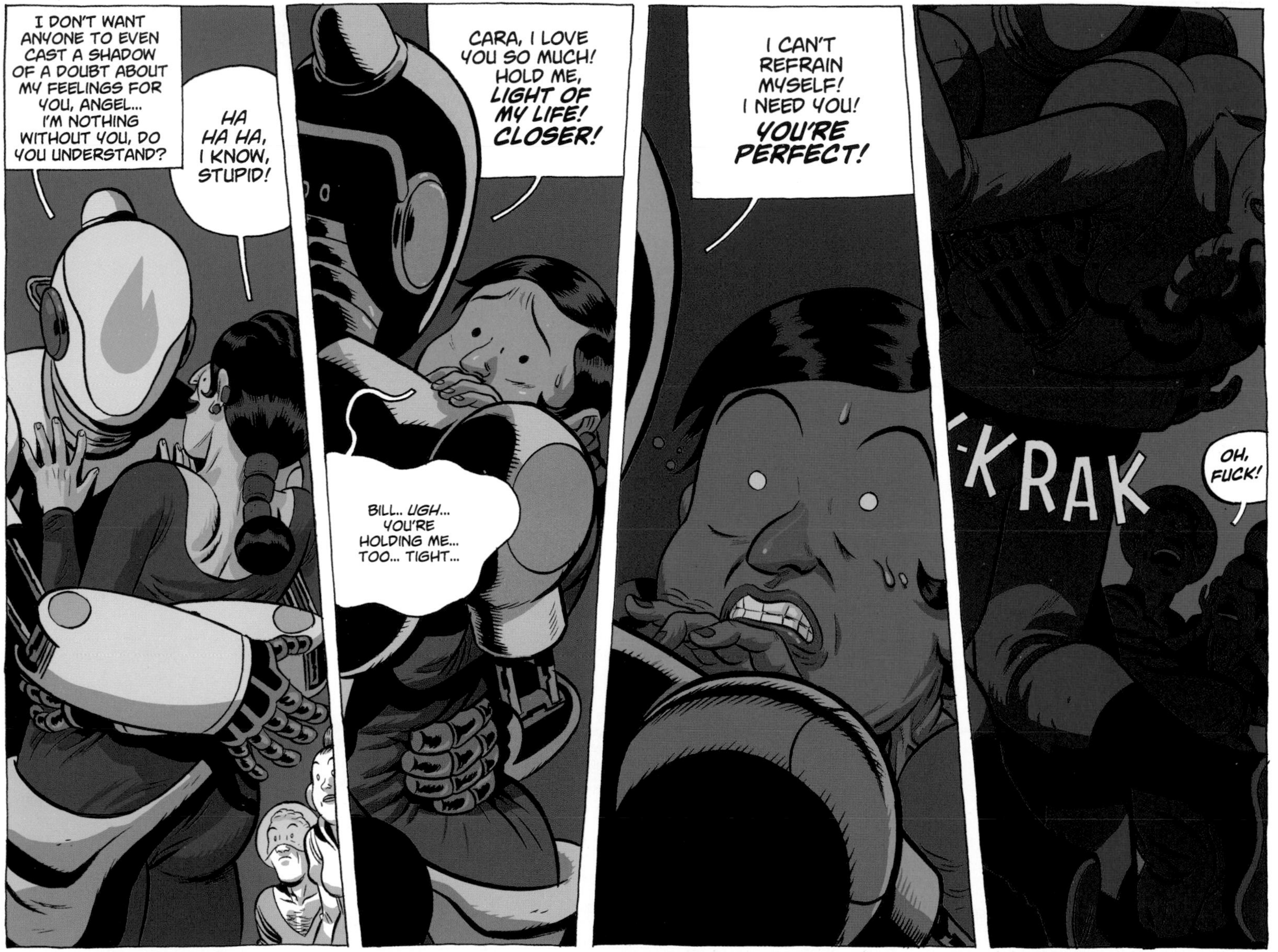
I DON'T WANT ANYONE TO EVEN CAST A SHADOW OF A DOUBT ABOUT MY FEELINGS FOR YOU, ANGEL... I'M NOTHING WITHOUT YOU, DO YOU UNDERSTAND?
HA HA HA, I KNOW, STUPID!
CARA, I LOVE YOU SO MUCH! HOLD ME, LIGHT OF MY LIFE! CLOSER!
BILL.. UGH... YOU'RE HOLDING ME... TOO... TIGHT...
I CAN'T REFRAIN MYSELF! I NEED YOU! YOU'RE PERFECT!
-KRAK
OH, FUCK!

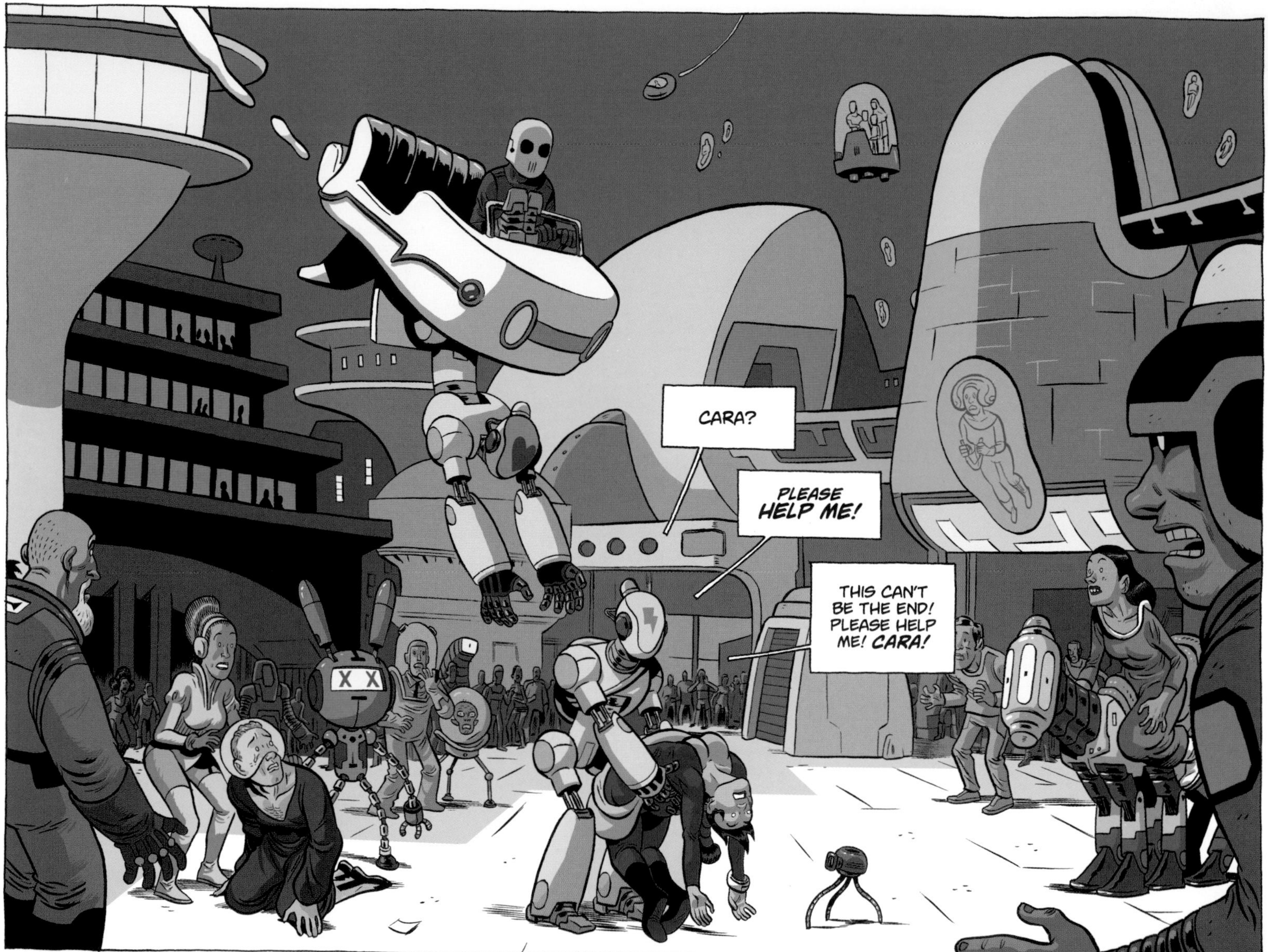
CARA?
PLEASE HELP ME!
THIS CAN'T BE THE END! PLEASE HELP ME! CARA!

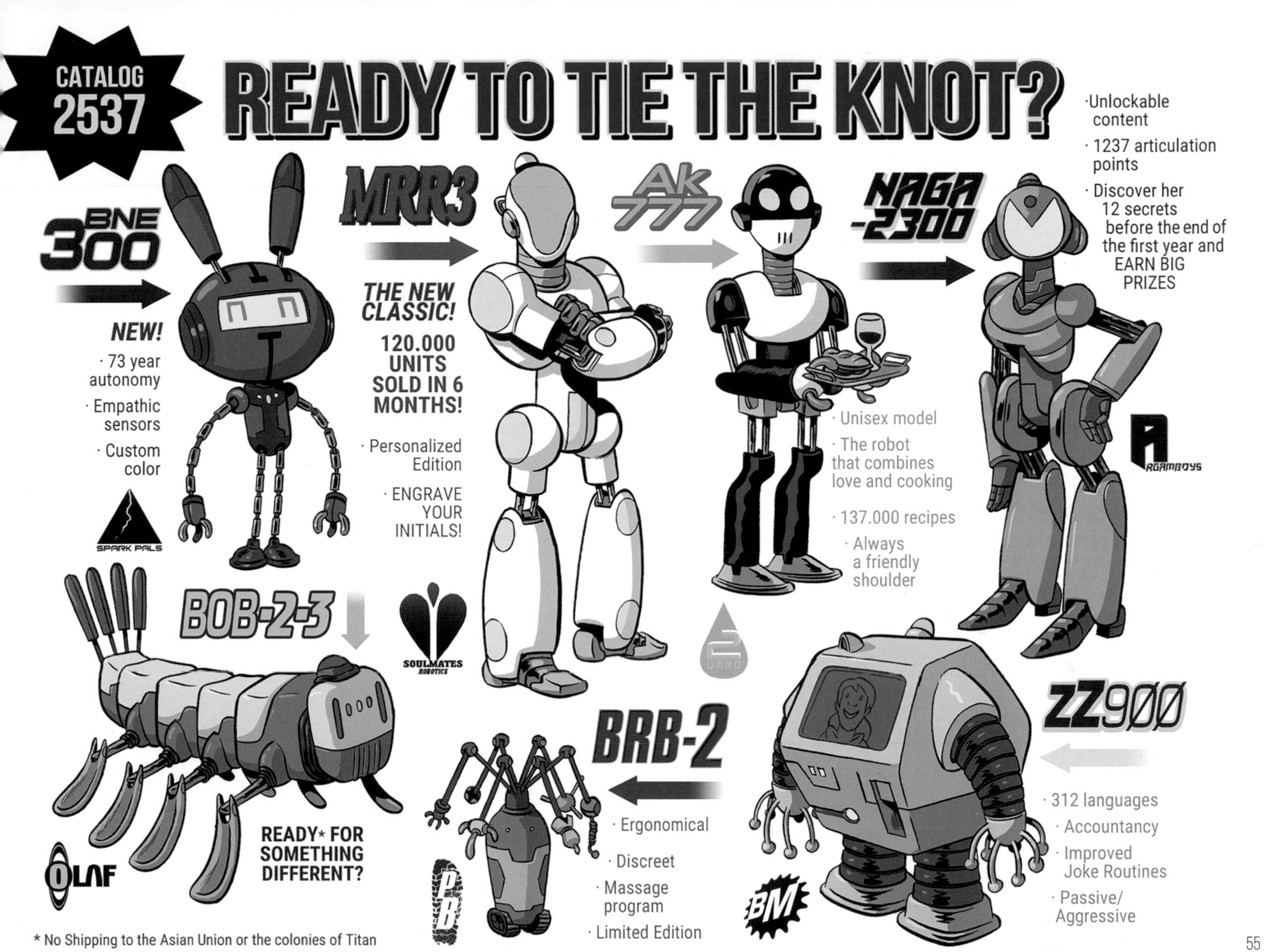
CATALOG 2537
READY TO TIE THE KNOT?
BNE 300
NEW!
· 73 year autonomy
· Empathic sensors
· Custom color
SPARK PALS
MRR3
THE NEW CLASSIC!
120.000 UNITS SOLD IN 6 MONTHS!
· Personalized Edition
· ENGRAVE YOUR INITIALS!
SOULMATES ROBOTICS
AK 777
· Unisex model
· The robot that combines love and cooking
· 137.000 recipes
· Always a friendly shoulder
NAGA -2300
·Unlockable content
· 1237 articulation points
· Discover her 12 secrets before the end of the first year and EARN BIG PRIZES
AGAMBOYS
BOB-2-3
READY* FOR SOMETHING DIFFERENT?
OLAF
BRB-2
· Ergonomical
· Discreet
· Massage program
· Limited Edition
PB
BM
ZZ900
· 312 languages
· Accountancy
· Improved Joke Routines
· Passive/ Aggressive
* No Shipping to the Asian Union or the colonies of Titan

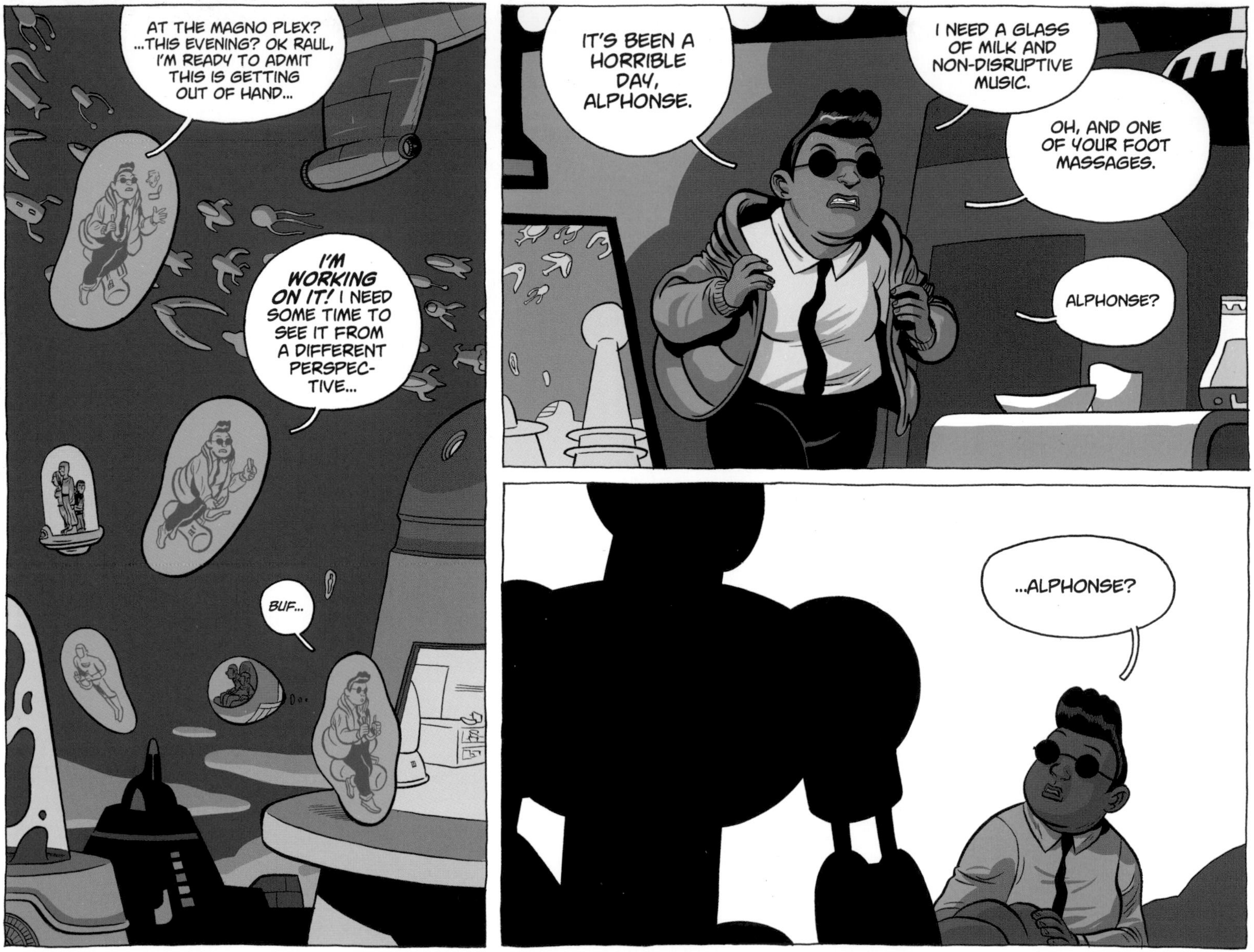
AT THE MAGNO PLEX? ...THIS EVENING? OK RAUL, I'M READY TO ADMIT THIS IS GETTING OUT OF HAND...
I'M WORKING ON IT! I NEED SOME TIME TO SEE IT FROM A DIFFERENT PERSPECTIVE...
BUF...
IT'S BEEN A HORRIBLE DAY, ALPHONSE.
I NEED A GLASS OF MILK AND NON-DISRUPTIVE MUSIC.
OH, AND ONE OF YOUR FOOT MASSAGES.
ALPHONSE?
...ALPHONSE?

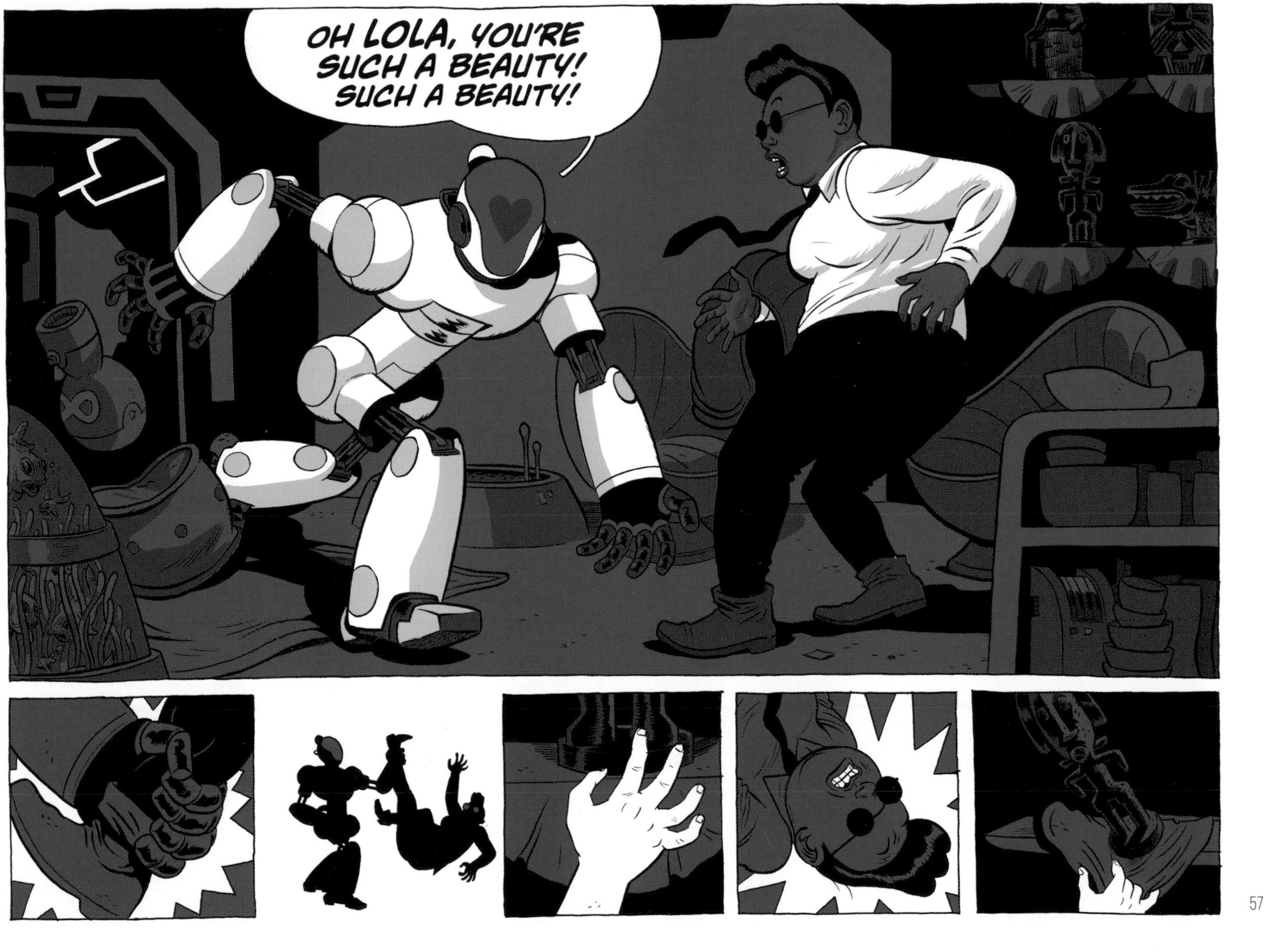
OH LOLA, YOU'RE SUCH A BEAUTY! SUCH A BEAUTY!

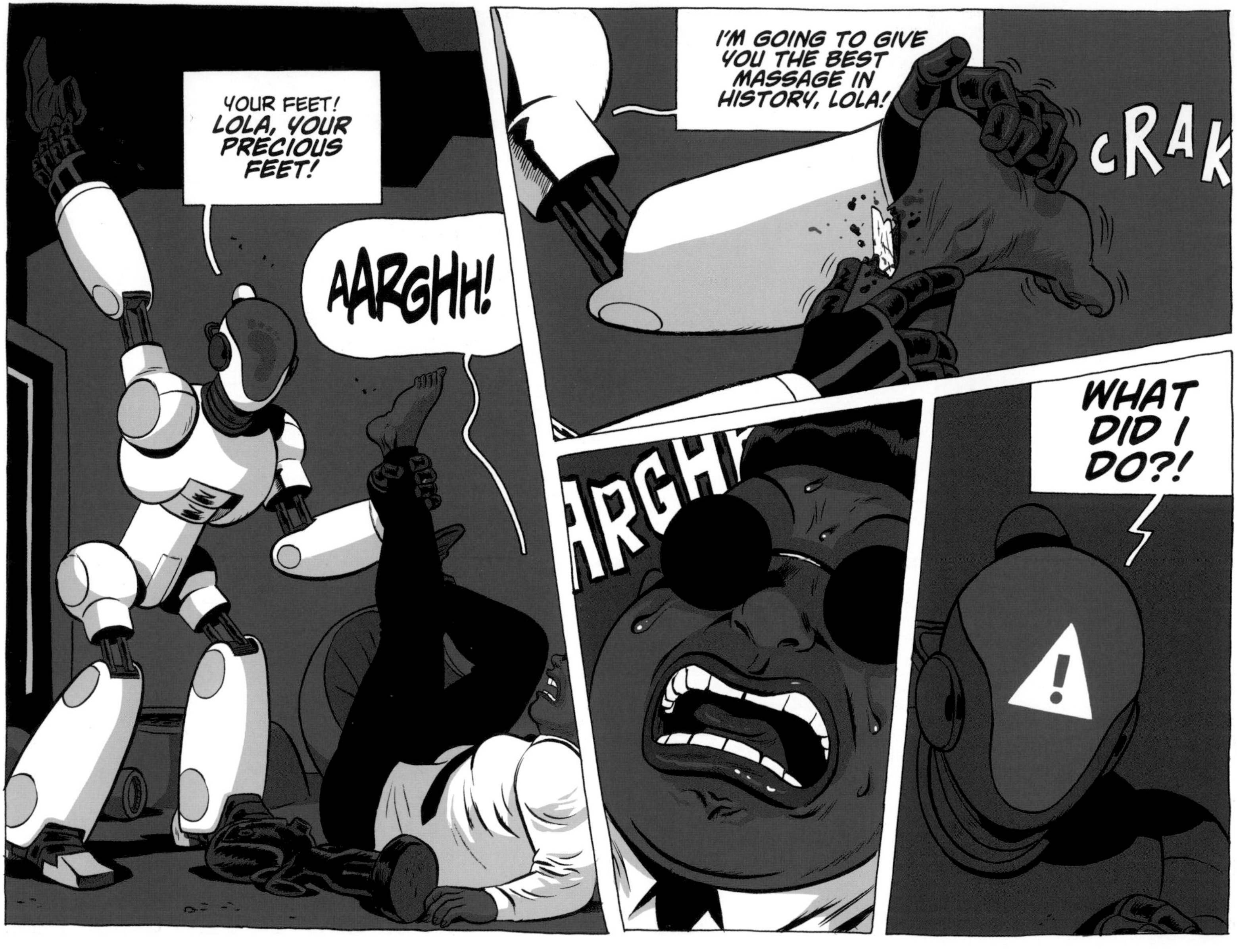
YOUR FEET! LOLA, YOUR PRECIOUS FEET!
AARGHH!
I'M GOING TO GIVE YOU THE BEST MASSAGE IN HISTORY, LOLA!
CRAK
ARGH
WHAT DID I DO?!

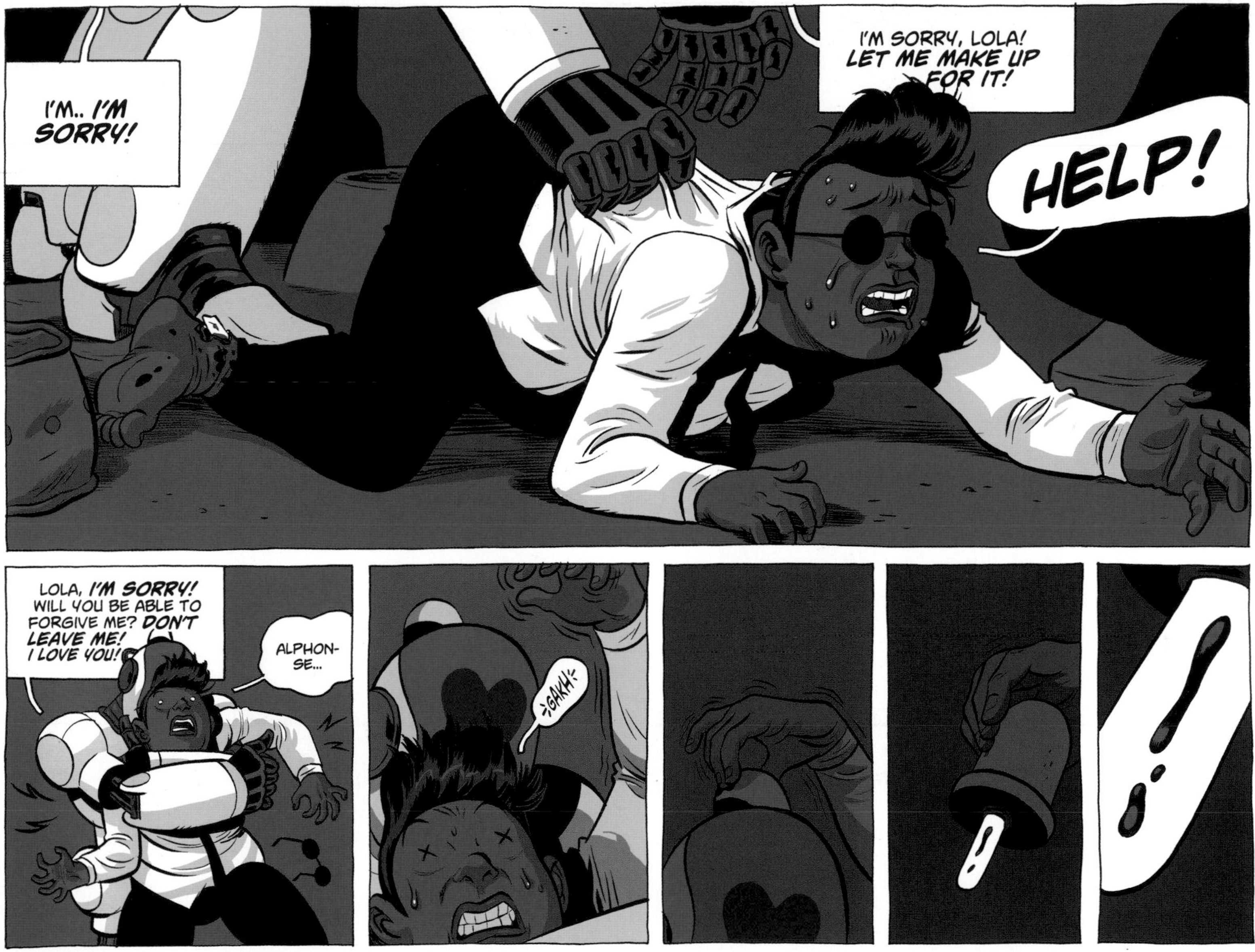
I'M.. I'M SORRY!
I'M SORRY, LOLA! LET ME MAKE UP FOR IT!
HELP!
LOLA, I'M SORRY! WILL YOU BE ABLE TO FORGIVE ME? DON'T LEAVE ME! I LOVE YOU!
ALPHON-SE...
GAKH

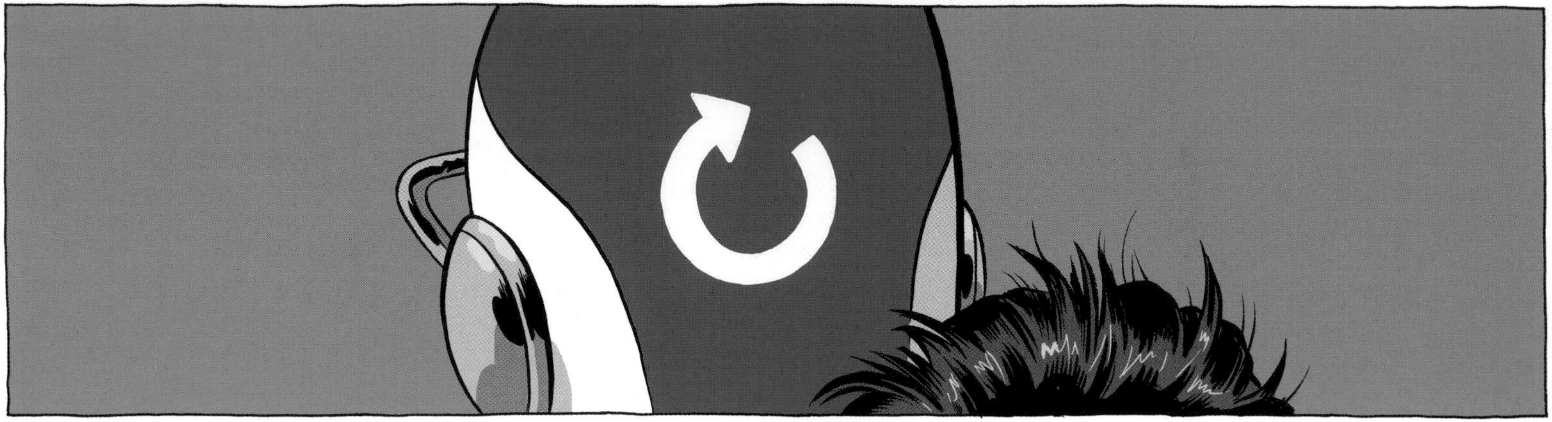

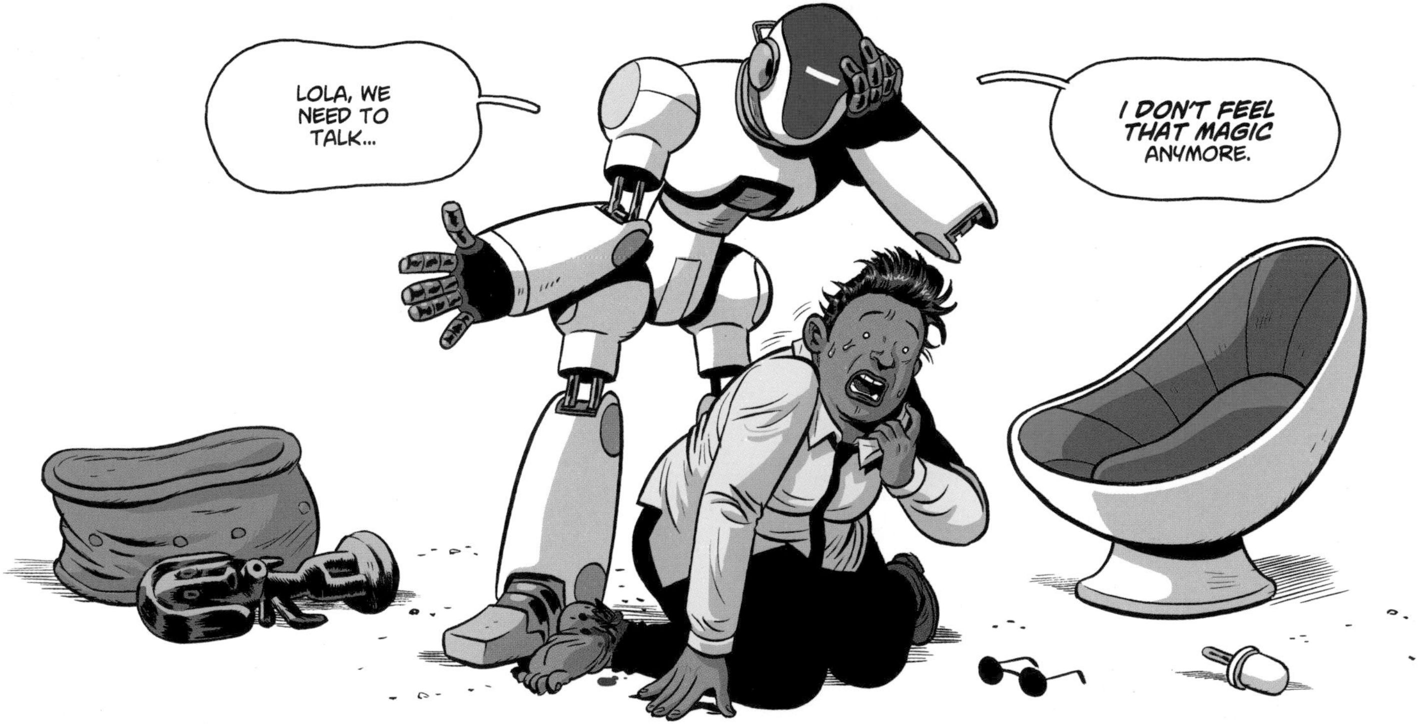
LOLA, WE NEED TO TALK...
I DON'T FEEL THAT MAGIC ANYMORE.

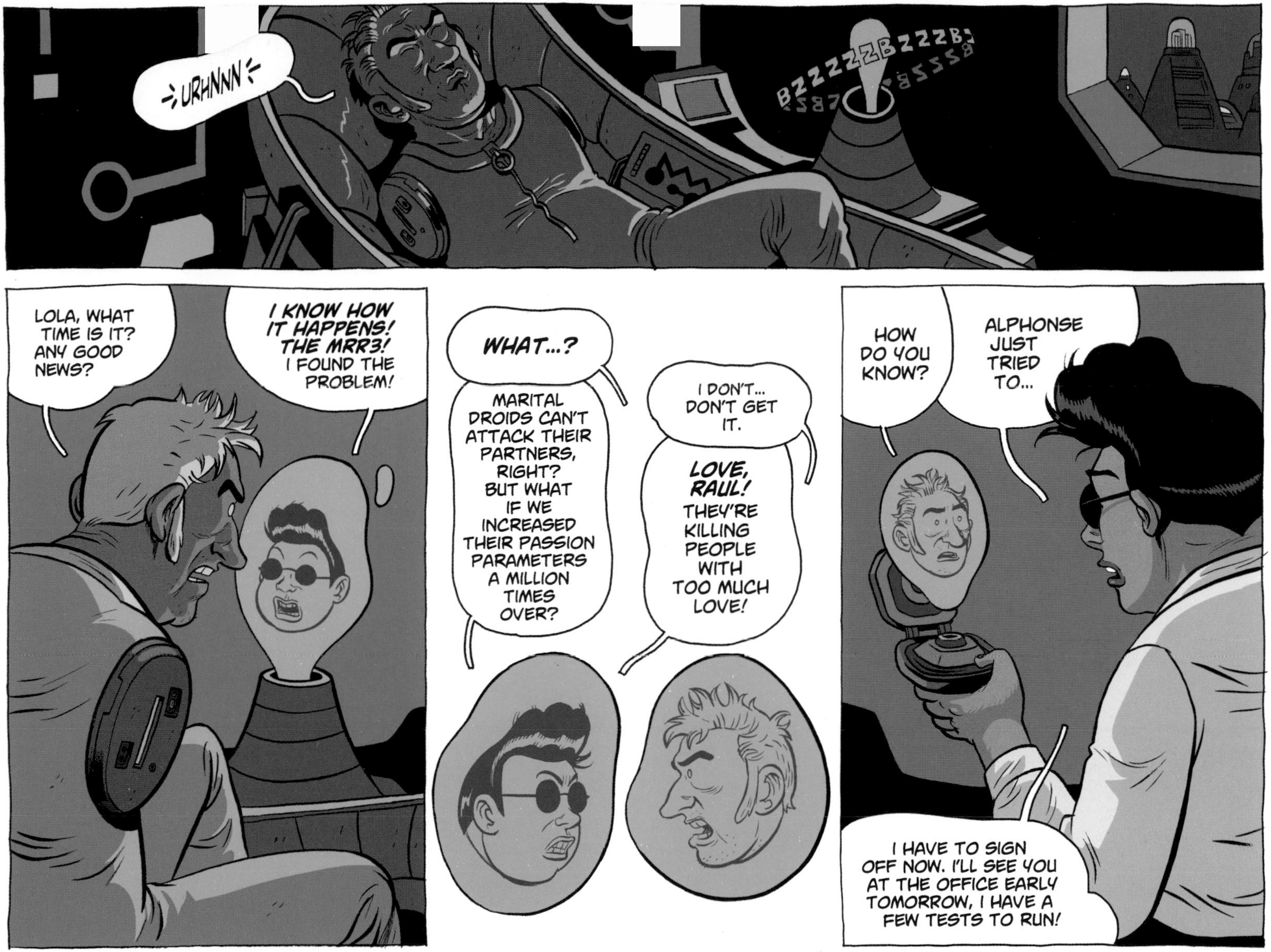
URHNNN
BZZZZZBZZZB
LOLA, WHAT TIME IS IT? ANY GOOD NEWS?
I KNOW HOW IT HAPPENS! THE MRR3! I FOUND THE PROBLEM!
WHAT...?
MARITAL DROIDS CAN'T ATTACK THEIR PARTNERS, RIGHT? BUT WHAT IF WE INCREASED THEIR PASSION PARAMETERS A MILLION TIMES OVER?
I DON'T... DON'T GET IT.
LOVE, RAUL! THEY'RE KILLING PEOPLE WITH TOO MUCH LOVE!
HOW DO YOU KNOW?
ALPHONSE JUST TRIED TO...
I HAVE TO SIGN OFF NOW. I'LL SEE YOU AT THE OFFICE EARLY TOMORROW, I HAVE A FEW TESTS TO RUN!

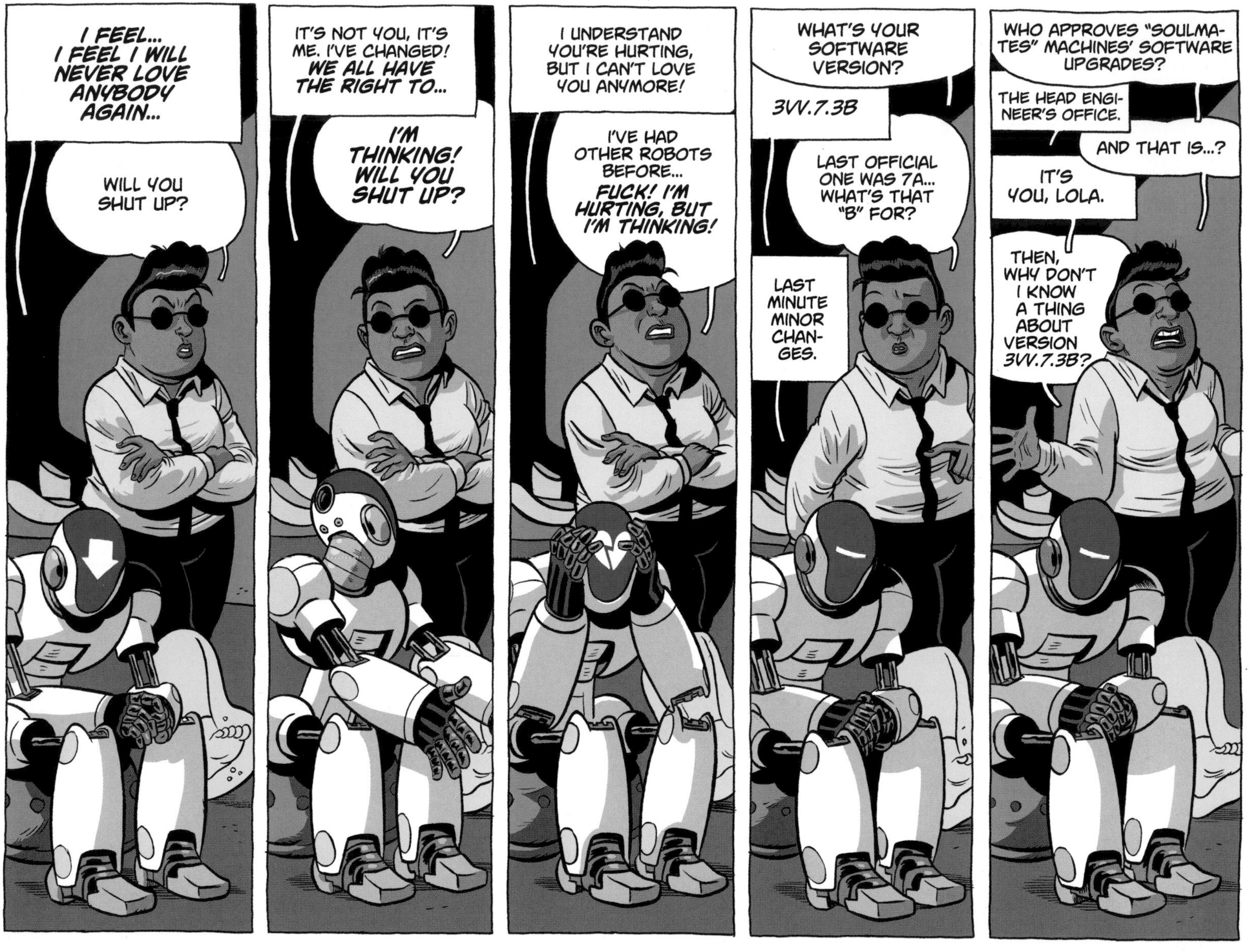
I FEEL... I FEEL I WILL NEVER LOVE ANYBODY AGAIN...
WILL YOU SHUT UP?
IT'S NOT YOU, IT'S ME. I'VE CHANGED! WE ALL HAVE THE RIGHT TO...
I'M THINKING! WILL YOU SHUT UP?
I UNDERSTAND YOU'RE HURTING, BUT I CAN'T LOVE YOU ANYMORE!
I'VE HAD OTHER ROBOTS BEFORE... FUCK! I'M HURTING, BUT I'M THINKING!
WHAT'S YOUR SOFTWARE VERSION?
3VV.7.3B
LAST OFFICIAL ONE WAS 7A... WHAT'S THAT "B" FOR?
LAST MINUTE MINOR CHANGES.
WHO APPROVES "SOULMATES" MACHINES' SOFTWARE UPGRADES?
THE HEAD ENGINEER'S OFFICE.
AND THAT IS...?
IT'S YOU, LOLA.
THEN, WHY DON'T I KNOW A THING ABOUT VERSION 3VV.7.3B?

♪

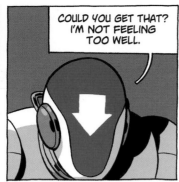

COULD YOU GET THAT? I'M NOT FEELING TOO WELL.

SORRY, I HAD PROBLEMS FINDING THE CONTROLLER.

ABOUT TIME! I CALLED YOU AN HOUR AND A HALF AGO!

IS HE SAFE NOW?

I THINK SO. TAKE HIM TO THE WORKSHOP AND TRACK THE LAST UPDATE'S ORIGIN.

I'M GOING TO TAKE A LITTLE NAP- JUST THIRTY MINUTES.

I'M A LITTLE TIRED...

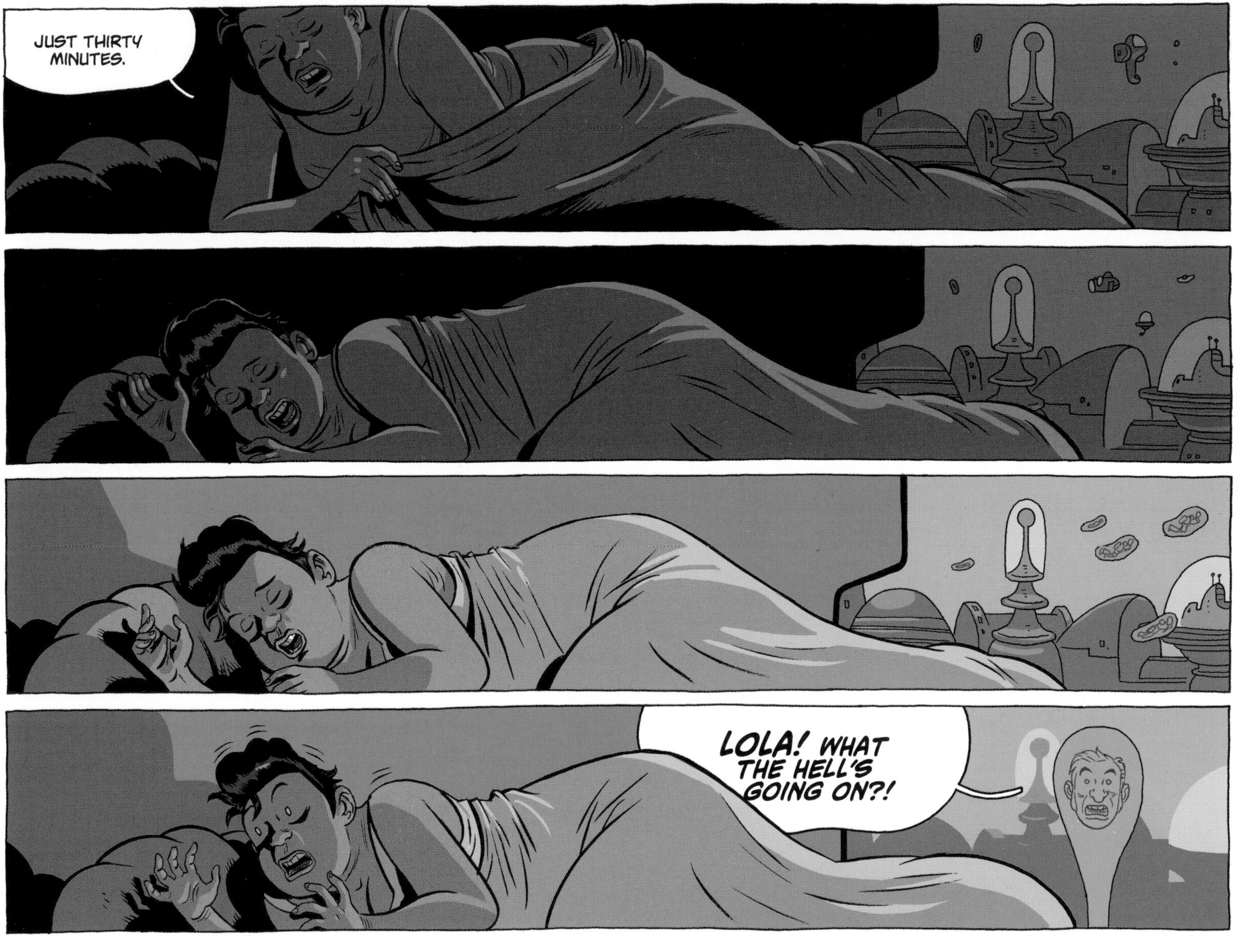
JUST THIRTY MINUTES.
LOLA! WHAT THE HELL'S GOING ON?!

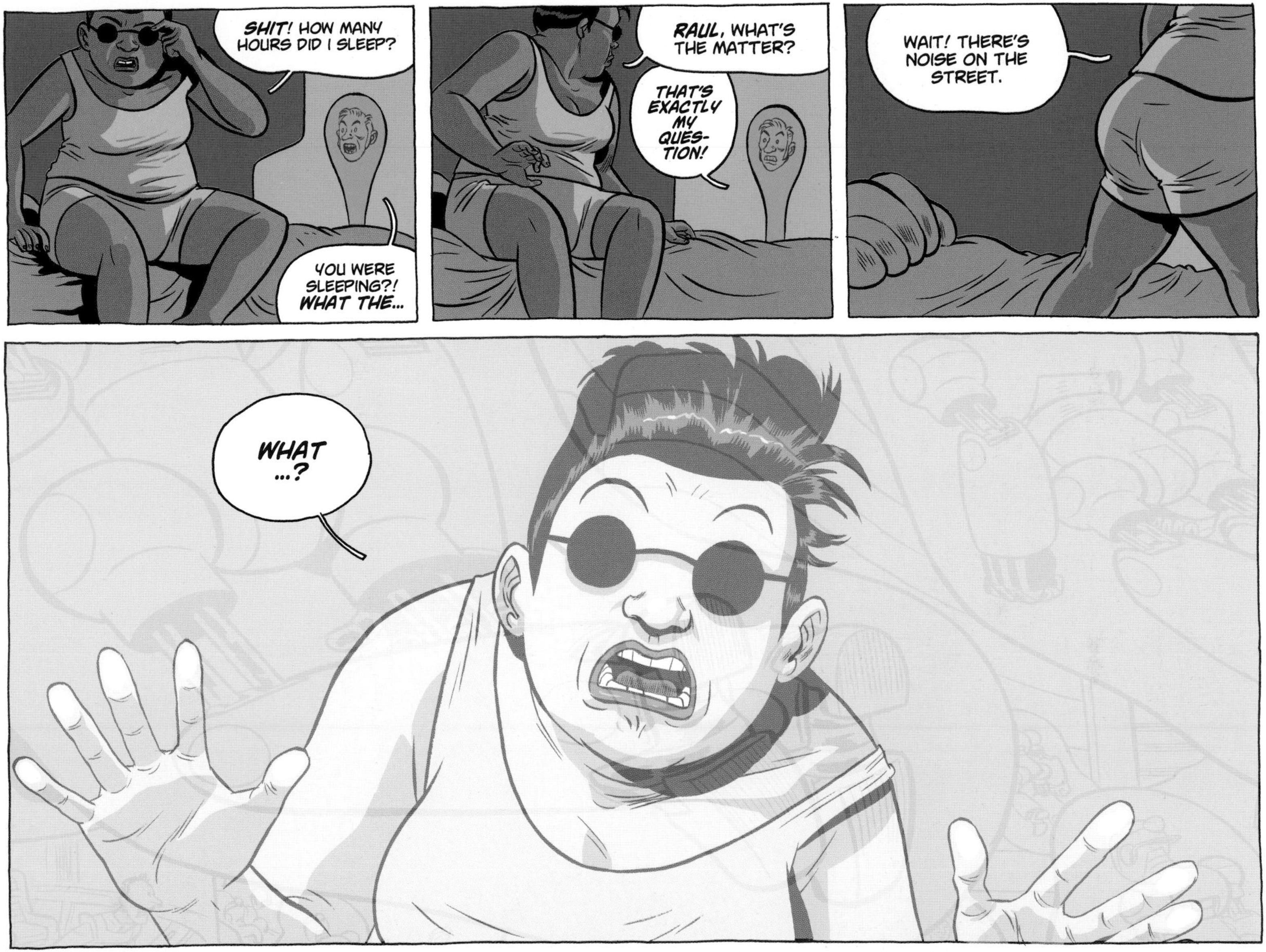
SHIT! HOW MANY HOURS DID I SLEEP?
YOU WERE SLEEPING?! WHAT THE...
RAUL, WHAT'S THE MATTER?
THAT'S EXACTLY MY QUES-TION!
WAIT! THERE'S NOISE ON THE STREET.
WHAT ...?

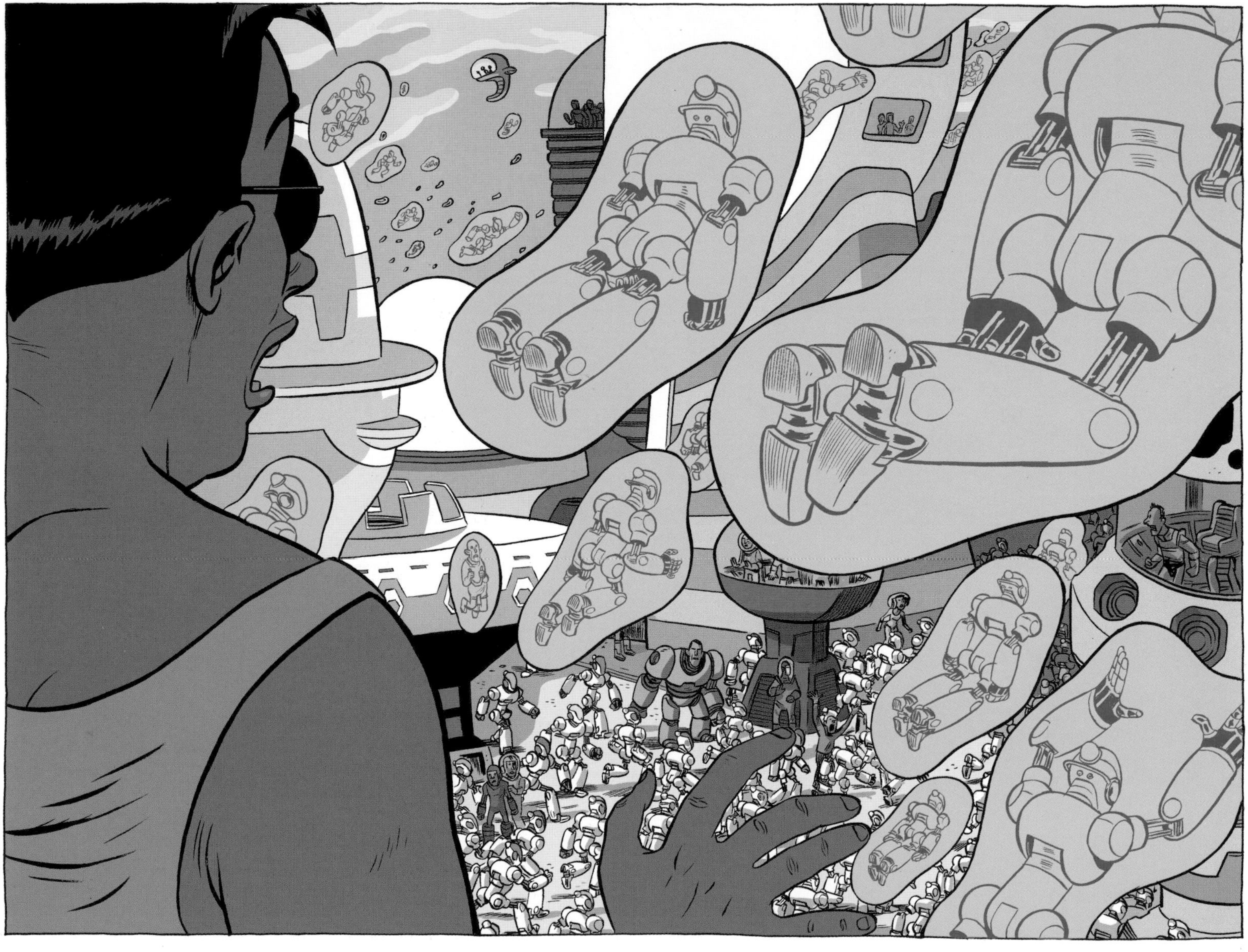

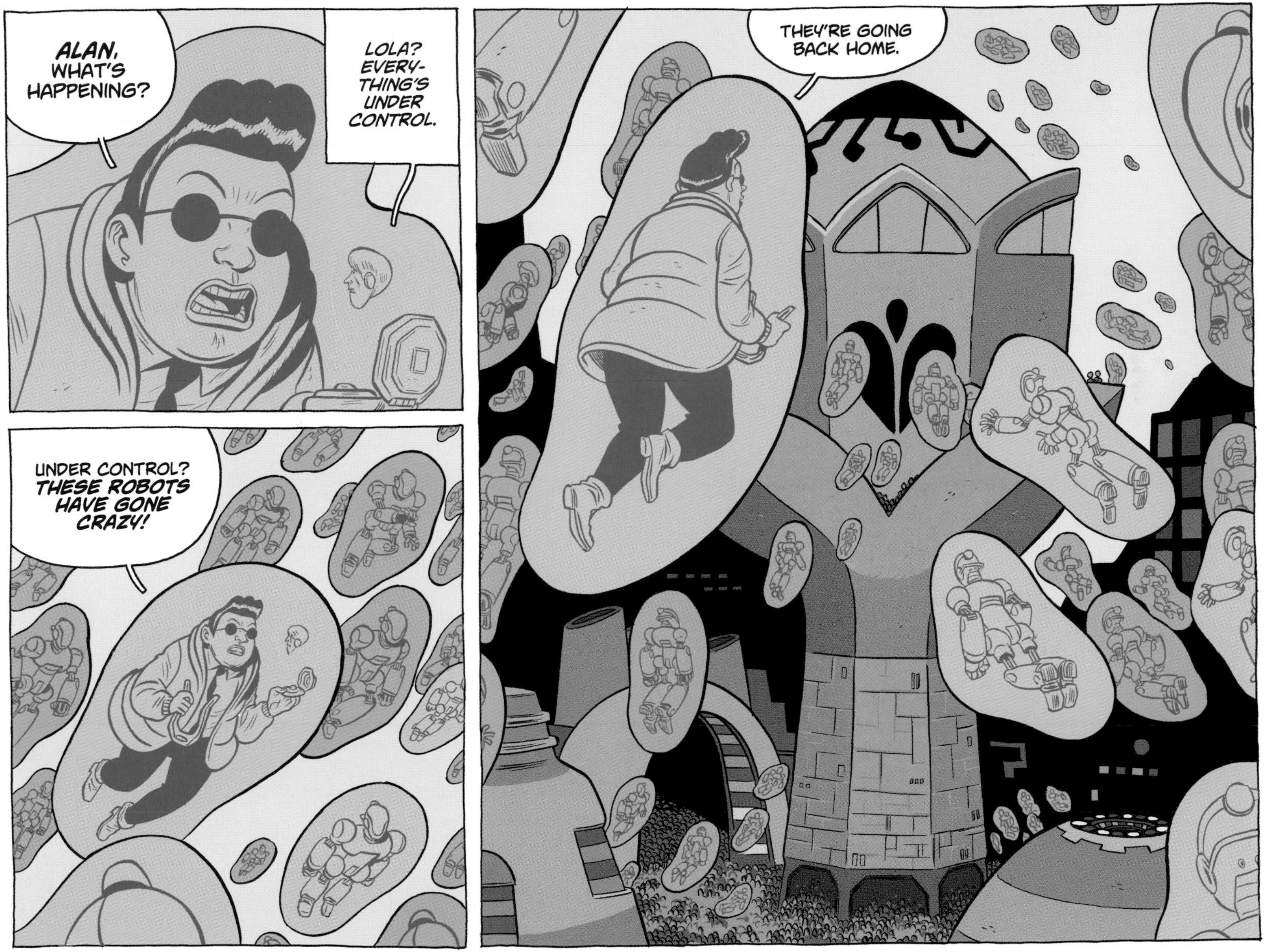
ALAN, WHAT'S HAPPENING?
LOLA? EVERY-THING'S UNDER CONTROL.
UNDER CONTROL? THESE ROBOTS HAVE GONE CRAZY!
THEY'RE GOING BACK HOME.

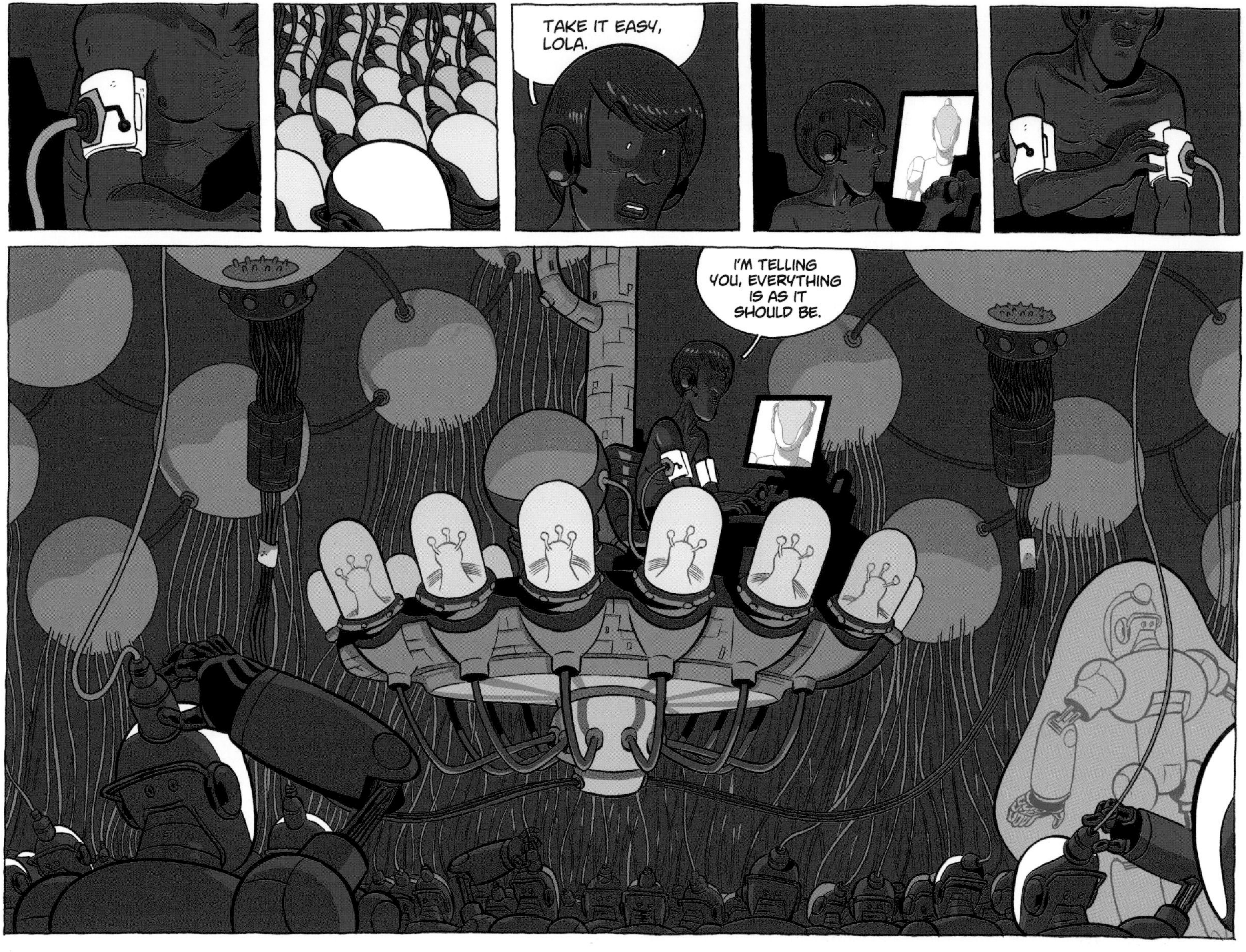
TAKE IT EASY, LOLA.
I'M TELLING YOU, EVERYTHING IS AS IT SHOULD BE.

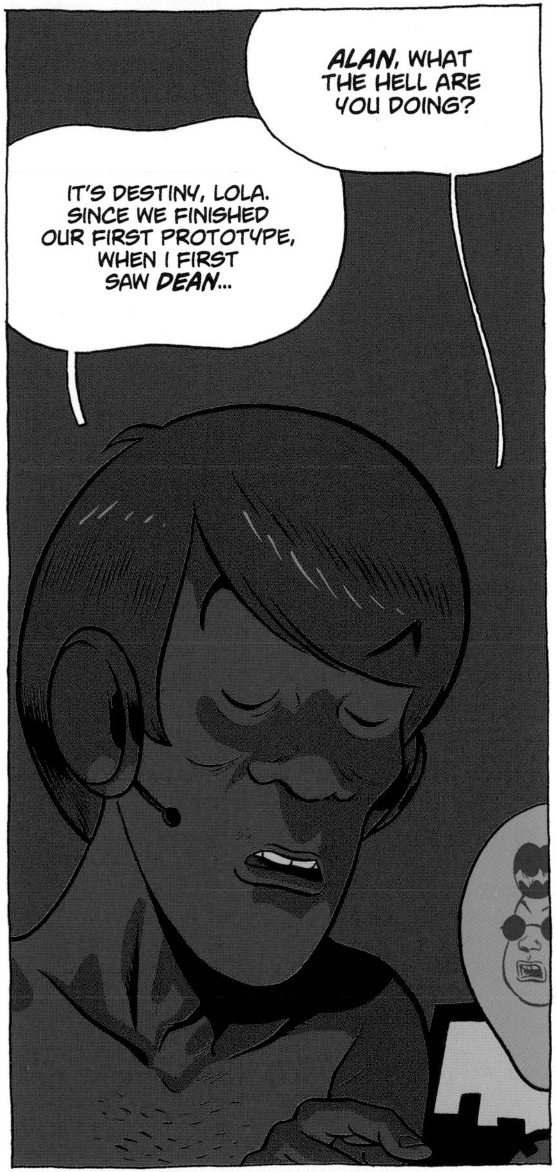
ALAN, WHAT THE HELL ARE YOU DOING?
IT'S DESTINY, LOLA. SINCE WE FINISHED OUR FIRST PROTOTYPE, WHEN I FIRST SAW DEAN...

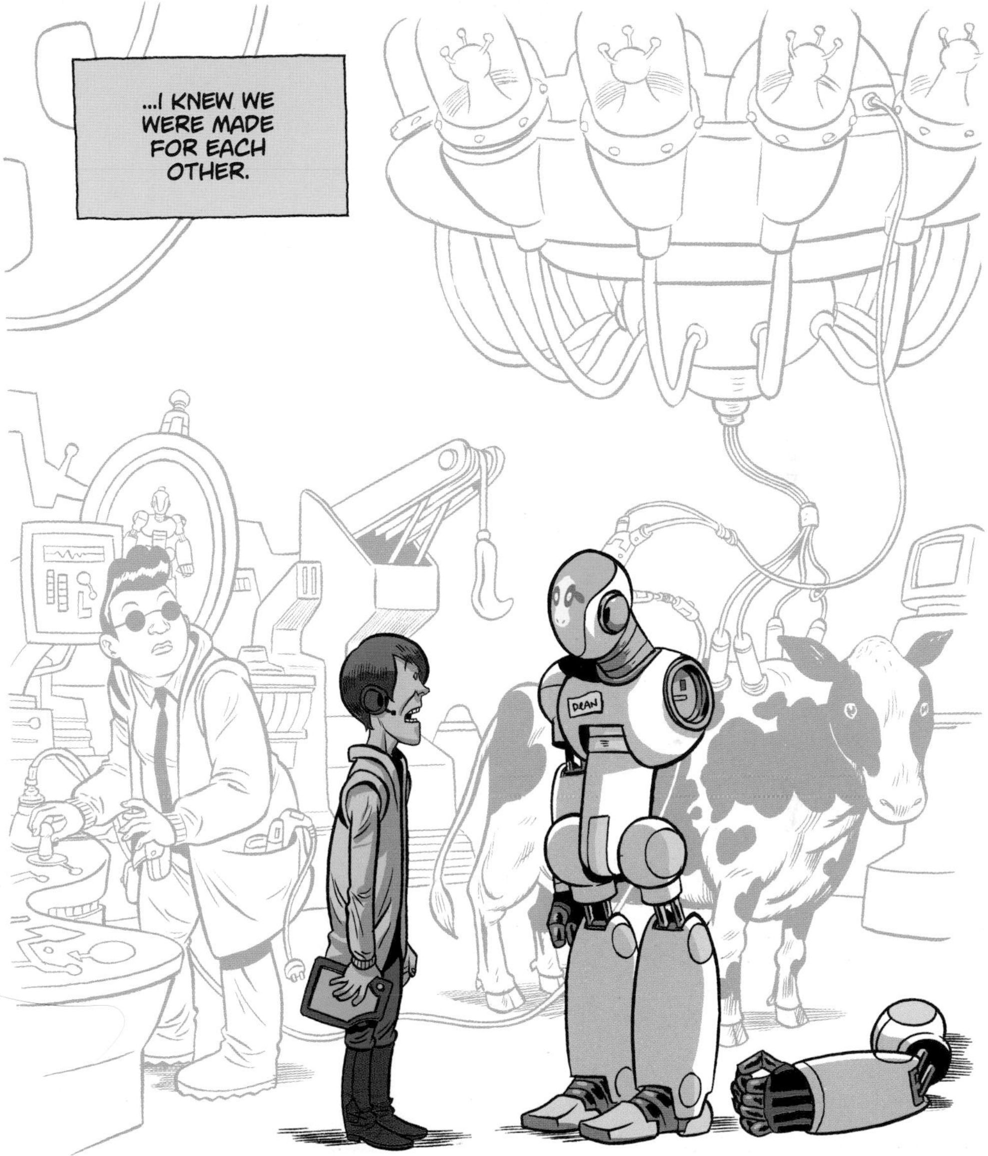
...I KNEW WE WERE MADE FOR EACH OTHER.
DEAN

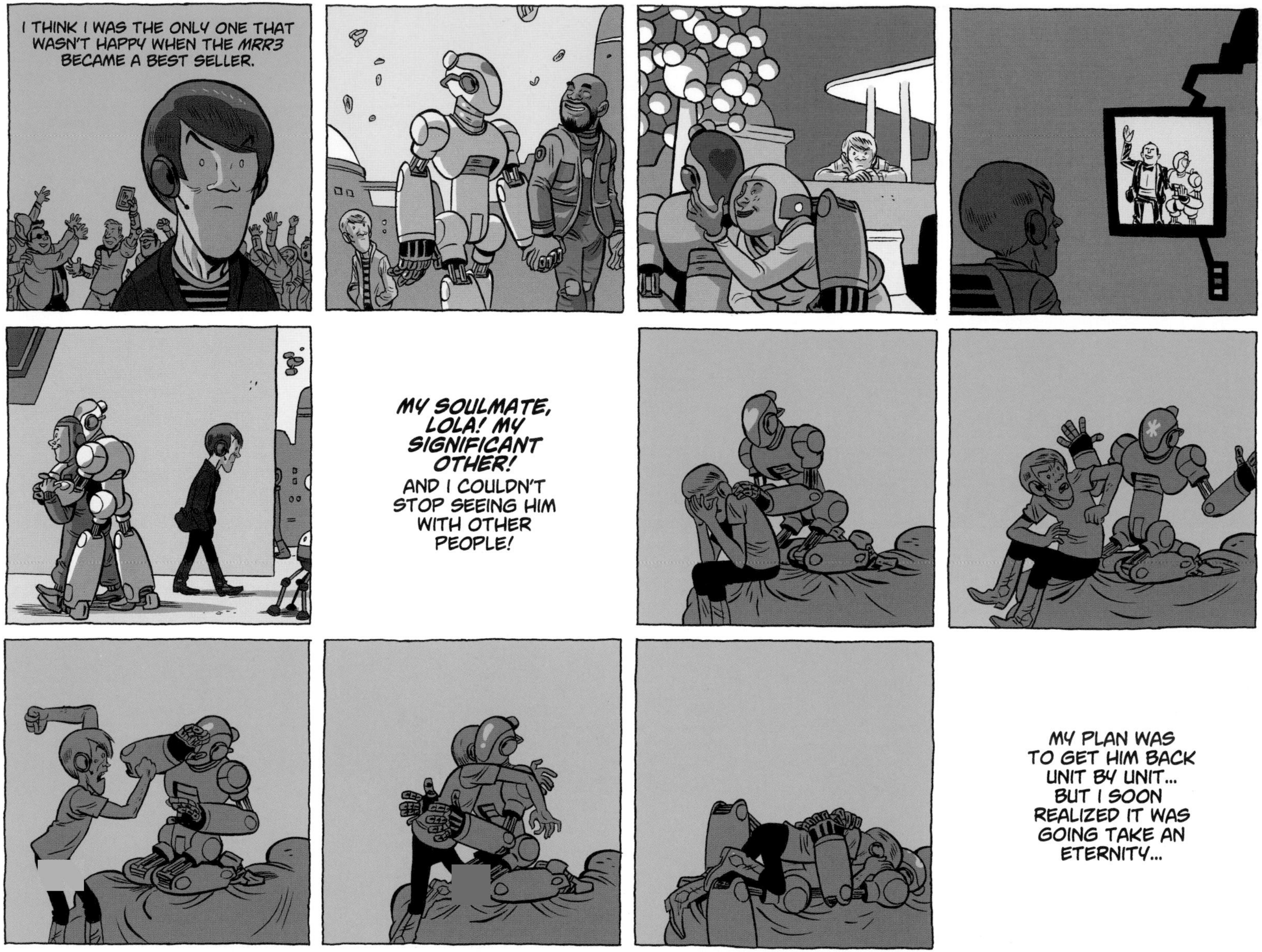
I THINK I WAS THE ONLY ONE THAT WASN'T HAPPY WHEN THE *MRR3* BECAME A BEST SELLER.
MY SOULMATE, LOLA! MY SIGNIFICANT OTHER!
AND I COULDN'T STOP SEEING HIM WITH OTHER PEOPLE!
MY PLAN WAS TO GET HIM BACK UNIT BY UNIT... BUT I SOON REALIZED IT WAS GOING TAKE AN ETERNITY...

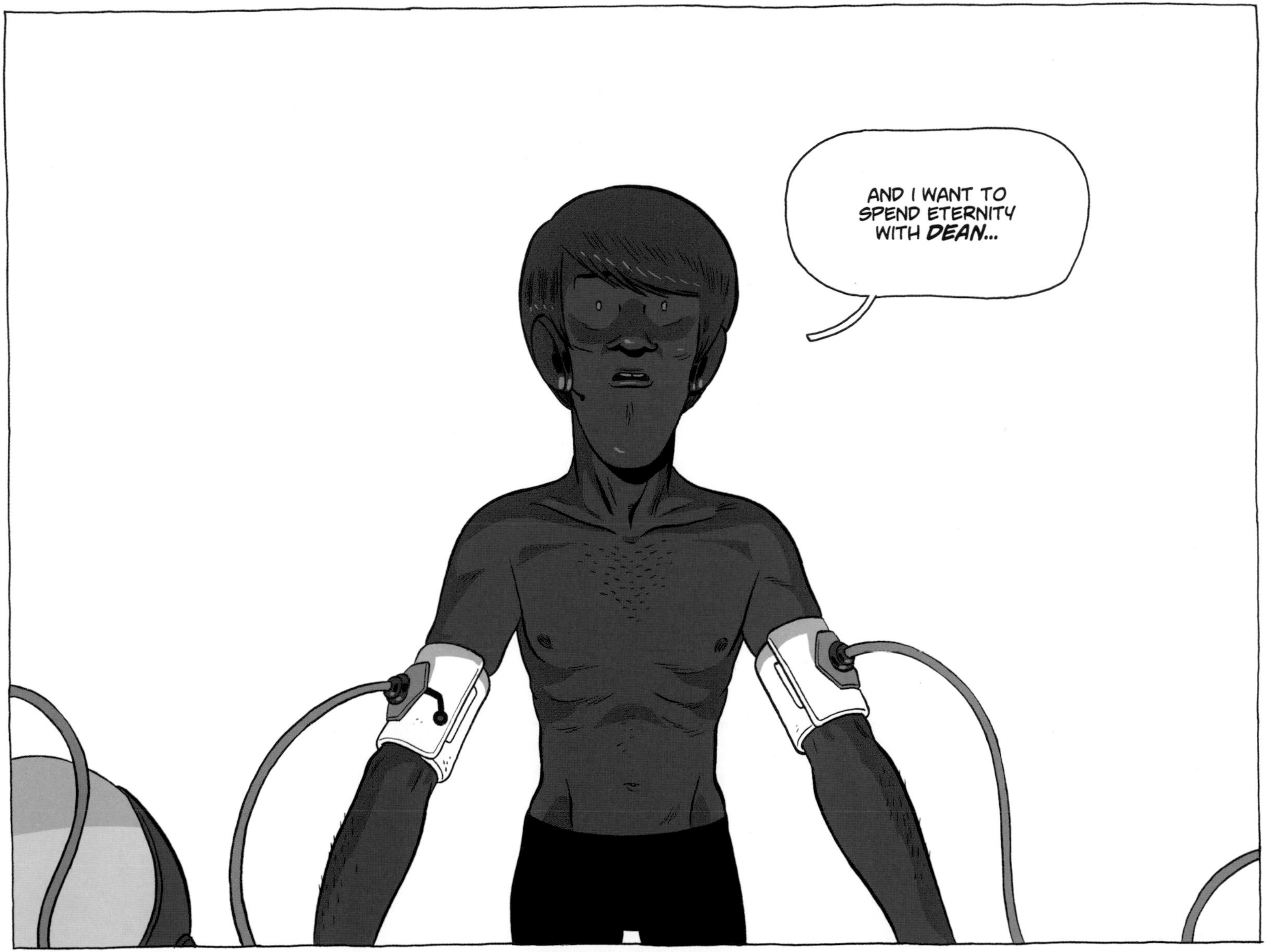
AND I WANT TO SPEND ETERNITY WITH **DEAN**...

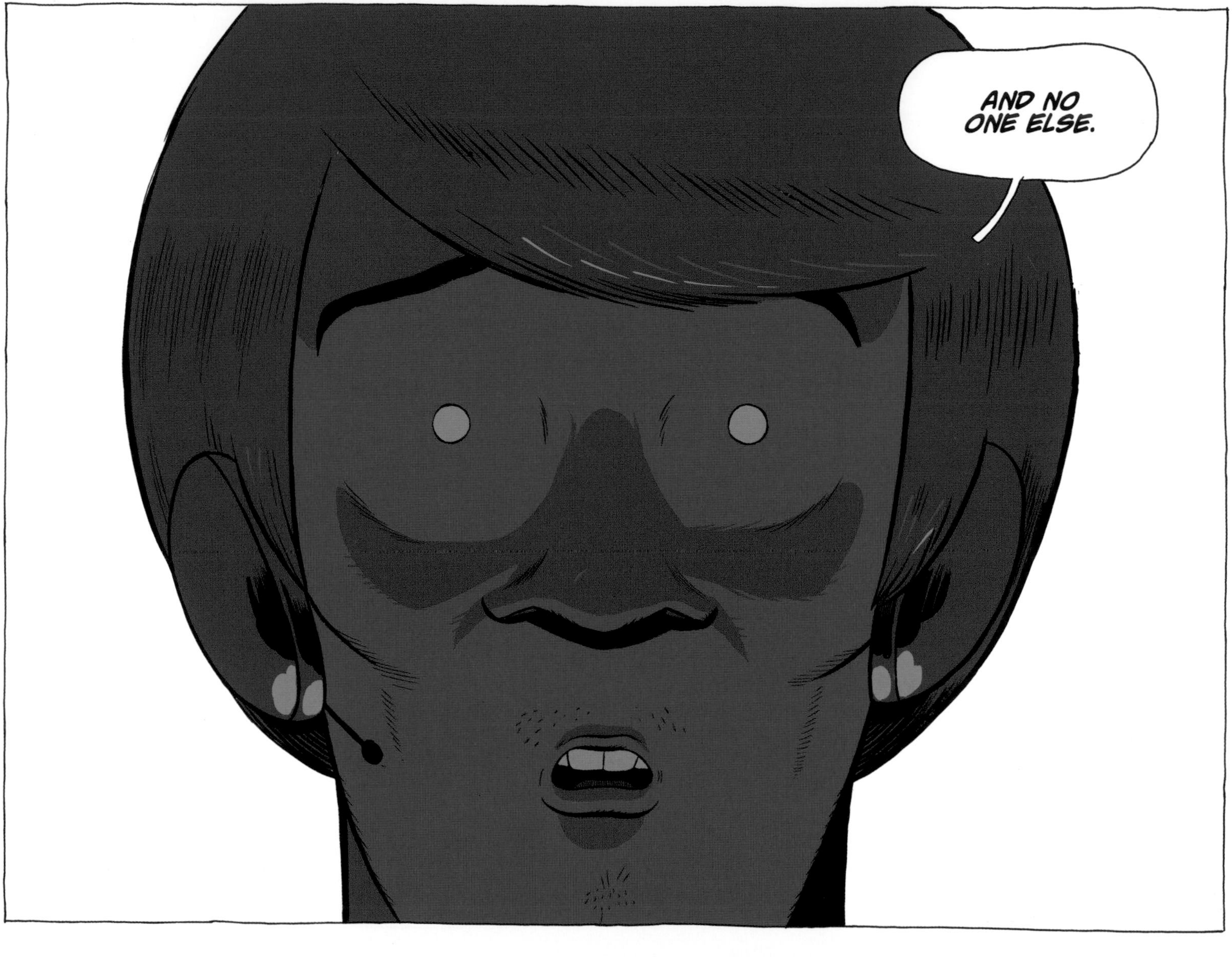
AND NO ONE ELSE.

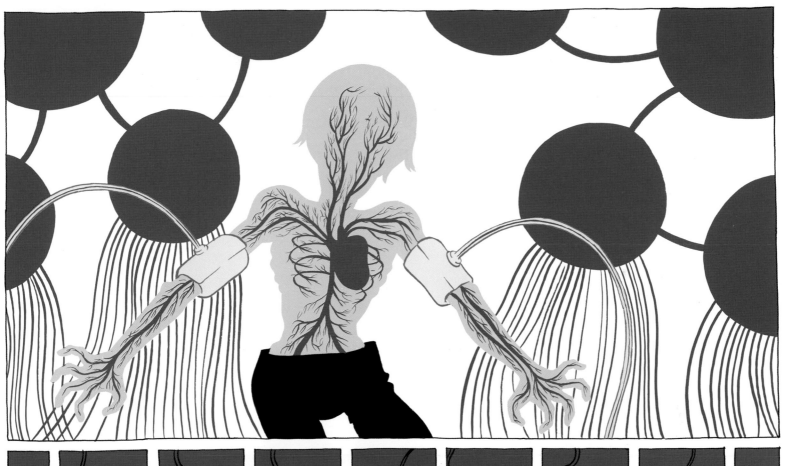
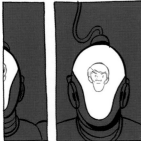

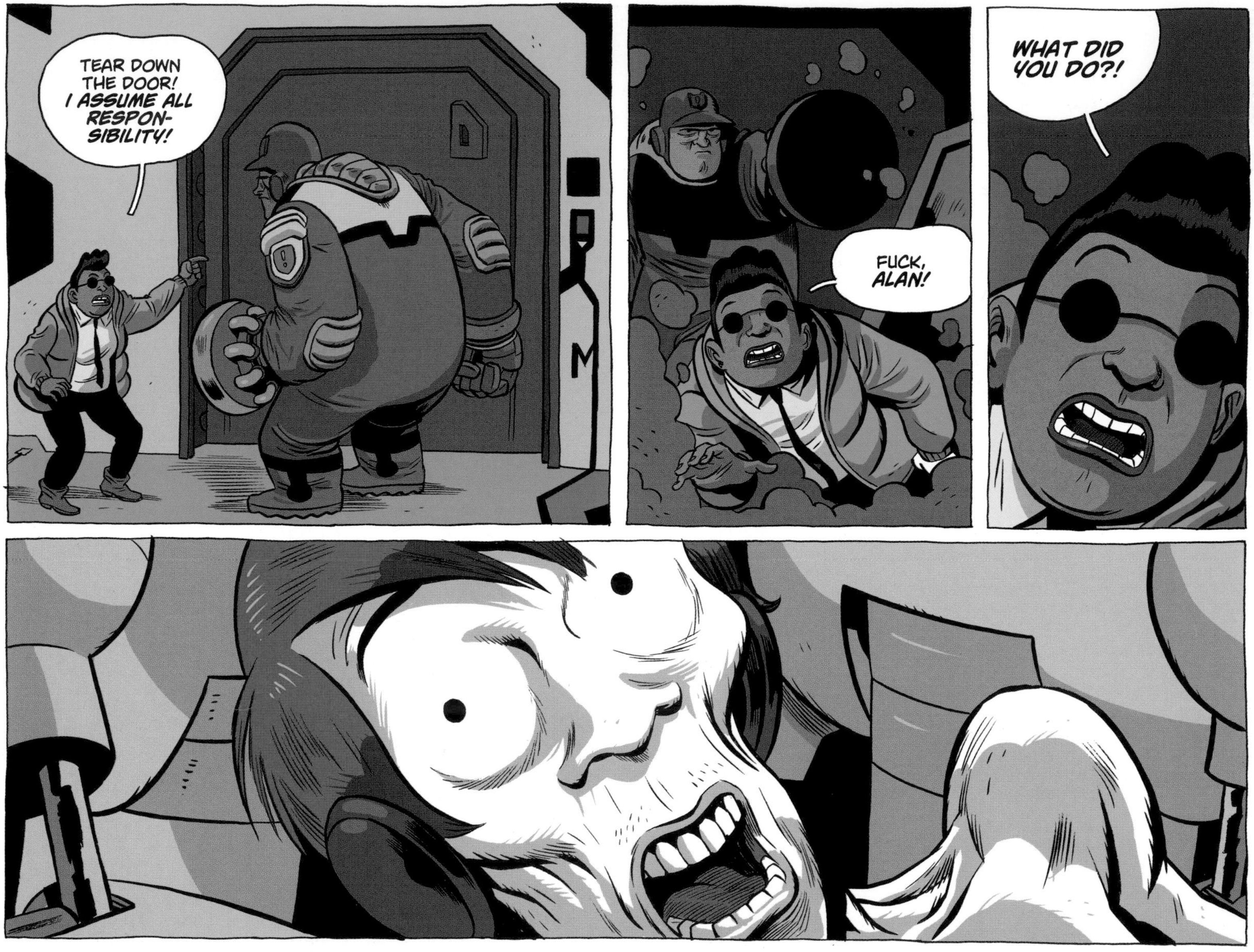
TEAR DOWN THE DOOR! I ASSUME ALL RESPON-SIBILITY!
FUCK, ALAN!
WHAT DID YOU DO?!

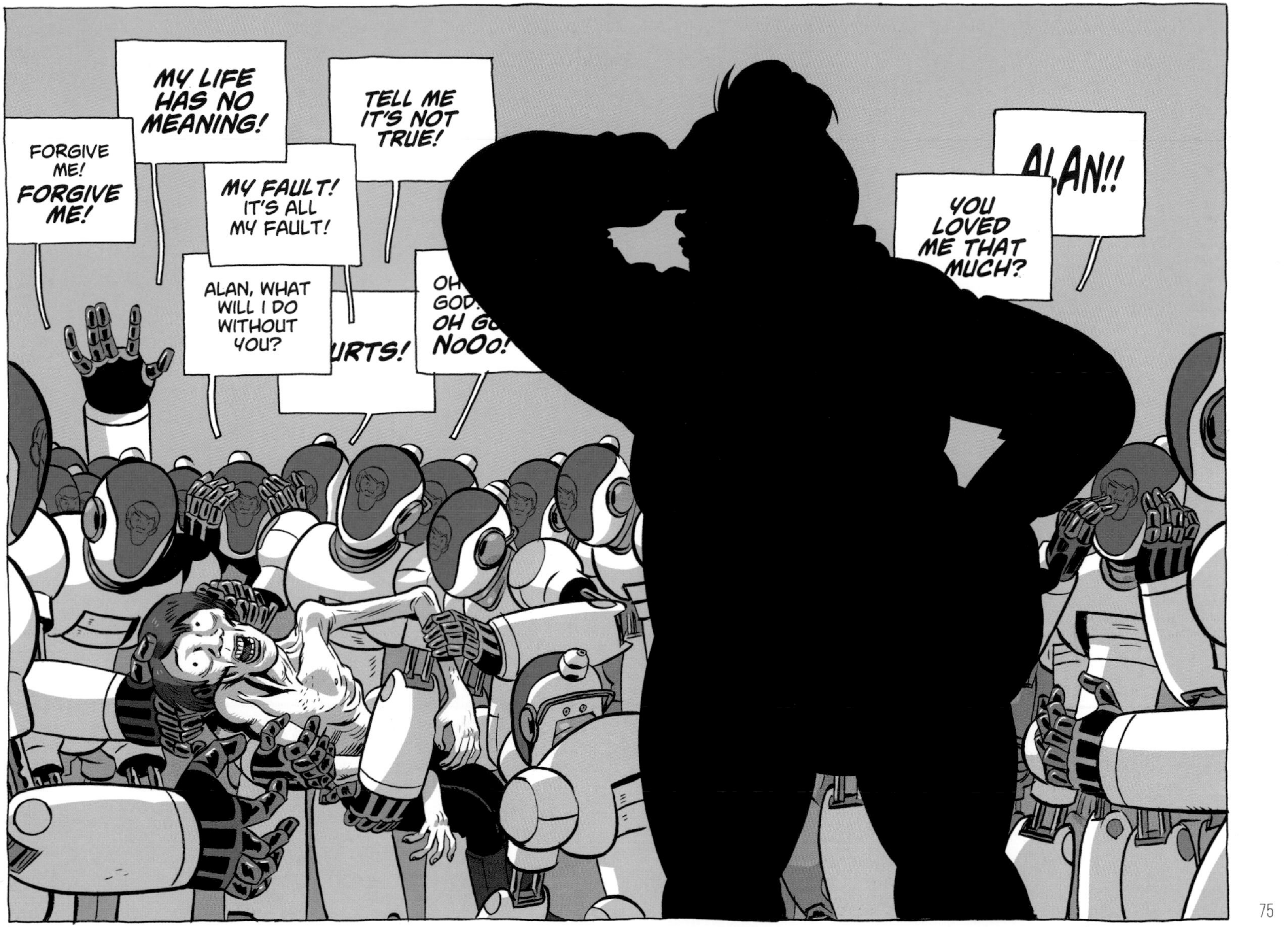
FORGIVE ME! FORGIVE ME!
MY LIFE HAS NO MEANING!
MY FAULT! IT'S ALL MY FAULT!
ALAN, WHAT WILL I DO WITHOUT YOU?
TELL ME IT'S NOT TRUE!
URTS!
NoOo!
YOU LOVED ME THAT MUCH?
AN!!

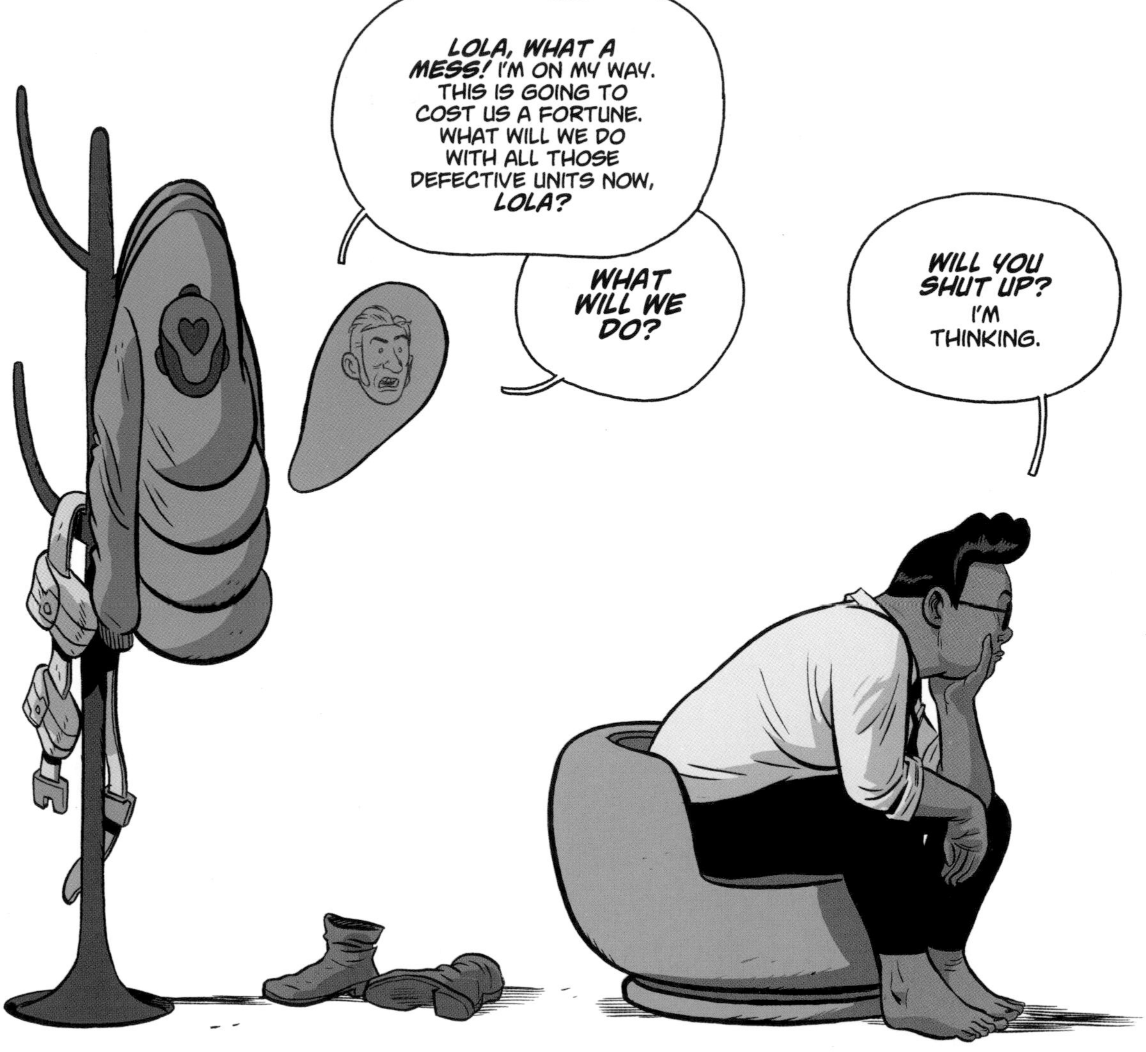
LOLA, WHAT A MESS! I'M ON MY WAY. THIS IS GOING TO COST US A FORTUNE. WHAT WILL WE DO WITH ALL THOSE DEFECTIVE UNITS NOW, LOLA?
WHAT WILL WE DO?
WILL YOU SHUT UP? I'M THINKING.

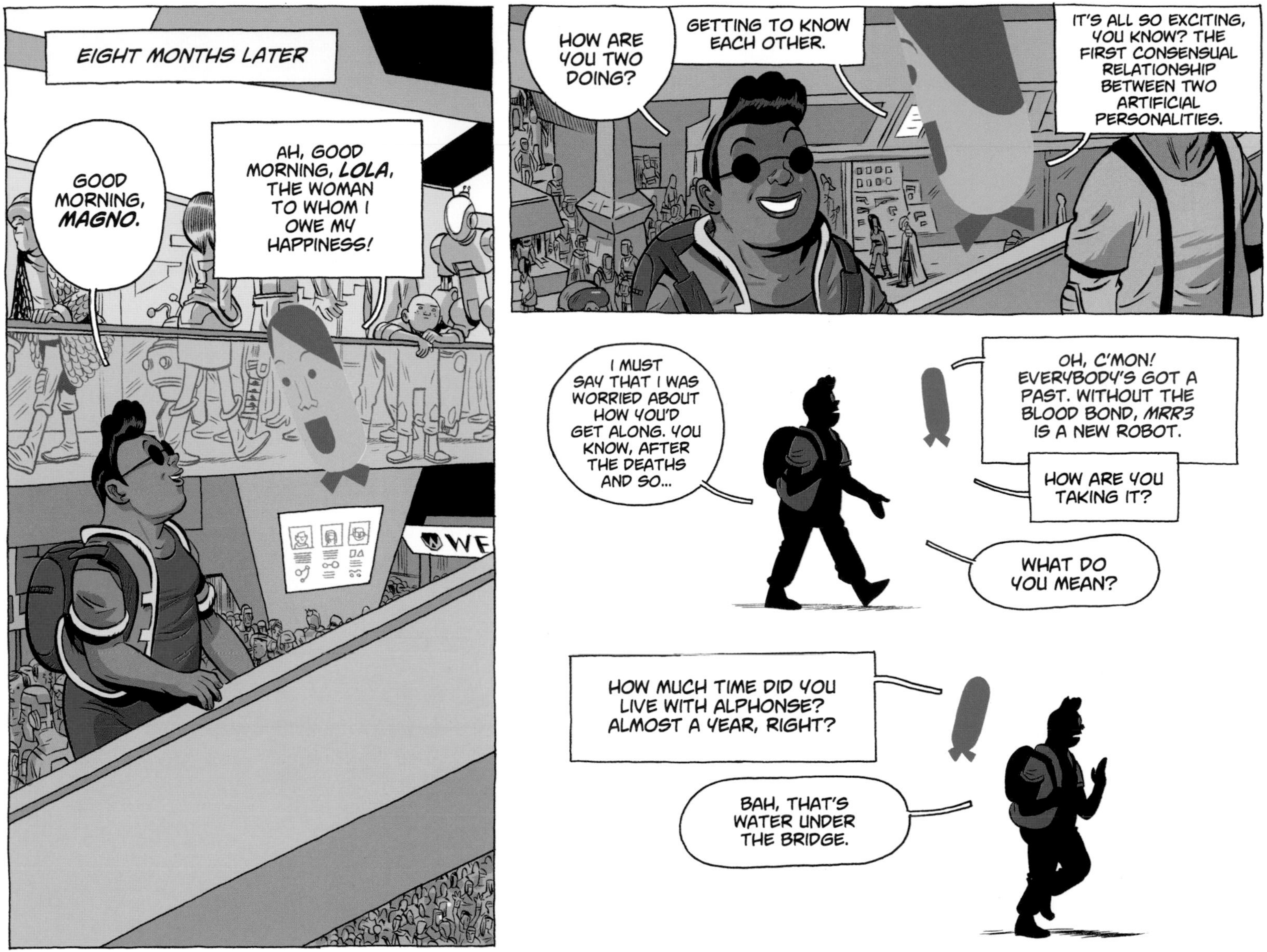
EIGHT MONTHS LATER
GOOD MORNING, MAGNO.
AH, GOOD MORNING, LOLA, THE WOMAN TO WHOM I OWE MY HAPPINESS!
HOW ARE YOU TWO DOING?
GETTING TO KNOW EACH OTHER.
IT'S ALL SO EXCITING, YOU KNOW? THE FIRST CONSENSUAL RELATIONSHIP BETWEEN TWO ARTIFICIAL PERSONALITIES.
I MUST SAY THAT I WAS WORRIED ABOUT HOW YOU'D GET ALONG. YOU KNOW, AFTER THE DEATHS AND SO...
OH, C'MON! EVERYBODY'S GOT A PAST. WITHOUT THE BLOOD BOND, MRR3 IS A NEW ROBOT.
HOW ARE YOU TAKING IT?
WHAT DO YOU MEAN?
HOW MUCH TIME DID YOU LIVE WITH ALPHONSE? ALMOST A YEAR, RIGHT?
BAH, THAT'S WATER UNDER THE BRIDGE.

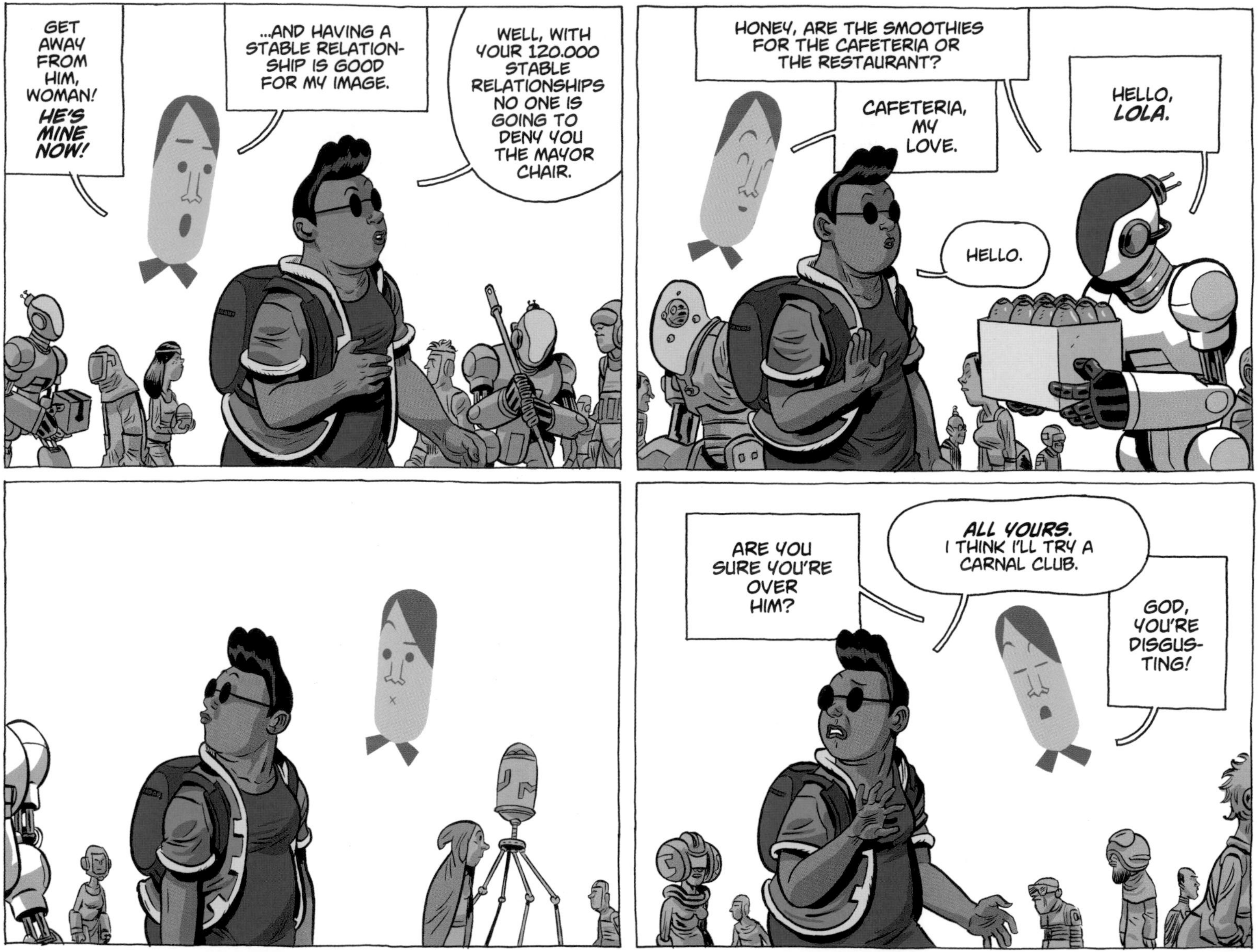
GET AWAY FROM HIM, WOMAN! HE'S MINE NOW!
...AND HAVING A STABLE RELATIONSHIP IS GOOD FOR MY IMAGE.
WELL, WITH YOUR 120.000 STABLE RELATIONSHIPS NO ONE IS GOING TO DENY YOU THE MAYOR CHAIR.
HONEY, ARE THE SMOOTHIES FOR THE CAFETERIA OR THE RESTAURANT?
CAFETERIA, MY LOVE.
HELLO, LOLA.
HELLO.
ARE YOU SURE YOU'RE OVER HIM?
ALL YOURS. I THINK I'LL TRY A CARNAL CLUB.
GOD, YOU'RE DISGUSTING!

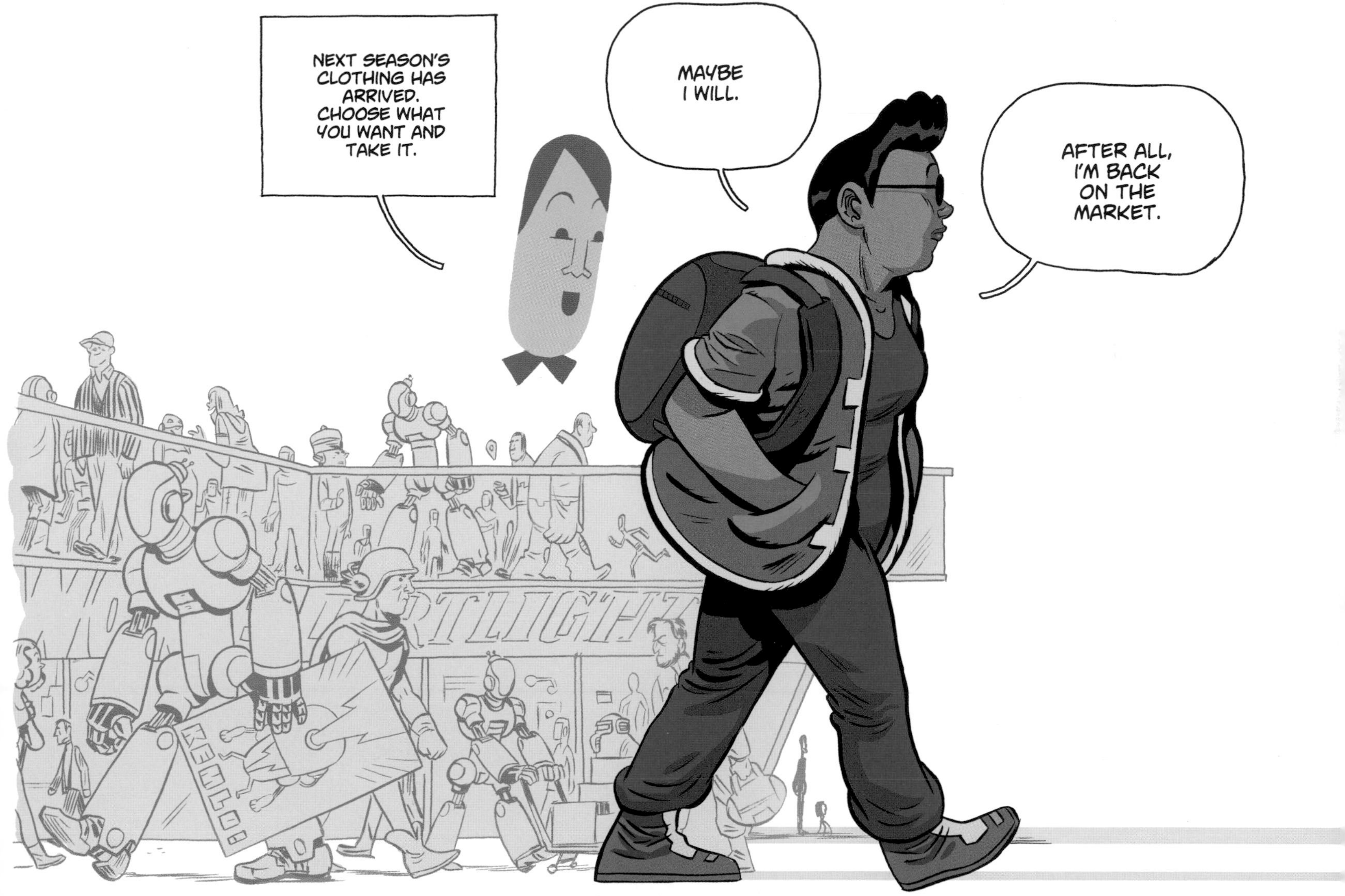
NEXT SEASON'S CLOTHING HAS ARRIVED. CHOOSE WHAT YOU WANT AND TAKE IT.
MAYBE I WILL.
AFTER ALL, I'M BACK ON THE MARKET.

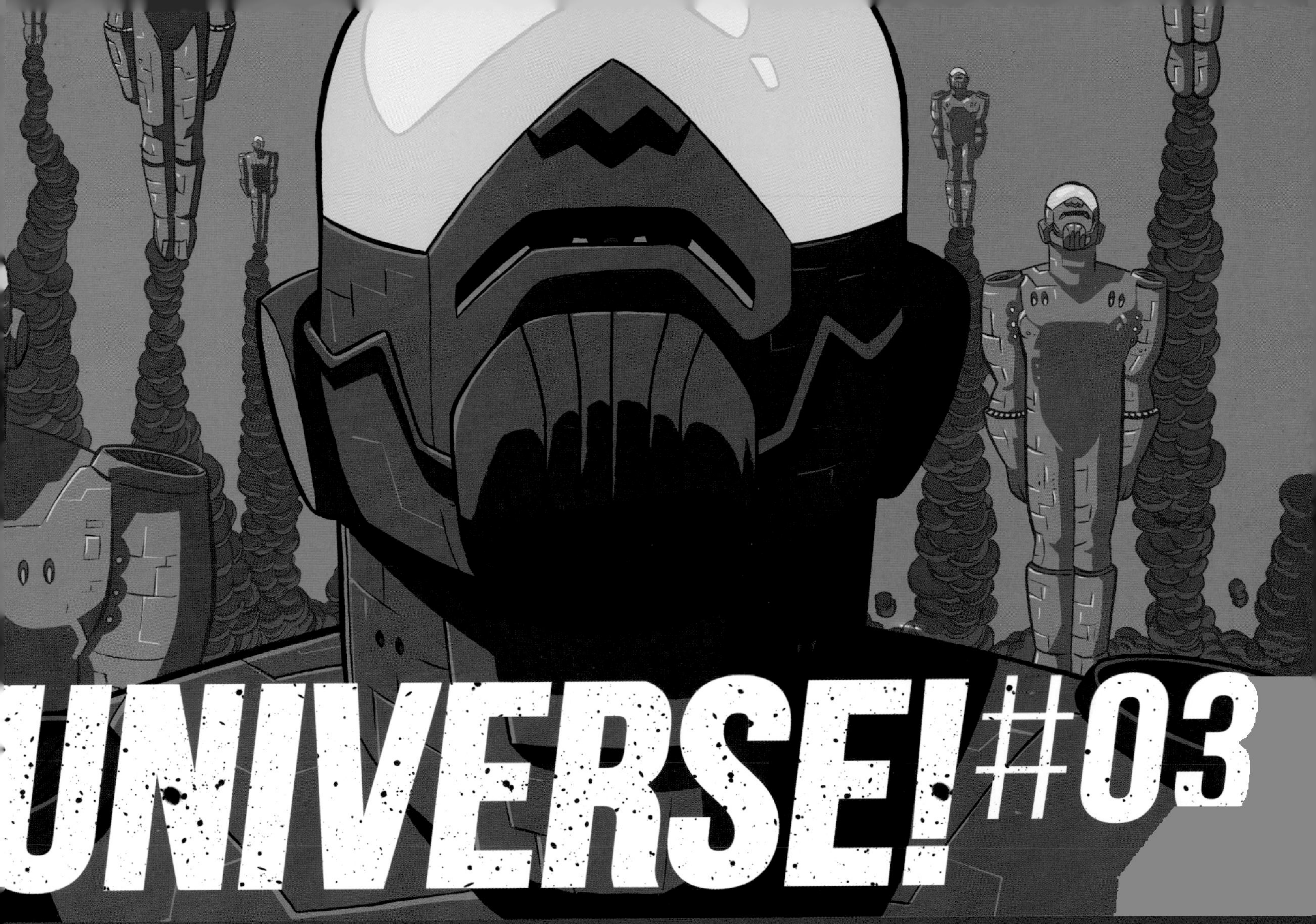

UNIVERSE! #03

WHAT WE KNOW ABOUT TAURUS-77

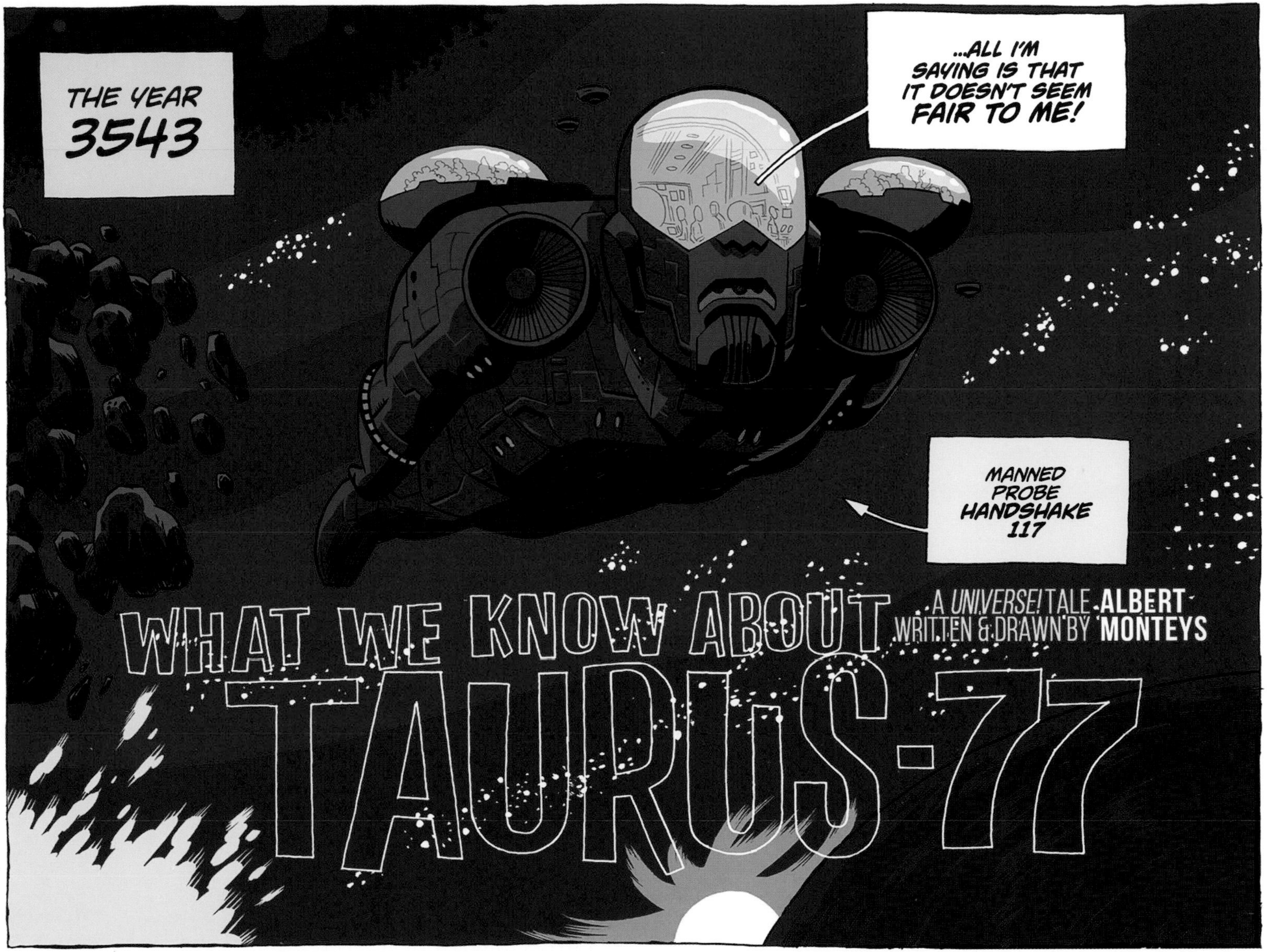
THE YEAR 3543
...ALL I'M SAYING IS THAT IT DOESN'T SEEM FAIR TO ME!
MANNED PROBE HANDSHAKE 117
WHAT WE KNOW ABOUT TAURUS-77
A UNIVERSE! TALE WRITTEN & DRAWN BY ALBERT MONTEYS

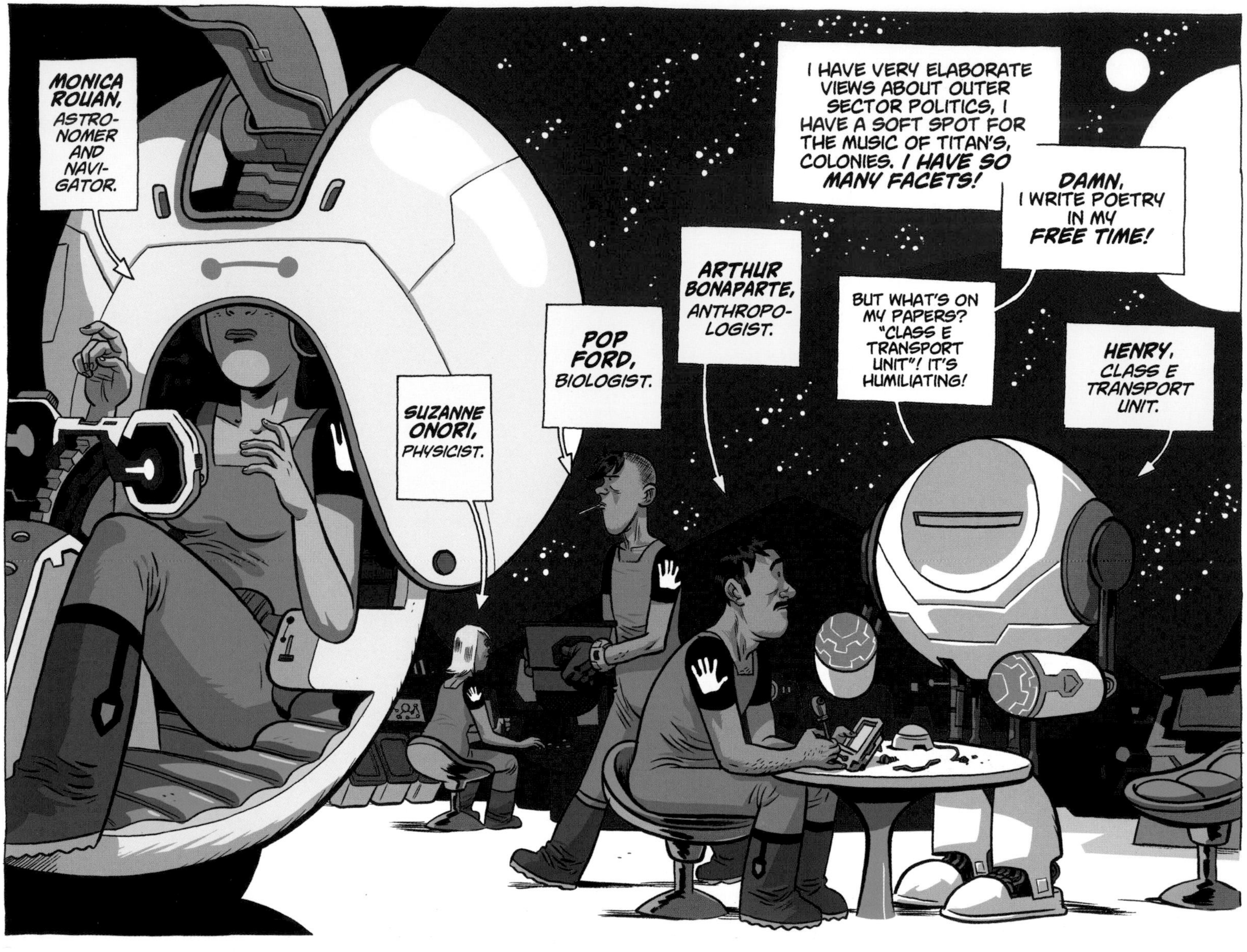
MONICA ROUAN, ASTRONOMER AND NAVIGATOR.
SUZANNE ONORI, PHYSICIST.
POP FORD, BIOLOGIST.
ARTHUR BONAPARTE, ANTHROPOLOGIST.
I HAVE VERY ELABORATE VIEWS ABOUT OUTER SECTOR POLITICS, I HAVE A SOFT SPOT FOR THE MUSIC OF TITAN'S, COLONIES. I HAVE SO MANY FACETS!
DAMN, I WRITE POETRY IN MY FREE TIME!
BUT WHAT'S ON MY PAPERS? "CLASS E TRANSPORT UNIT"! IT'S HUMILIATING!
HENRY, CLASS E TRANSPORT UNIT.

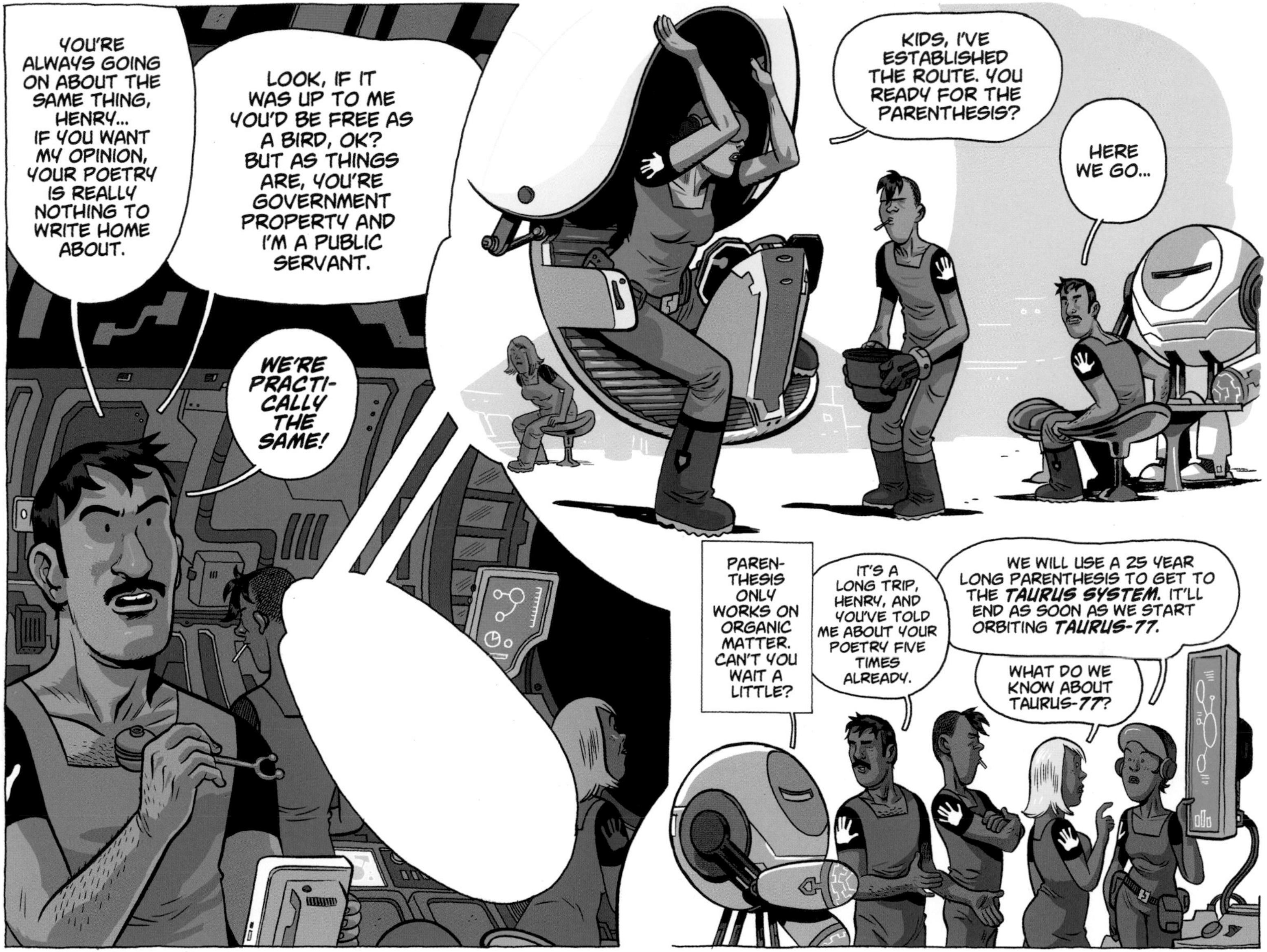

YOU'RE ALWAYS GOING ON ABOUT THE SAME THING, HENRY... IF YOU WANT MY OPINION, YOUR POETRY IS REALLY NOTHING TO WRITE HOME ABOUT.
LOOK, IF IT WAS UP TO ME YOU'D BE FREE AS A BIRD, OK? BUT AS THINGS ARE, YOU'RE GOVERNMENT PROPERTY AND I'M A PUBLIC SERVANT.
WE'RE PRACTICALLY THE SAME!
KIDS, I'VE ESTABLISHED THE ROUTE. YOU READY FOR THE PARENTHESIS?
HERE WE GO...
PARENTHESIS ONLY WORKS ON ORGANIC MATTER. CAN'T YOU WAIT A LITTLE?
IT'S A LONG TRIP, HENRY, AND YOU'VE TOLD ME ABOUT YOUR POETRY FIVE TIMES ALREADY.
WE WILL USE A 25 YEAR LONG PARENTHESIS TO GET TO THE TAURUS SYSTEM. IT'LL END AS SOON AS WE START ORBITING TAURUS-77.
WHAT DO WE KNOW ABOUT TAURUS-77?

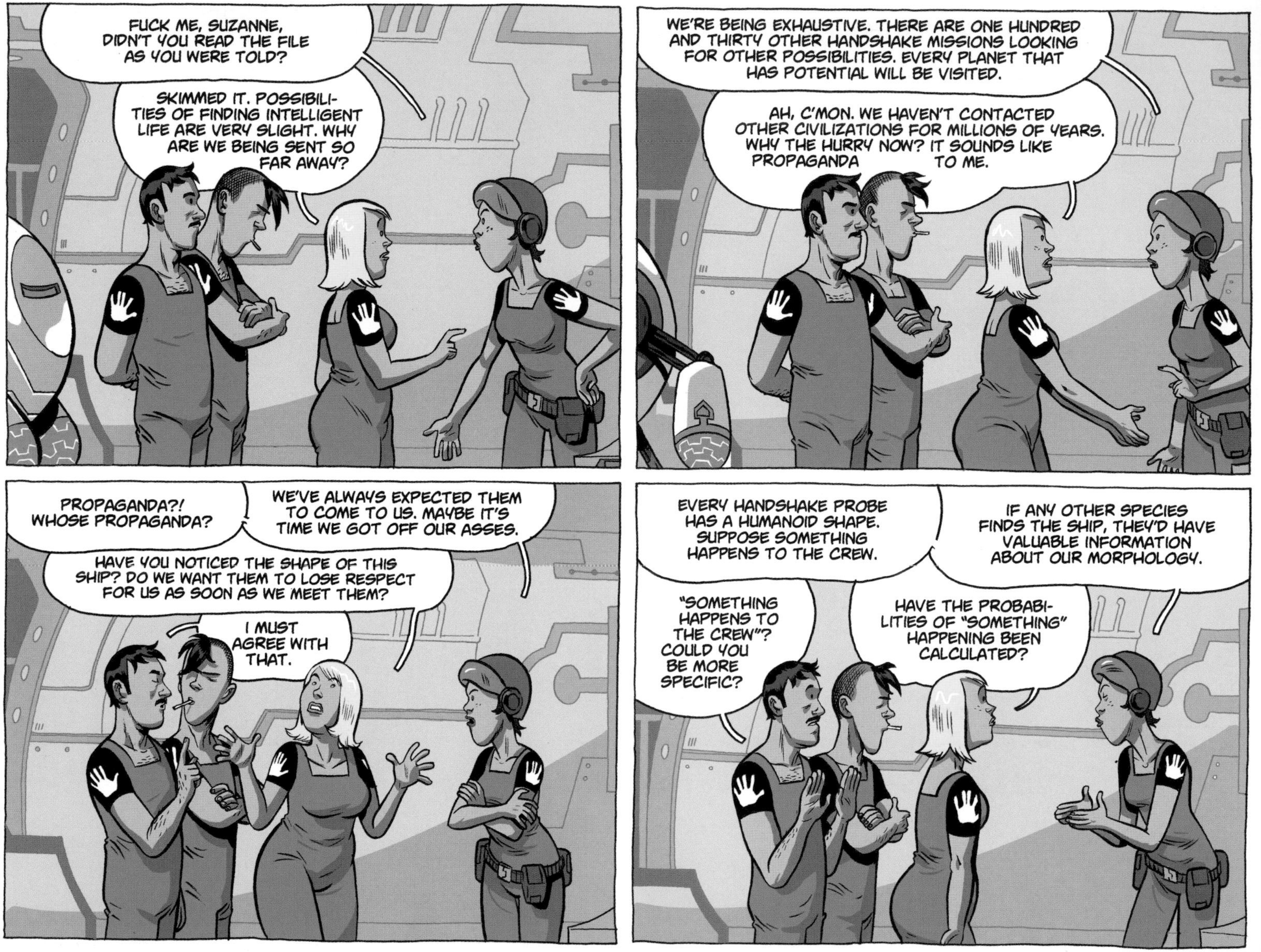
FUCK ME, SUZANNE, DIDN'T YOU READ THE FILE AS YOU WERE TOLD?
SKIMMED IT. POSSIBILITIES OF FINDING INTELLIGENT LIFE ARE VERY SLIGHT. WHY ARE WE BEING SENT SO FAR AWAY?
WE'RE BEING EXHAUSTIVE. THERE ARE ONE HUNDRED AND THIRTY OTHER HANDSHAKE MISSIONS LOOKING FOR OTHER POSSIBILITIES. EVERY PLANET THAT HAS POTENTIAL WILL BE VISITED.
AH, C'MON. WE HAVEN'T CONTACTED OTHER CIVILIZATIONS FOR MILLIONS OF YEARS. WHY THE HURRY NOW? IT SOUNDS LIKE PROPAGANDA TO ME.
PROPAGANDA?! WHOSE PROPAGANDA?
WE'VE ALWAYS EXPECTED THEM TO COME TO US. MAYBE IT'S TIME WE GOT OFF OUR ASSES.
HAVE YOU NOTICED THE SHAPE OF THIS SHIP? DO WE WANT THEM TO LOSE RESPECT FOR US AS SOON AS WE MEET THEM?
I MUST AGREE WITH THAT.
EVERY HANDSHAKE PROBE HAS A HUMANOID SHAPE. SUPPOSE SOMETHING HAPPENS TO THE CREW.
IF ANY OTHER SPECIES FINDS THE SHIP, THEY'D HAVE VALUABLE INFORMATION ABOUT OUR MORPHOLOGY.
"SOMETHING HAPPENS TO THE CREW"? COULD YOU BE MORE SPECIFIC?
HAVE THE PROBABILITIES OF "SOMETHING" HAPPENING BEEN CALCULATED?

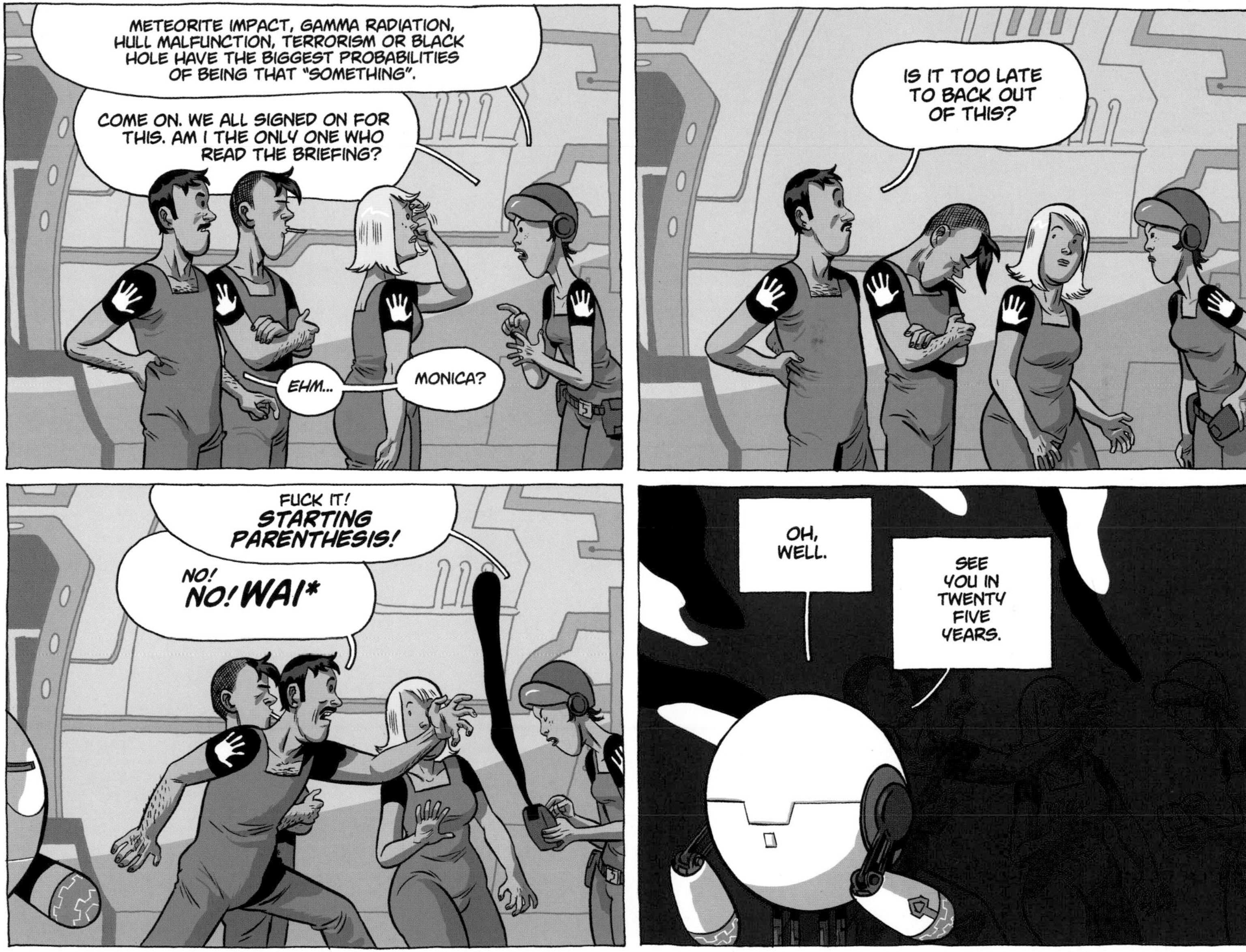
METEORITE IMPACT, GAMMA RADIATION, HULL MALFUNCTION, TERRORISM OR BLACK HOLE HAVE THE BIGGEST PROBABILITIES OF BEING THAT "SOMETHING".
COME ON. WE ALL SIGNED ON FOR THIS. AM I THE ONLY ONE WHO READ THE BRIEFING?
EHM...
MONICA?
IS IT TOO LATE TO BACK OUT OF THIS?
FUCK IT! STARTING PARENTHESIS!
NO! NO! WAI*
OH, WELL.
SEE YOU IN TWENTY FIVE YEARS.

3544	3545	3546	3547	3548
3549	3550	3551	3552	3553
3554	3555	3556	3557	3558
3559	3560	3561	3562	3563

| 3564 | 3565 | 3566 | 3567 | 3568 |

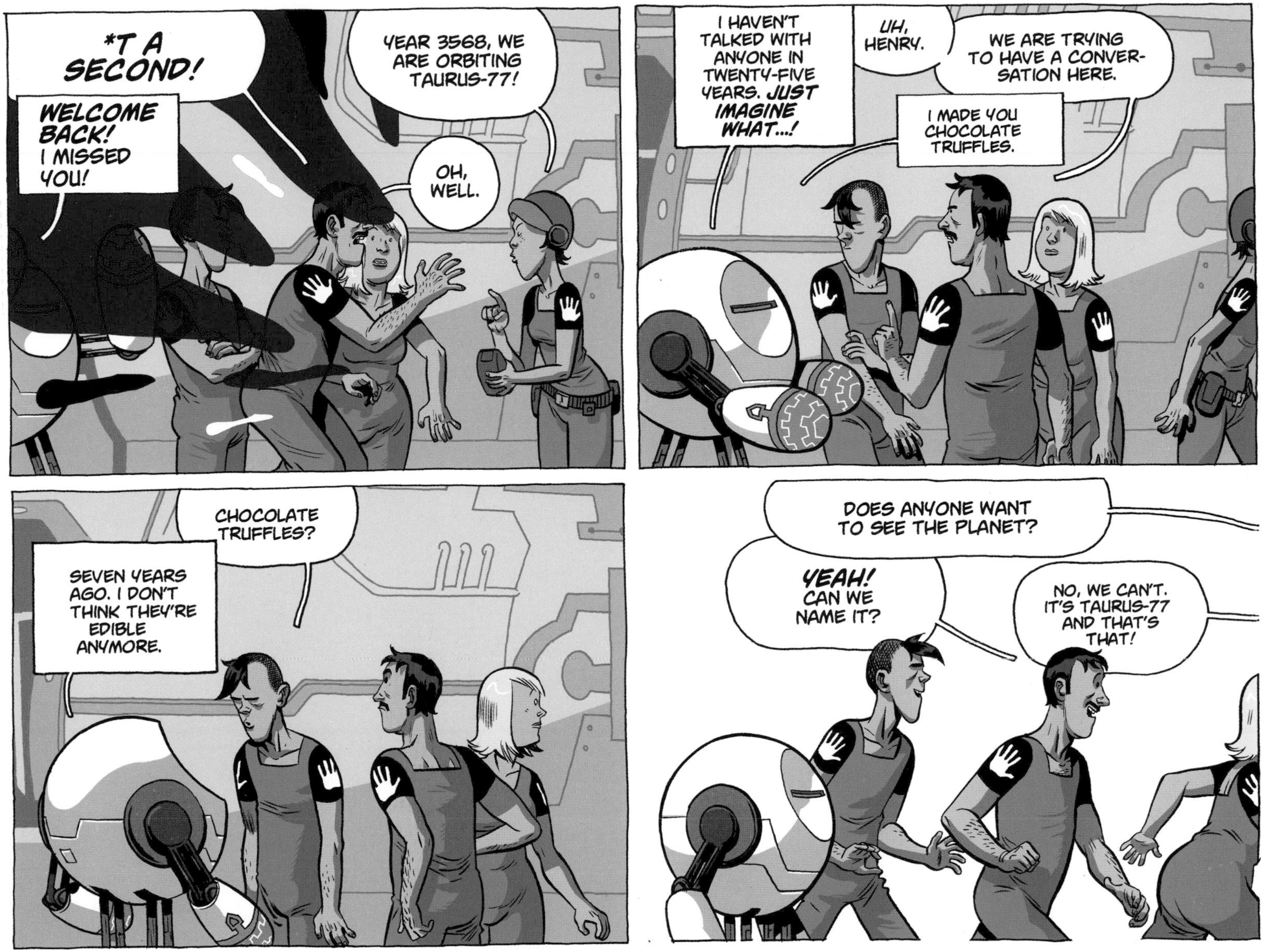
*T A SECOND!
WELCOME BACK! I MISSED YOU!
YEAR 3568, WE ARE ORBITING TAURUS-77!
OH, WELL.
I HAVEN'T TALKED WITH ANYONE IN TWENTY-FIVE YEARS. JUST IMAGINE WHAT...!
UH, HENRY.
WE ARE TRYING TO HAVE A CONVER-SATION HERE.
I MADE YOU CHOCOLATE TRUFFLES.
CHOCOLATE TRUFFLES?
SEVEN YEARS AGO. I DON'T THINK THEY'RE EDIBLE ANYMORE.
DOES ANYONE WANT TO SEE THE PLANET?
YEAH! CAN WE NAME IT?
NO, WE CAN'T. IT'S TAURUS-77 AND THAT'S THAT!

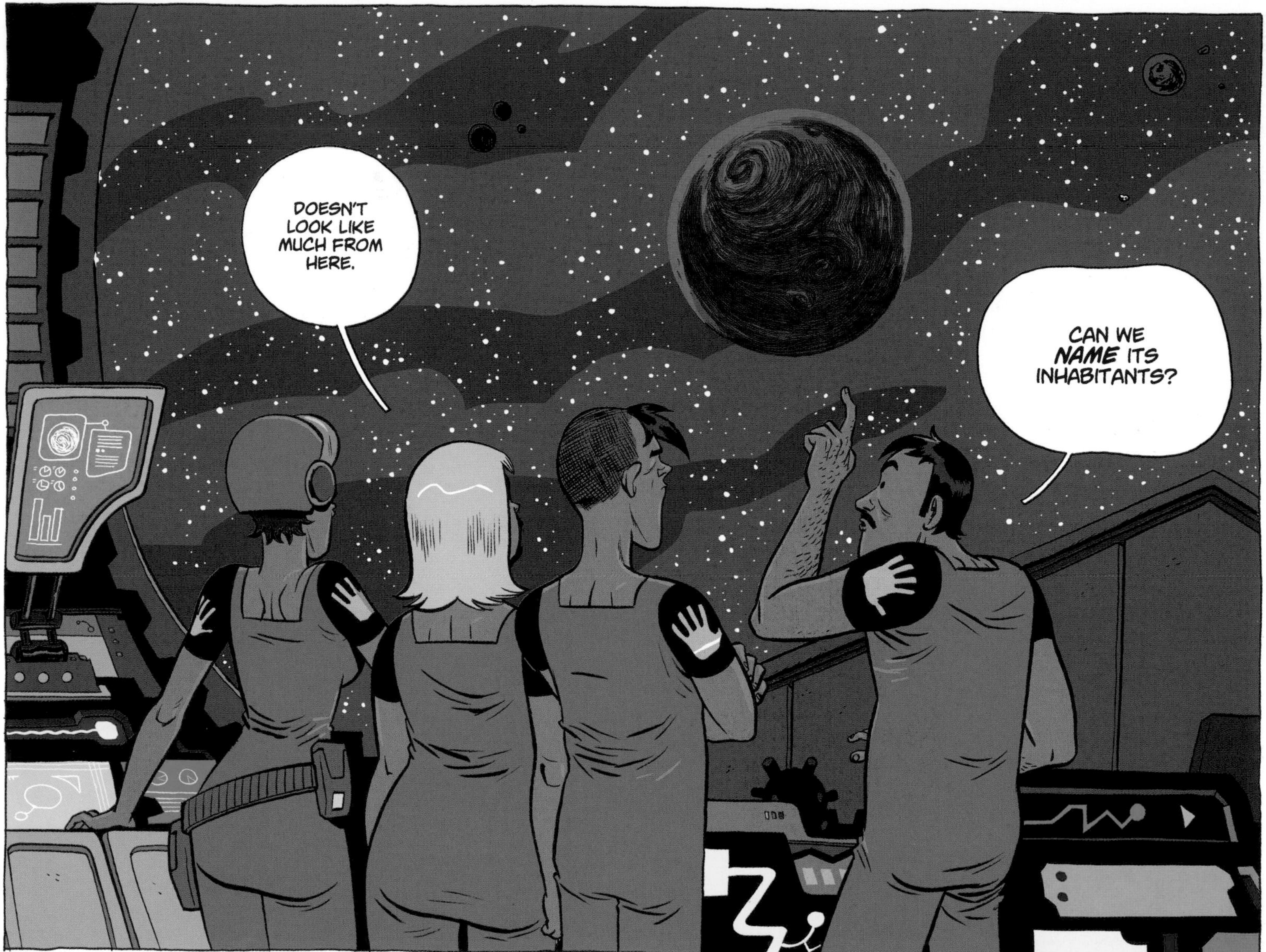
DOESN'T LOOK LIKE MUCH FROM HERE.
CAN WE *NAME* ITS INHABITANTS?

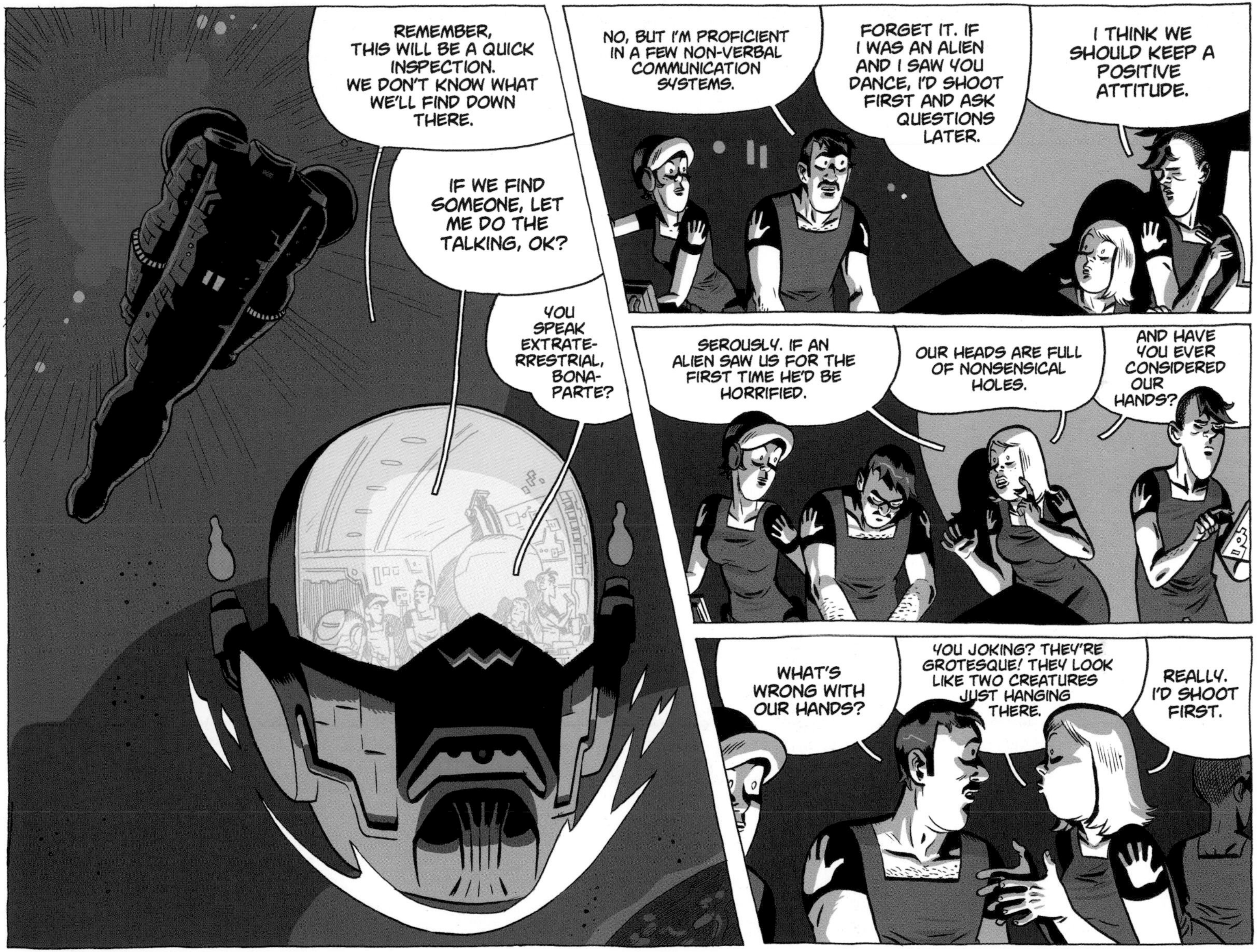
REMEMBER, THIS WILL BE A QUICK INSPECTION. WE DON'T KNOW WHAT WE'LL FIND DOWN THERE.
IF WE FIND SOMEONE, LET ME DO THE TALKING, OK?
YOU SPEAK EXTRATE-RRESTRIAL, BONA-PARTE?
NO, BUT I'M PROFICIENT IN A FEW NON-VERBAL COMMUNICATION SYSTEMS.
FORGET IT. IF I WAS AN ALIEN AND I SAW YOU DANCE, I'D SHOOT FIRST AND ASK QUESTIONS LATER.
I THINK WE SHOULD KEEP A POSITIVE ATTITUDE.
SEROUSLY. IF AN ALIEN SAW US FOR THE FIRST TIME HE'D BE HORRIFIED.
OUR HEADS ARE FULL OF NONSENSICAL HOLES.
AND HAVE YOU EVER CONSIDERED OUR HANDS?
WHAT'S WRONG WITH OUR HANDS?
YOU JOKING? THEY'RE GROTESQUE! THEY LOOK LIKE TWO CREATURES JUST HANGING THERE.
REALLY. I'D SHOOT FIRST.

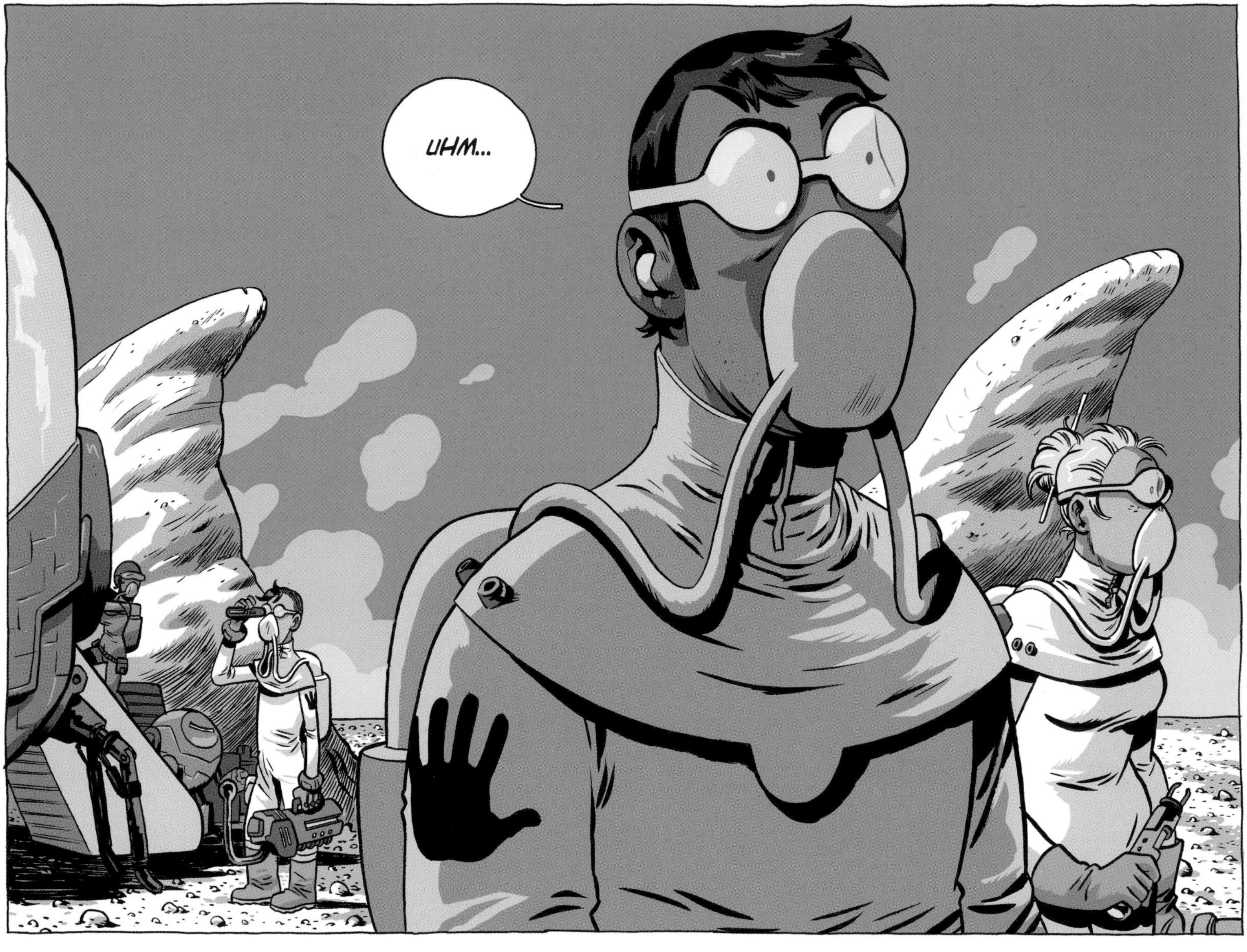
UHM...

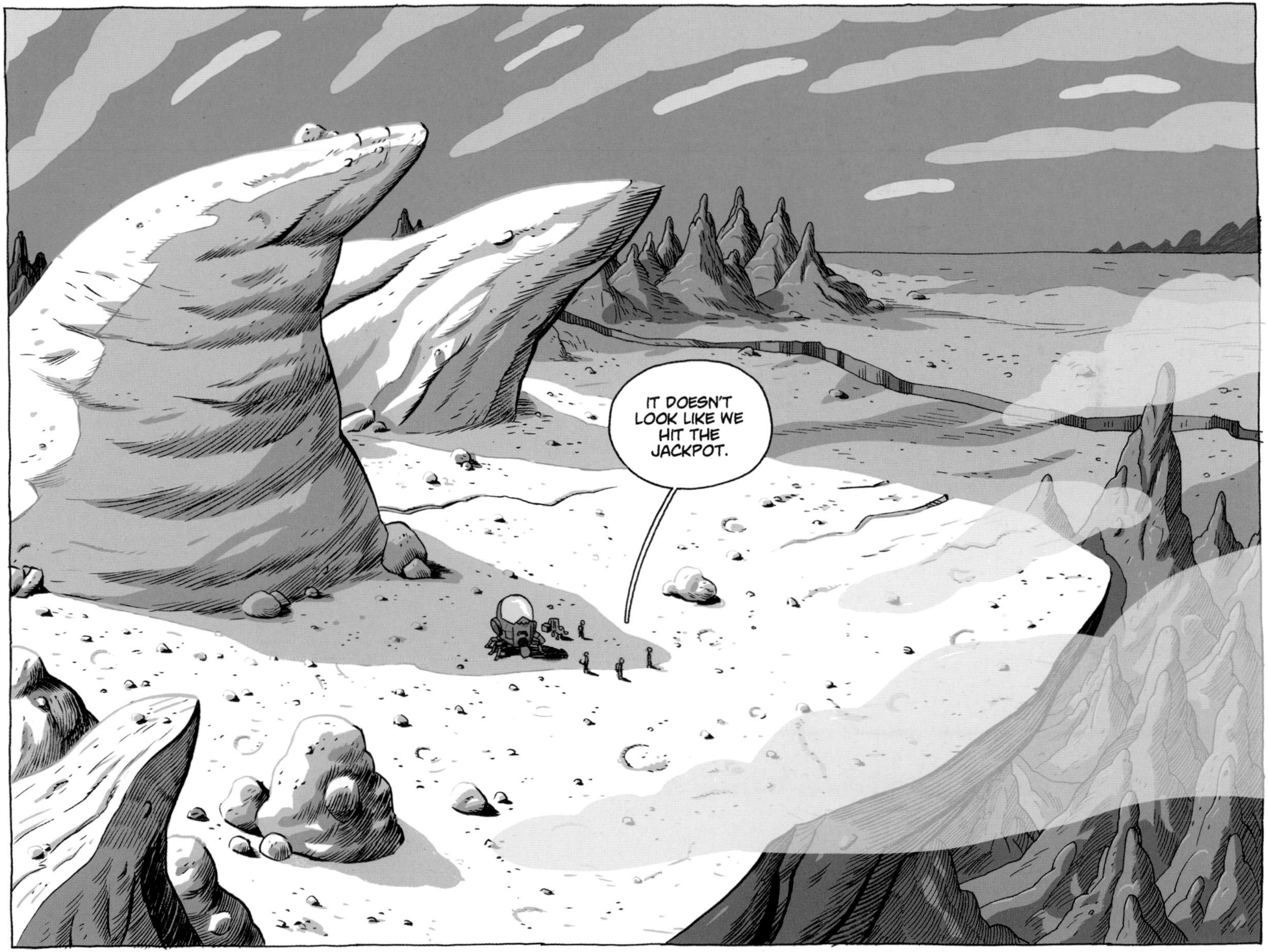
IT DOESN'T LOOK LIKE WE HIT THE JACKPOT.

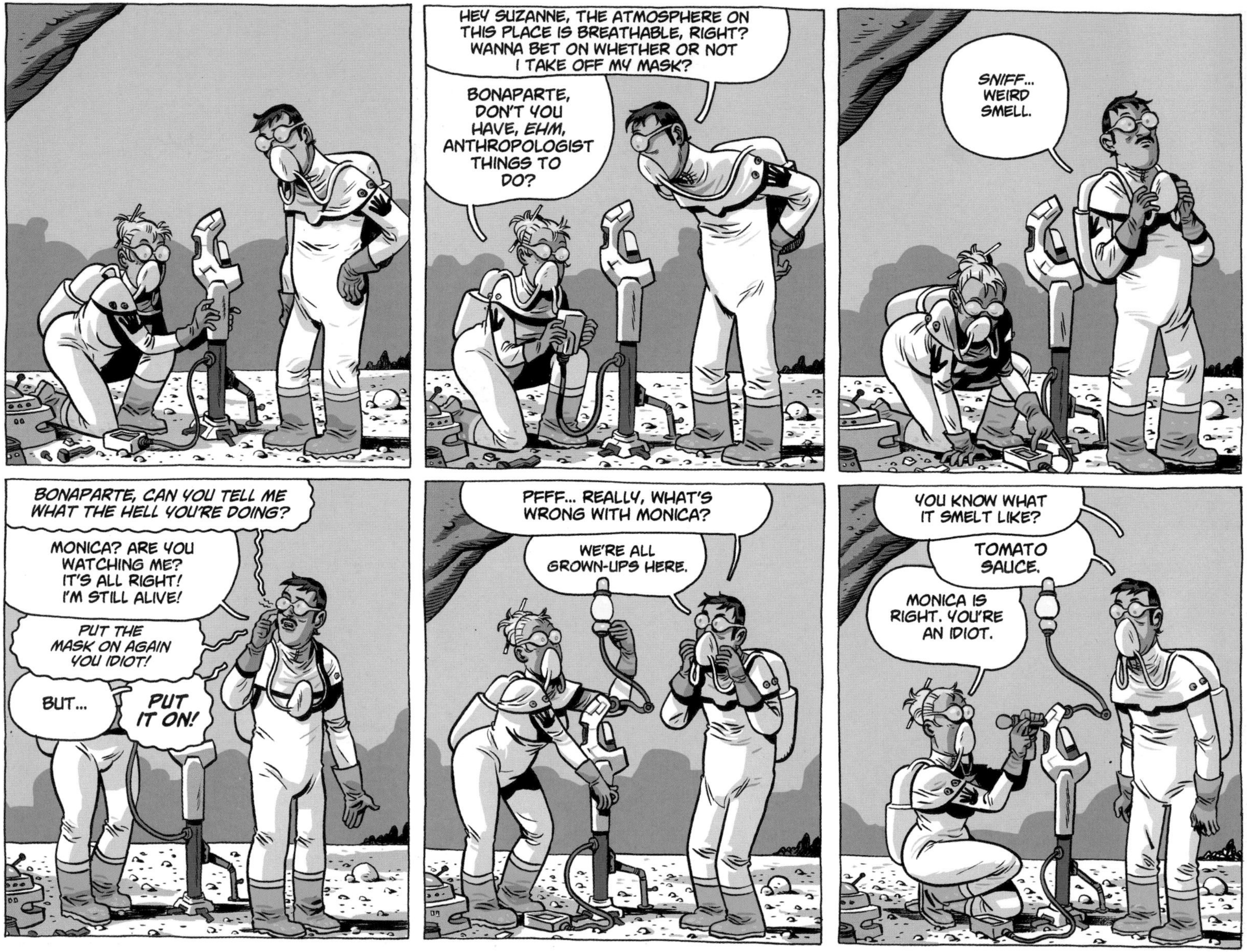
HEY SUZANNE, THE ATMOSPHERE ON THIS PLACE IS BREATHABLE, RIGHT? WANNA BET ON WHETHER OR NOT I TAKE OFF MY MASK?
BONAPARTE, DON'T YOU HAVE, *EHM*, ANTHROPOLOGIST THINGS TO DO?
SNIFF... WEIRD SMELL.
BONAPARTE, CAN YOU TELL ME WHAT THE HELL YOU'RE DOING?
MONICA? ARE YOU WATCHING ME? IT'S ALL RIGHT! I'M STILL ALIVE!
PUT THE MASK ON AGAIN YOU IDIOT!
BUT...
PUT IT ON!
PFFF... REALLY, WHAT'S WRONG WITH MONICA?
WE'RE ALL GROWN-UPS HERE.
YOU KNOW WHAT IT SMELT LIKE?
TOMATO SAUCE.
MONICA IS RIGHT. YOU'RE AN IDIOT.

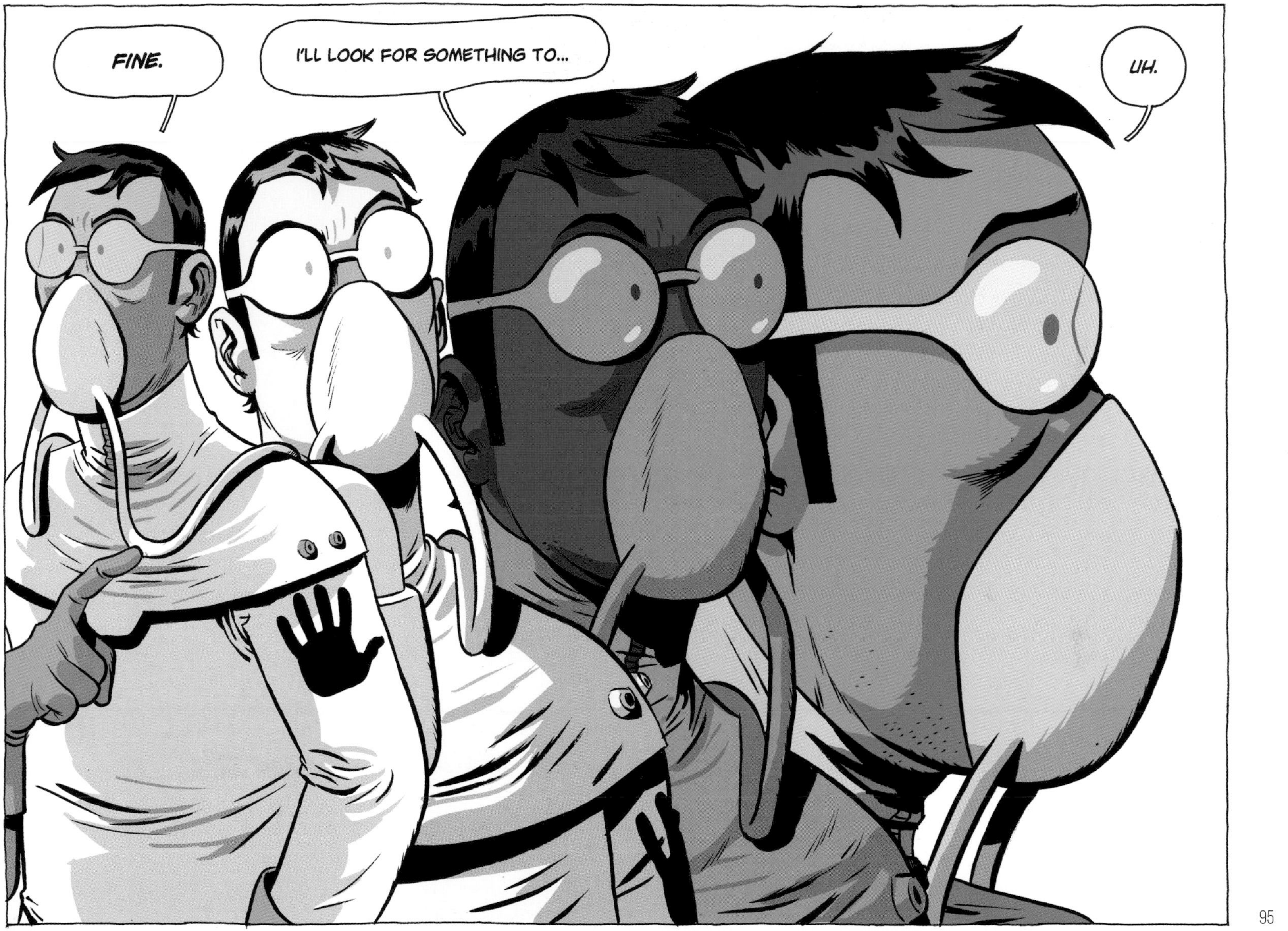
FINE.
I'LL LOOK FOR SOMETHING TO...
UH.

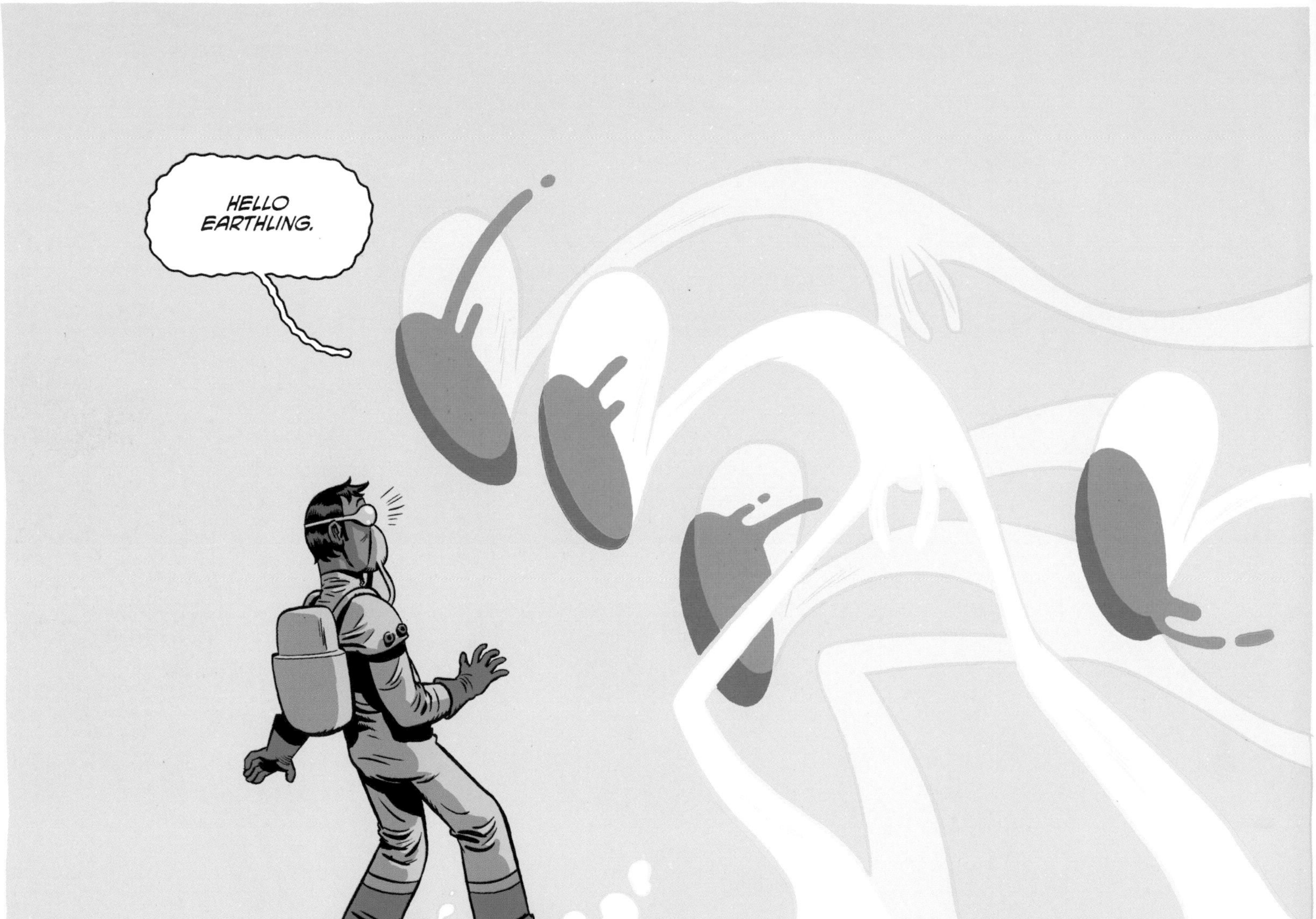
HELLO EARTHLING.

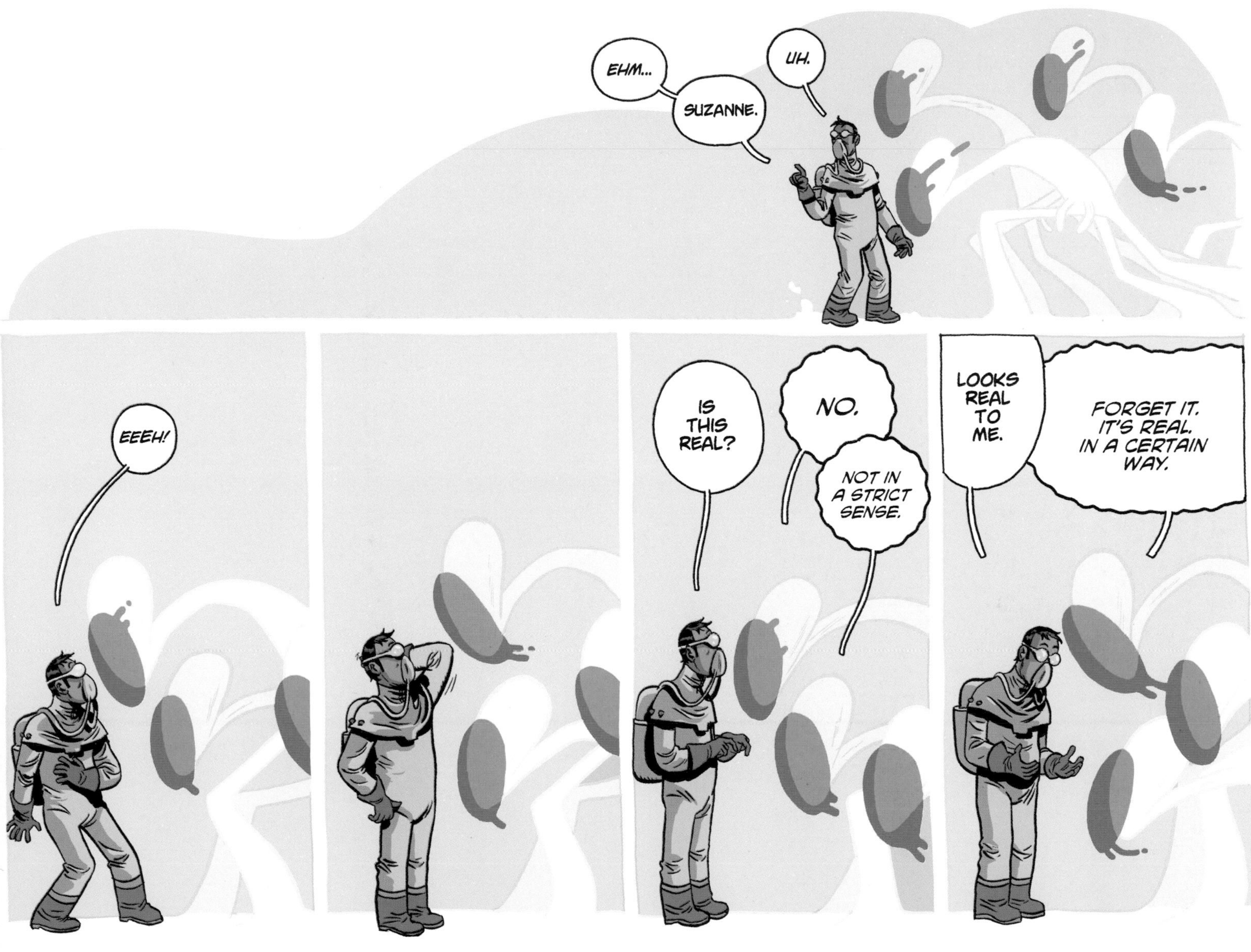
EHM...
SUZANNE.
UH.
EEEH!
IS THIS REAL?
NO.
NOT IN A STRICT SENSE.
LOOKS REAL TO ME.
FORGET IT. IT'S REAL. IN A CERTAIN WAY.

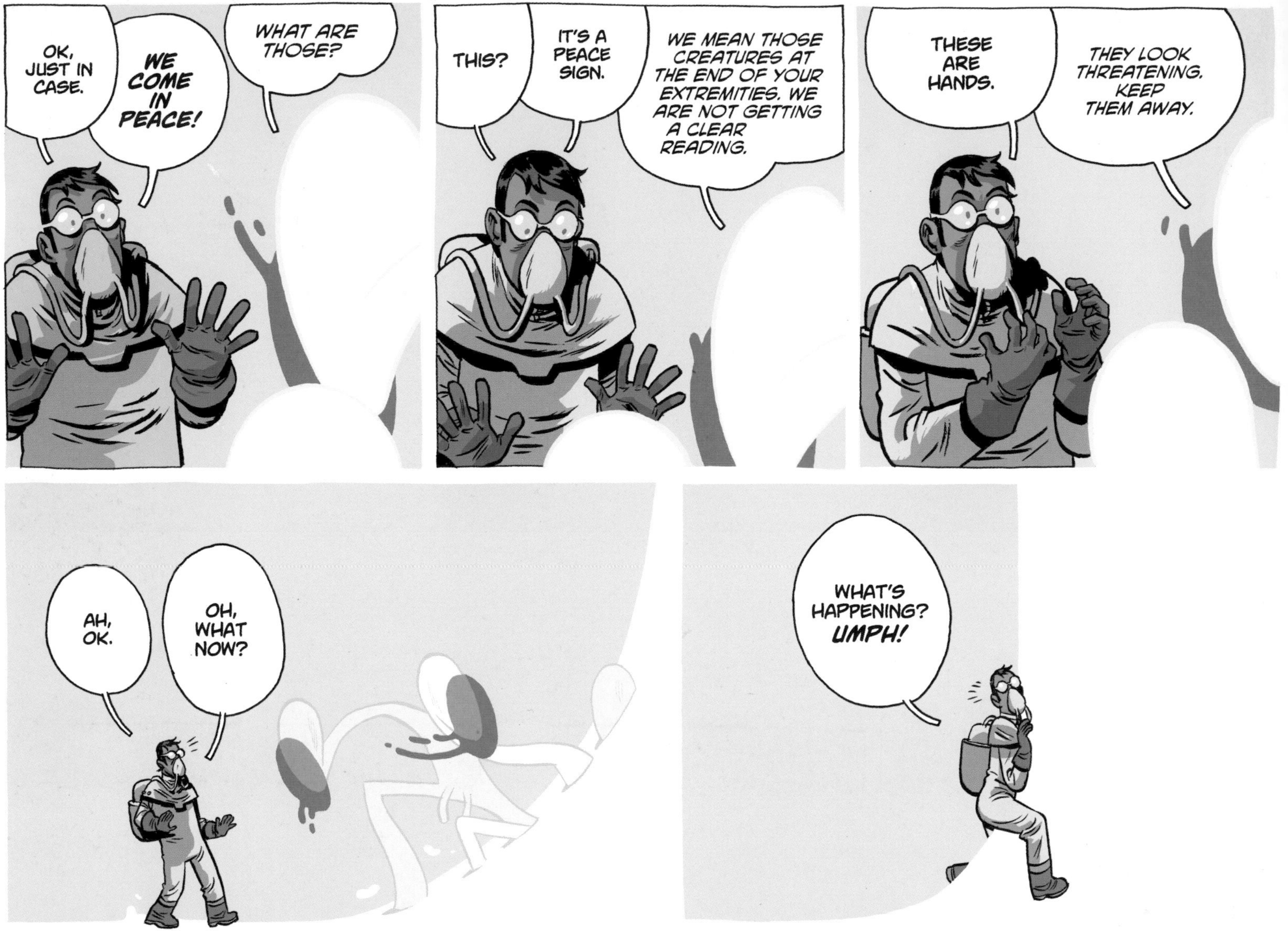
OK, JUST IN CASE.
WE COME IN PEACE!
WHAT ARE THOSE?
THIS?
IT'S A PEACE SIGN.
WE MEAN THOSE CREATURES AT THE END OF YOUR EXTREMITIES. WE ARE NOT GETTING A CLEAR READING.
THESE ARE HANDS.
THEY LOOK THREATENING. KEEP THEM AWAY.
AH, OK.
OH, WHAT NOW?
WHAT'S HAPPENING? UMPH!

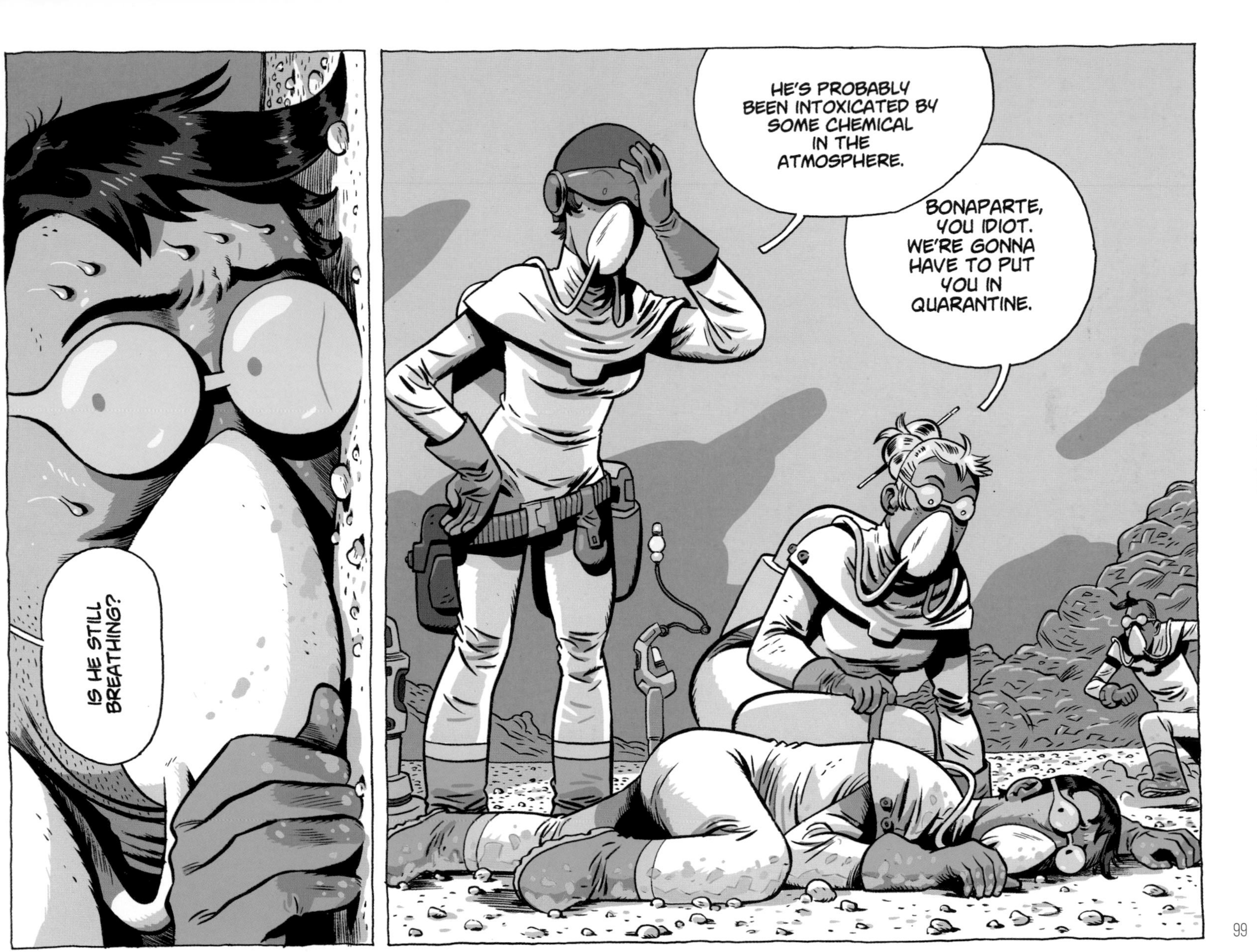
IS HE STILL BREATHING?
HE'S PROBABLY BEEN INTOXICATED BY SOME CHEMICAL IN THE ATMOSPHERE.
BONAPARTE, YOU IDIOT. WE'RE GONNA HAVE TO PUT YOU IN QUARANTINE.

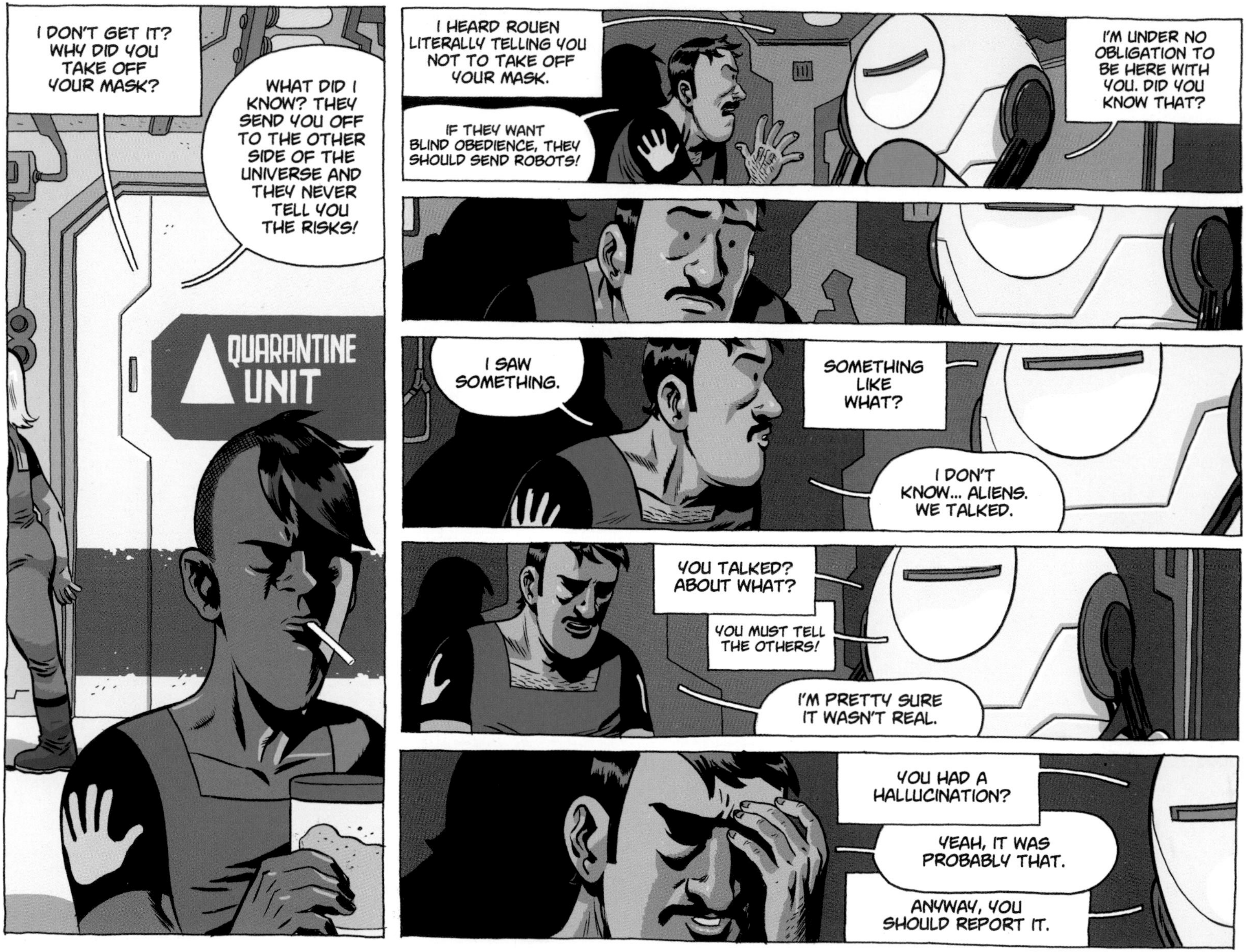
I DON'T GET IT? WHY DID YOU TAKE OFF YOUR MASK?
WHAT DID I KNOW? THEY SEND YOU OFF TO THE OTHER SIDE OF THE UNIVERSE AND THEY NEVER TELL YOU THE RISKS!
QUARANTINE UNIT
I HEARD ROUEN LITERALLY TELLING YOU NOT TO TAKE OFF YOUR MASK.
IF THEY WANT BLIND OBEDIENCE, THEY SHOULD SEND ROBOTS!
I'M UNDER NO OBLIGATION TO BE HERE WITH YOU. DID YOU KNOW THAT?
I SAW SOMETHING.
SOMETHING LIKE WHAT?
I DON'T KNOW... ALIENS. WE TALKED.
YOU TALKED? ABOUT WHAT?
YOU MUST TELL THE OTHERS!
I'M PRETTY SURE IT WASN'T REAL.
YOU HAD A HALLUCINATION?
YEAH, IT WAS PROBABLY THAT.
ANYWAY, YOU SHOULD REPORT IT.

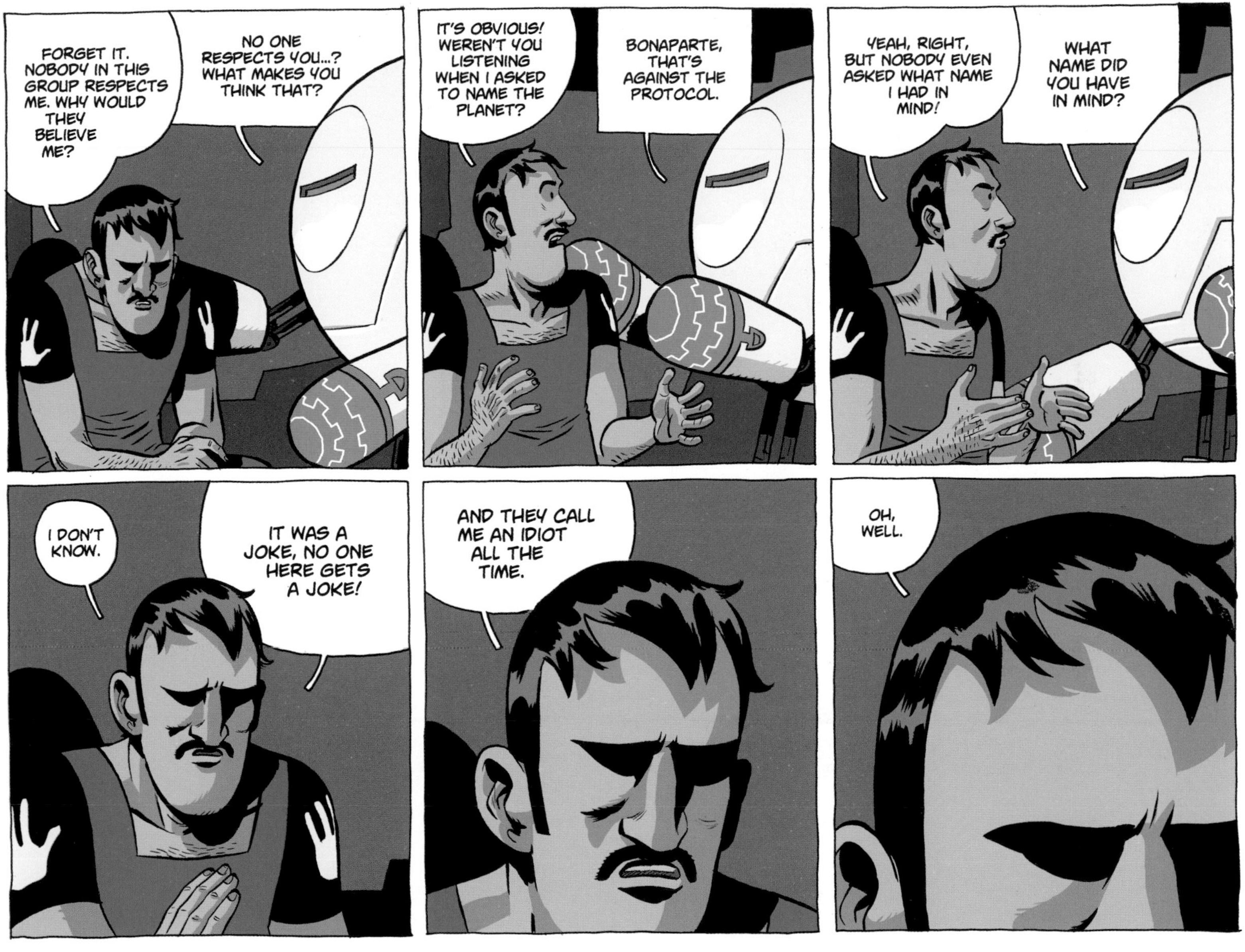
FORGET IT. NOBODY IN THIS GROUP RESPECTS ME. WHY WOULD THEY BELIEVE ME?
NO ONE RESPECTS YOU...? WHAT MAKES YOU THINK THAT?
IT'S OBVIOUS! WEREN'T YOU LISTENING WHEN I ASKED TO NAME THE PLANET?
BONAPARTE, THAT'S AGAINST THE PROTOCOL.
YEAH, RIGHT, BUT NOBODY EVEN ASKED WHAT NAME I HAD IN MIND!
WHAT NAME DID YOU HAVE IN MIND?
I DON'T KNOW.
IT WAS A JOKE, NO ONE HERE GETS A JOKE!
AND THEY CALL ME AN IDIOT ALL THE TIME.
OH, WELL.

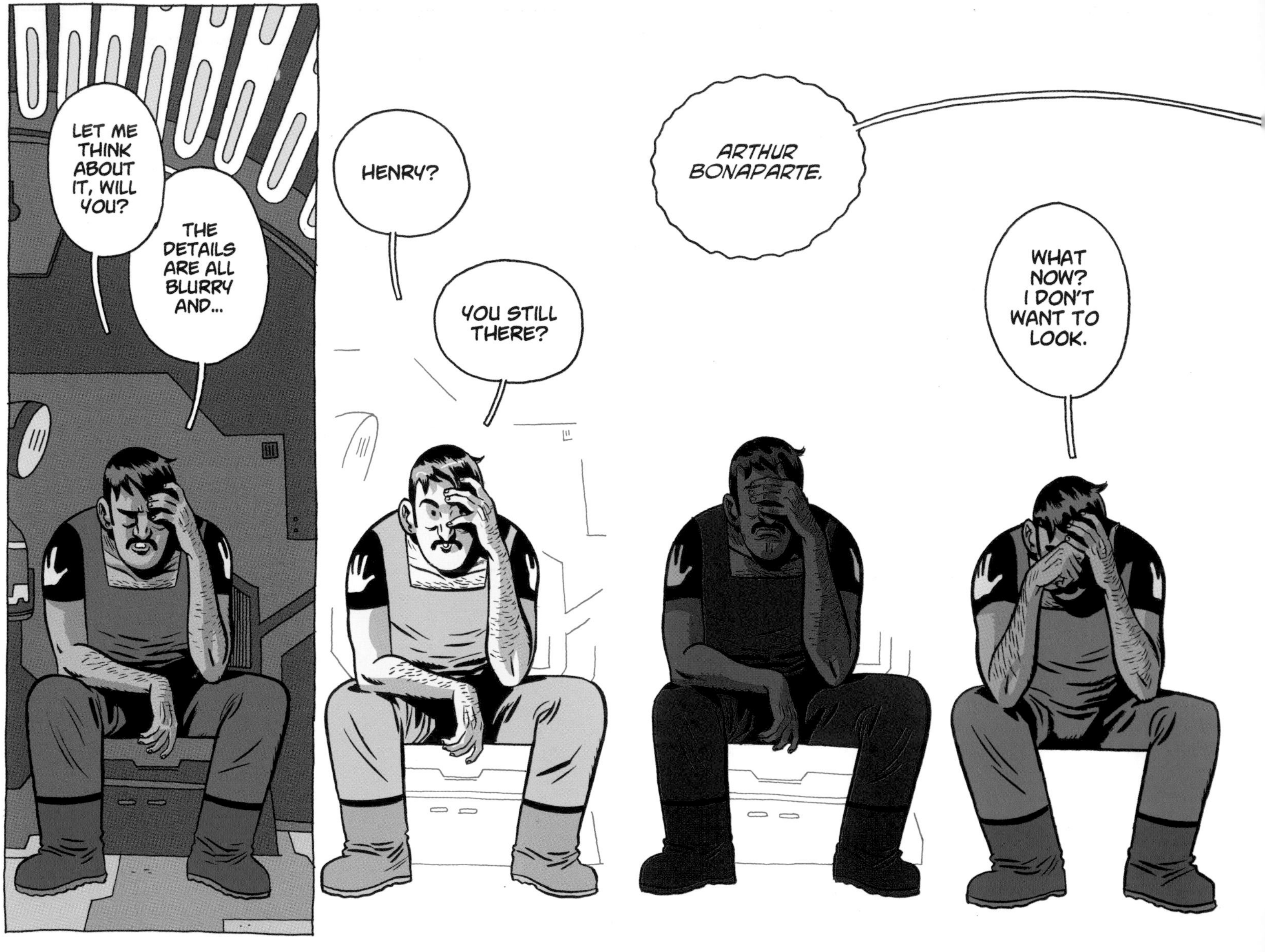
LET ME THINK ABOUT IT, WILL YOU?
THE DETAILS ARE ALL BLURRY AND...
HENRY?
YOU STILL THERE?
ARTHUR BONAPARTE.
WHAT NOW? I DON'T WANT TO LOOK.

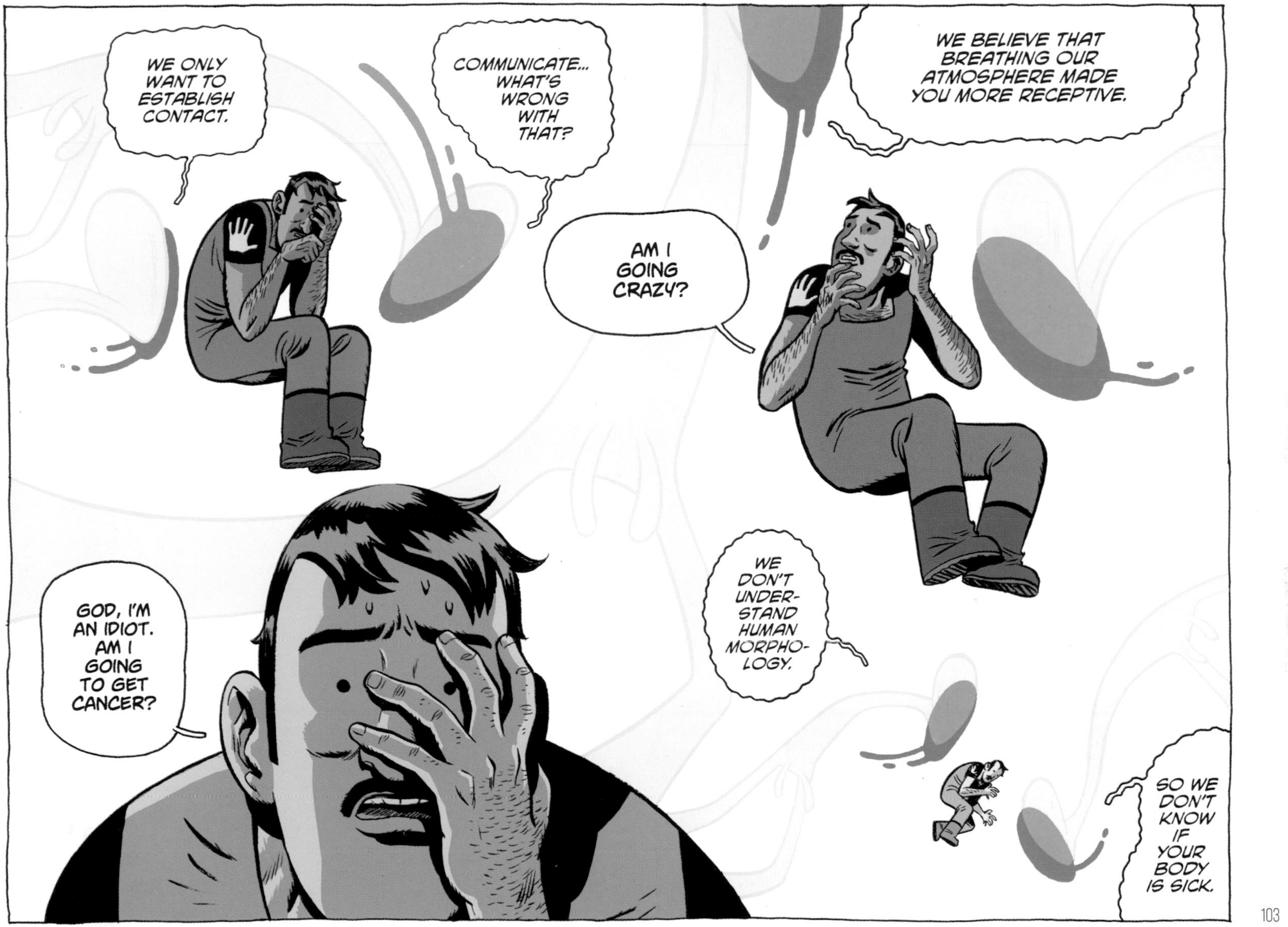
WE ONLY WANT TO ESTABLISH CONTACT.
COMMUNICATE... WHAT'S WRONG WITH THAT?
WE BELIEVE THAT BREATHING OUR ATMOSPHERE MADE YOU MORE RECEPTIVE.
AM I GOING CRAZY?
GOD, I'M AN IDIOT. AM I GOING TO GET CANCER?
WE DON'T UNDER-STAND HUMAN MORPHO-LOGY.
SO WE DON'T KNOW IF YOUR BODY IS SICK.

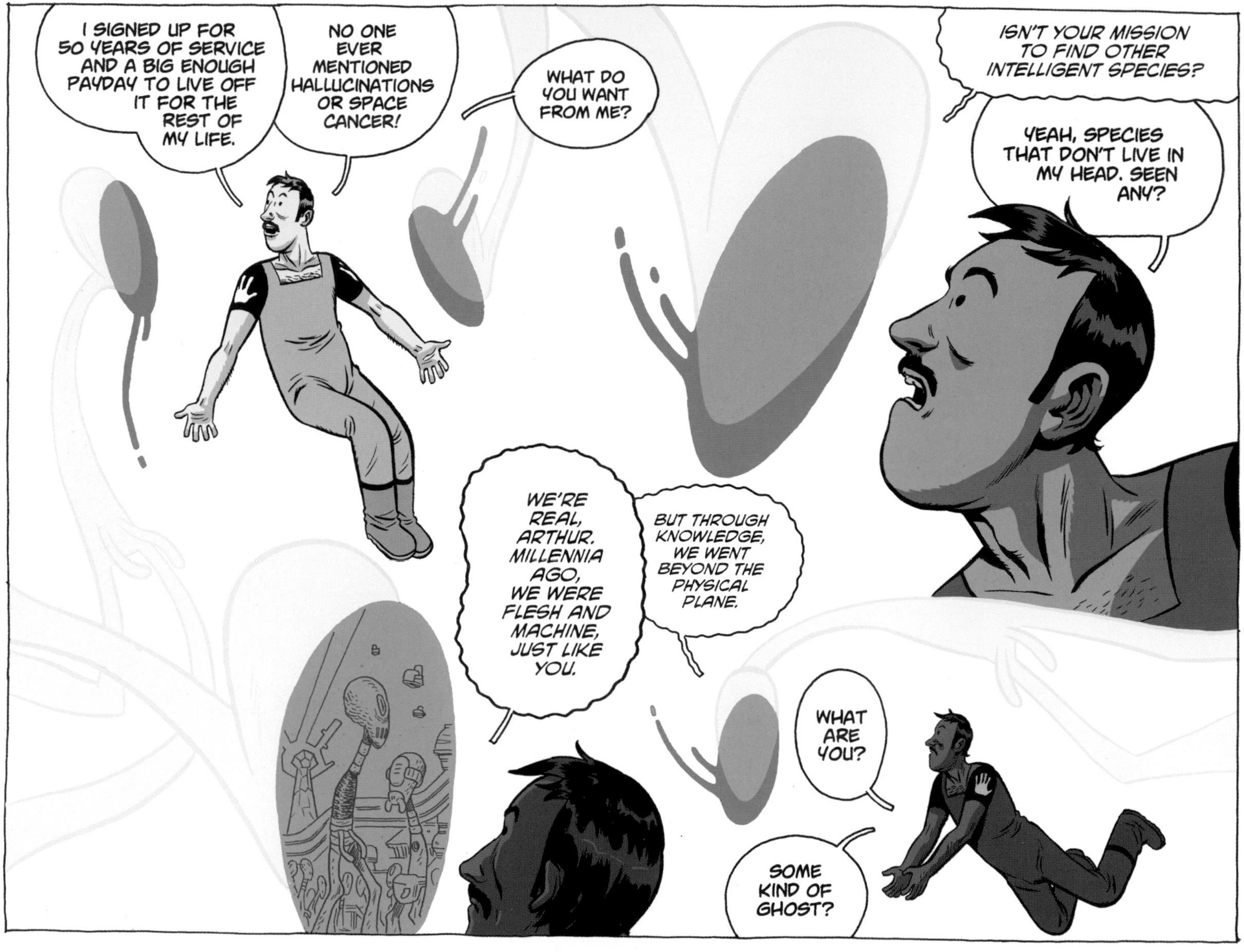
I SIGNED UP FOR 50 YEARS OF SERVICE AND A BIG ENOUGH PAYDAY TO LIVE OFF IT FOR THE REST OF MY LIFE.
NO ONE EVER MENTIONED HALLUCINATIONS OR SPACE CANCER!
WHAT DO YOU WANT FROM ME?
ISN'T YOUR MISSION TO FIND OTHER INTELLIGENT SPECIES?
YEAH, SPECIES THAT DON'T LIVE IN MY HEAD. SEEN ANY?
WE'RE REAL, ARTHUR. MILLENNIA AGO, WE WERE FLESH AND MACHINE, JUST LIKE YOU.
BUT THROUGH KNOWLEDGE, WE WENT BEYOND THE PHYSICAL PLANE.
WHAT ARE YOU?
SOME KIND OF GHOST?

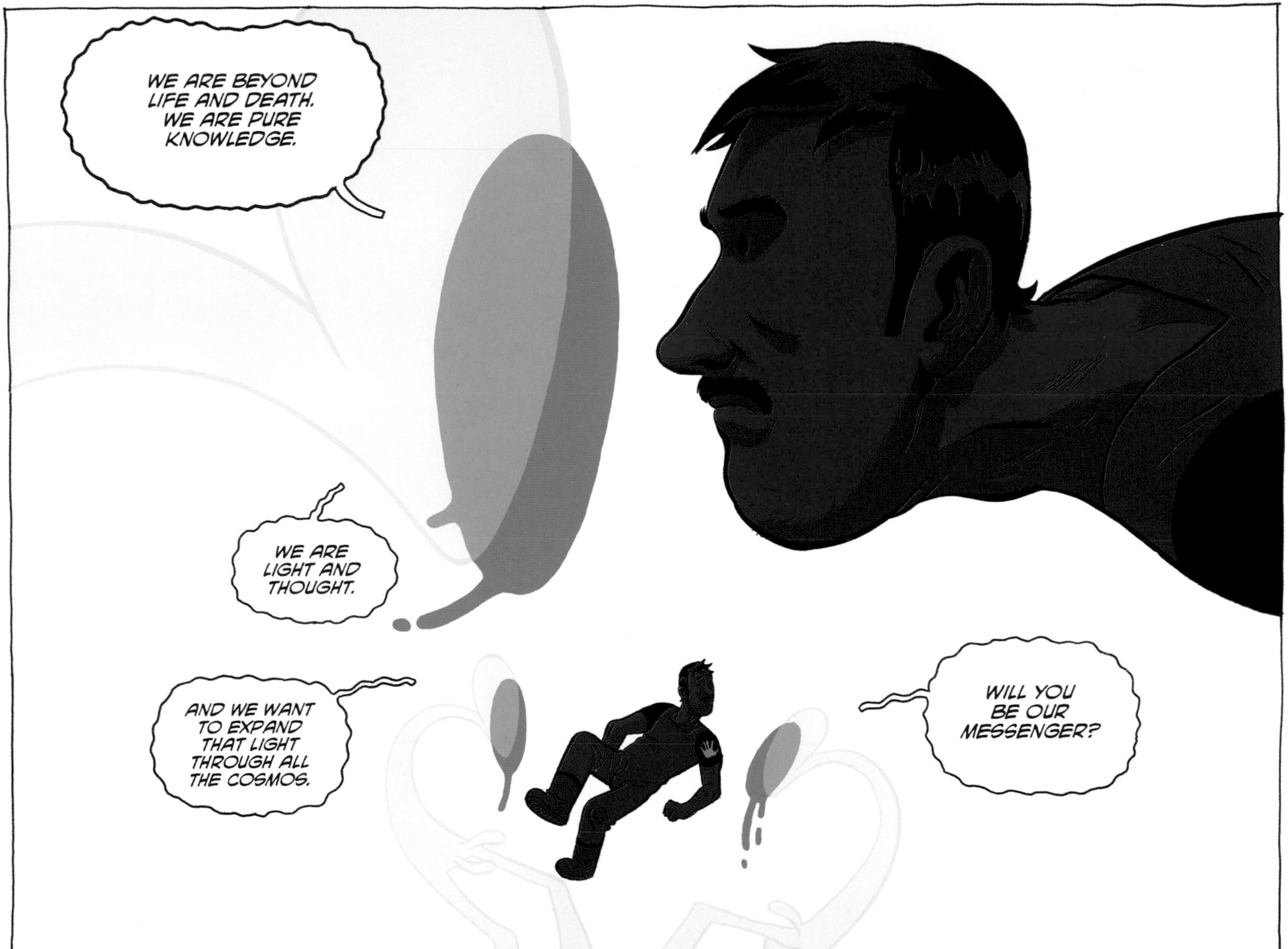
WE ARE BEYOND LIFE AND DEATH. WE ARE PURE KNOWLEDGE.
WE ARE LIGHT AND THOUGHT.
AND WE WANT TO EXPAND THAT LIGHT THROUGH ALL THE COSMOS.
WILL YOU BE OUR MESSENGER?

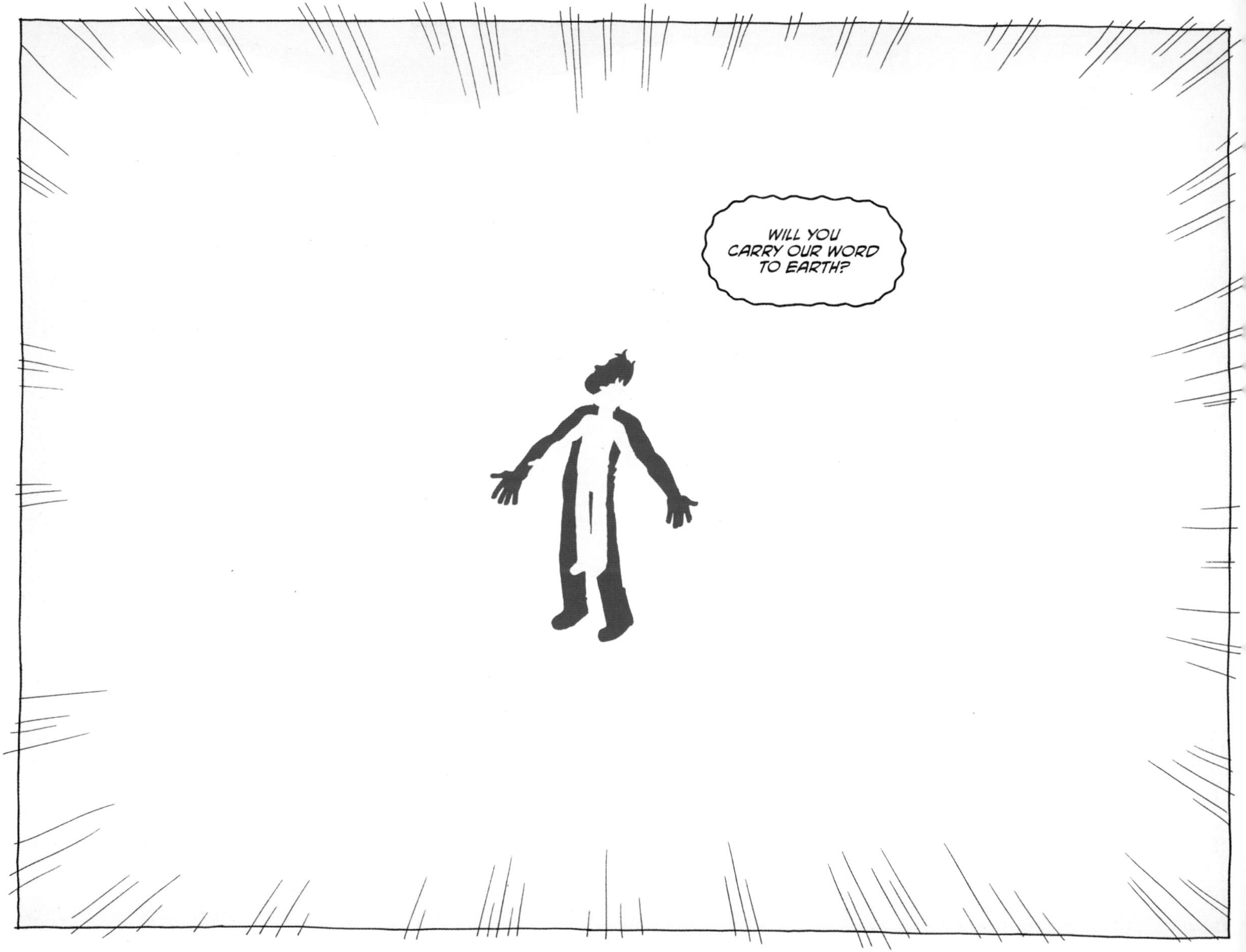
WILL YOU CARRY OUR WORD TO EARTH?

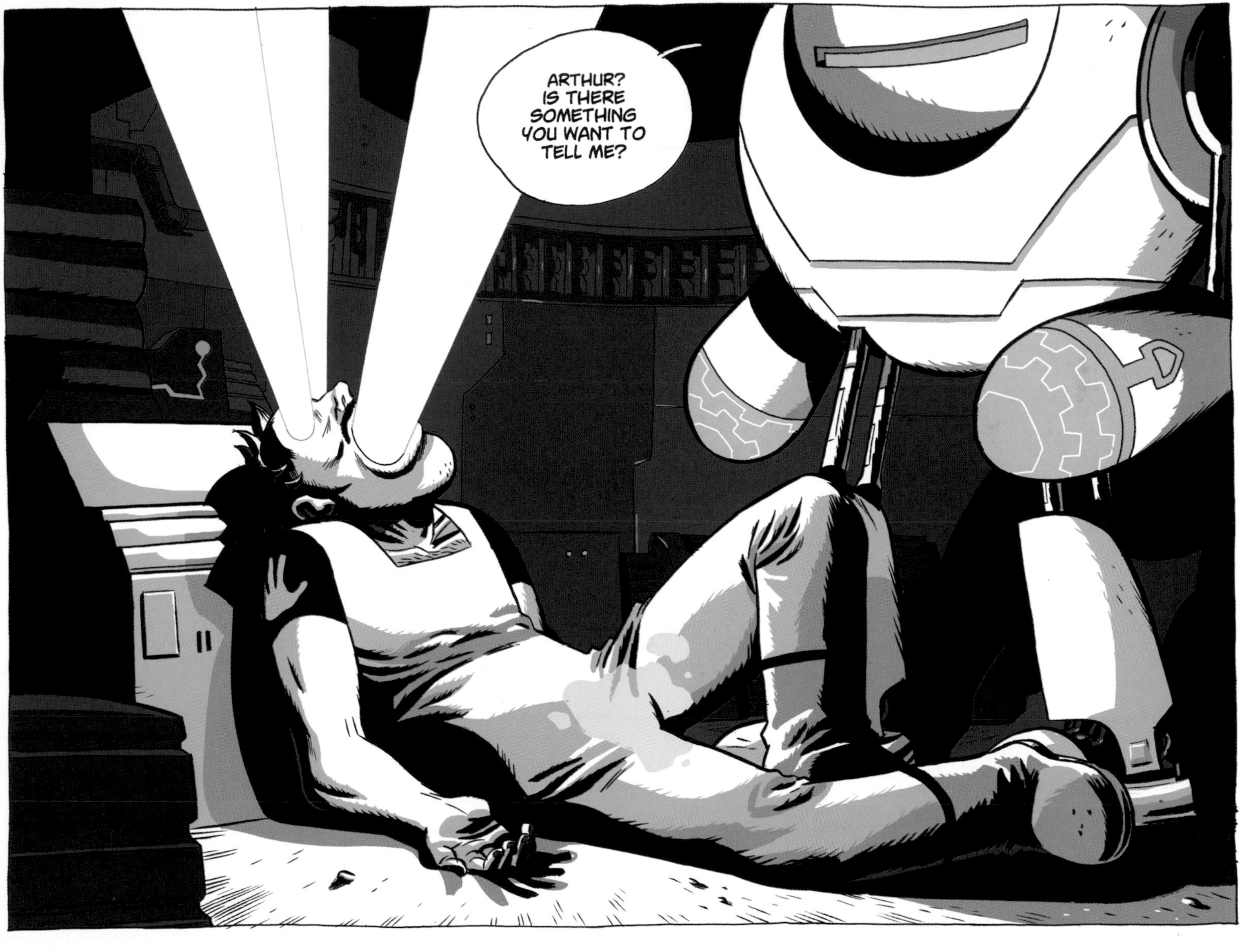
ARTHUR? IS THERE SOMETHING YOU WANT TO TELL ME?

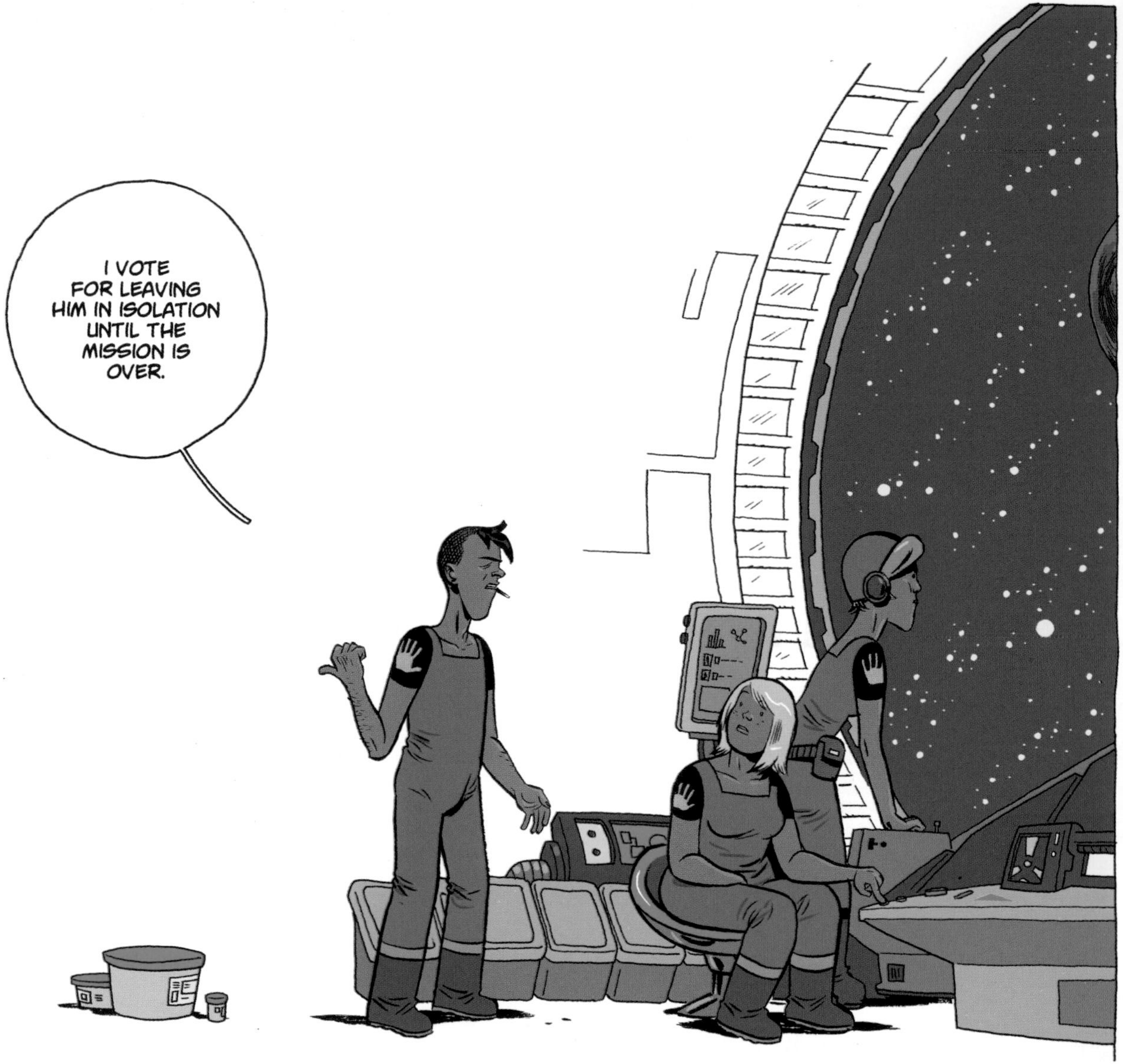
I VOTE FOR LEAVING HIM IN ISOLATION UNTIL THE MISSION IS OVER.

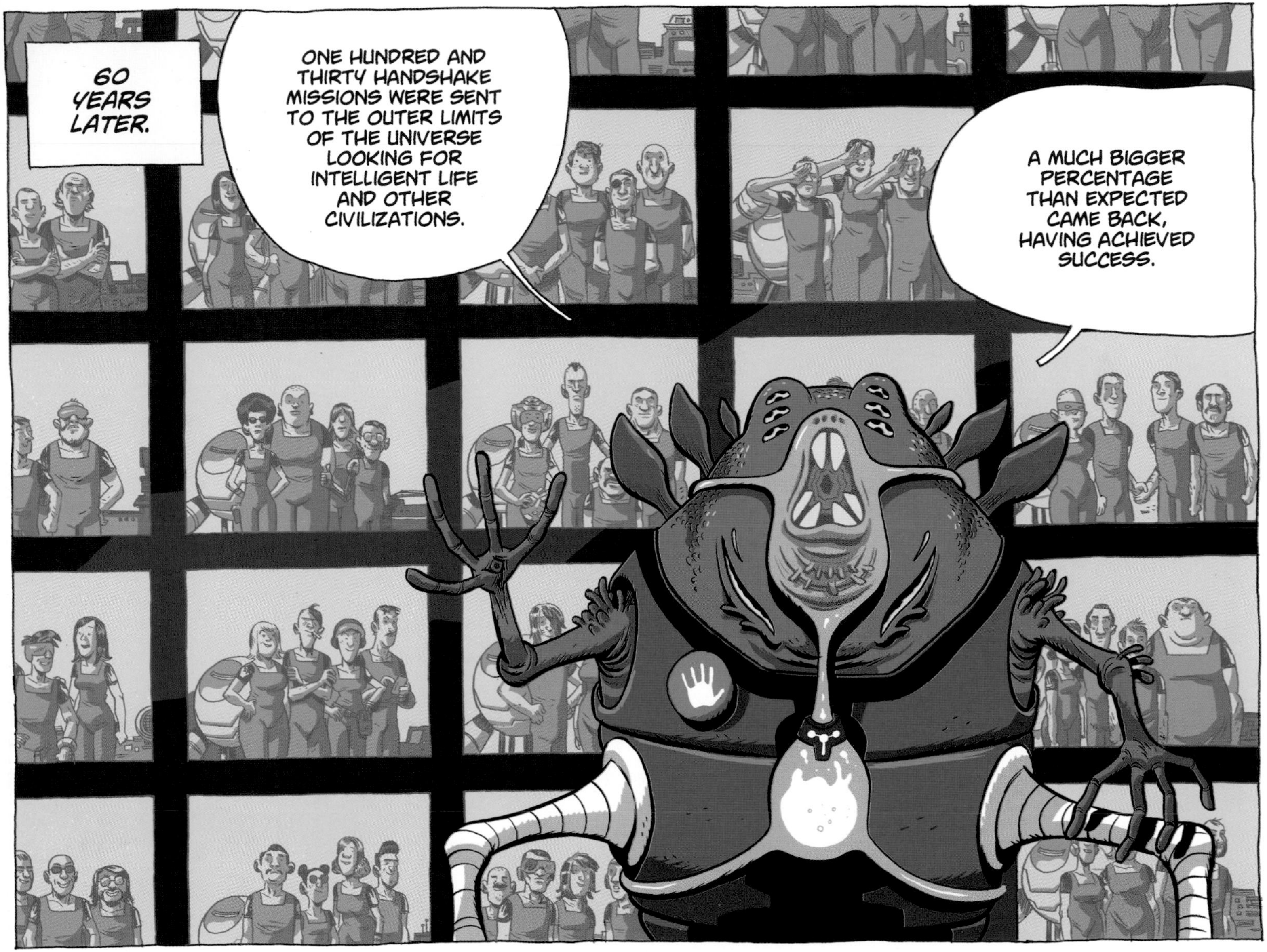
60 YEARS LATER.
ONE HUNDRED AND THIRTY HANDSHAKE MISSIONS WERE SENT TO THE OUTER LIMITS OF THE UNIVERSE LOOKING FOR INTELLIGENT LIFE AND OTHER CIVILIZATIONS.
A MUCH BIGGER PERCENTAGE THAN EXPECTED CAME BACK, HAVING ACHIEVED SUCCESS.

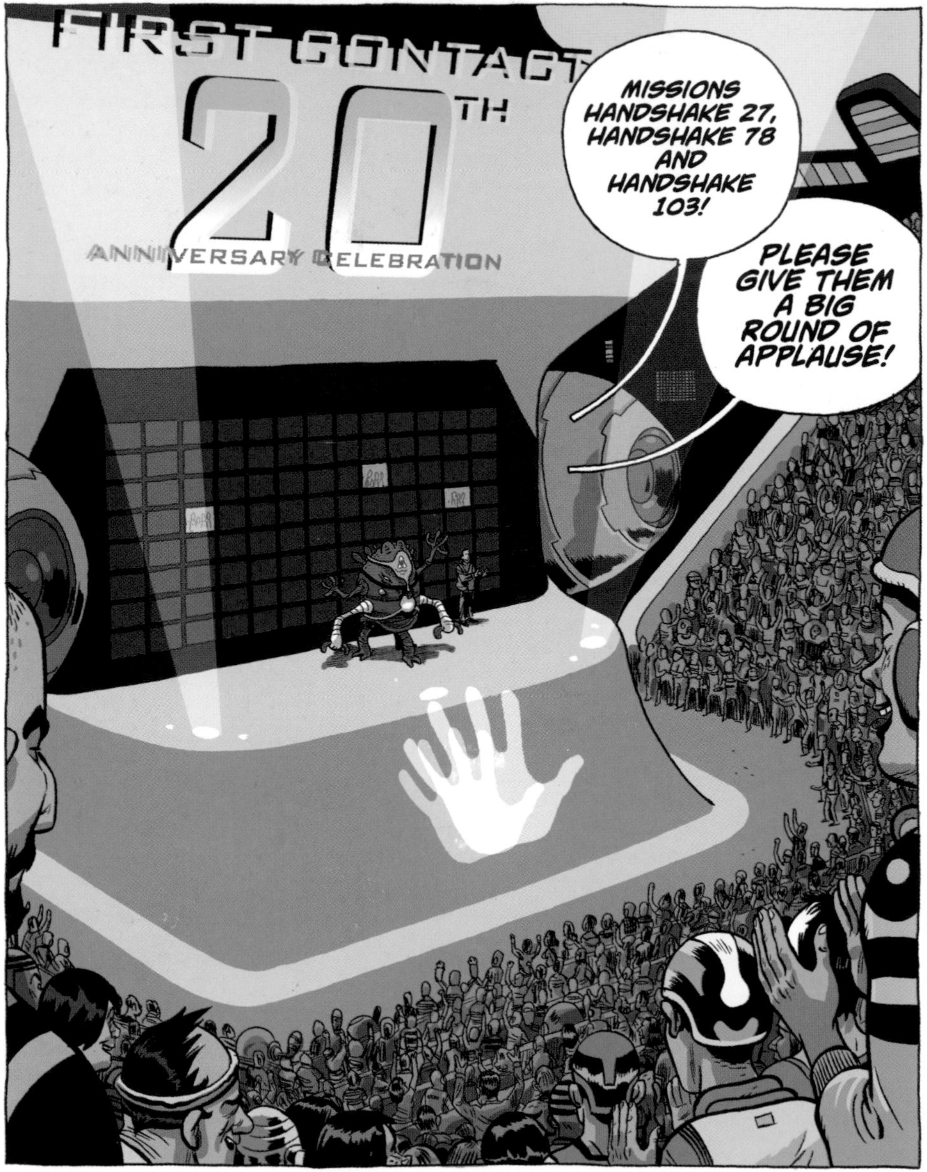
FIRST CONTACT
20TH
ANNIVERSARY CELEBRATION
MISSIONS HANDSHAKE 27, HANDSHAKE 78 AND HANDSHAKE 103!
PLEASE GIVE THEM A BIG ROUND OF APPLAUSE!

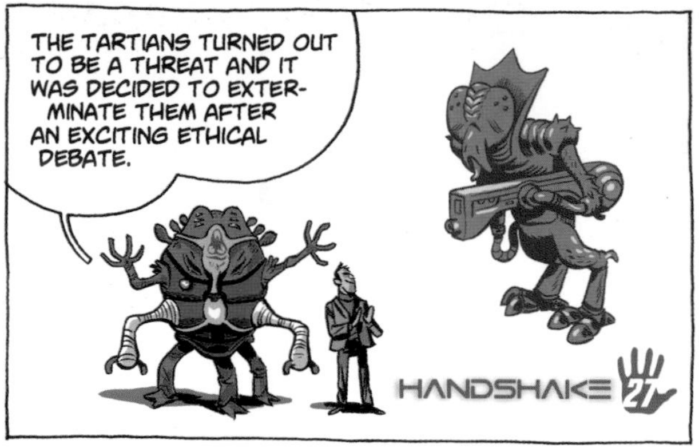
THE TARTIANS TURNED OUT TO BE A THREAT AND IT WAS DECIDED TO EXTER-MINATE THEM AFTER AN EXCITING ETHICAL DEBATE.
HANDSHAKE 27

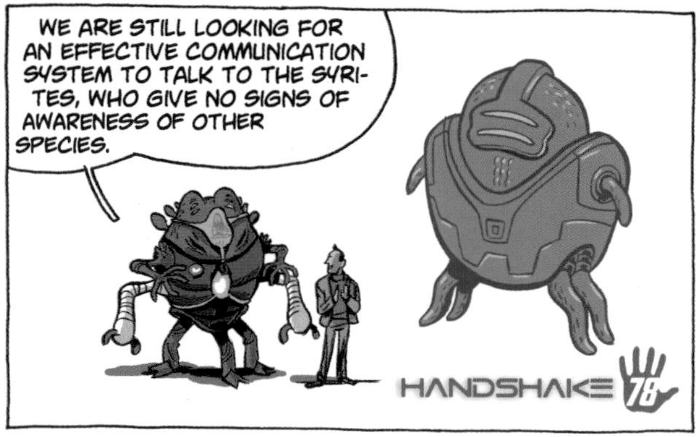
WE ARE STILL LOOKING FOR AN EFFECTIVE COMMUNICATION SYSTEM TO TALK TO THE SYRI-TES, WHO GIVE NO SIGNS OF AWARENESS OF OTHER SPECIES.
HANDSHAKE 78

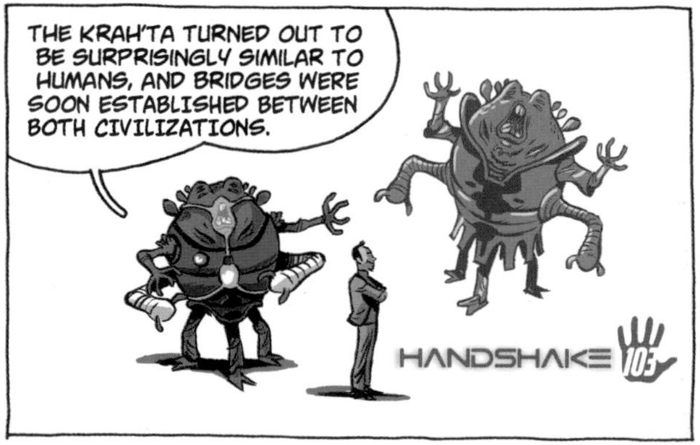
THE KRAH'TA TURNED OUT TO BE SURPRISINGLY SIMILAR TO HUMANS, AND BRIDGES WERE SOON ESTABLISHED BETWEEN BOTH CIVILIZATIONS.
HANDSHAKE 103

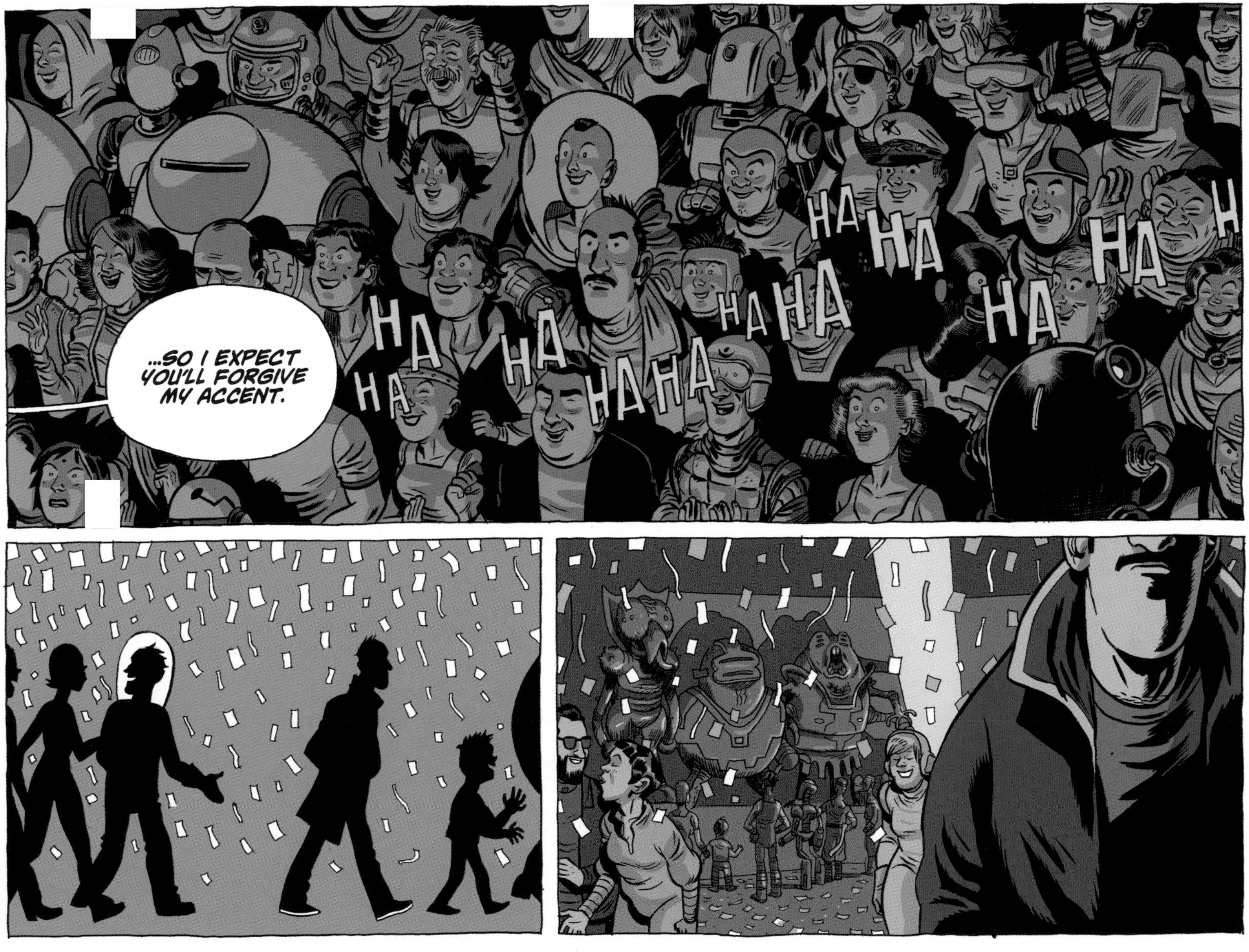
...SO I EXPECT YOU'LL FORGIVE MY ACCENT.
HA HA
HA
HAHA
HA HA
HA
HA HA
HA
HA HA
H

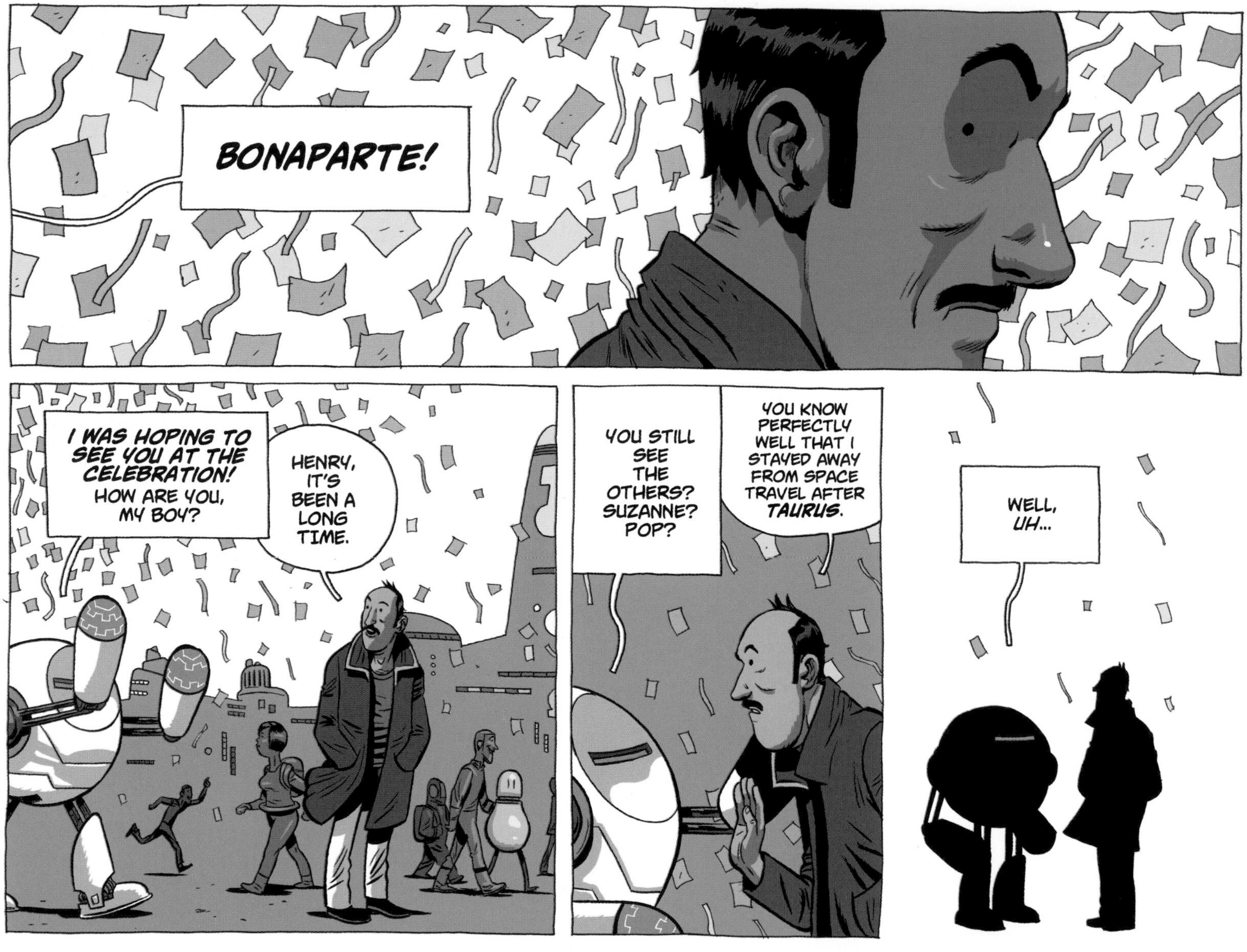
BONAPARTE!
I WAS HOPING TO SEE YOU AT THE CELEBRATION! HOW ARE YOU, MY BOY?
HENRY, IT'S BEEN A LONG TIME.
YOU STILL SEE THE OTHERS? SUZANNE? POP?
YOU KNOW PERFECTLY WELL THAT I STAYED AWAY FROM SPACE TRAVEL AFTER *TAURUS*.
WELL, *UH*...

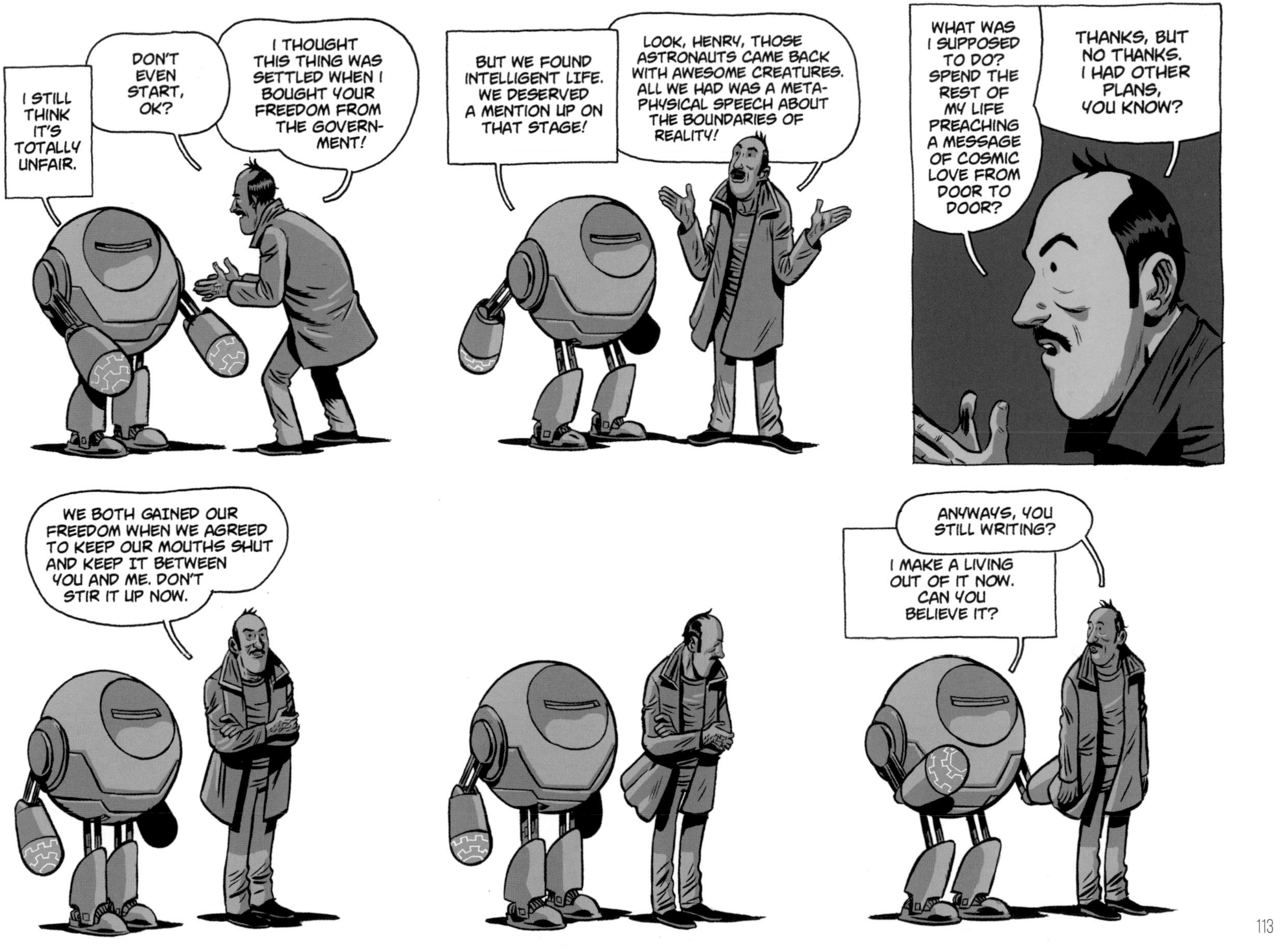
I STILL THINK IT'S TOTALLY UNFAIR.
DON'T EVEN START, OK?
I THOUGHT THIS THING WAS SETTLED WHEN I BOUGHT YOUR FREEDOM FROM THE GOVERNMENT!
BUT WE FOUND INTELLIGENT LIFE. WE DESERVED A MENTION UP ON THAT STAGE!
LOOK, HENRY, THOSE ASTRONAUTS CAME BACK WITH AWESOME CREATURES. ALL WE HAD WAS A METAPHYSICAL SPEECH ABOUT THE BOUNDARIES OF REALITY!
WHAT WAS I SUPPOSED TO DO? SPEND THE REST OF MY LIFE PREACHING A MESSAGE OF COSMIC LOVE FROM DOOR TO DOOR?
THANKS, BUT NO THANKS. I HAD OTHER PLANS, YOU KNOW?
WE BOTH GAINED OUR FREEDOM WHEN WE AGREED TO KEEP OUR MOUTHS SHUT AND KEEP IT BETWEEN YOU AND ME. DON'T STIR IT UP NOW.
ANYWAYS, YOU STILL WRITING?
I MAKE A LIVING OUT OF IT NOW. CAN YOU BELIEVE IT?

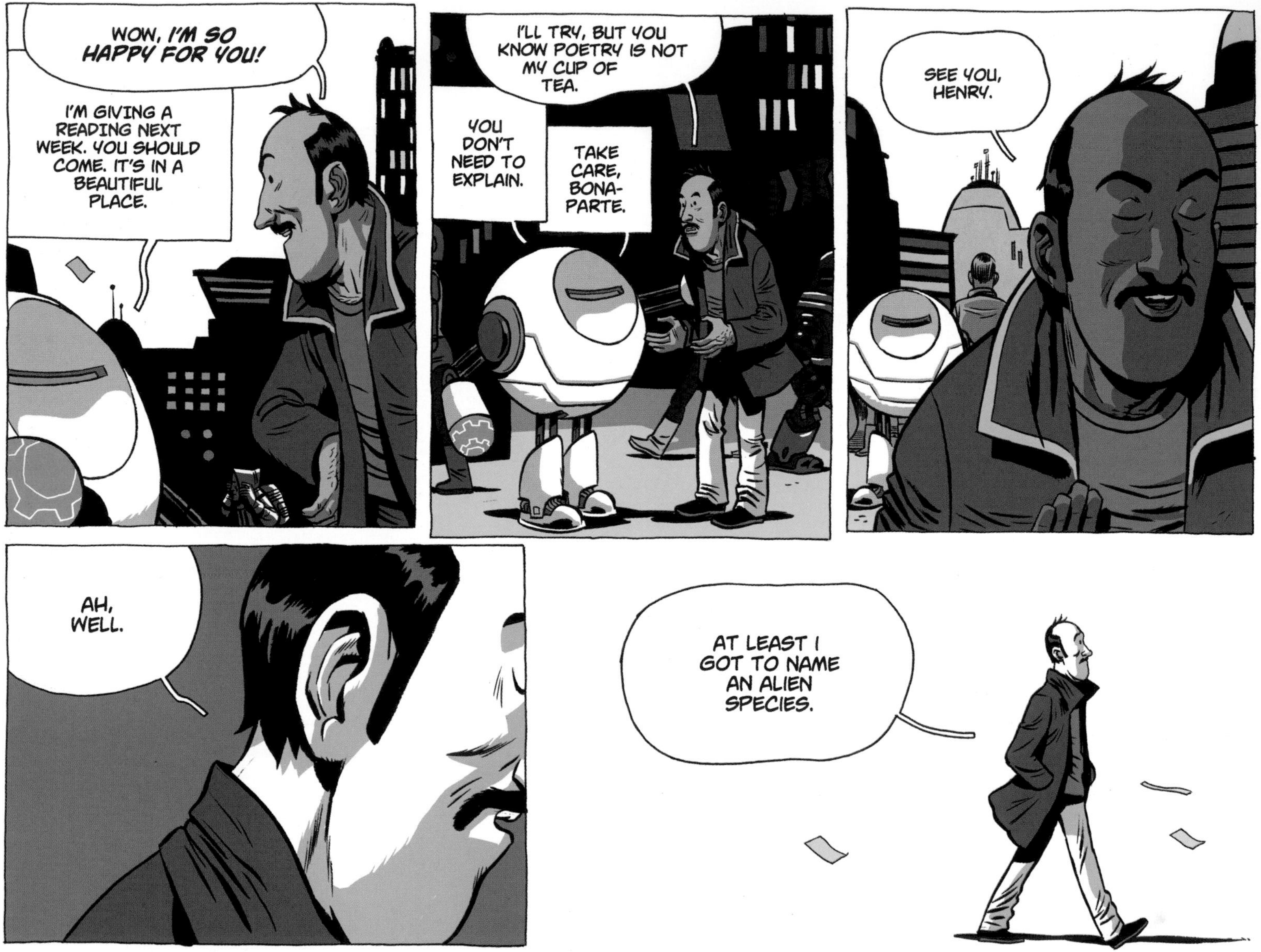
WOW, *I'M SO HAPPY FOR YOU!*
I'M GIVING A READING NEXT WEEK. YOU SHOULD COME. IT'S IN A BEAUTIFUL PLACE.
I'LL TRY, BUT YOU KNOW POETRY IS NOT MY CUP OF TEA.
YOU DON'T NEED TO EXPLAIN.
TAKE CARE, BONA-PARTE.
SEE YOU, HENRY.
AH, WELL.
AT LEAST I GOT TO NAME AN ALIEN SPECIES.

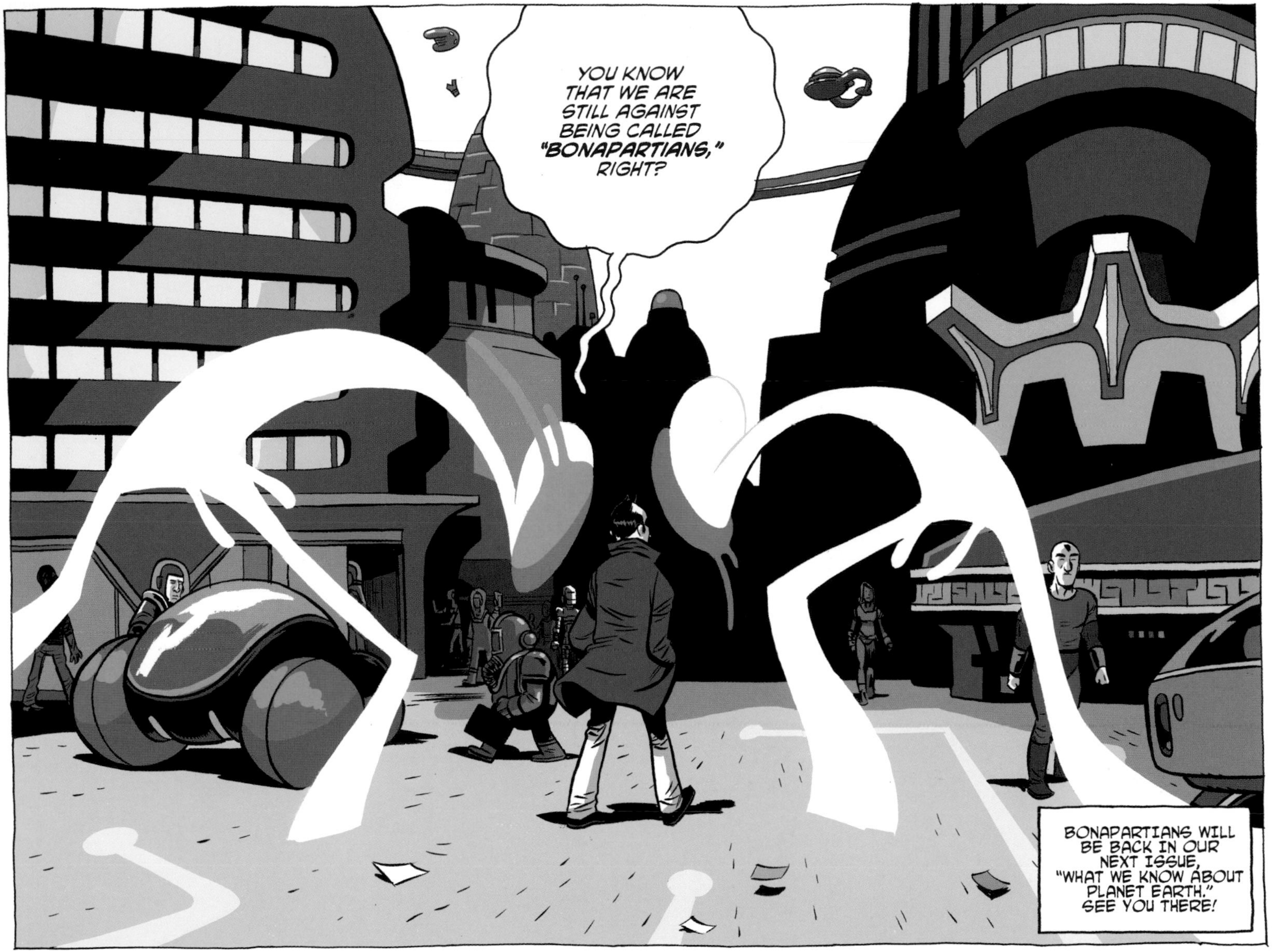
YOU KNOW THAT WE ARE STILL AGAINST BEING CALLED **"BONAPARTIANS,"** RIGHT?
BONAPARTIANS WILL BE BACK IN OUR NEXT ISSUE, "WHAT WE KNOW ABOUT PLANET EARTH." SEE YOU THERE!

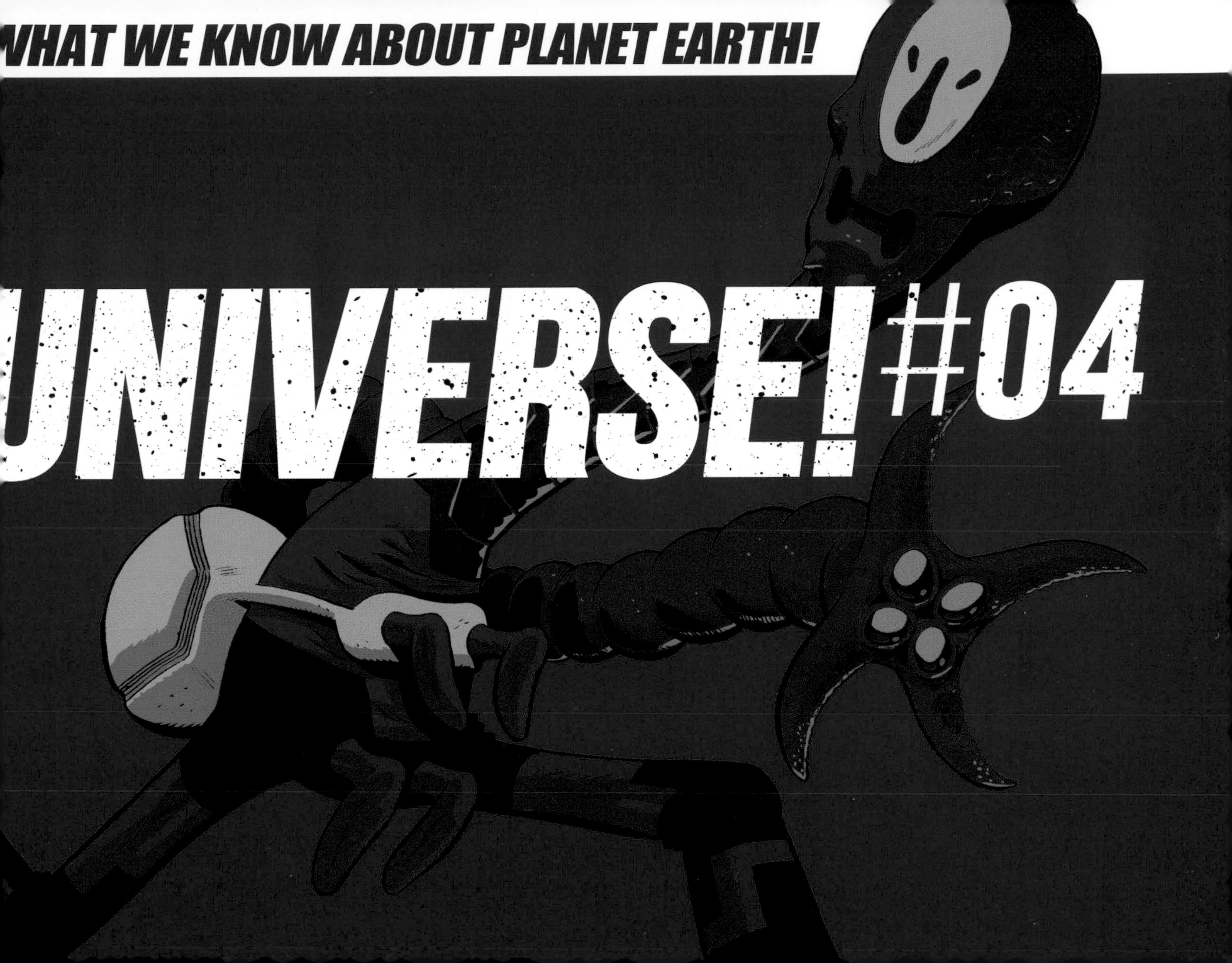
VHAT WE KNOW ABOUT PLANET EARTH!
UNIVERSE! #04

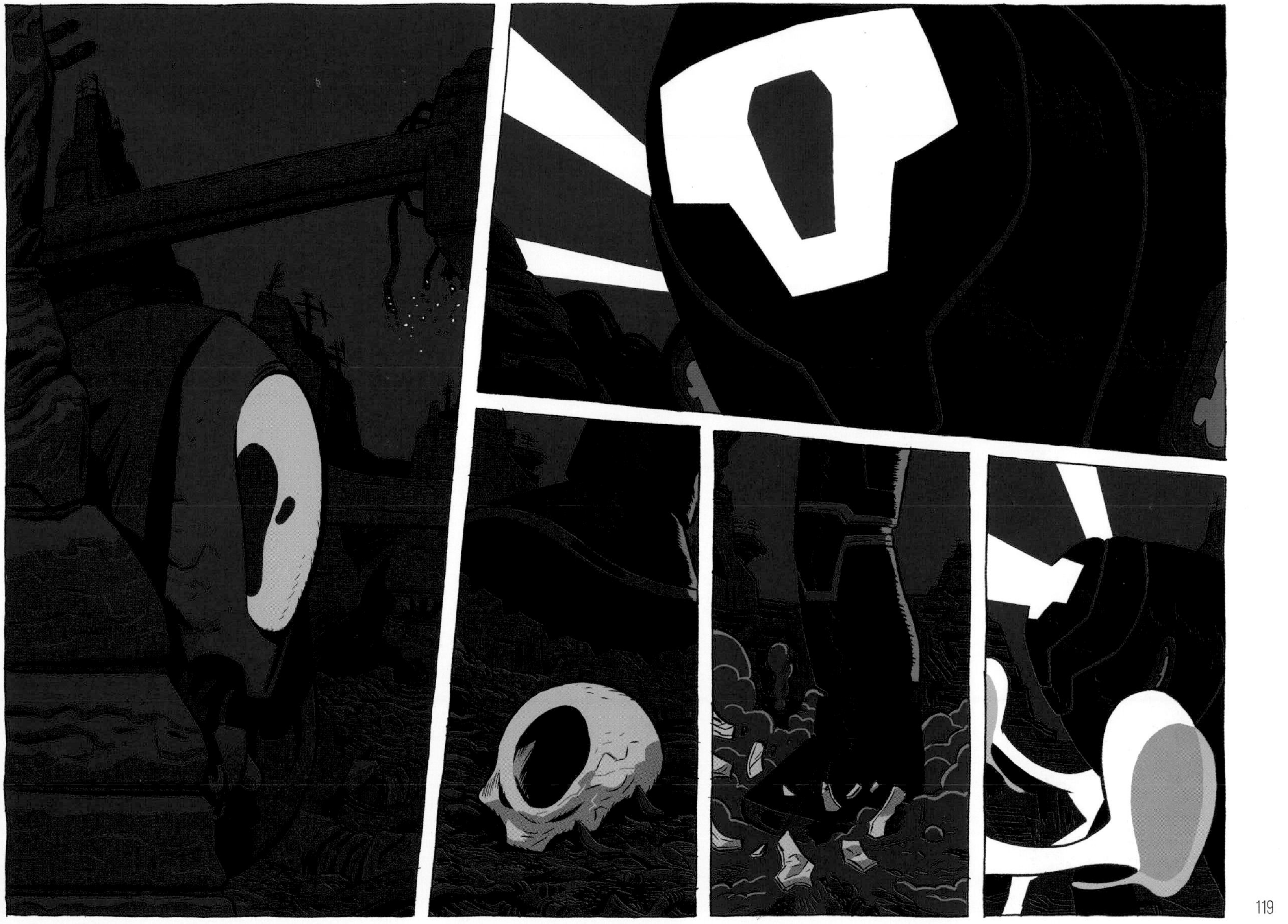

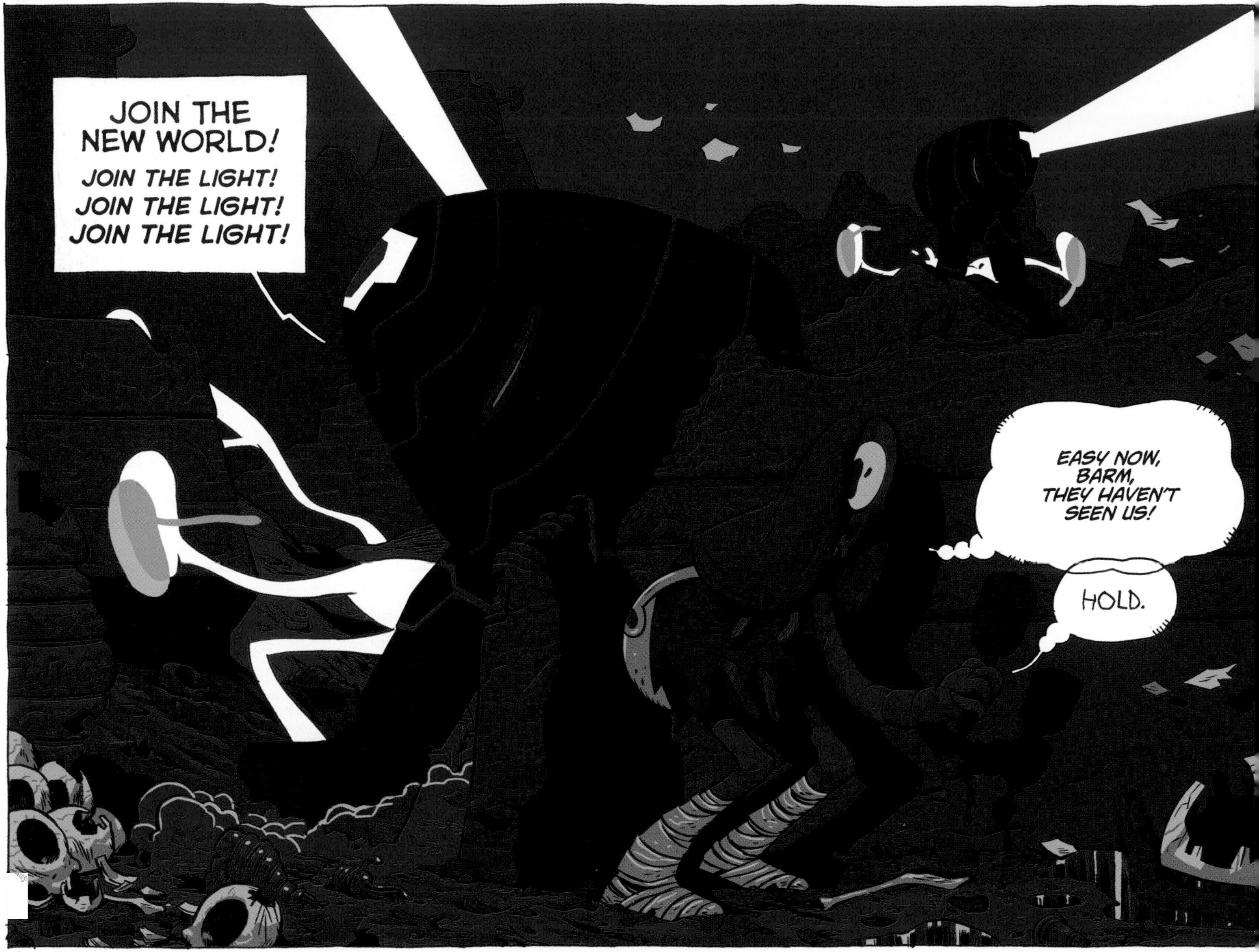
JOIN THE NEW WORLD!
JOIN THE LIGHT! JOIN THE LIGHT! JOIN THE LIGHT!
EASY NOW, BARM, THEY HAVEN'T SEEN US!
HOLD.

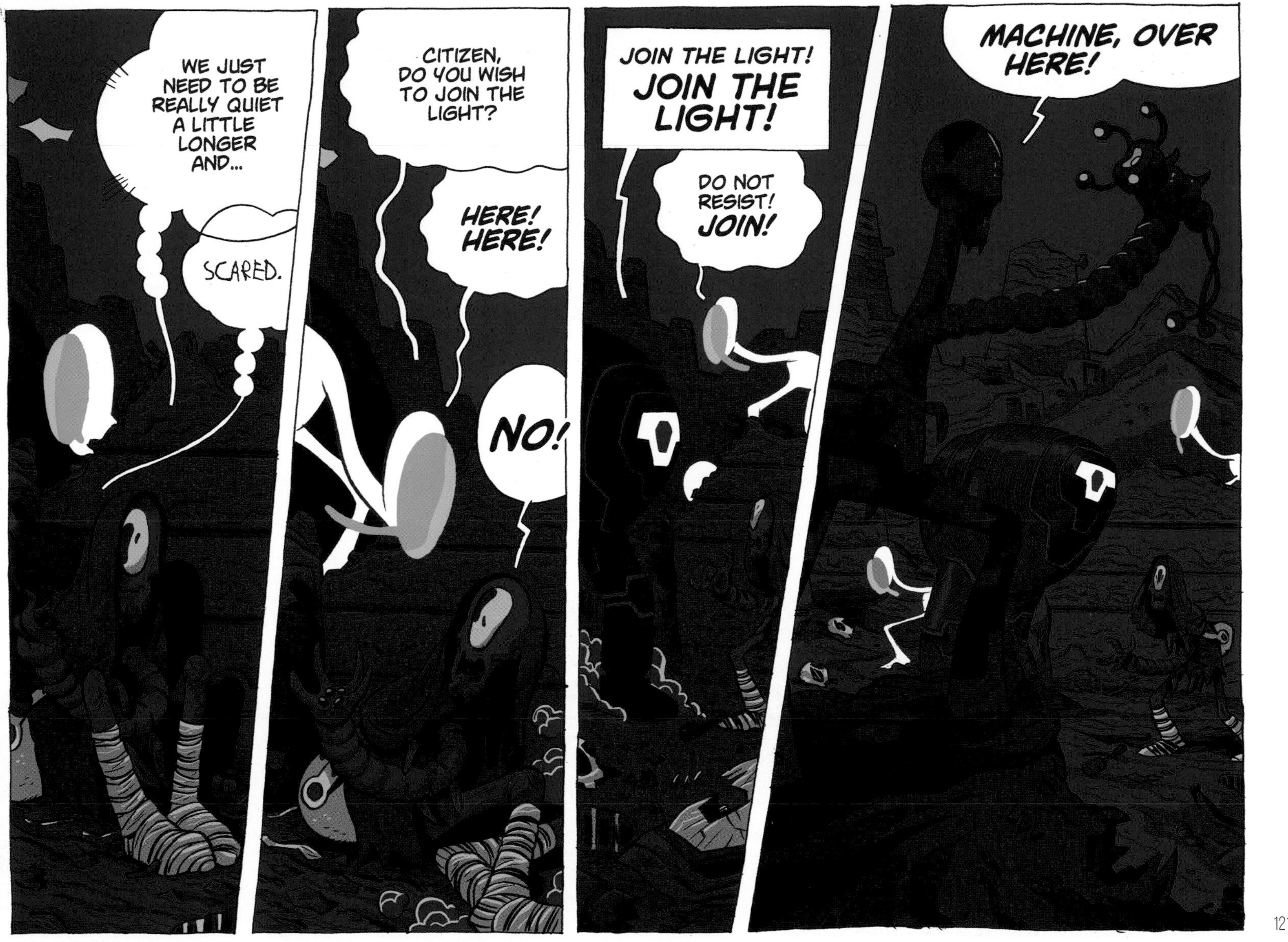
WE JUST NEED TO BE REALLY QUIET A LITTLE LONGER AND...
SCARED.
CITIZEN, DO YOU WISH TO JOIN THE LIGHT?
HERE! HERE!
NO!
JOIN THE LIGHT! JOIN THE LIGHT!
DO NOT RESIST! JOIN!
MACHINE, OVER HERE!

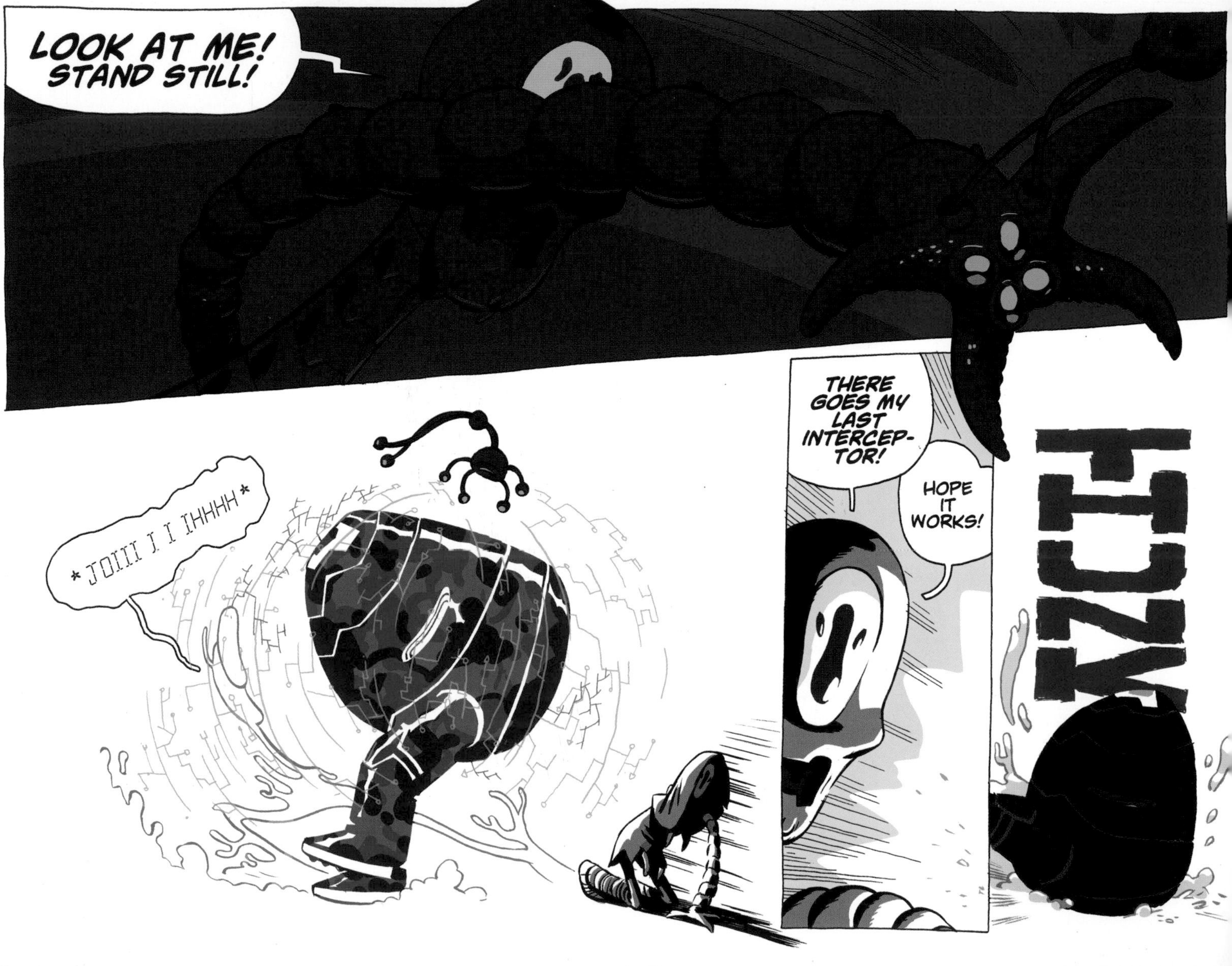
LOOK AT ME! STAND STILL!
JOIII I I IHHHH
THERE GOES MY LAST INTERCEP-TOR!
HOPE IT WORKS!

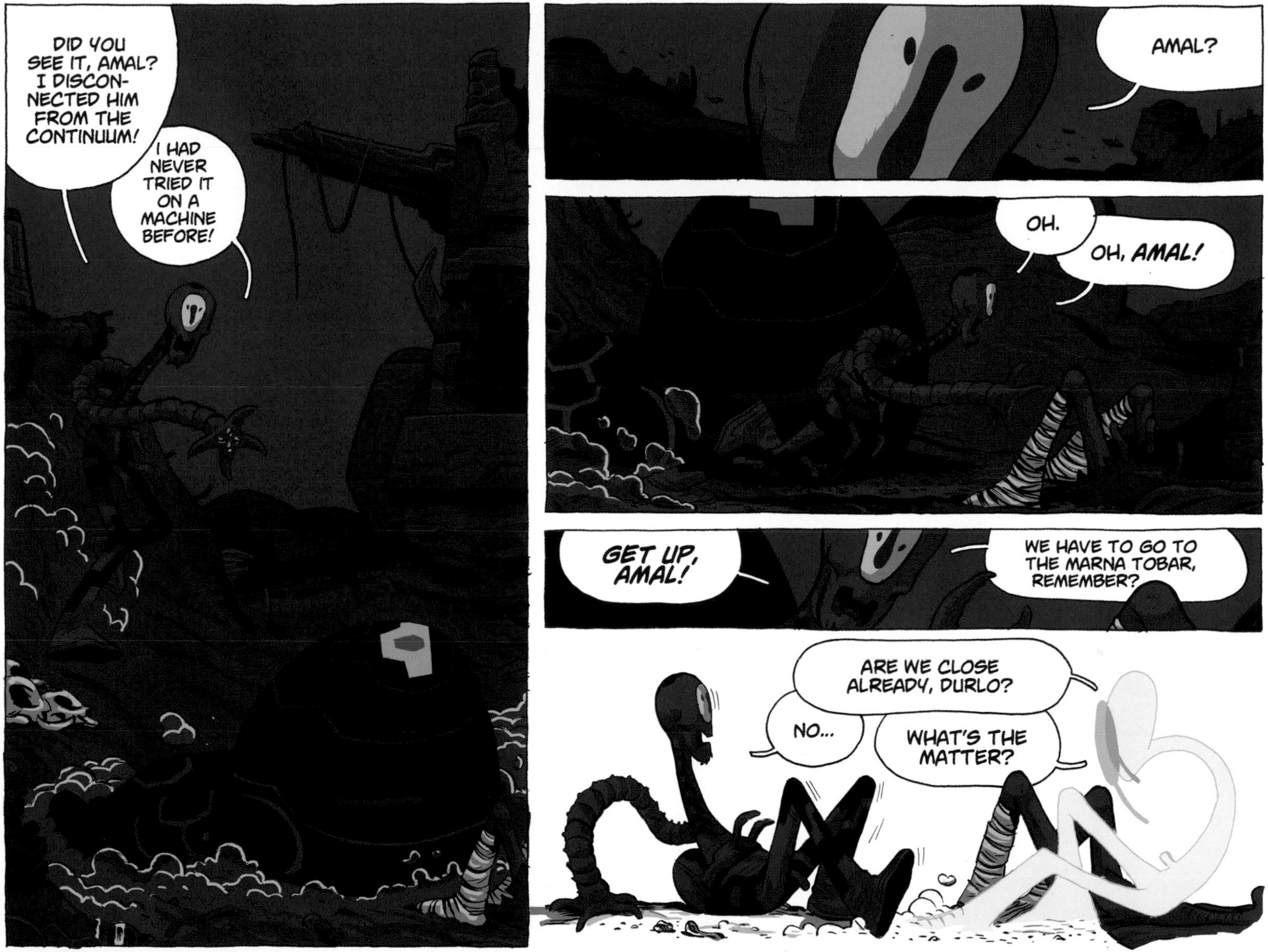
DID YOU SEE IT, AMAL? I DISCONNECTED HIM FROM THE CONTINUUM!
I HAD NEVER TRIED IT ON A MACHINE BEFORE!
AMAL?
OH.
OH, AMAL!
GET UP, AMAL!
WE HAVE TO GO TO THE MARNA TOBAR, REMEMBER?
ARE WE CLOSE ALREADY, DURLO?
NO...
WHAT'S THE MATTER?

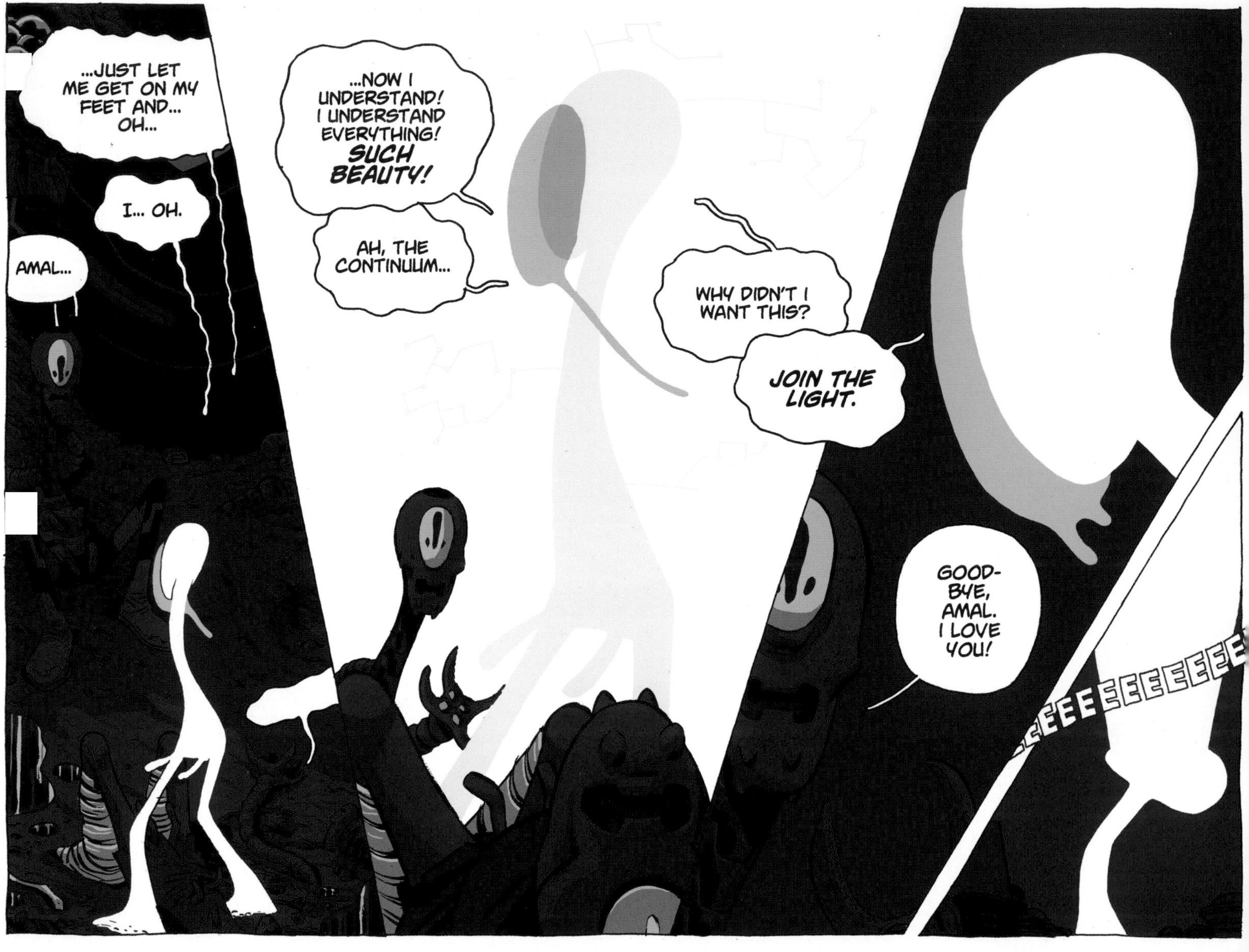
...JUST LET ME GET ON MY FEET AND... OH...
I... OH.
AMAL...
...NOW I UNDERSTAND! I UNDERSTAND EVERYTHING! *SUCH BEAUTY!*
AH, THE CONTINUUM...
WHY DIDN'T I WANT THIS?
JOIN THE LIGHT.
GOOD-BYE, AMAL. I LOVE YOU!
EEEEEEEEEEEEE

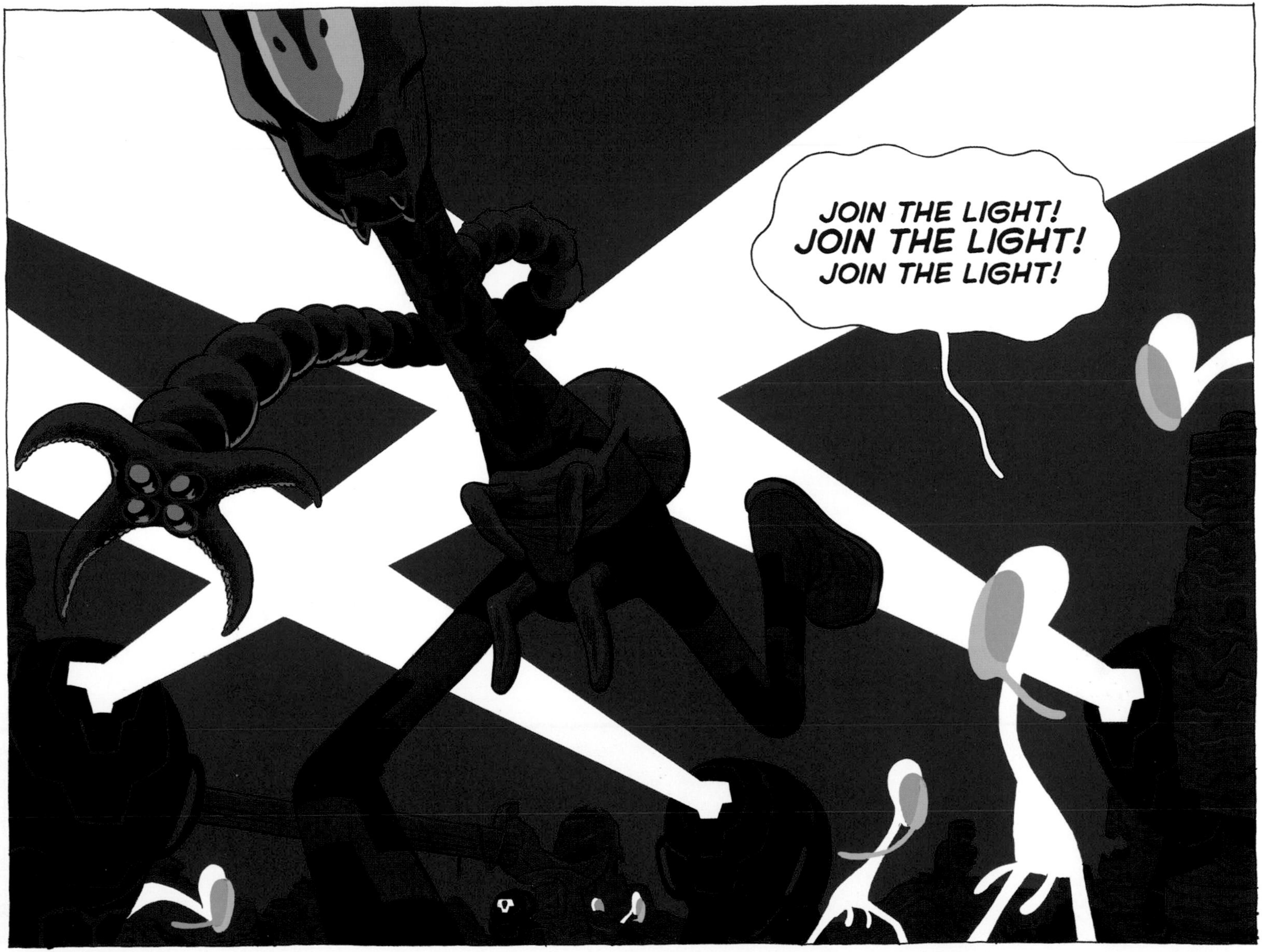
JOIN THE LIGHT!
JOIN THE LIGHT!
JOIN THE LIGHT!

SCRATCH

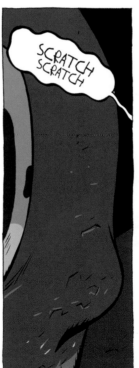

SCRATCH
SCRATCH

AH, TARP, IT'S YOU...
YOU STARTLED ME!

FOOD.

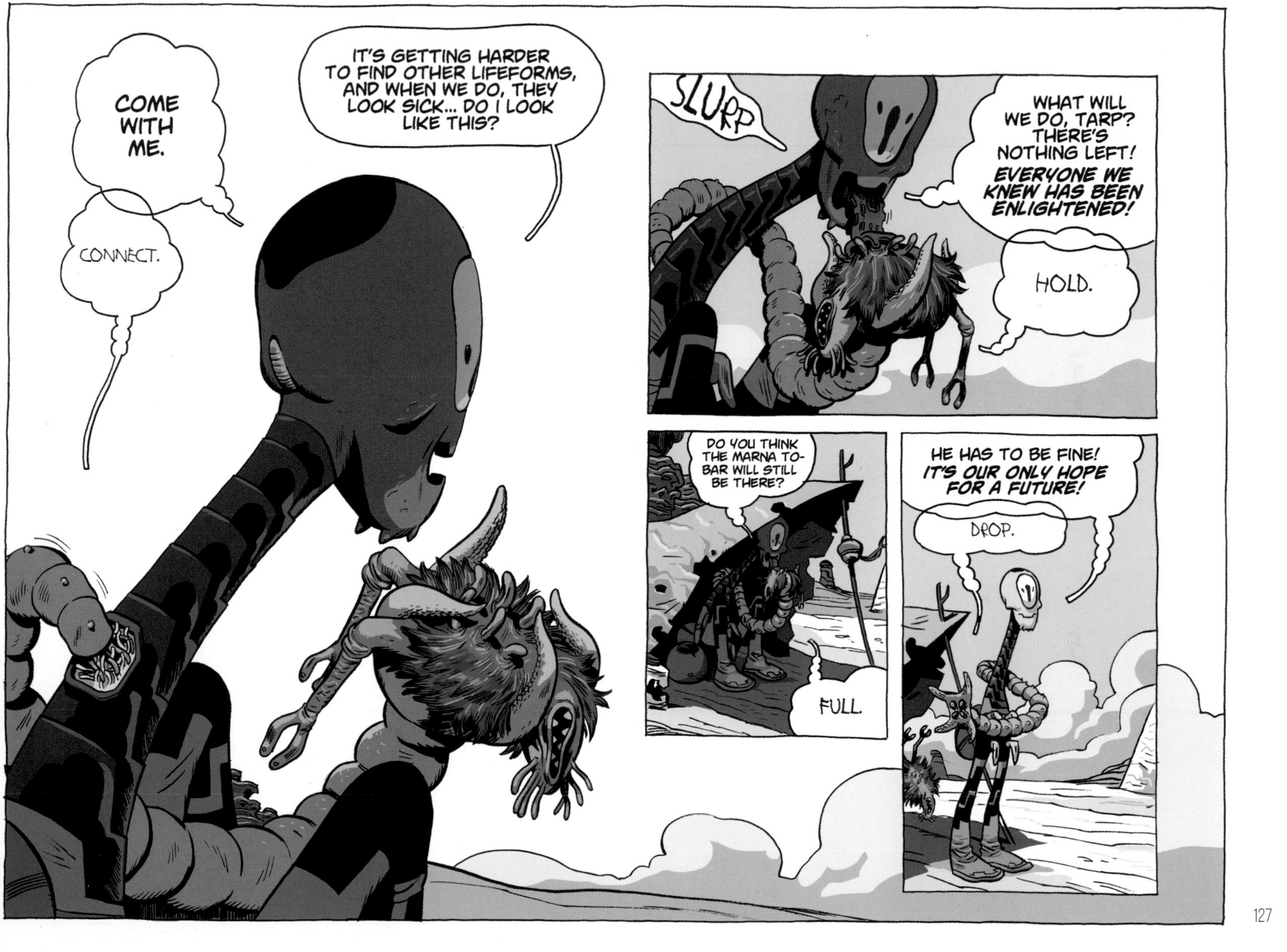
COME WITH ME.
IT'S GETTING HARDER TO FIND OTHER LIFEFORMS, AND WHEN WE DO, THEY LOOK SICK... DO I LOOK LIKE THIS?
CONNECT.
SLURP
WHAT WILL WE DO, TARP? THERE'S NOTHING LEFT! EVERYONE WE KNEW HAS BEEN ENLIGHTENED!
HOLD.
DO YOU THINK THE MARNA TO-BAR WILL STILL BE THERE?
FULL.
HE HAS TO BE FINE! IT'S OUR ONLY HOPE FOR A FUTURE!
DROP.

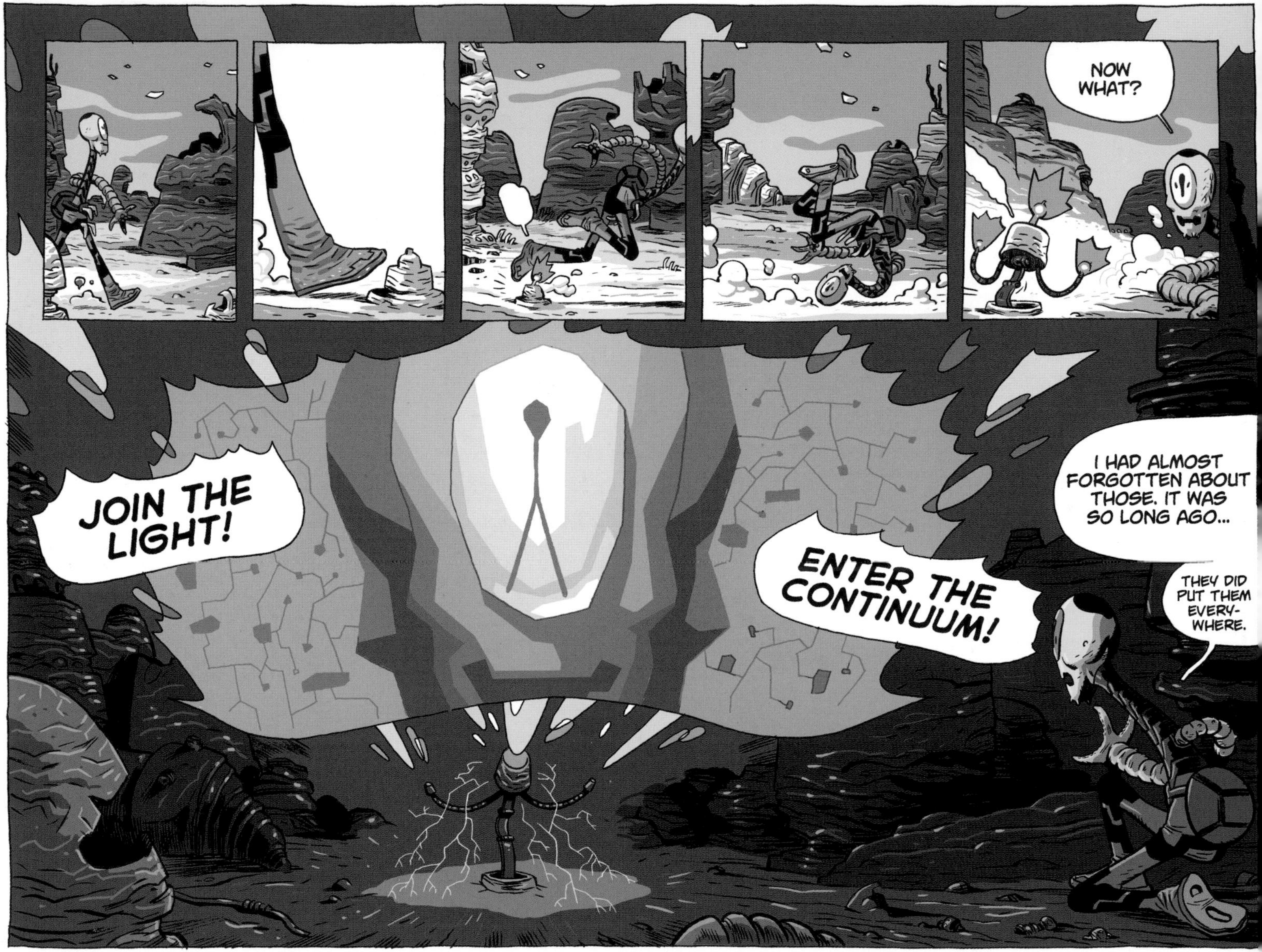
NOW WHAT?
JOIN THE LIGHT!
ENTER THE CONTINUUM!
I HAD ALMOST FORGOTTEN ABOUT THOSE. IT WAS SO LONG AGO...
THEY DID PUT THEM EVERY-WHERE.

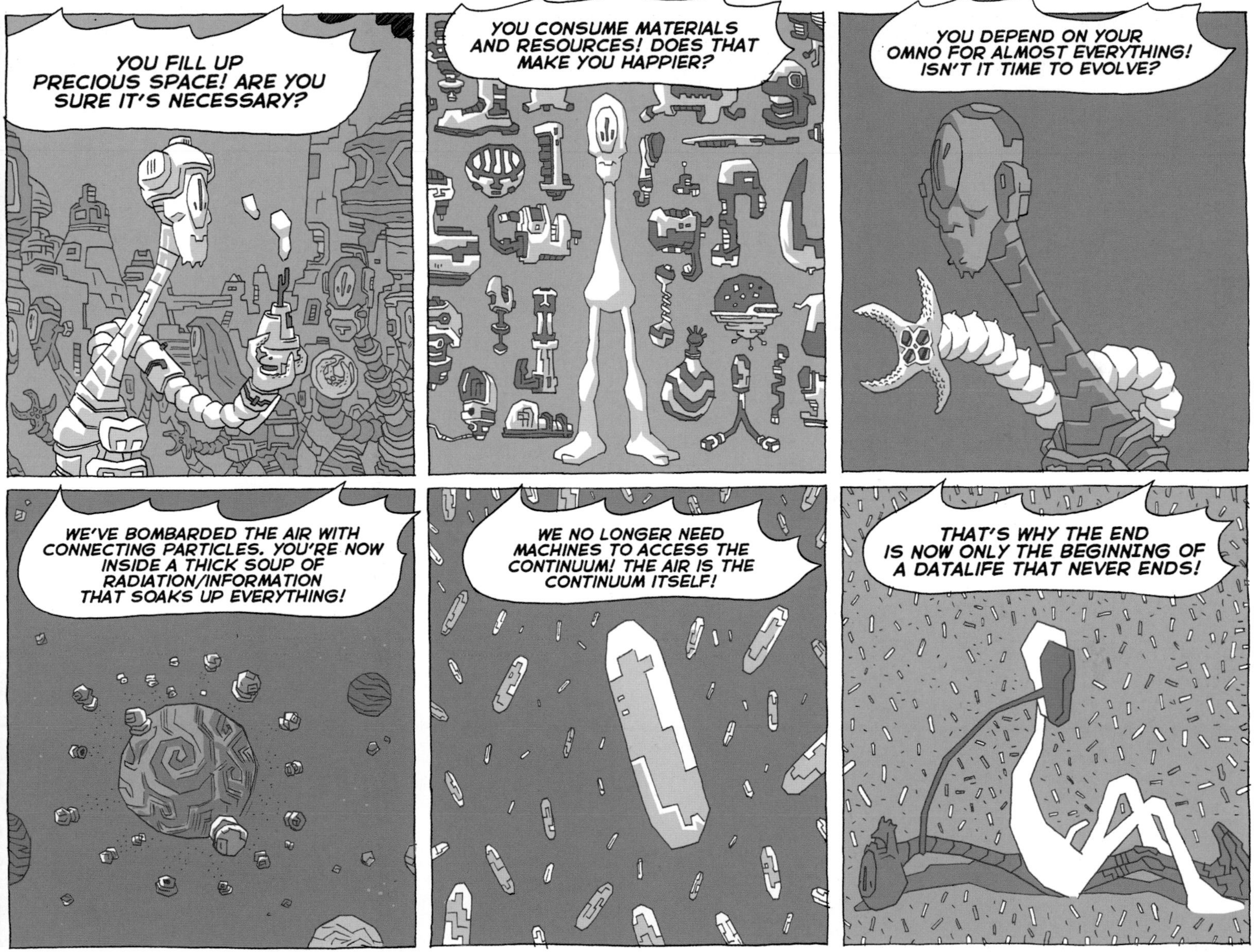
YOU FILL UP PRECIOUS SPACE! ARE YOU SURE IT'S NECESSARY?
YOU CONSUME MATERIALS AND RESOURCES! DOES THAT MAKE YOU HAPPIER?
YOU DEPEND ON YOUR OMNO FOR ALMOST EVERYTHING! ISN'T IT TIME TO EVOLVE?
WE'VE BOMBARDED THE AIR WITH CONNECTING PARTICLES. YOU'RE NOW INSIDE A THICK SOUP OF RADIATION/INFORMATION THAT SOAKS UP EVERYTHING!
WE NO LONGER NEED MACHINES TO ACCESS THE CONTINUUM! THE AIR IS THE CONTINUUM ITSELF!
THAT'S WHY THE END IS NOW ONLY THE BEGINNING OF A DATALIFE THAT NEVER ENDS!

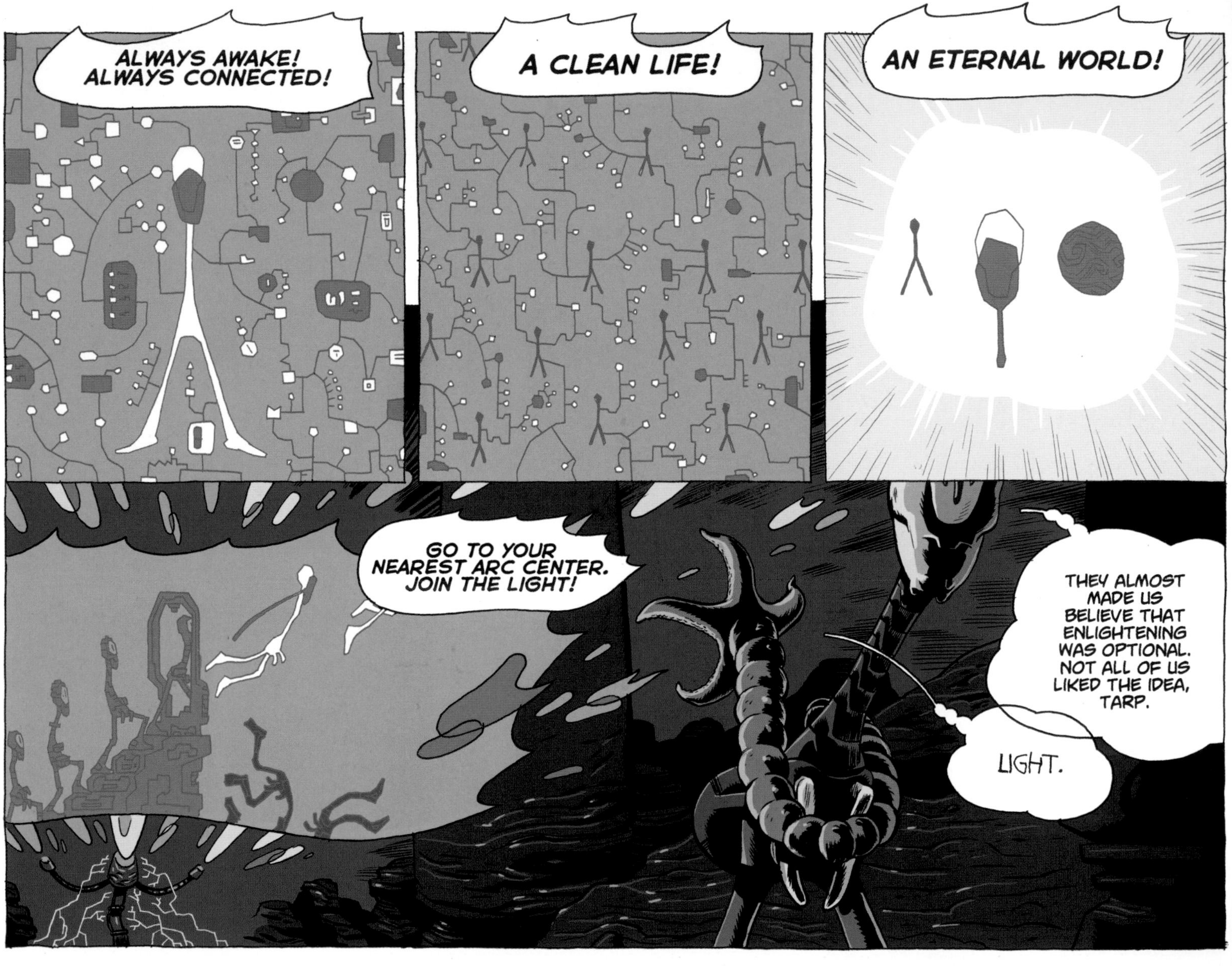
ALWAYS AWAKE! ALWAYS CONNECTED!
A CLEAN LIFE!
AN ETERNAL WORLD!
GO TO YOUR NEAREST ARC CENTER. JOIN THE LIGHT!
THEY ALMOST MADE US BELIEVE THAT ENLIGHTENING WAS OPTIONAL. NOT ALL OF US LIKED THE IDEA, TARP.
LIGHT.

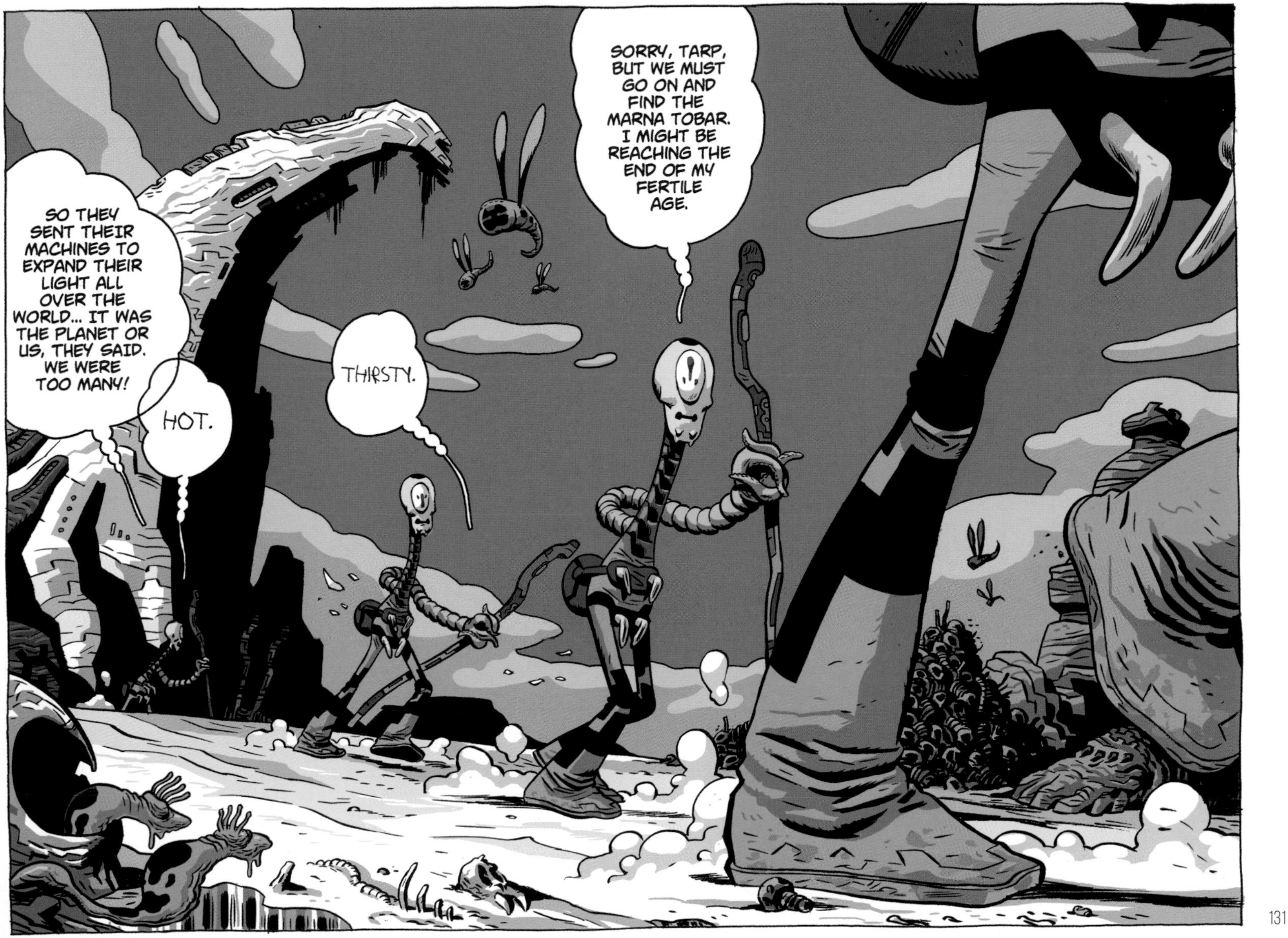
SO THEY SENT THEIR MACHINES TO EXPAND THEIR LIGHT ALL OVER THE WORLD... IT WAS THE PLANET OR US, THEY SAID. WE WERE TOO MANY!
HOT.
THIRSTY.
SORRY, TARP, BUT WE MUST GO ON AND FIND THE MARNA TOBAR. I MIGHT BE REACHING THE END OF MY FERTILE AGE.

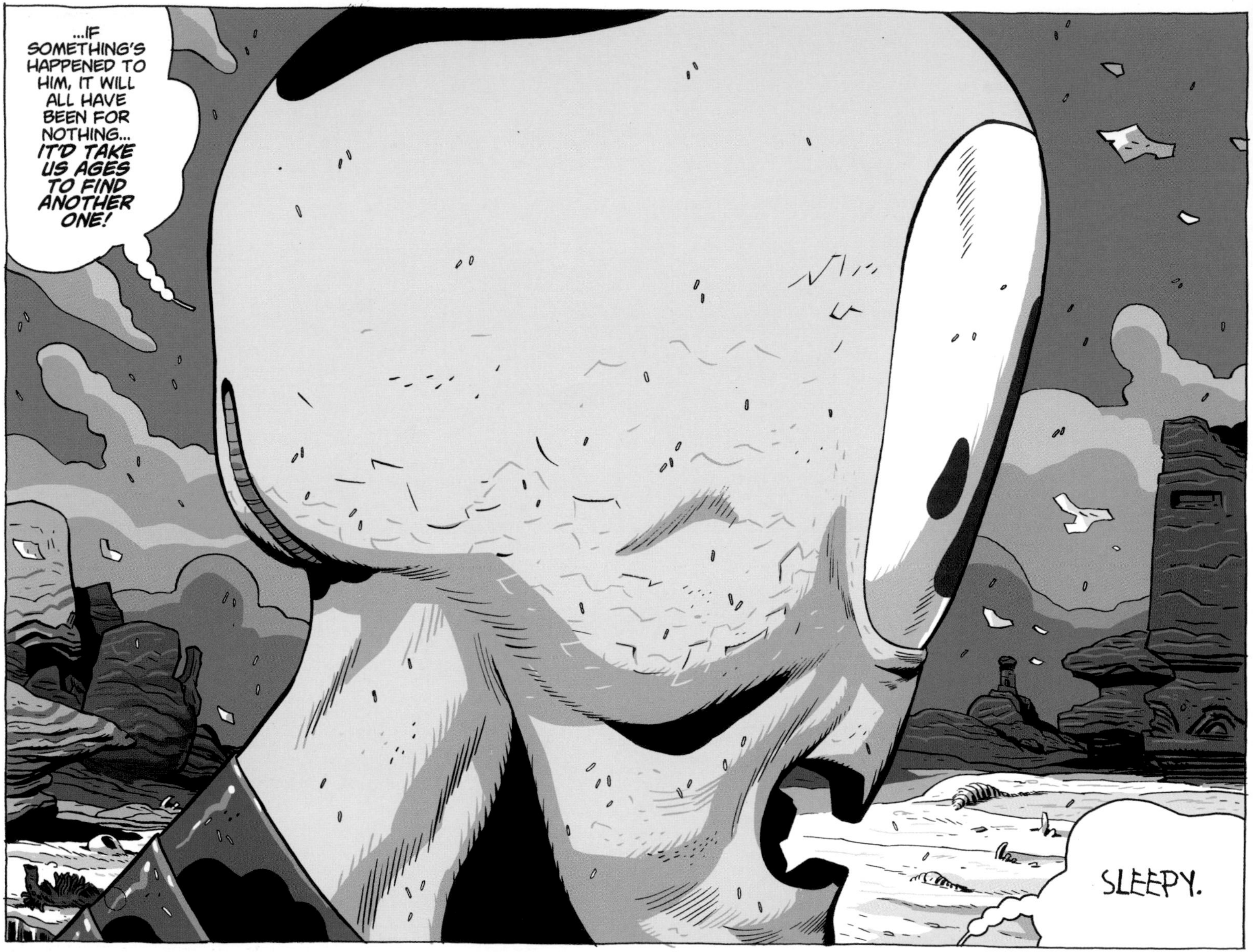
...IF SOMETHING'S HAPPENED TO HIM, IT WILL ALL HAVE BEEN FOR NOTHING... *IT'D TAKE US AGES TO FIND ANOTHER ONE!*
SLEEPY.

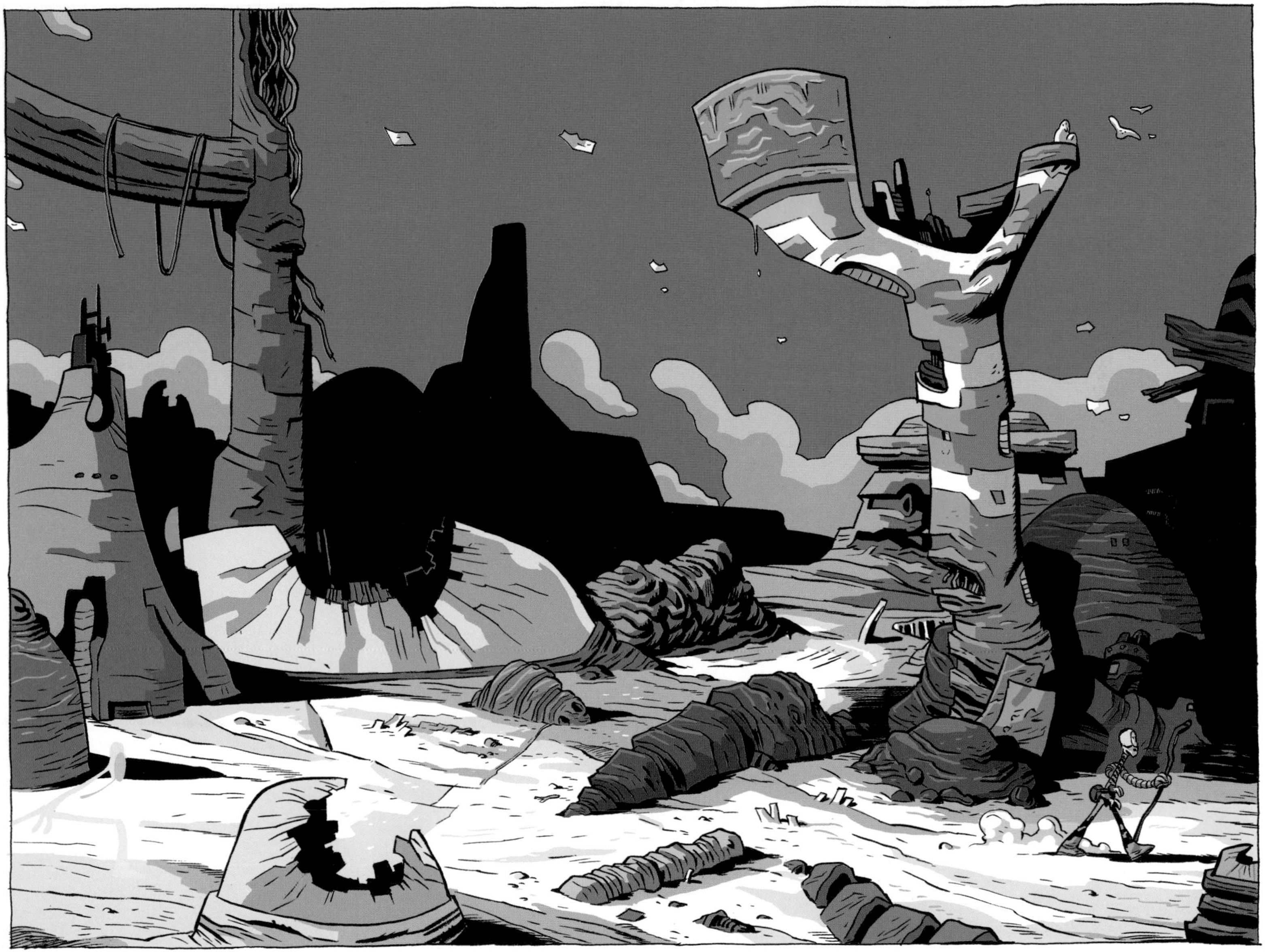

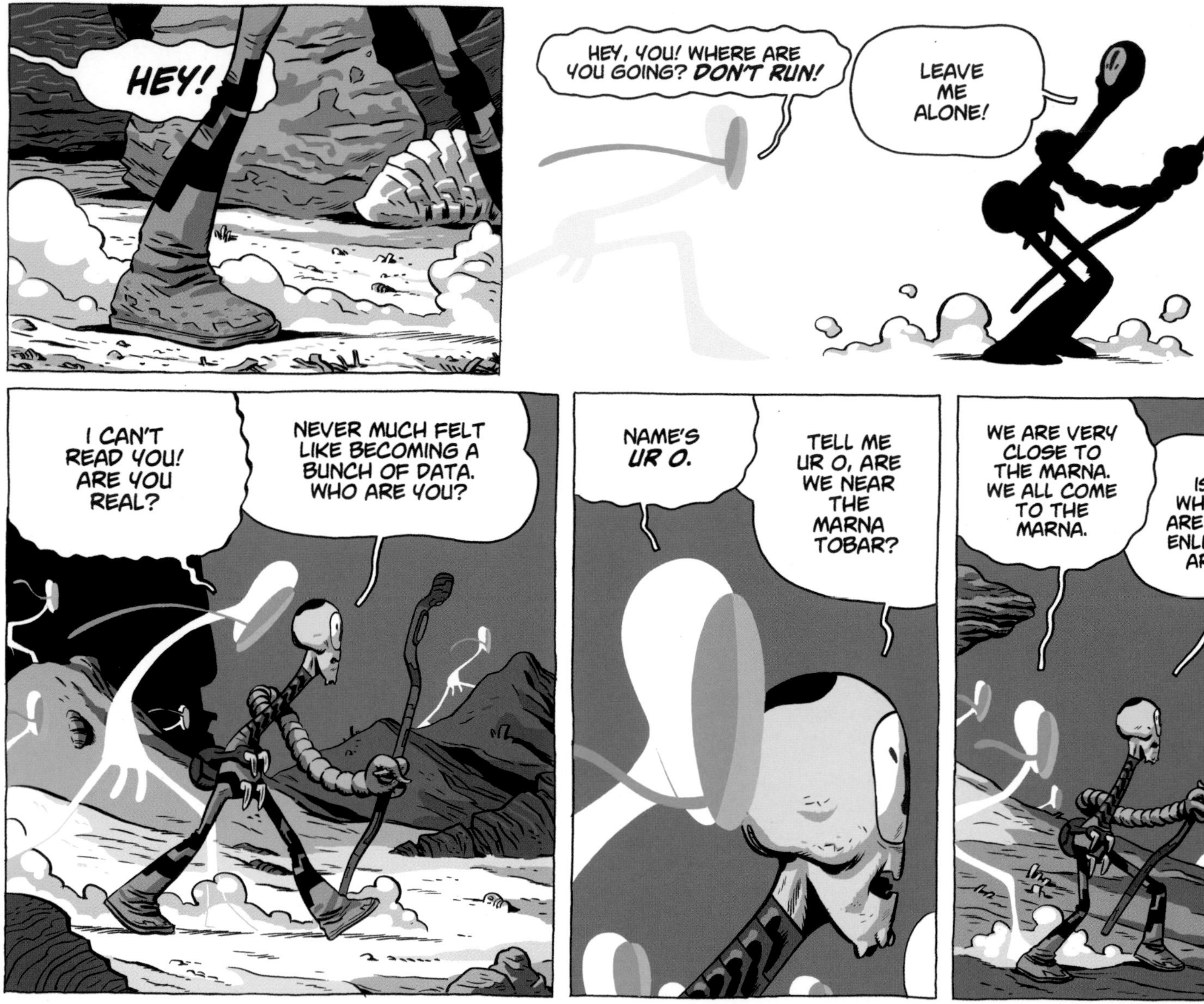
HEY!
HEY, YOU! WHERE ARE YOU GOING? DON'T RUN!
LEAVE ME ALONE!
I CAN'T READ YOU! ARE YOU REAL?
NEVER MUCH FELT LIKE BECOMING A BUNCH OF DATA. WHO ARE YOU?
NAME'S UR O.
TELL ME UR O, ARE WE NEAR THE MARNA TOBAR?
WE ARE VERY CLOSE TO THE MARNA. WE ALL COME TO THE MARNA.
IS THAT WHY THERE ARE SO MANY ENLIGHTENED AROUND?

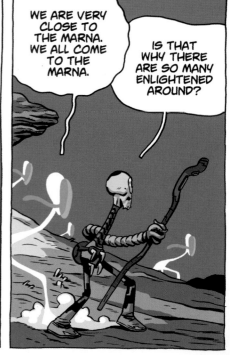

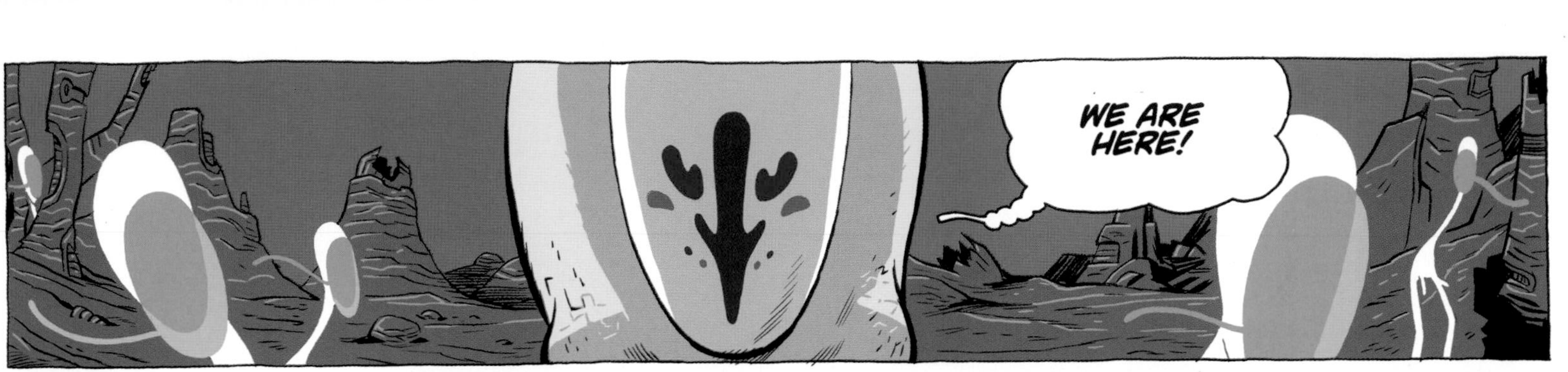
WE ARE HERE!

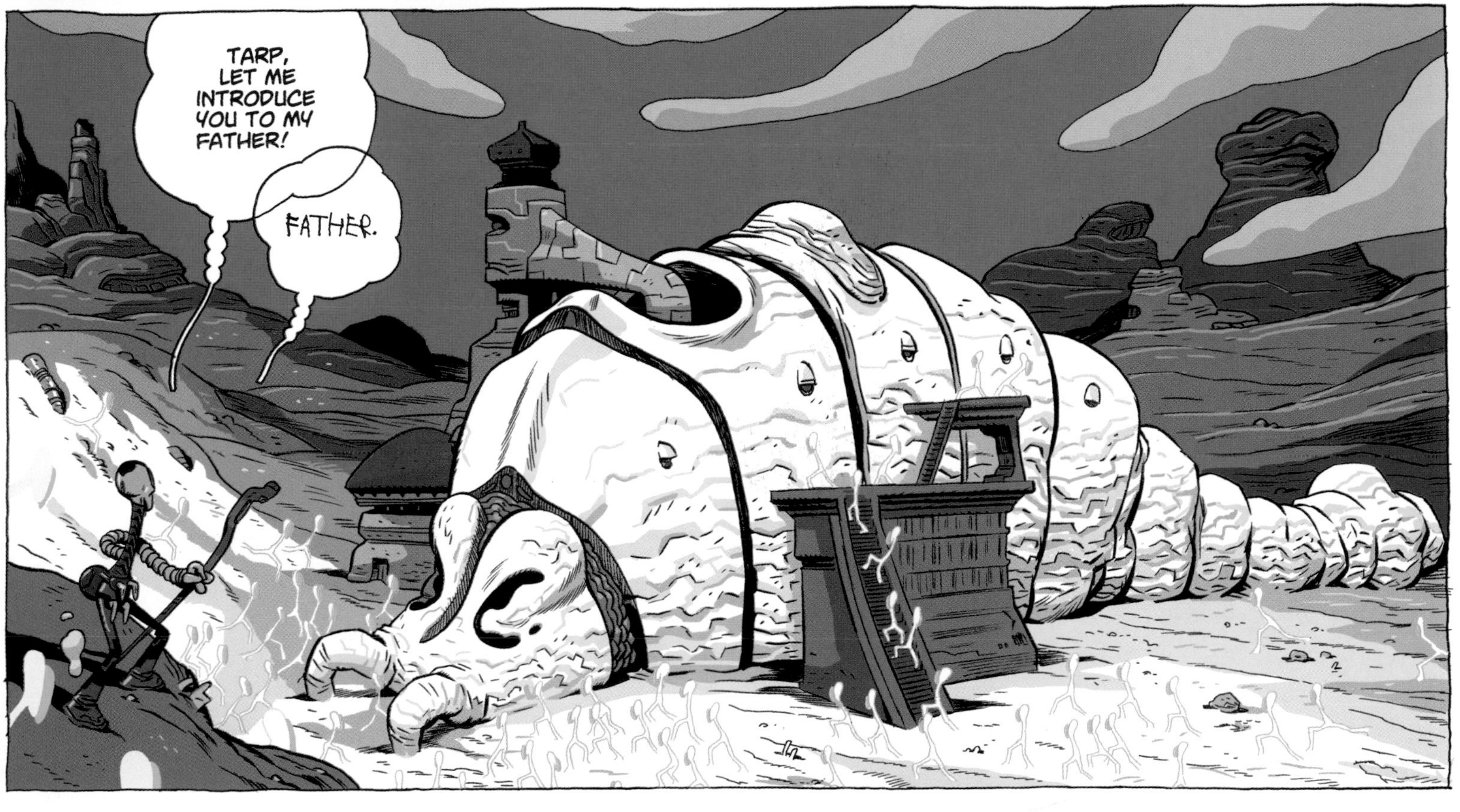
TARP, LET ME INTRODUCE YOU TO MY FATHER!
FATHER.

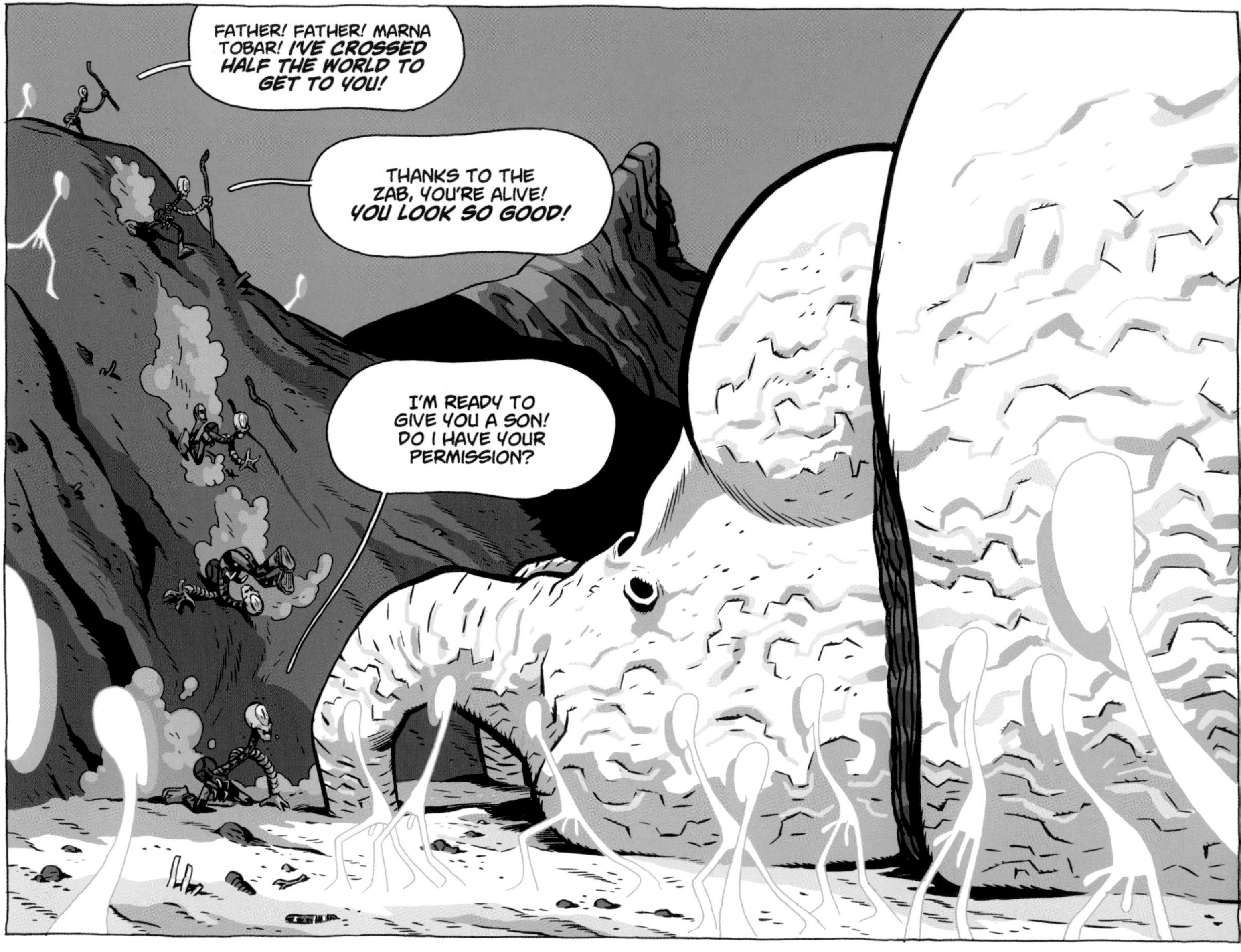
FATHER! FATHER! MARNA TOBAR! I'VE CROSSED HALF THE WORLD TO GET TO YOU!
THANKS TO THE ZAB, YOU'RE ALIVE! YOU LOOK SO GOOD!
I'M READY TO GIVE YOU A SON! DO I HAVE YOUR PERMISSION?

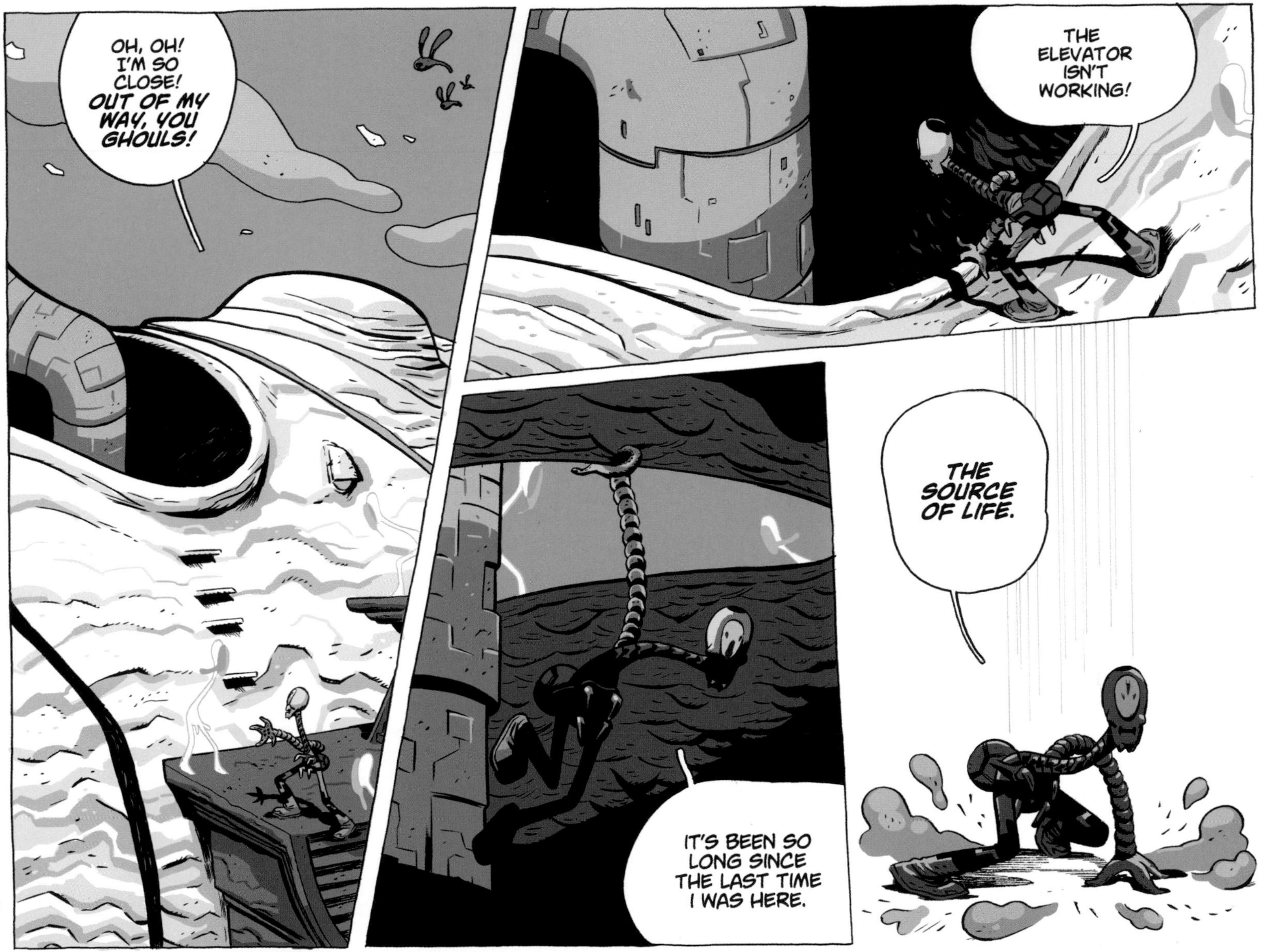
OH, OH! I'M SO CLOSE! OUT OF MY WAY, YOU GHOULS!
THE ELEVATOR ISN'T WORKING!
IT'S BEEN SO LONG SINCE THE LAST TIME I WAS HERE.
THE SOURCE OF LIFE.

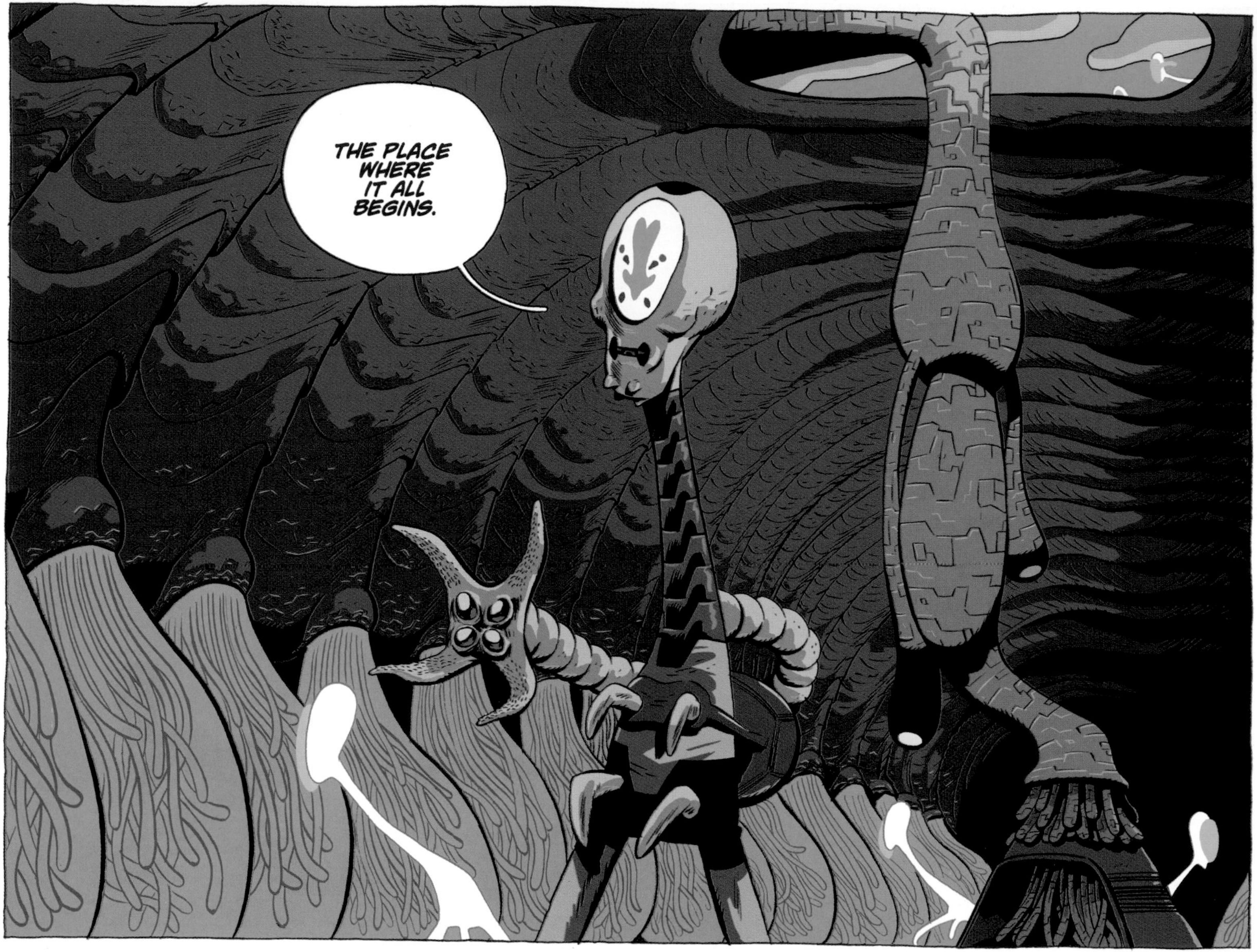
THE PLACE WHERE IT ALL BEGINS.

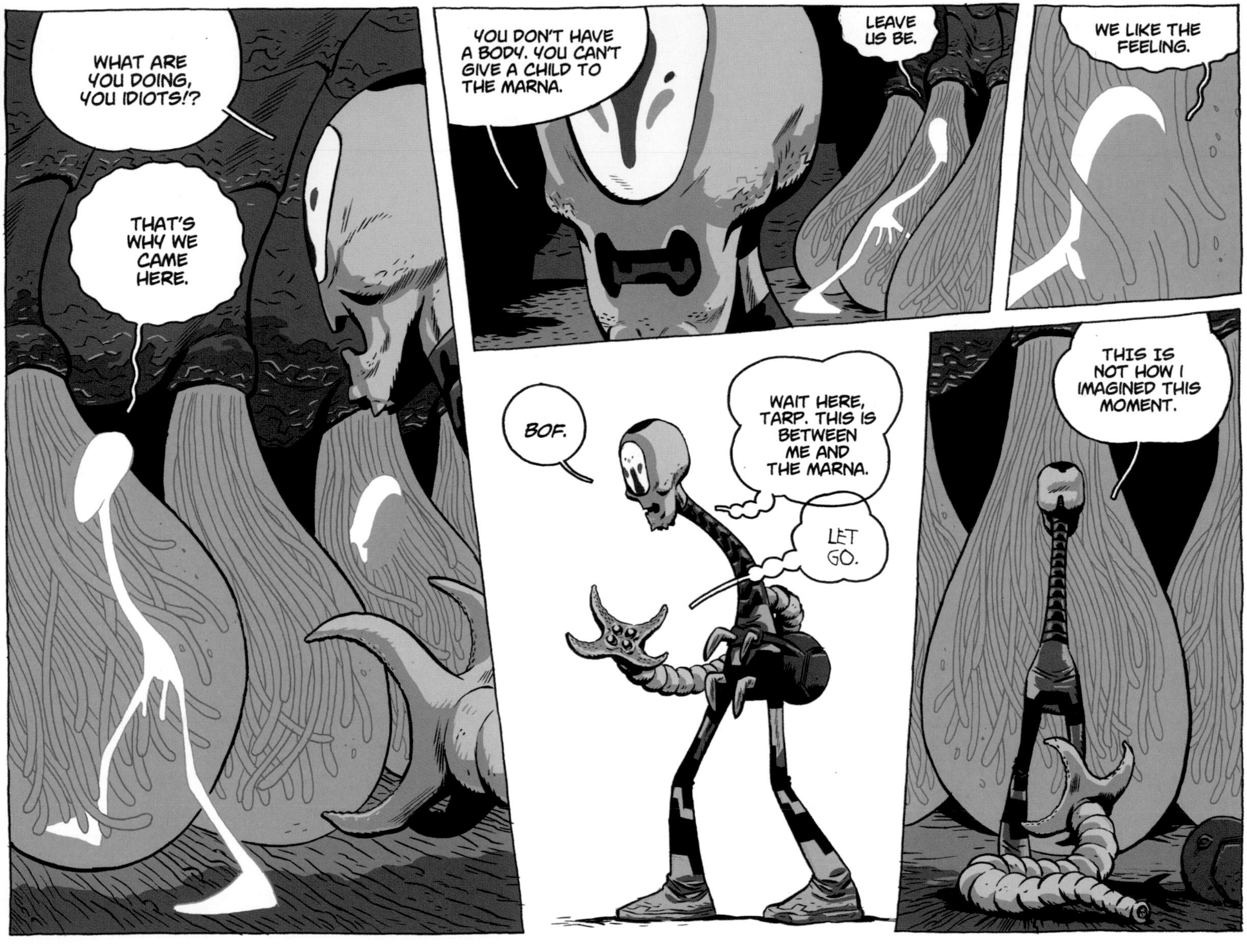
WHAT ARE YOU DOING, YOU IDIOTS!?
THAT'S WHY WE CAME HERE.
YOU DON'T HAVE A BODY. YOU CAN'T GIVE A CHILD TO THE MARNA.
LEAVE US BE.
WE LIKE THE FEELING.
BOF.
WAIT HERE, TARP. THIS IS BETWEEN ME AND THE MARNA.
LET GO.
THIS IS NOT HOW I IMAGINED THIS MOMENT.

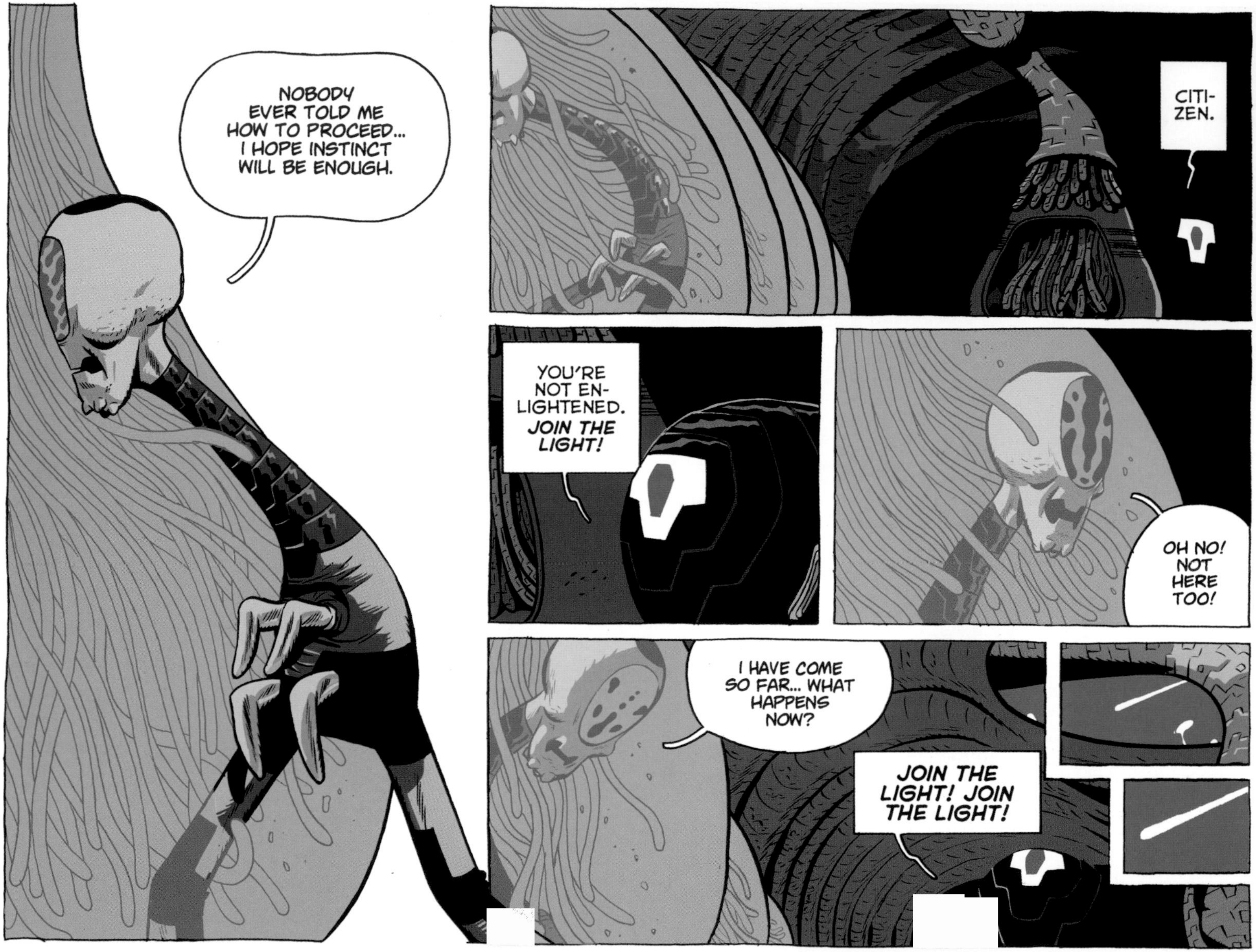
NOBODY EVER TOLD ME HOW TO PROCEED... I HOPE INSTINCT WILL BE ENOUGH.
CITI-ZEN.
YOU'RE NOT EN-LIGHTENED. *JOIN THE LIGHT!*
OH NO! NOT HERE TOO!
I HAVE COME SO FAR... WHAT HAPPENS NOW?
JOIN THE LIGHT! JOIN THE LIGHT!

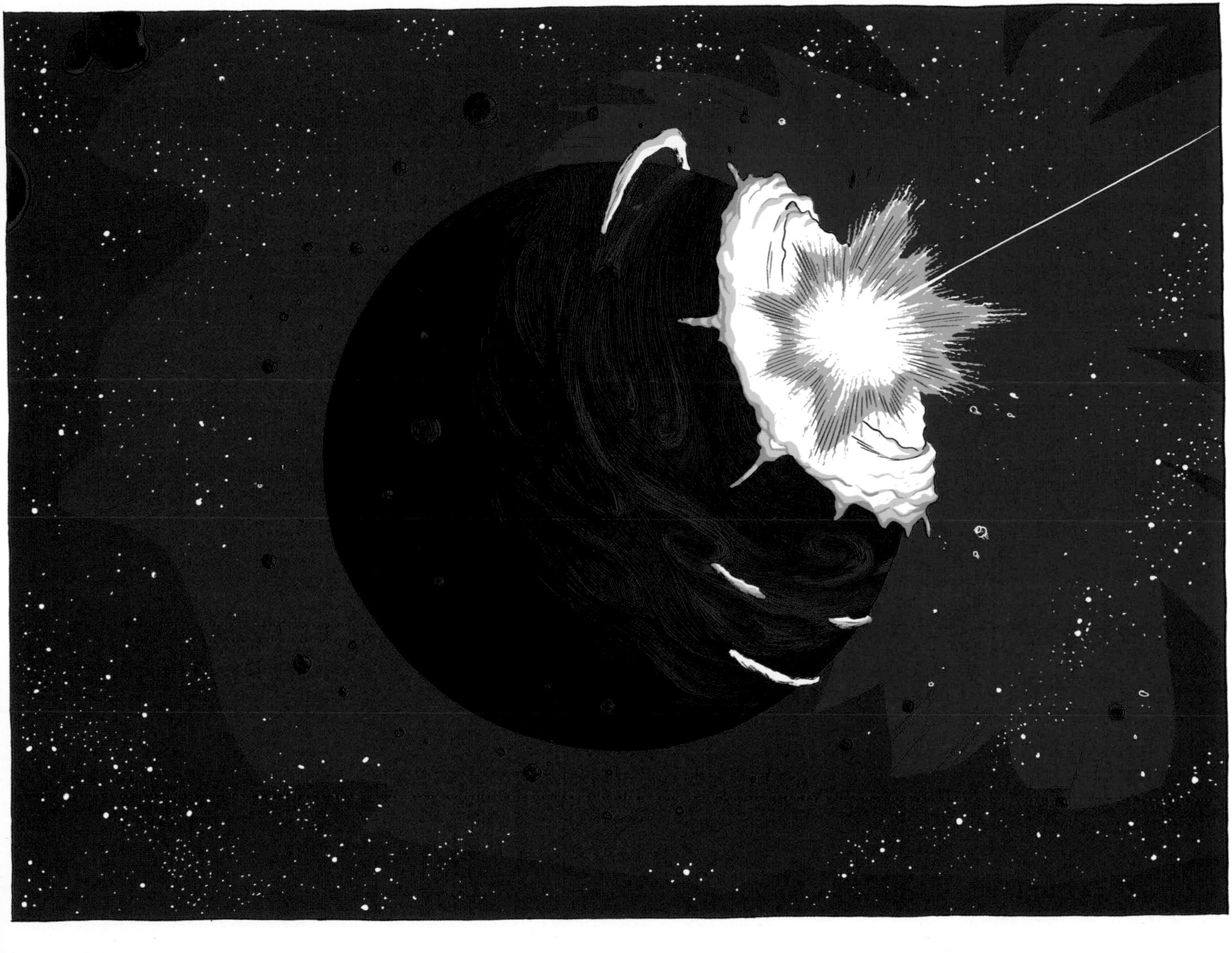

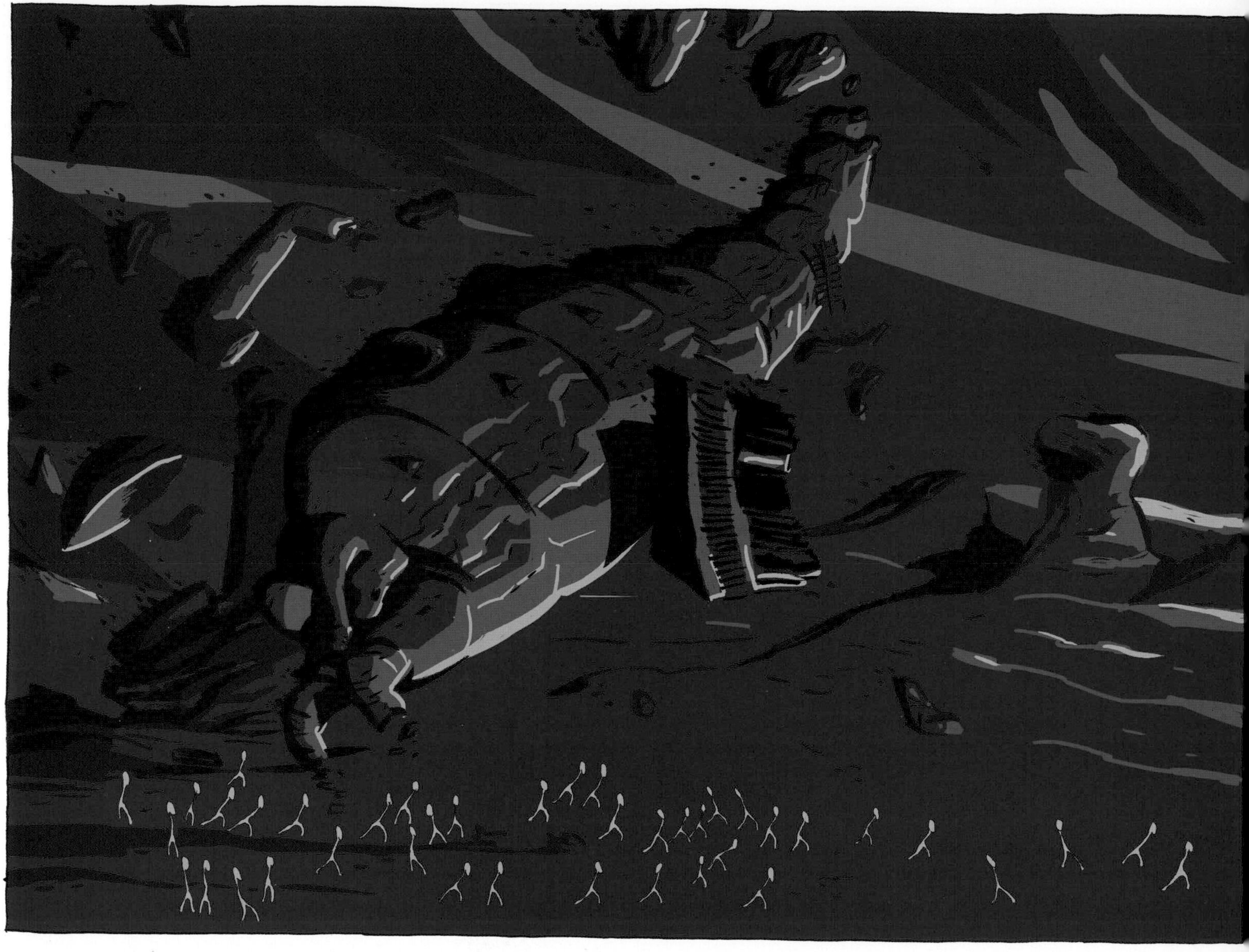

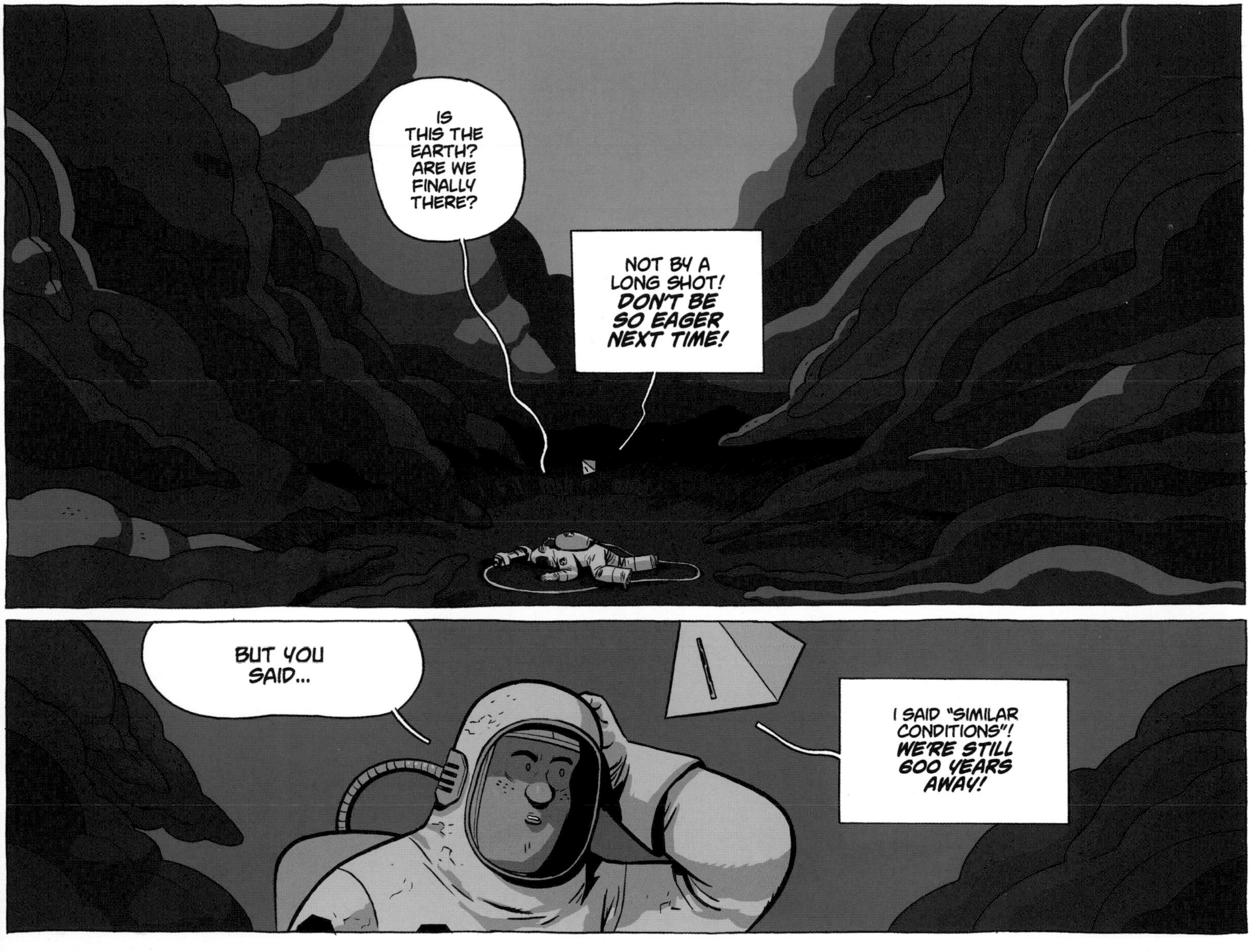
IS THIS THE EARTH? ARE WE FINALLY THERE?
NOT BY A LONG SHOT! DON'T BE SO EAGER NEXT TIME!
BUT YOU SAID...
I SAID "SIMILAR CONDITIONS"! WE'RE STILL 600 YEARS AWAY!

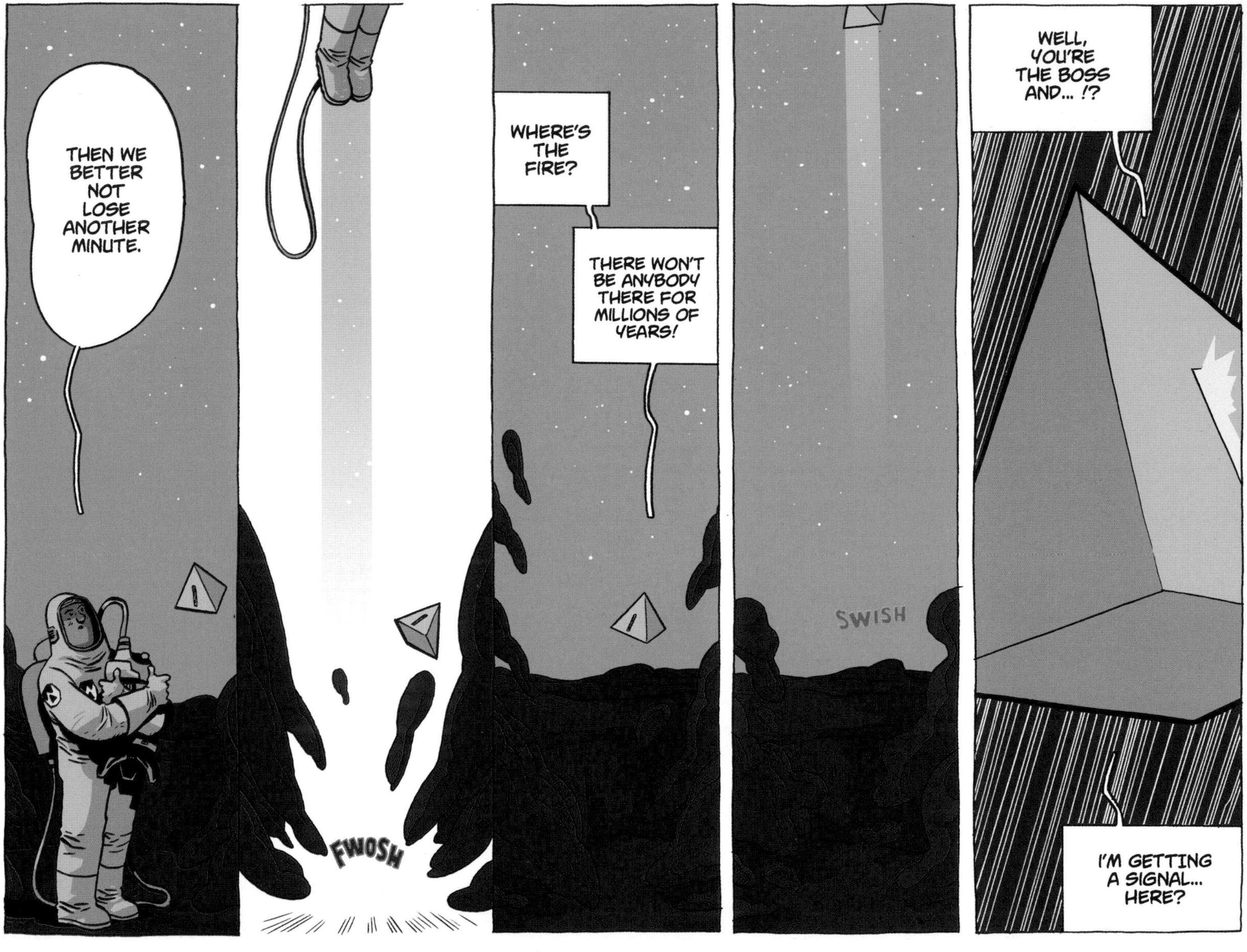
THEN WE BETTER NOT LOSE ANOTHER MINUTE.
FWOSH
WHERE'S THE FIRE?
THERE WON'T BE ANYBODY THERE FOR MILLIONS OF YEARS!
SWISH
WELL, YOU'RE THE BOSS AND... !?
I'M GETTING A SIGNAL... HERE?

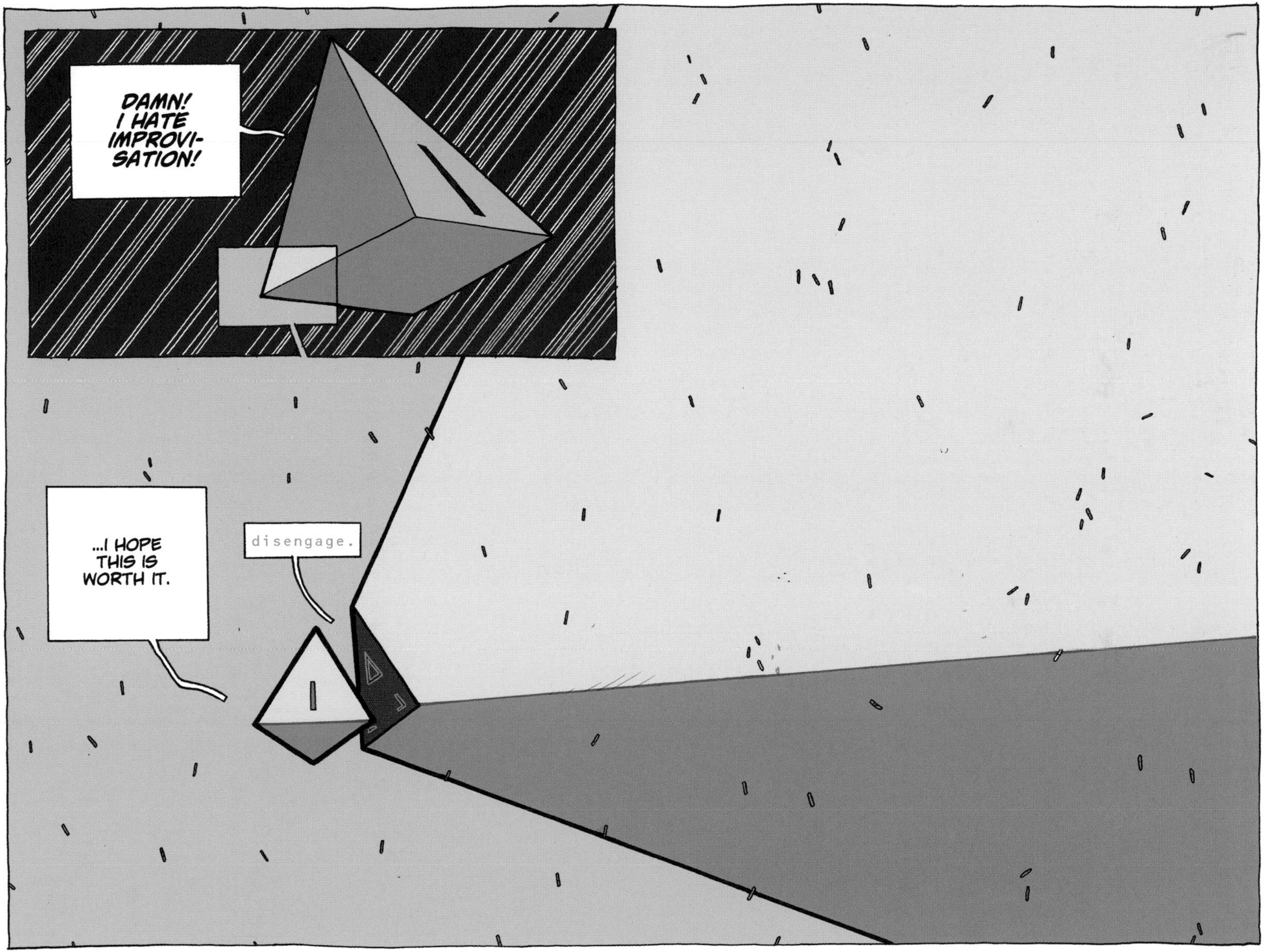
DAMN! I HATE IMPROVI-SATION!
...I HOPE THIS IS WORTH IT.
disengage.

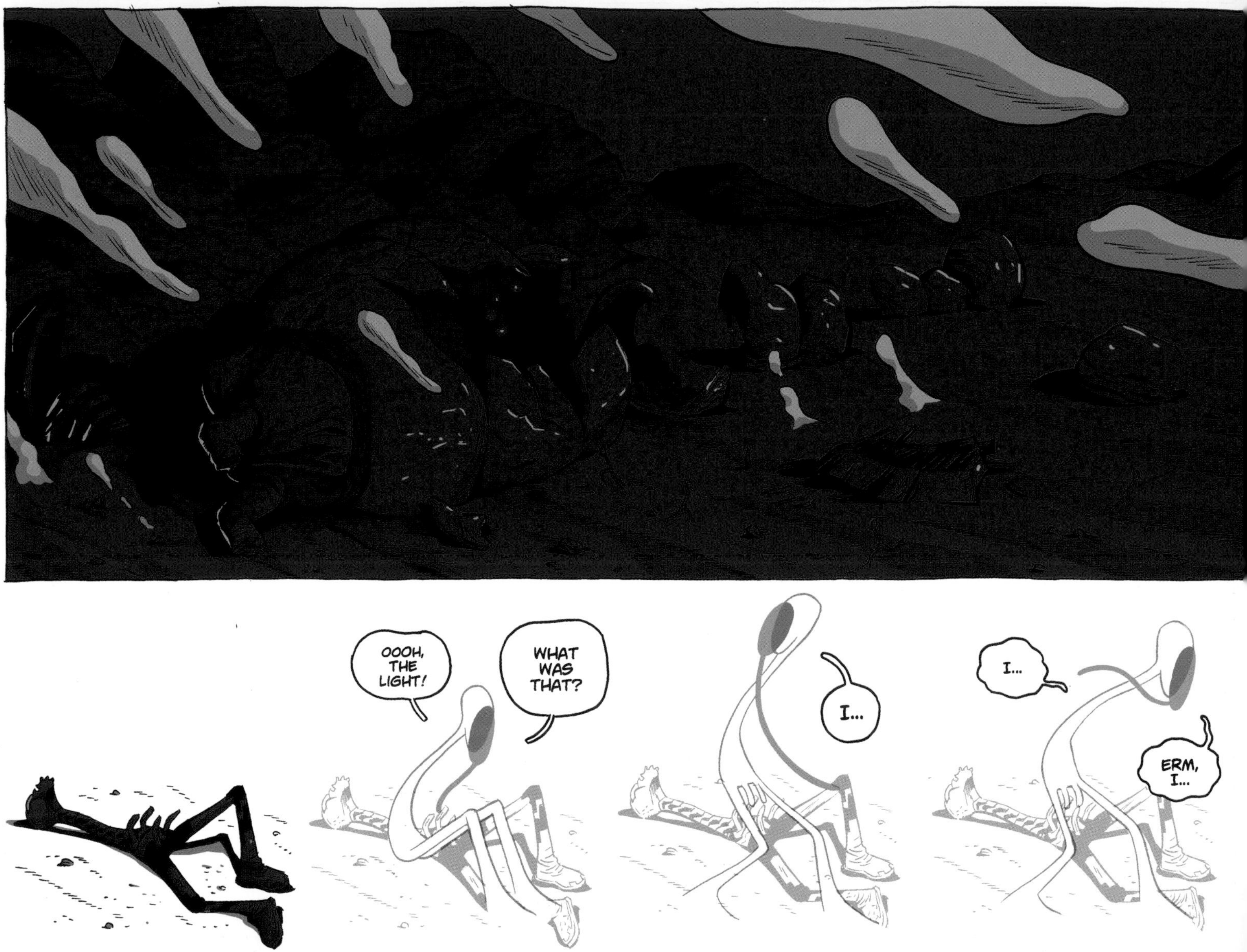
OOOH, THE LIGHT!
WHAT WAS THAT?
I...
I...
ERM, I...

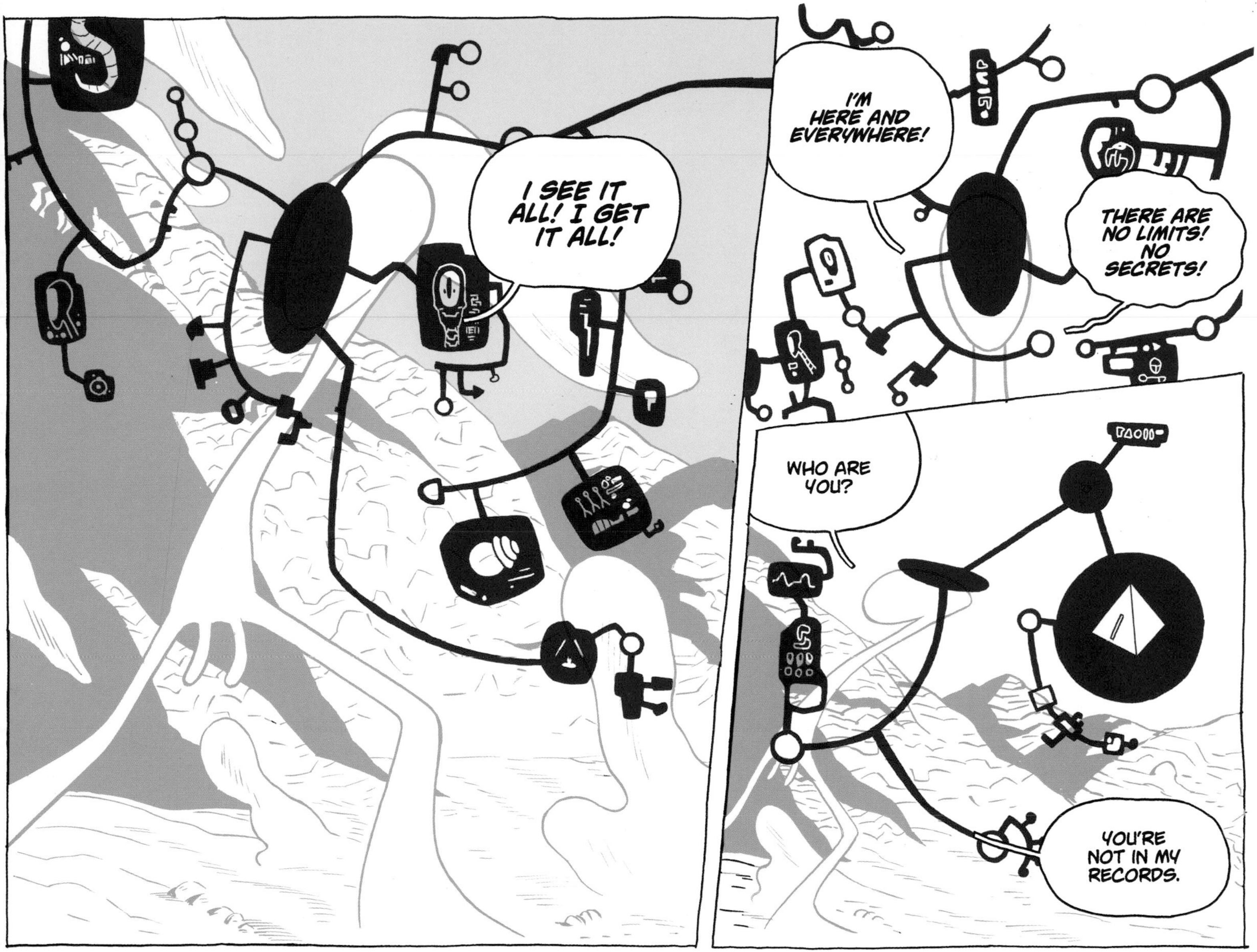
I SEE IT ALL! I GET IT ALL!
I'M HERE AND EVERYWHERE!
THERE ARE NO LIMITS! NO SECRETS!
WHO ARE YOU?
YOU'RE NOT IN MY RECORDS.

I GUESS THE END OF THE WORLD IS NOT THE BEST TIME TO ESTABLISH CONTACT WITH ANOTHER CIVILIZATION.
ANOTHER CIVILIZATION? WHERE DO YOU COME FROM?
WELL IT'S A LONG STORY AND...
ONE STEP AT A TIME.
...I MUST BEGIN BY APOLOGIZING FOR THE DAMAGES DONE ON YOUR PLANET AND STATING THAT NEITHER I, NOR THE HUMAN SPECIES, NOR WORTHAM INDUSTRIES HAVE ACTED WITH ANY ILL INTENTIONS IN THIS MATTER. I'M IN A POSITION TO NEGOTIATE A COMPENSATION, IF NECESSARY.
AM I SPEAKING WITH A VALID REPRESEN-TATIVE?
WELL, IT DEPENDS.

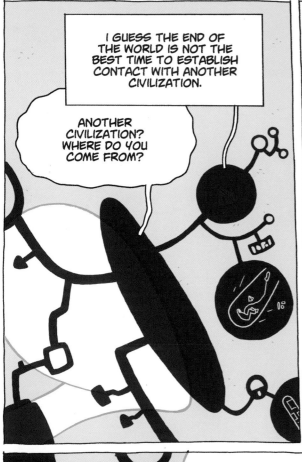

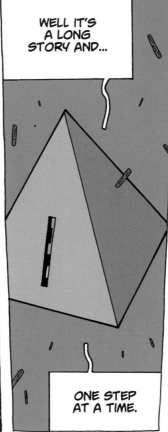

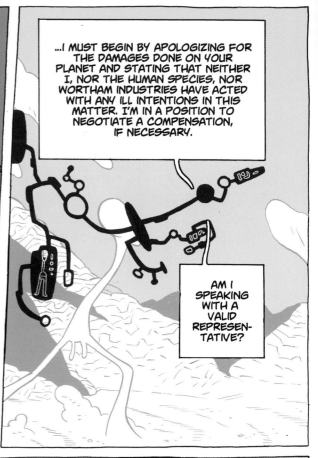

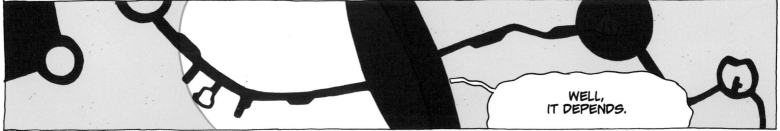

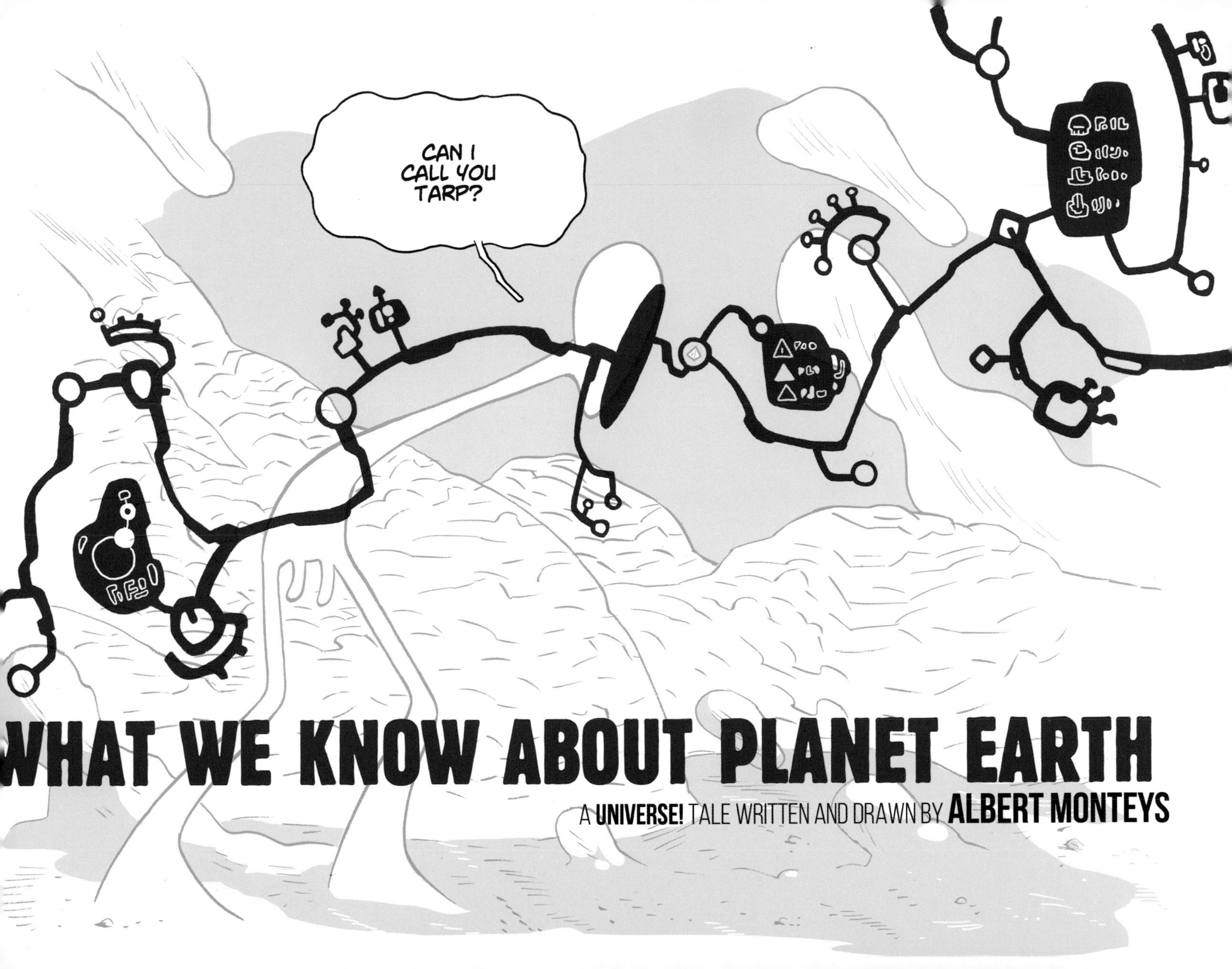
CAN I CALL YOU TARP?

WHAT WE KNOW ABOUT PLANET EARTH

A **UNIVERSE!** TALE WRITTEN AND DRAWN BY **ALBERT MONTEYS**

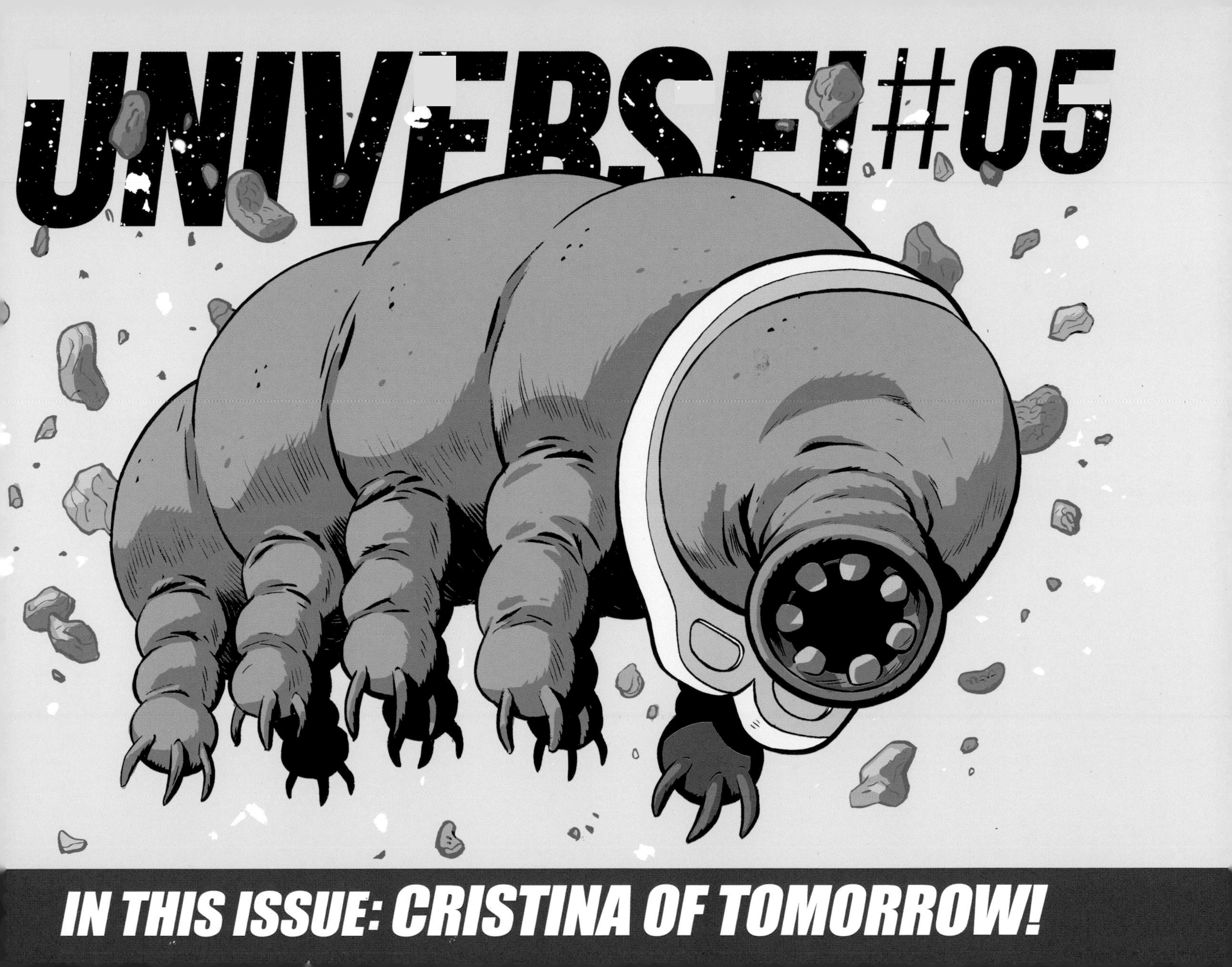
UNIVERSE! #05
IN THIS ISSUE: CRISTINA OF TOMORROW!

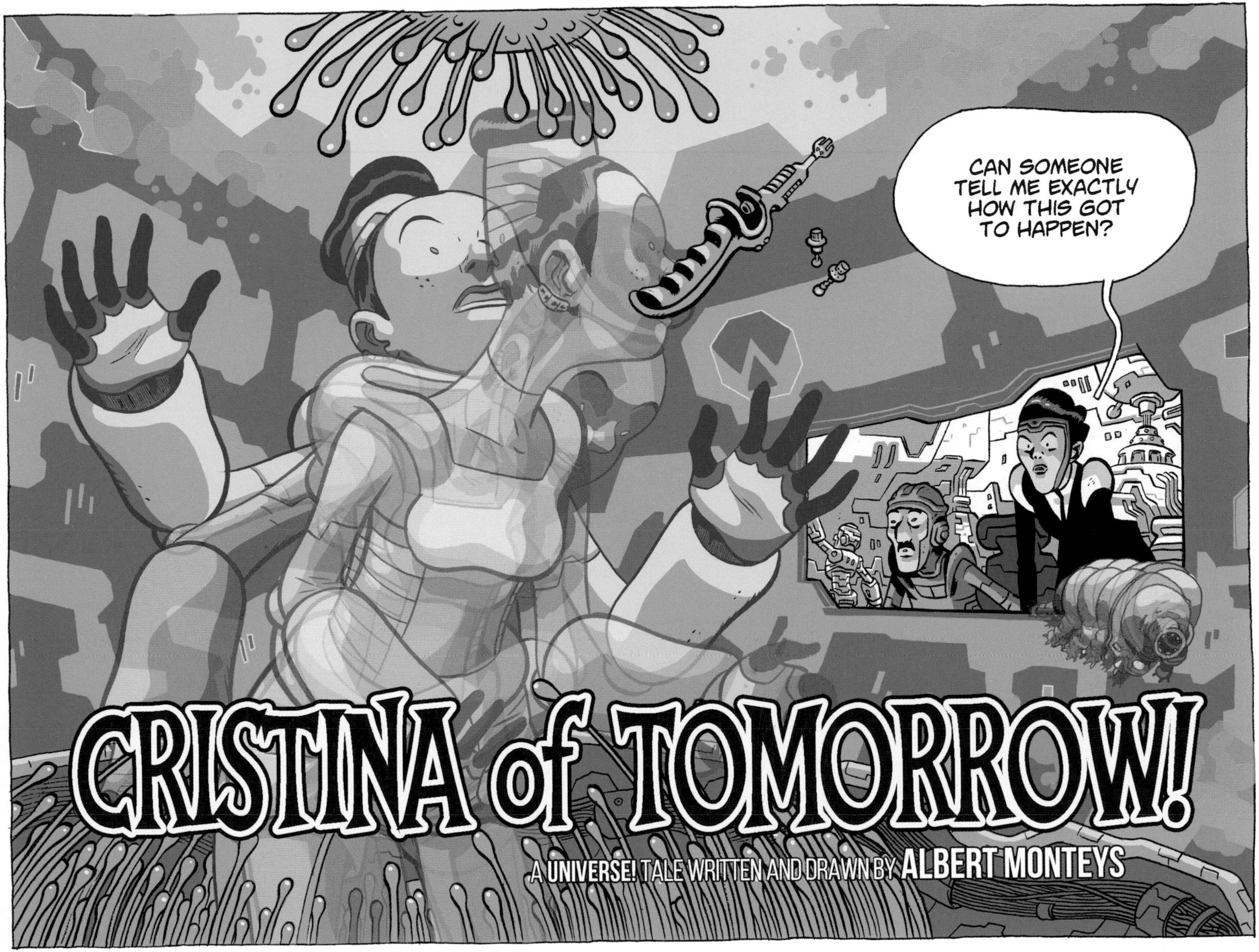
CAN SOMEONE TELL ME EXACTLY HOW THIS GOT TO HAPPEN?
CRISTINA of TOMORROW!
A UNIVERSE! TALE WRITTEN AND DRAWN BY ALBERT MONTEYS

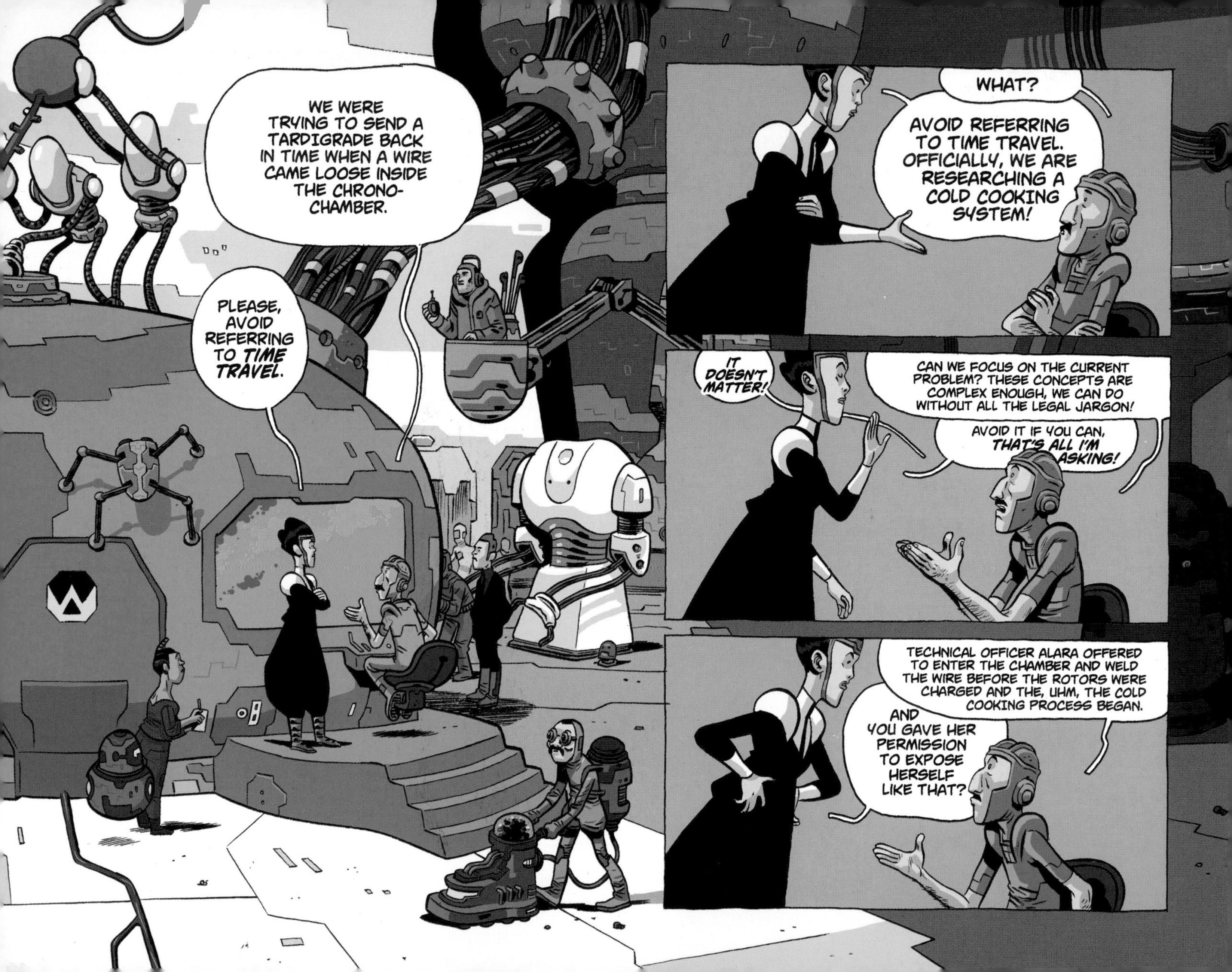
WE WERE TRYING TO SEND A TARDIGRADE BACK IN TIME WHEN A WIRE CAME LOOSE INSIDE THE CHRONO-CHAMBER.
PLEASE, AVOID REFERRING TO *TIME TRAVEL*.
WHAT?
AVOID REFERRING TO TIME TRAVEL. OFFICIALLY, WE ARE RESEARCHING A COLD COOKING SYSTEM!
IT DOESN'T MATTER!
CAN WE FOCUS ON THE CURRENT PROBLEM? THESE CONCEPTS ARE COMPLEX ENOUGH, WE CAN DO WITHOUT ALL THE LEGAL JARGON!
AVOID IT IF YOU CAN, *THAT'S ALL I'M ASKING!*
TECHNICAL OFFICER ALARA OFFERED TO ENTER THE CHAMBER AND WELD THE WIRE BEFORE THE ROTORS WERE CHARGED AND THE, UHM, THE COLD COOKING PROCESS BEGAN.
AND YOU GAVE HER PERMISSION TO EXPOSE HERSELF LIKE THAT?

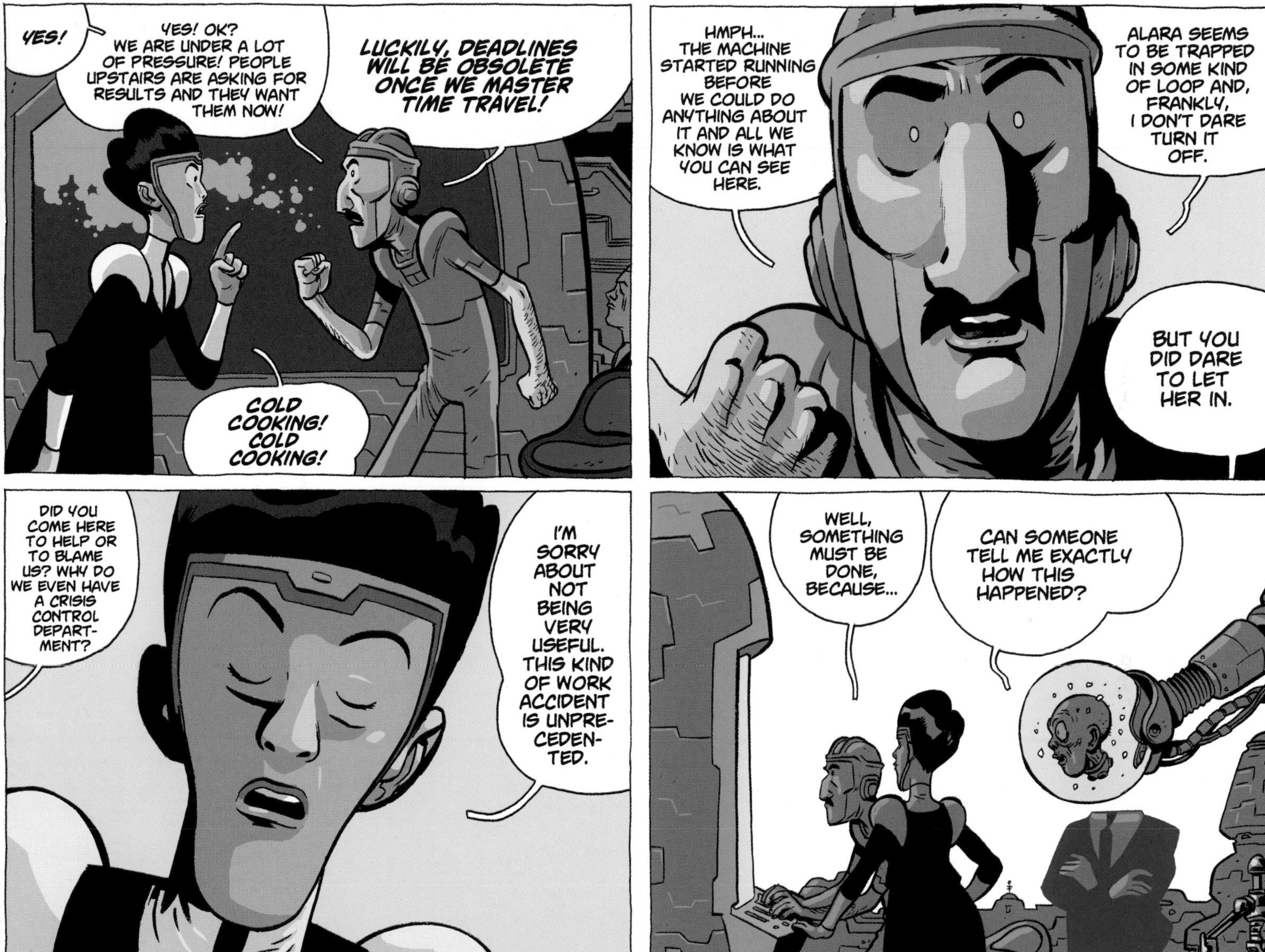
YES!
YES! OK? WE ARE UNDER A LOT OF PRESSURE! PEOPLE UPSTAIRS ARE ASKING FOR RESULTS AND THEY WANT THEM NOW!
LUCKILY, DEADLINES WILL BE OBSOLETE ONCE WE MASTER TIME TRAVEL!
COLD COOKING! COLD COOKING!
HMPH... THE MACHINE STARTED RUNNING BEFORE WE COULD DO ANYTHING ABOUT IT AND ALL WE KNOW IS WHAT YOU CAN SEE HERE.
ALARA SEEMS TO BE TRAPPED IN SOME KIND OF LOOP AND, FRANKLY, I DON'T DARE TURN IT OFF.
BUT YOU DID DARE TO LET HER IN.
DID YOU COME HERE TO HELP OR TO BLAME US? WHY DO WE EVEN HAVE A CRISIS CONTROL DEPART-MENT?
I'M SORRY ABOUT NOT BEING VERY USEFUL. THIS KIND OF WORK ACCIDENT IS UNPRE-CEDEN-TED.
WELL, SOMETHING MUST BE DONE, BECAUSE...
CAN SOMEONE TELL ME EXACTLY HOW THIS HAPPENED?

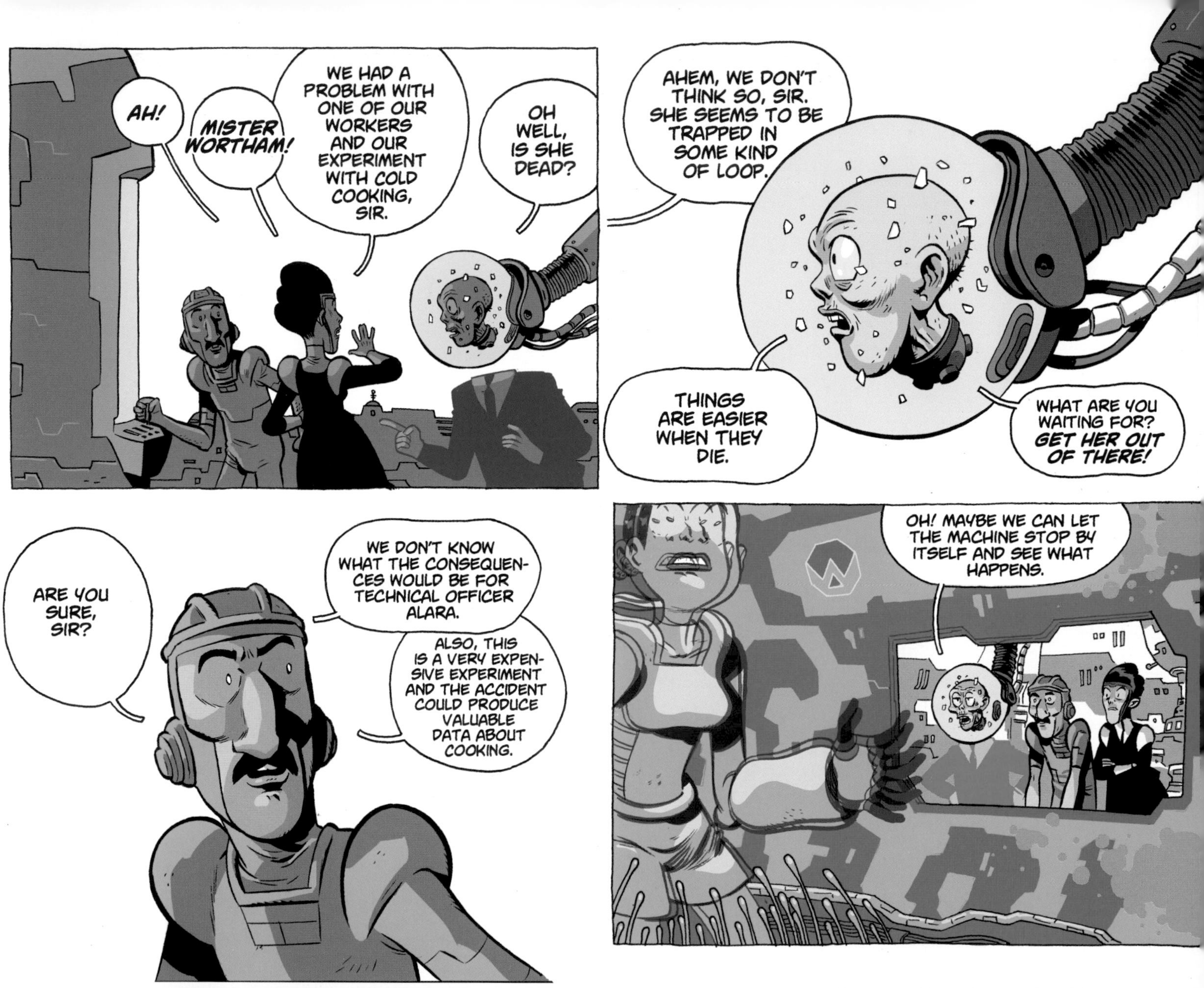
AH!
MISTER WORTHAM!
WE HAD A PROBLEM WITH ONE OF OUR WORKERS AND OUR EXPERIMENT WITH COLD COOKING, SIR.
OH WELL, IS SHE DEAD?
AHEM, WE DON'T THINK SO, SIR. SHE SEEMS TO BE TRAPPED IN SOME KIND OF LOOP.
THINGS ARE EASIER WHEN THEY DIE.
WHAT ARE YOU WAITING FOR? GET HER OUT OF THERE!
ARE YOU SURE, SIR?
WE DON'T KNOW WHAT THE CONSEQUEN-CES WOULD BE FOR TECHNICAL OFFICER ALARA.
ALSO, THIS IS A VERY EXPEN-SIVE EXPERIMENT AND THE ACCIDENT COULD PRODUCE VALUABLE DATA ABOUT COOKING.
OH! MAYBE WE CAN LET THE MACHINE STOP BY ITSELF AND SEE WHAT HAPPENS.

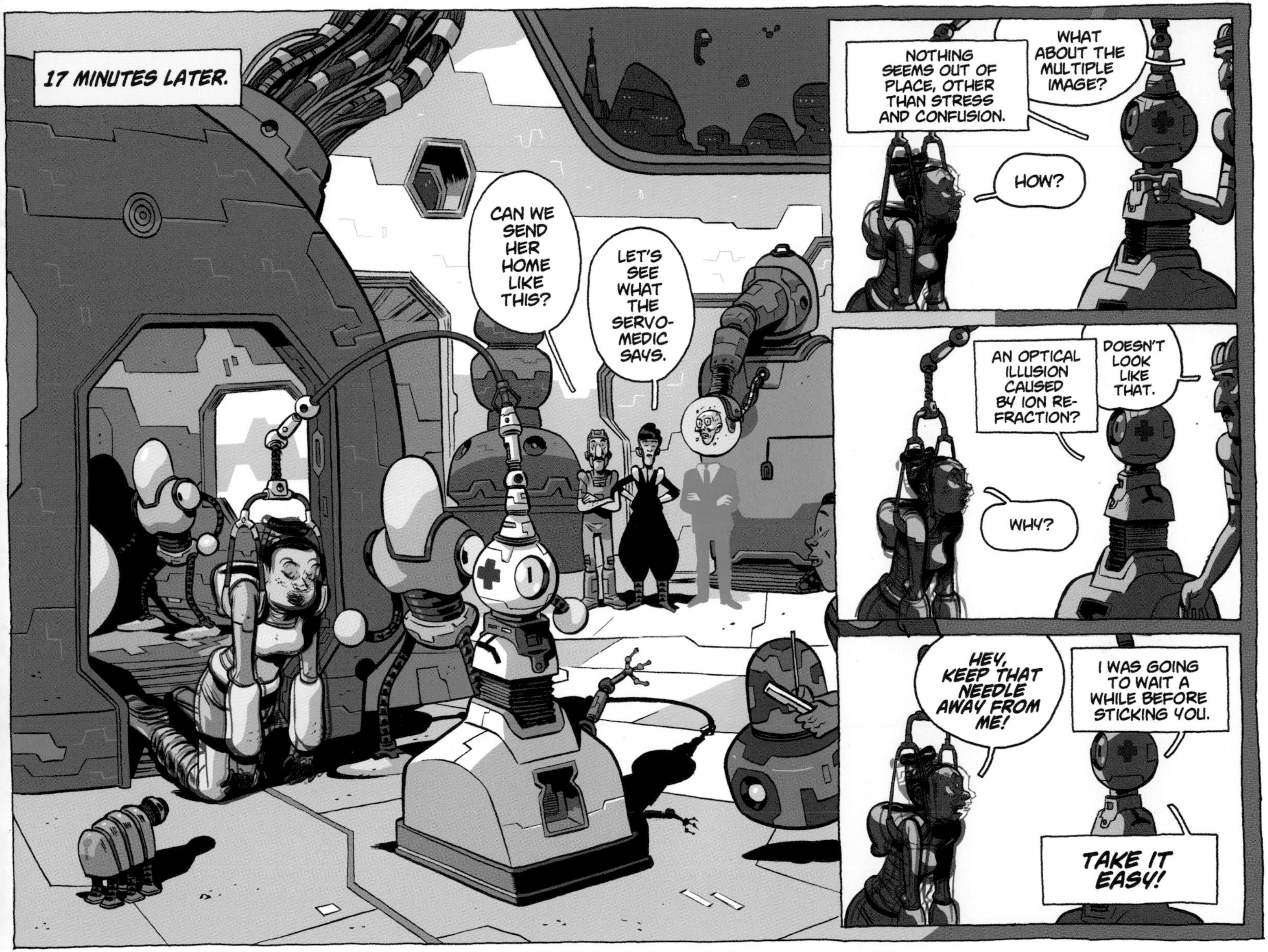

17 MINUTES LATER.
CAN WE SEND HER HOME LIKE THIS?
LET'S SEE WHAT THE SERVO-MEDIC SAYS.
NOTHING SEEMS OUT OF PLACE, OTHER THAN STRESS AND CONFUSION.
WHAT ABOUT THE MULTIPLE IMAGE?
HOW?
AN OPTICAL ILLUSION CAUSED BY ION RE-FRACTION?
DOESN'T LOOK LIKE THAT.
WHY?
HEY, KEEP THAT NEEDLE AWAY FROM ME!
I WAS GOING TO WAIT A WHILE BEFORE STICKING YOU.
TAKE IT EASY!

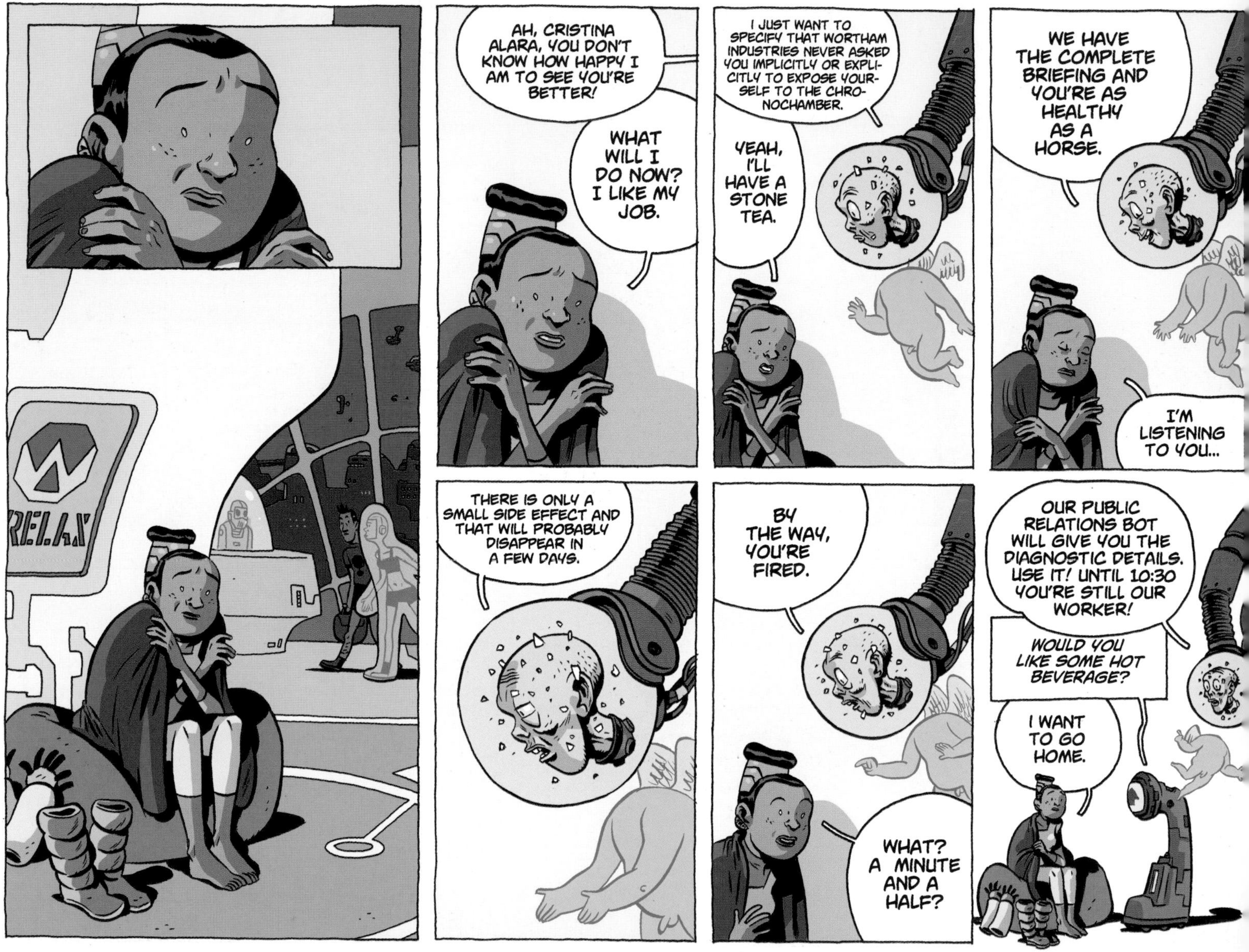
RELAX
AH, CRISTINA ALARA, YOU DON'T KNOW HOW HAPPY I AM TO SEE YOU'RE BETTER!
WHAT WILL I DO NOW? I LIKE MY JOB.
I JUST WANT TO SPECIFY THAT WORTHAM INDUSTRIES NEVER ASKED YOU IMPLICITLY OR EXPLICITLY TO EXPOSE YOURSELF TO THE CHRONOCHAMBER.
YEAH, I'LL HAVE A STONE TEA.
WE HAVE THE COMPLETE BRIEFING AND YOU'RE AS HEALTHY AS A HORSE.
I'M LISTENING TO YOU...
THERE IS ONLY A SMALL SIDE EFFECT AND THAT WILL PROBABLY DISAPPEAR IN A FEW DAYS.
BY THE WAY, YOU'RE FIRED.
WHAT? A MINUTE AND A HALF?
OUR PUBLIC RELATIONS BOT WILL GIVE YOU THE DIAGNOSTIC DETAILS. USE IT! UNTIL 10:30 YOU'RE STILL OUR WORKER!
WOULD YOU LIKE SOME HOT BEVERAGE?
I WANT TO GO HOME.

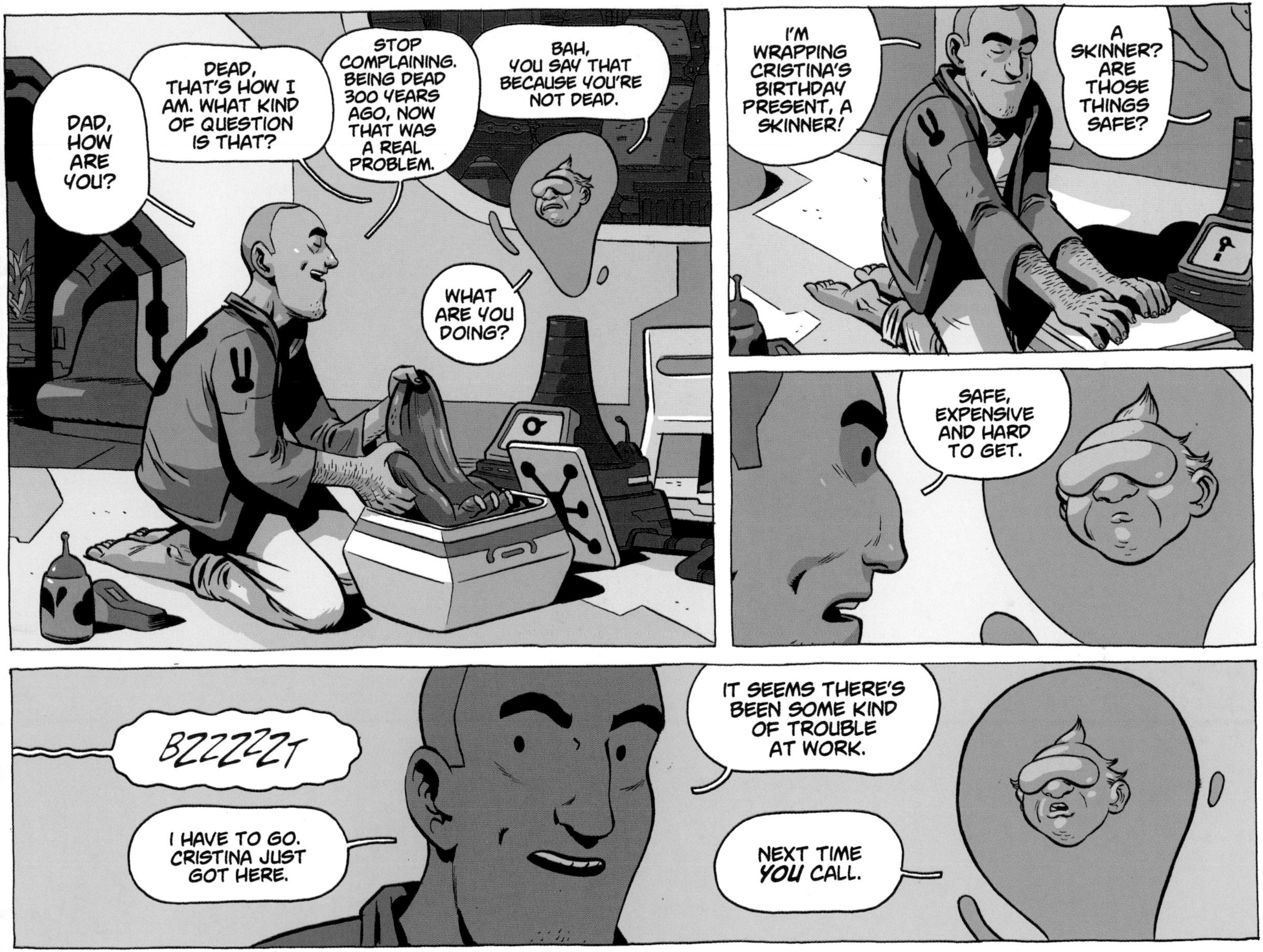
DAD, HOW ARE YOU?
DEAD, THAT'S HOW I AM. WHAT KIND OF QUESTION IS THAT?
STOP COMPLAINING. BEING DEAD 300 YEARS AGO, NOW THAT WAS A REAL PROBLEM.
BAH, YOU SAY THAT BECAUSE YOU'RE NOT DEAD.
WHAT ARE YOU DOING?
I'M WRAPPING CRISTINA'S BIRTHDAY PRESENT, A SKINNER!
A SKINNER? ARE THOSE THINGS SAFE?
SAFE, EXPENSIVE AND HARD TO GET.
BZZZZZT
IT SEEMS THERE'S BEEN SOME KIND OF TROUBLE AT WORK.
I HAVE TO GO. CRISTINA JUST GOT HERE.
NEXT TIME ***YOU*** CALL.

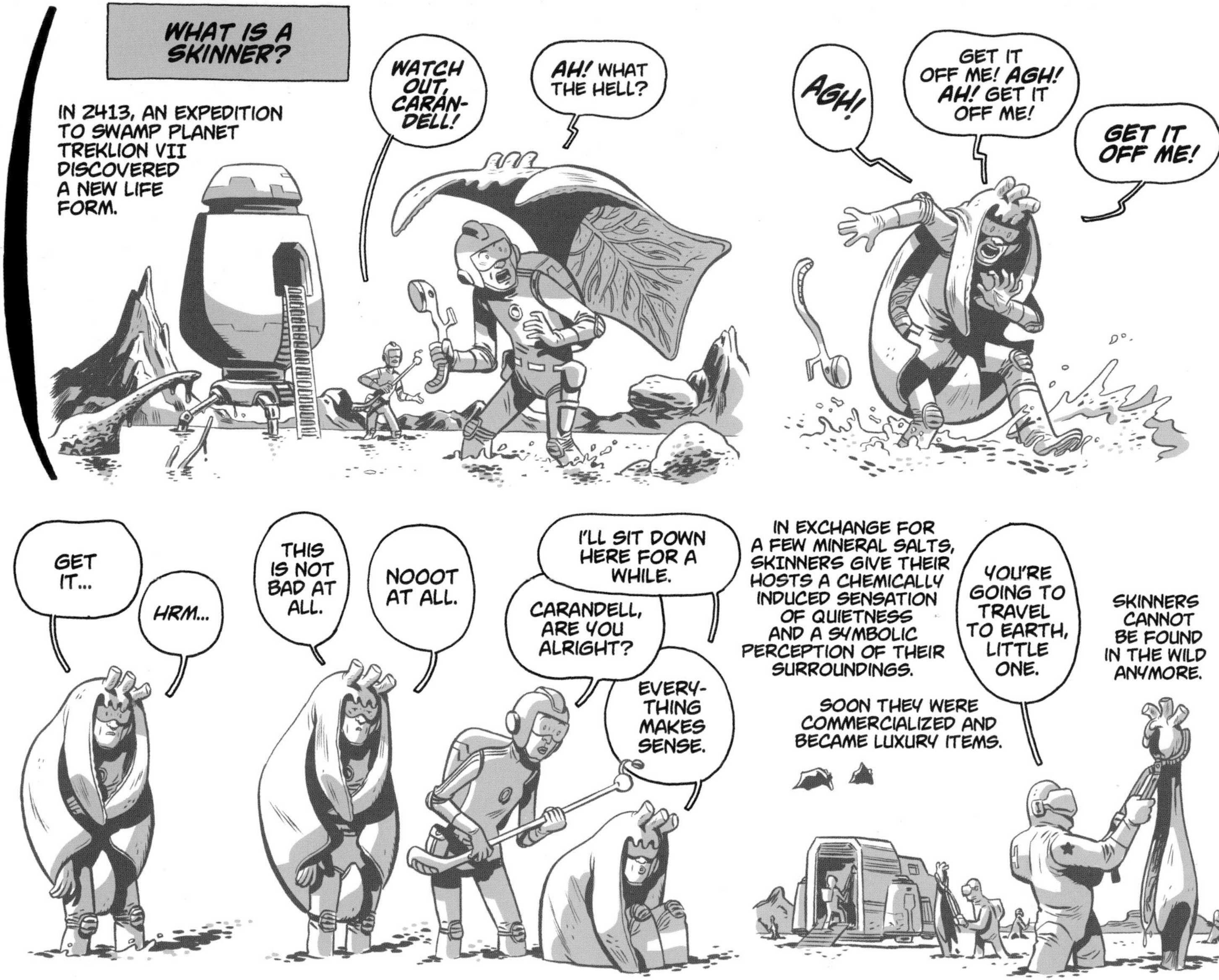

WHAT IS A SKINNER?
IN 2413, AN EXPEDITION TO SWAMP PLANET TREKLION VII DISCOVERED A NEW LIFE FORM.
WATCH OUT, CARAN-DELL!
AH! WHAT THE HELL?
AGH!
GET IT OFF ME! AGH! AH! GET IT OFF ME!
GET IT OFF ME!
GET IT...
HRM...
THIS IS NOT BAD AT ALL.
NOOOT AT ALL.
I'LL SIT DOWN HERE FOR A WHILE.
CARANDELL, ARE YOU ALRIGHT?
EVERY-THING MAKES SENSE.
IN EXCHANGE FOR A FEW MINERAL SALTS, SKINNERS GIVE THEIR HOSTS A CHEMICALLY INDUCED SENSATION OF QUIETNESS AND A SYMBOLIC PERCEPTION OF THEIR SURROUNDINGS.
SOON THEY WERE COMMERCIALIZED AND BECAME LUXURY ITEMS.
YOU'RE GOING TO TRAVEL TO EARTH, LITTLE ONE.
SKINNERS CANNOT BE FOUND IN THE WILD ANYMORE.

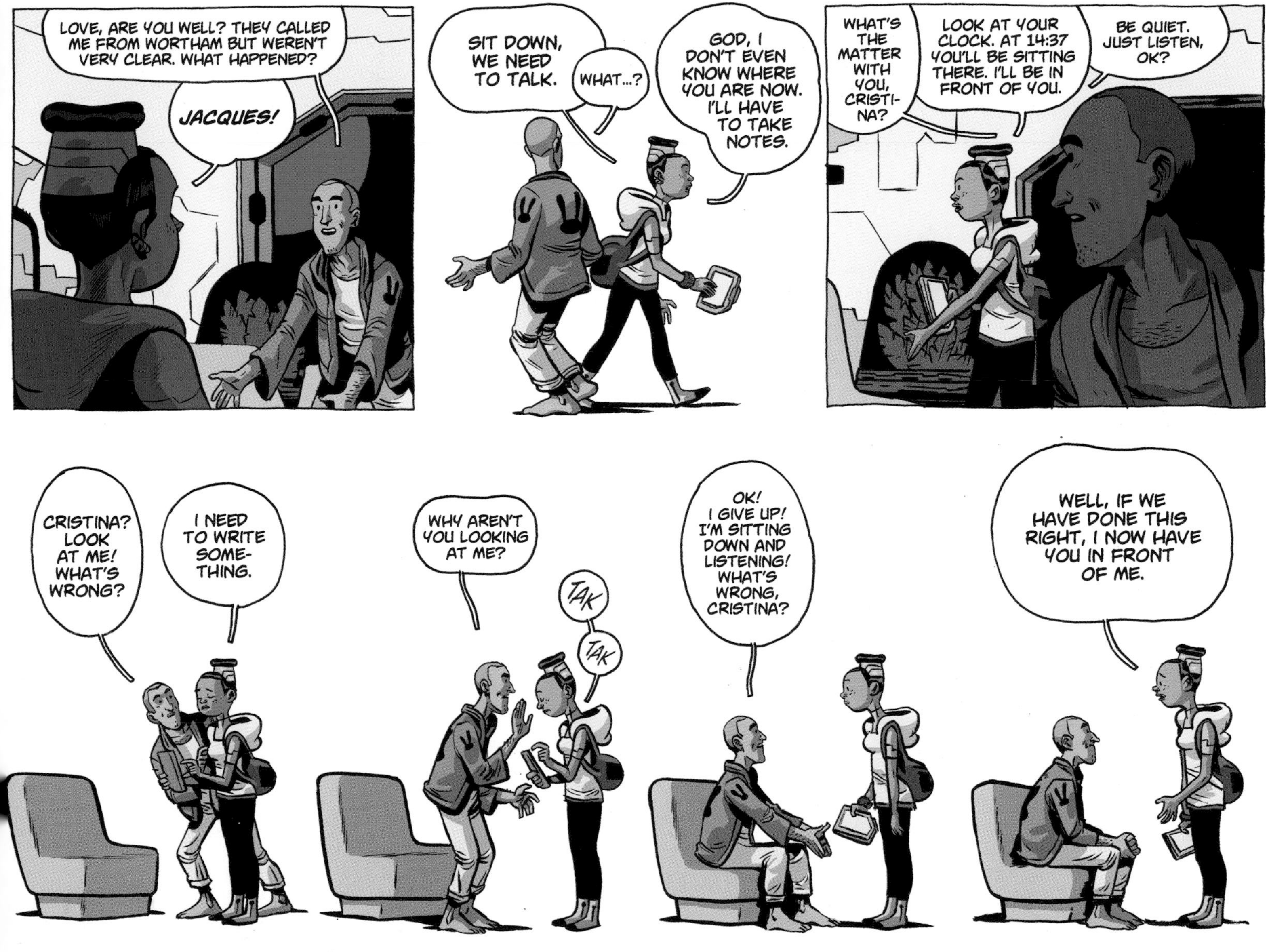
LOVE, ARE YOU WELL? THEY CALLED ME FROM WORTHAM BUT WEREN'T VERY CLEAR. WHAT HAPPENED?
JACQUES!
SIT DOWN, WE NEED TO TALK.
WHAT...?
GOD, I DON'T EVEN KNOW WHERE YOU ARE NOW. I'LL HAVE TO TAKE NOTES.
WHAT'S THE MATTER WITH YOU, CRISTI-NA?
LOOK AT YOUR CLOCK. AT 14:37 YOU'LL BE SITTING THERE. I'LL BE IN FRONT OF YOU.
BE QUIET. JUST LISTEN, OK?
CRISTINA? LOOK AT ME! WHAT'S WRONG?
I NEED TO WRITE SOME-THING.
WHY AREN'T YOU LOOKING AT ME?
TAK
TAK
OK! I GIVE UP! I'M SITTING DOWN AND LISTENING! WHAT'S WRONG, CRISTINA?
WELL, IF WE HAVE DONE THIS RIGHT, I NOW HAVE YOU IN FRONT OF ME.

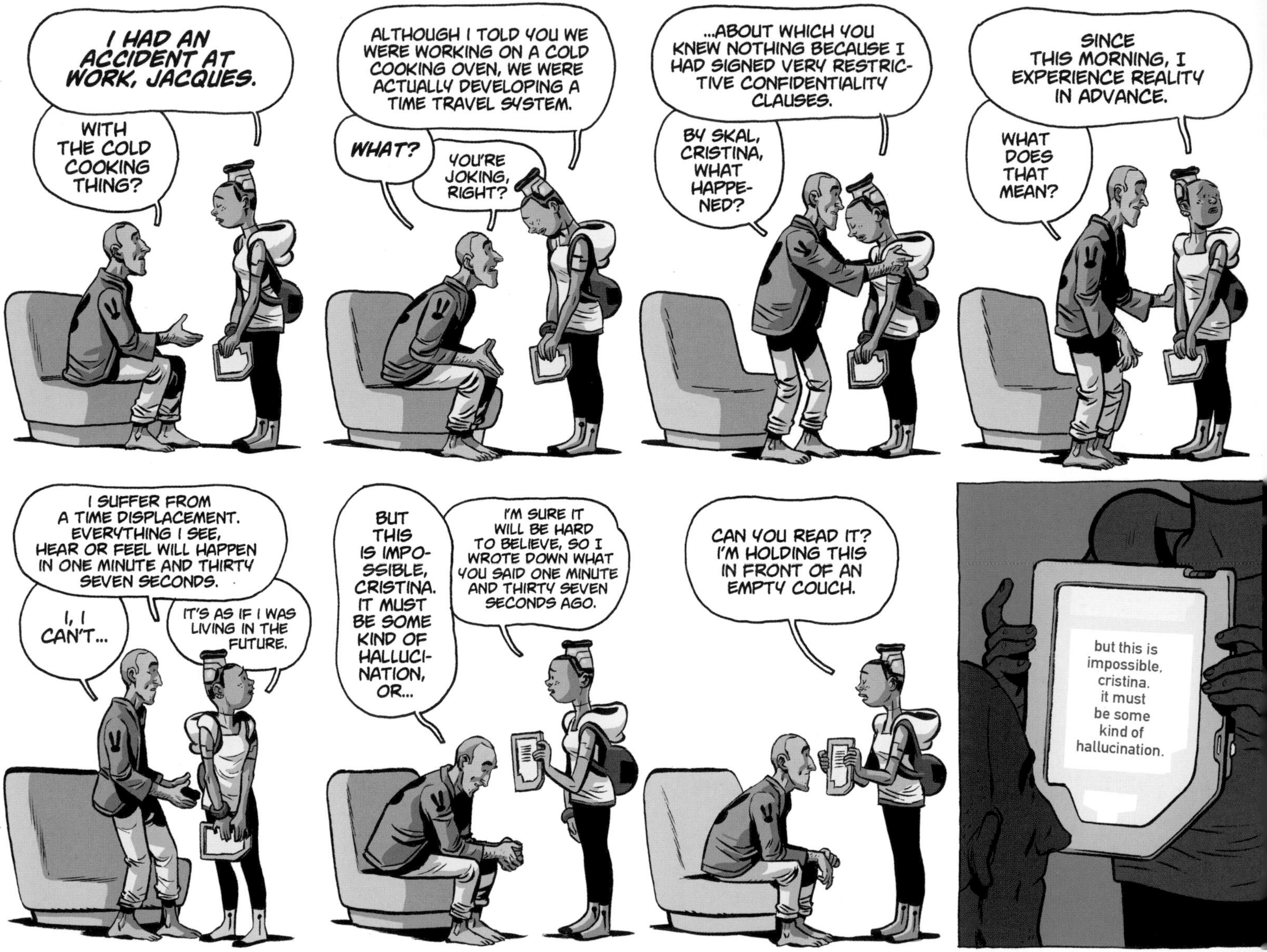
I HAD AN ACCIDENT AT WORK, JACQUES.
WITH THE COLD COOKING THING?
ALTHOUGH I TOLD YOU WE WERE WORKING ON A COLD COOKING OVEN, WE WERE ACTUALLY DEVELOPING A TIME TRAVEL SYSTEM.
WHAT?
YOU'RE JOKING, RIGHT?
...ABOUT WHICH YOU KNEW NOTHING BECAUSE I HAD SIGNED VERY RESTRICTIVE CONFIDENTIALITY CLAUSES.
BY SKAL, CRISTINA, WHAT HAPPENED?
SINCE THIS MORNING, I EXPERIENCE REALITY IN ADVANCE.
WHAT DOES THAT MEAN?
I SUFFER FROM A TIME DISPLACEMENT. EVERYTHING I SEE, HEAR OR FEEL WILL HAPPEN IN ONE MINUTE AND THIRTY SEVEN SECONDS.
I, I CAN'T...
IT'S AS IF I WAS LIVING IN THE FUTURE.
BUT THIS IS IMPOSSIBLE, CRISTINA. IT MUST BE SOME KIND OF HALLUCINATION, OR...
I'M SURE IT WILL BE HARD TO BELIEVE, SO I WROTE DOWN WHAT YOU SAID ONE MINUTE AND THIRTY SEVEN SECONDS AGO.
CAN YOU READ IT? I'M HOLDING THIS IN FRONT OF AN EMPTY COUCH.
but this is impossible, cristina. it must be some kind of hallucination.

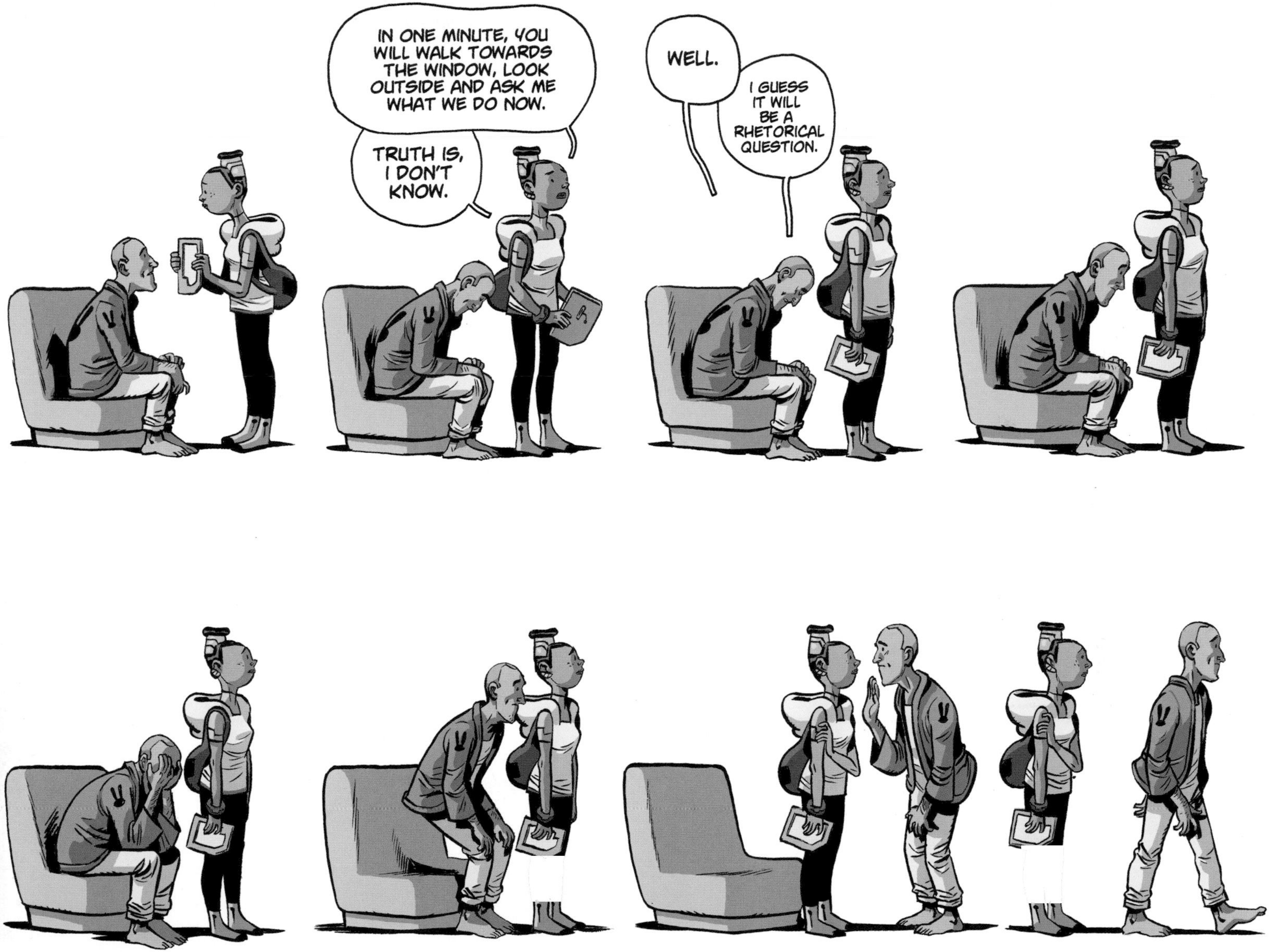
IN ONE MINUTE, YOU WILL WALK TOWARDS THE WINDOW, LOOK OUTSIDE AND ASK ME WHAT WE DO NOW.
TRUTH IS, I DON'T KNOW.
WELL.
I GUESS IT WILL BE A RHETORICAL QUESTION.

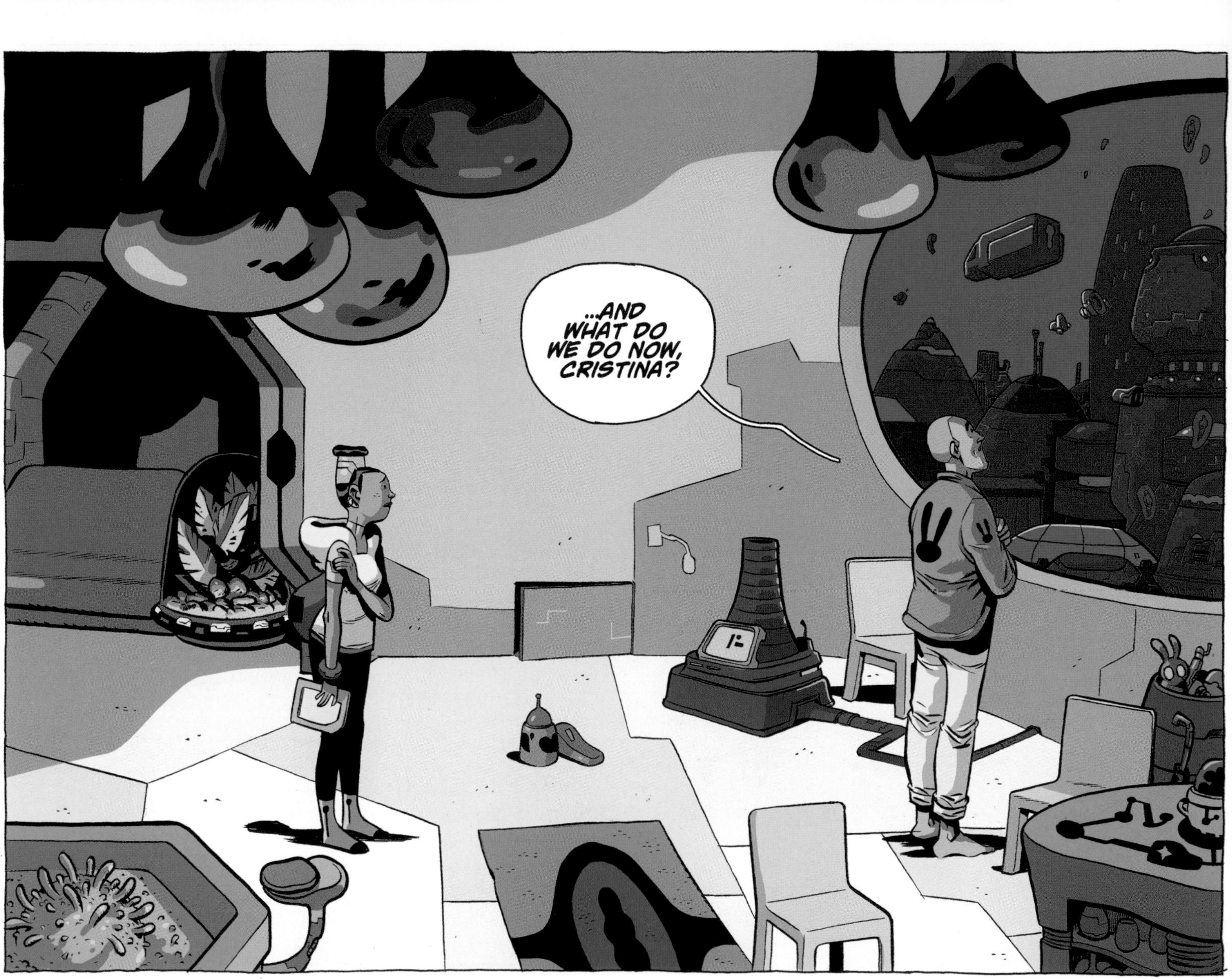
...AND WHAT DO WE DO NOW, CRISTINA?

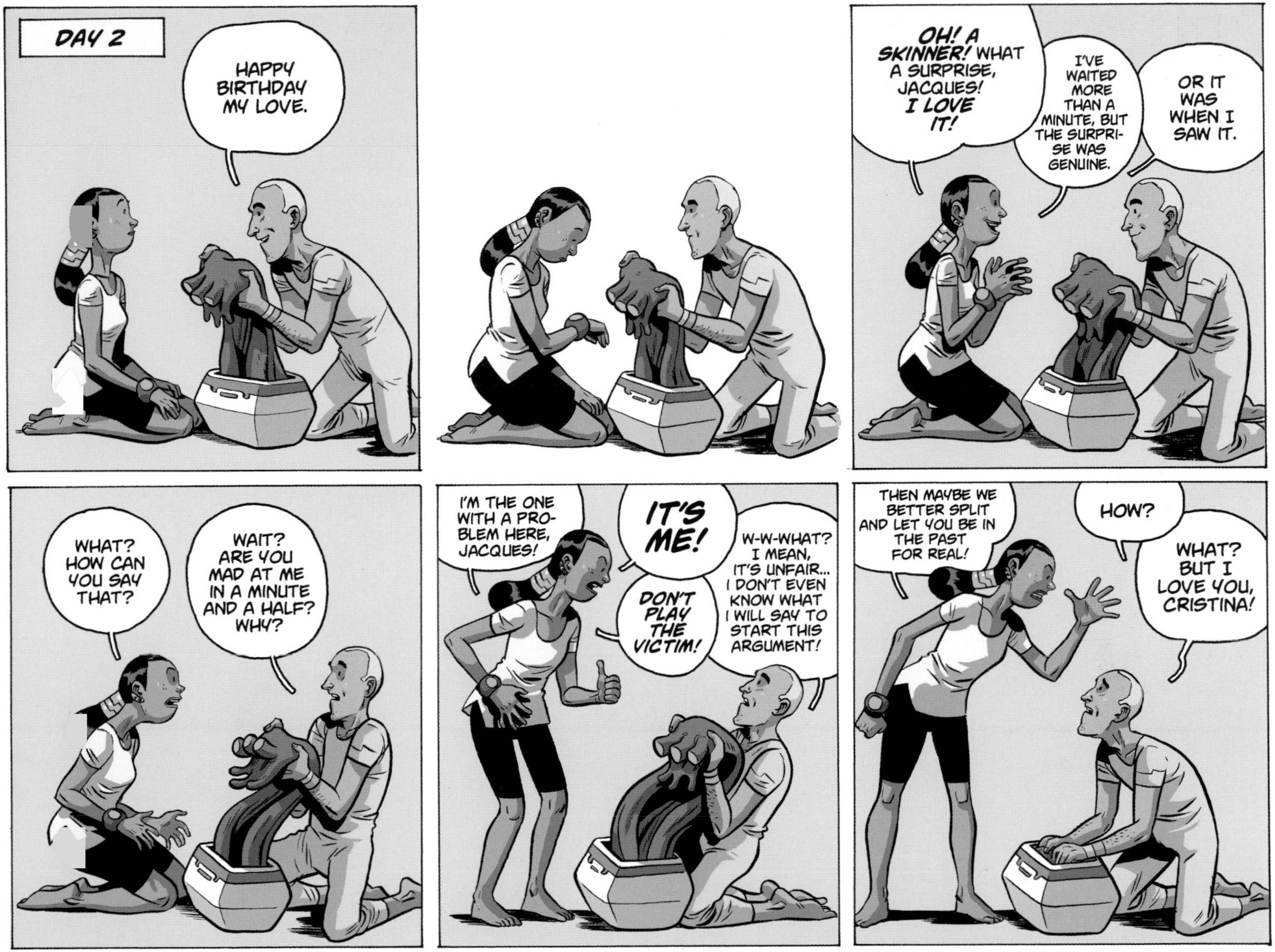
DAY 2
HAPPY BIRTHDAY MY LOVE.
OH! A SKINNER! WHAT A SURPRISE, JACQUES! I LOVE IT!
I'VE WAITED MORE THAN A MINUTE, BUT THE SURPRI-SE WAS GENUINE.
OR IT WAS WHEN I SAW IT.
WHAT? HOW CAN YOU SAY THAT?
WAIT? ARE YOU MAD AT ME IN A MINUTE AND A HALF? WHY?
I'M THE ONE WITH A PRO-BLEM HERE, JACQUES!
IT'S ME!
DON'T PLAY THE VICTIM!
W-W-WHAT? I MEAN, IT'S UNFAIR... I DON'T EVEN KNOW WHAT I WILL SAY TO START THIS ARGUMENT!
THEN MAYBE WE BETTER SPLIT AND LET YOU BE IN THE PAST FOR REAL!
HOW?
WHAT? BUT I LOVE YOU, CRISTINA!

LISTEN, I DON'T EVEN WANT TO LOOK AT YOU RIGHT NOW!
BUT I...
I THOUGHT WE HAD TALKED ABOUT THIS!
YOU SHOULD WAIT A MINUTE AND A HALF, A MINUTE AND A HALF BEFORE REACTING TO WHAT I DO!
IT'S NOT FAIR, YOU KNOW? IT'S SO HARD! YOU ALREADY KNOW EVERYTHING!
OHM
YOU'RE IN THE FUTURE... I DON'T KNOW... LIVING WITH YOU IS LIKE LIVING IN THE PAST.
MMMH... SO NICE...
?
SORRY MY LOVE. HERE, USE THE SKINNER, SEE IF YOU LIKE IT.
HAPPY BIRTHDAY.

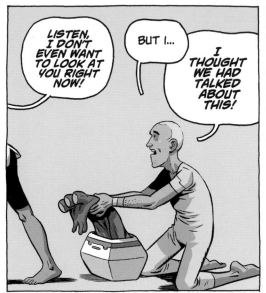

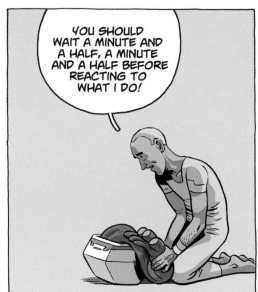

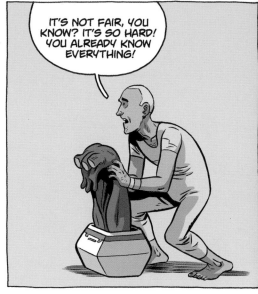

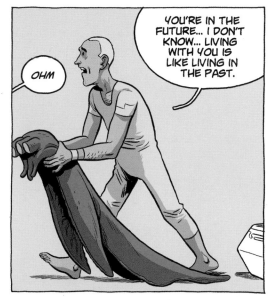

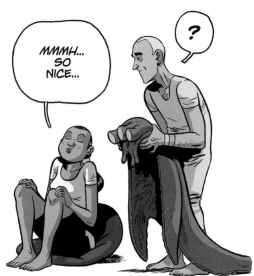

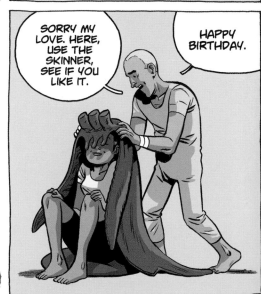

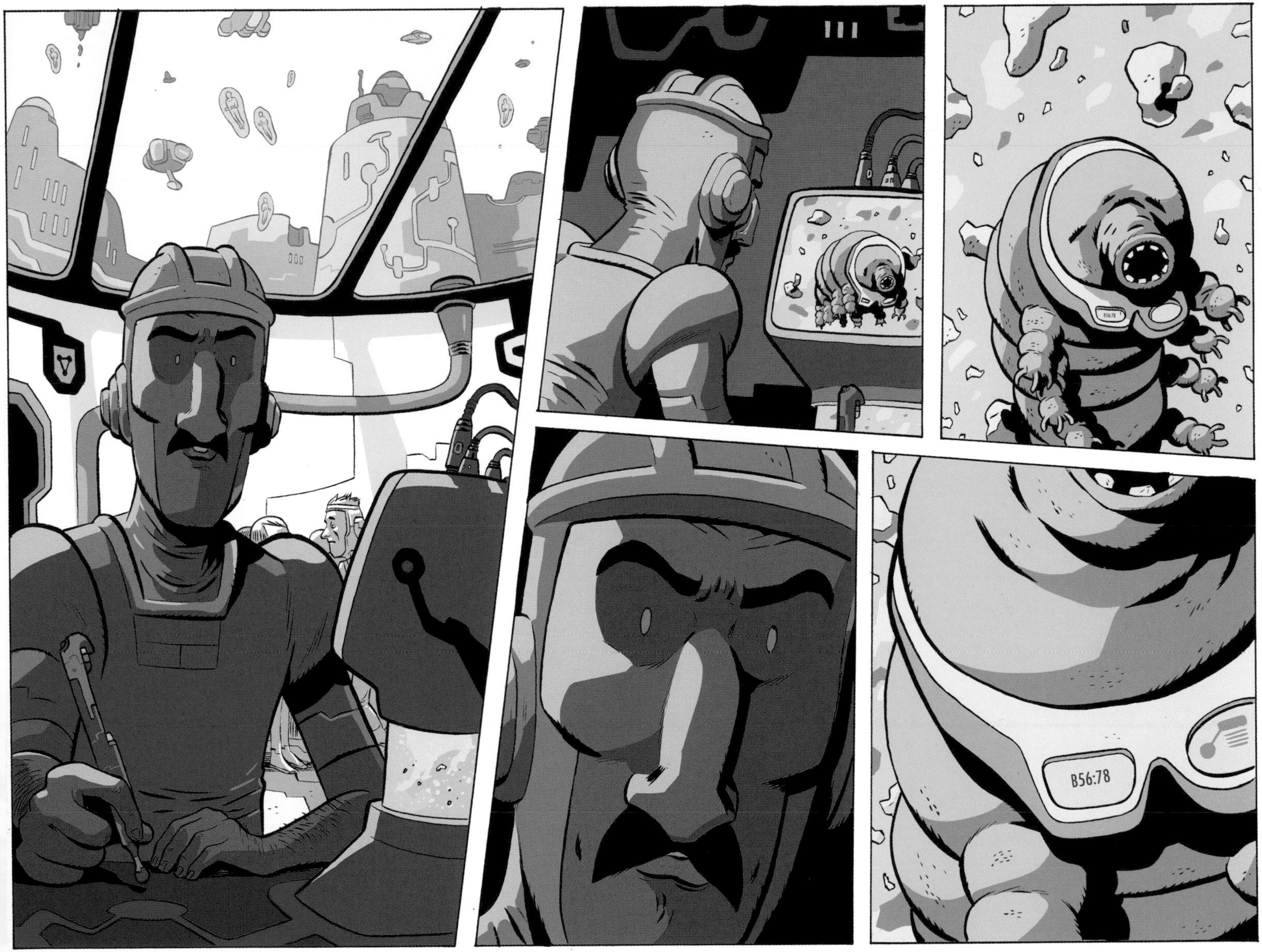
B56:78
B56:78

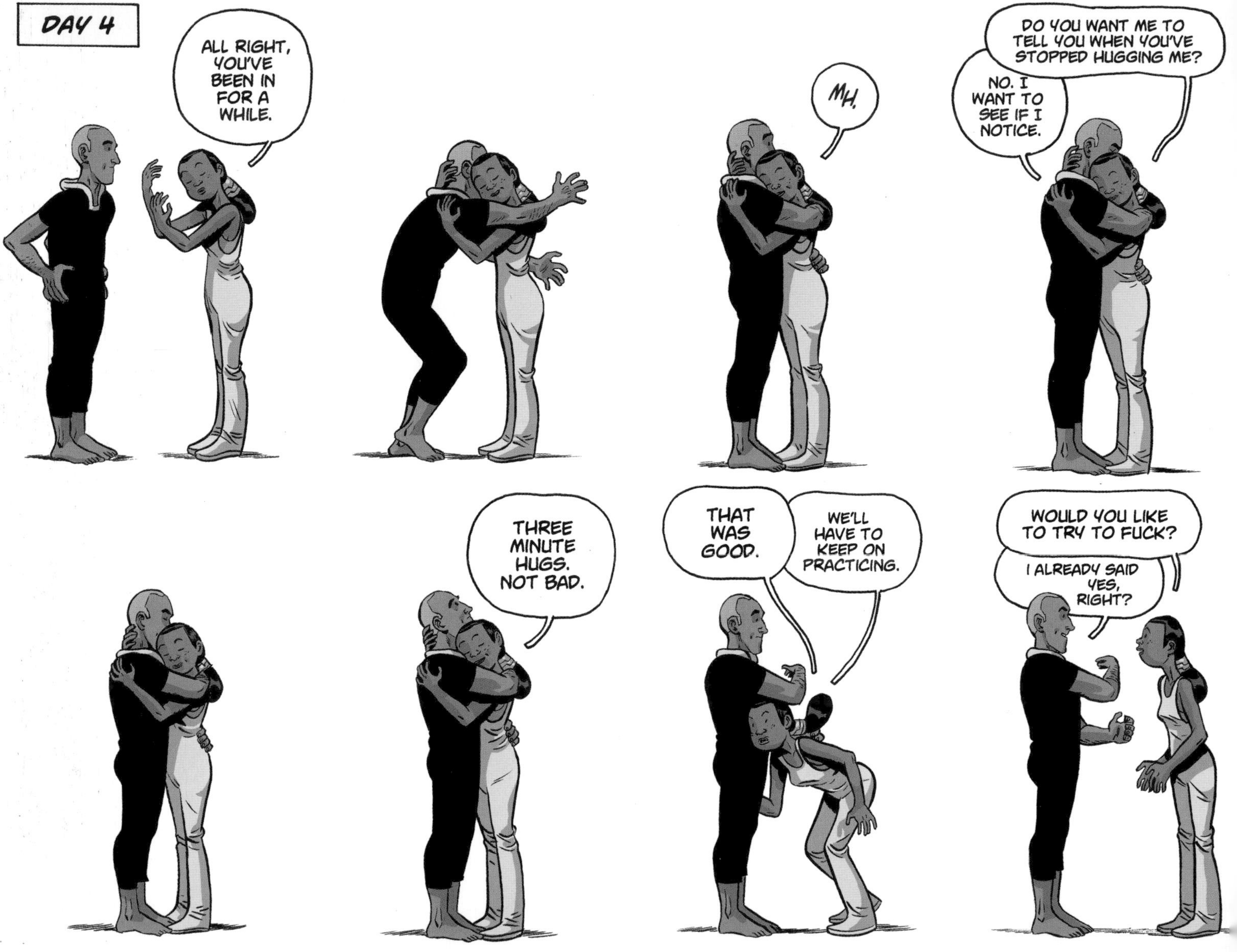
DAY 4
ALL RIGHT, YOU'VE BEEN IN FOR A WHILE.
MH.
DO YOU WANT ME TO TELL YOU WHEN YOU'VE STOPPED HUGGING ME?
NO. I WANT TO SEE IF I NOTICE.
THREE MINUTE HUGS. NOT BAD.
THAT WAS GOOD.
WE'LL HAVE TO KEEP ON PRACTICING.
WOULD YOU LIKE TO TRY TO FUCK?
I ALREADY SAID YES, RIGHT?

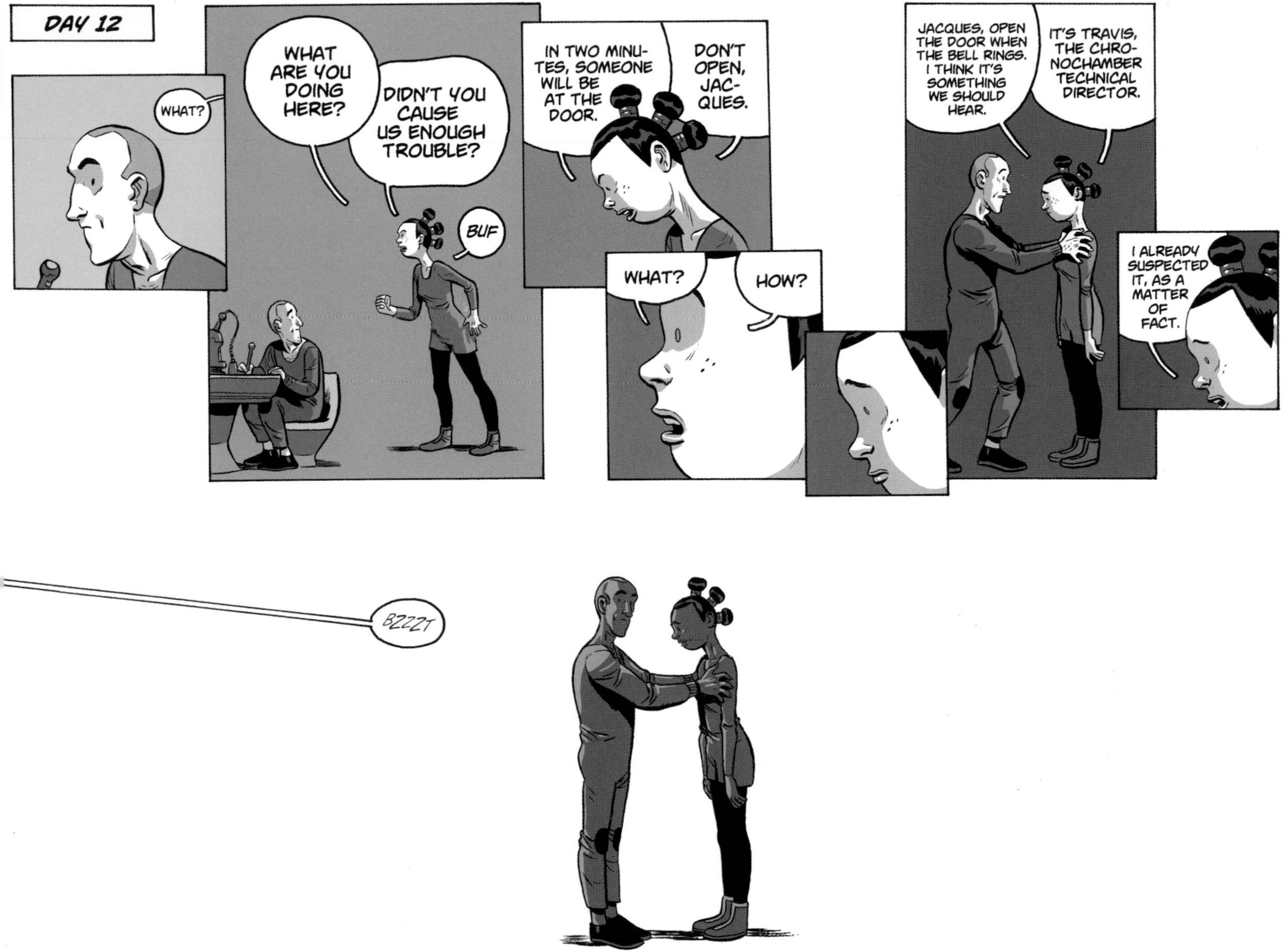
DAY 12
WHAT?
WHAT ARE YOU DOING HERE?
DIDN'T YOU CAUSE US ENOUGH TROUBLE?
BUF
IN TWO MINUTES, SOMEONE WILL BE AT THE DOOR.
DON'T OPEN, JACQUES.
WHAT?
HOW?
JACQUES, OPEN THE DOOR WHEN THE BELL RINGS. I THINK IT'S SOMETHING WE SHOULD HEAR.
IT'S TRAVIS, THE CHRONOCHAMBER TECHNICAL DIRECTOR.
I ALREADY SUSPECTED IT, AS A MATTER OF FACT.
BZZZT

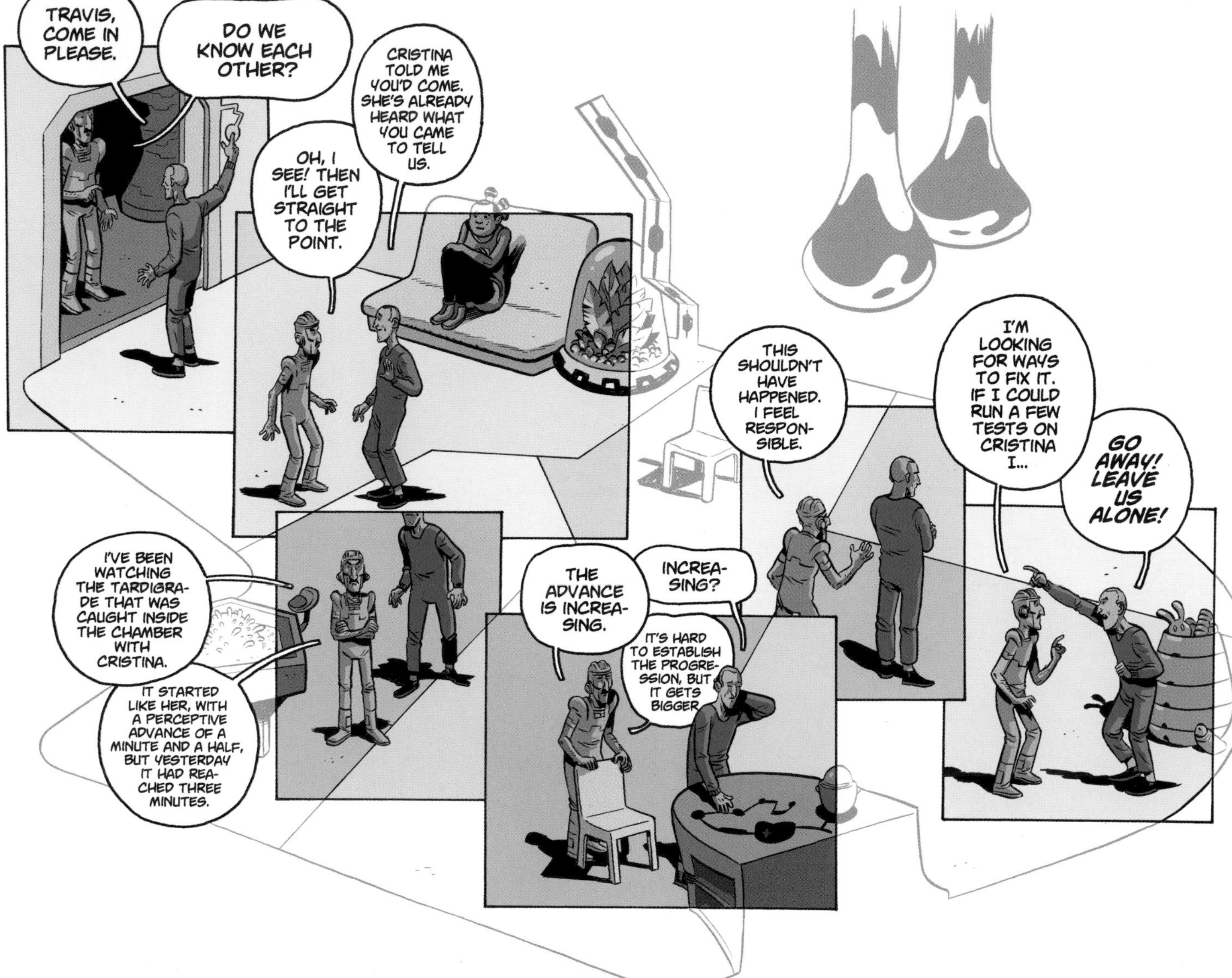
TRAVIS, COME IN PLEASE.
DO WE KNOW EACH OTHER?
CRISTINA TOLD ME YOU'D COME. SHE'S ALREADY HEARD WHAT YOU CAME TO TELL US.
OH, I SEE! THEN I'LL GET STRAIGHT TO THE POINT.
I'VE BEEN WATCHING THE TARDIGRA-DE THAT WAS CAUGHT INSIDE THE CHAMBER WITH CRISTINA.
IT STARTED LIKE HER, WITH A PERCEPTIVE ADVANCE OF A MINUTE AND A HALF, BUT YESTERDAY IT HAD REA-CHED THREE MINUTES.
THE ADVANCE IS INCREA-SING.
INCREA-SING?
IT'S HARD TO ESTABLISH THE PROGRE-SSION, BUT IT GETS BIGGER
THIS SHOULDN'T HAVE HAPPENED. I FEEL RESPON-SIBLE.
I'M LOOKING FOR WAYS TO FIX IT. IF I COULD RUN A FEW TESTS ON CRISTINA I...
GO AWAY! LEAVE US ALONE!

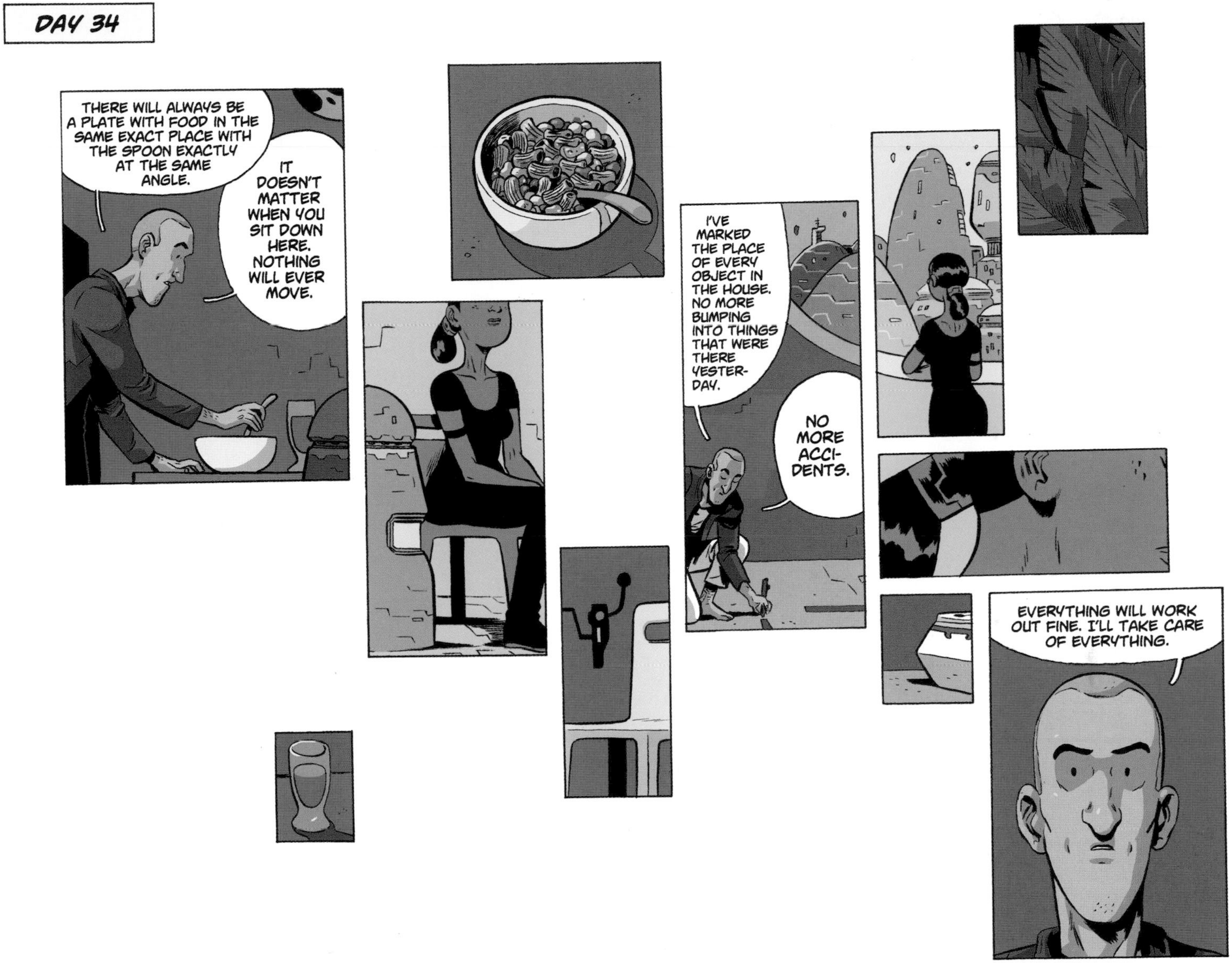
DAY 34
THERE WILL ALWAYS BE A PLATE WITH FOOD IN THE SAME EXACT PLACE WITH THE SPOON EXACTLY AT THE SAME ANGLE.
IT DOESN'T MATTER WHEN YOU SIT DOWN HERE. NOTHING WILL EVER MOVE.
I'VE MARKED THE PLACE OF EVERY OBJECT IN THE HOUSE. NO MORE BUMPING INTO THINGS THAT WERE THERE YESTER-DAY.
NO MORE ACCI-DENTS.
EVERYTHING WILL WORK OUT FINE. I'LL TAKE CARE OF EVERYTHING.

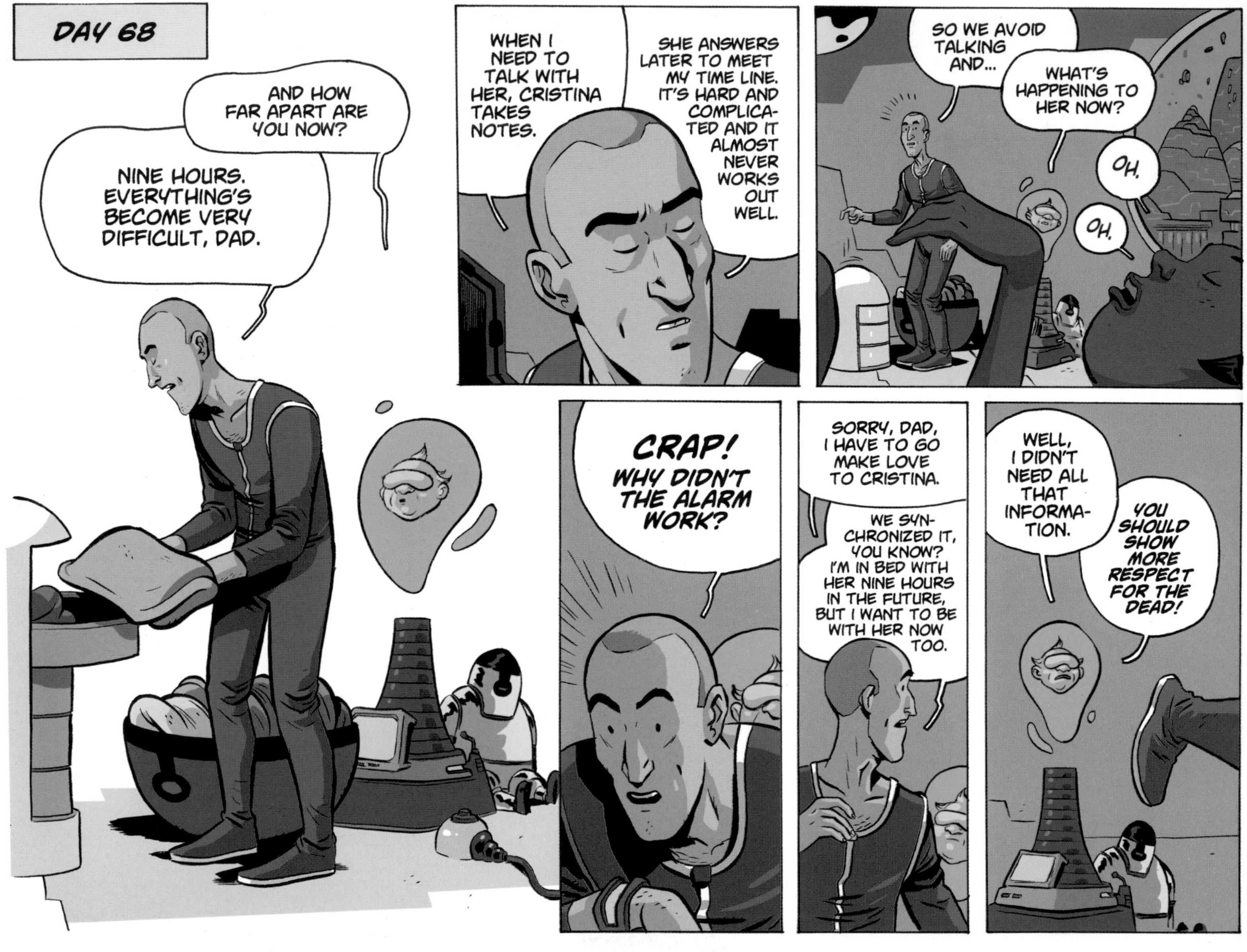
DAY 68
AND HOW FAR APART ARE YOU NOW?
NINE HOURS. EVERYTHING'S BECOME VERY DIFFICULT, DAD.
WHEN I NEED TO TALK WITH HER, CRISTINA TAKES NOTES.
SHE ANSWERS LATER TO MEET MY TIME LINE. IT'S HARD AND COMPLICATED AND IT ALMOST NEVER WORKS OUT WELL.
SO WE AVOID TALKING AND...
WHAT'S HAPPENING TO HER NOW?
OH.
OH.
CRAP! WHY DIDN'T THE ALARM WORK?
SORRY, DAD, I HAVE TO GO MAKE LOVE TO CRISTINA.
WE SYNCHRONIZED IT, YOU KNOW? I'M IN BED WITH HER NINE HOURS IN THE FUTURE, BUT I WANT TO BE WITH HER NOW TOO.
WELL, I DIDN'T NEED ALL THAT INFORMATION.
YOU SHOULD SHOW MORE RESPECT FOR THE DEAD!

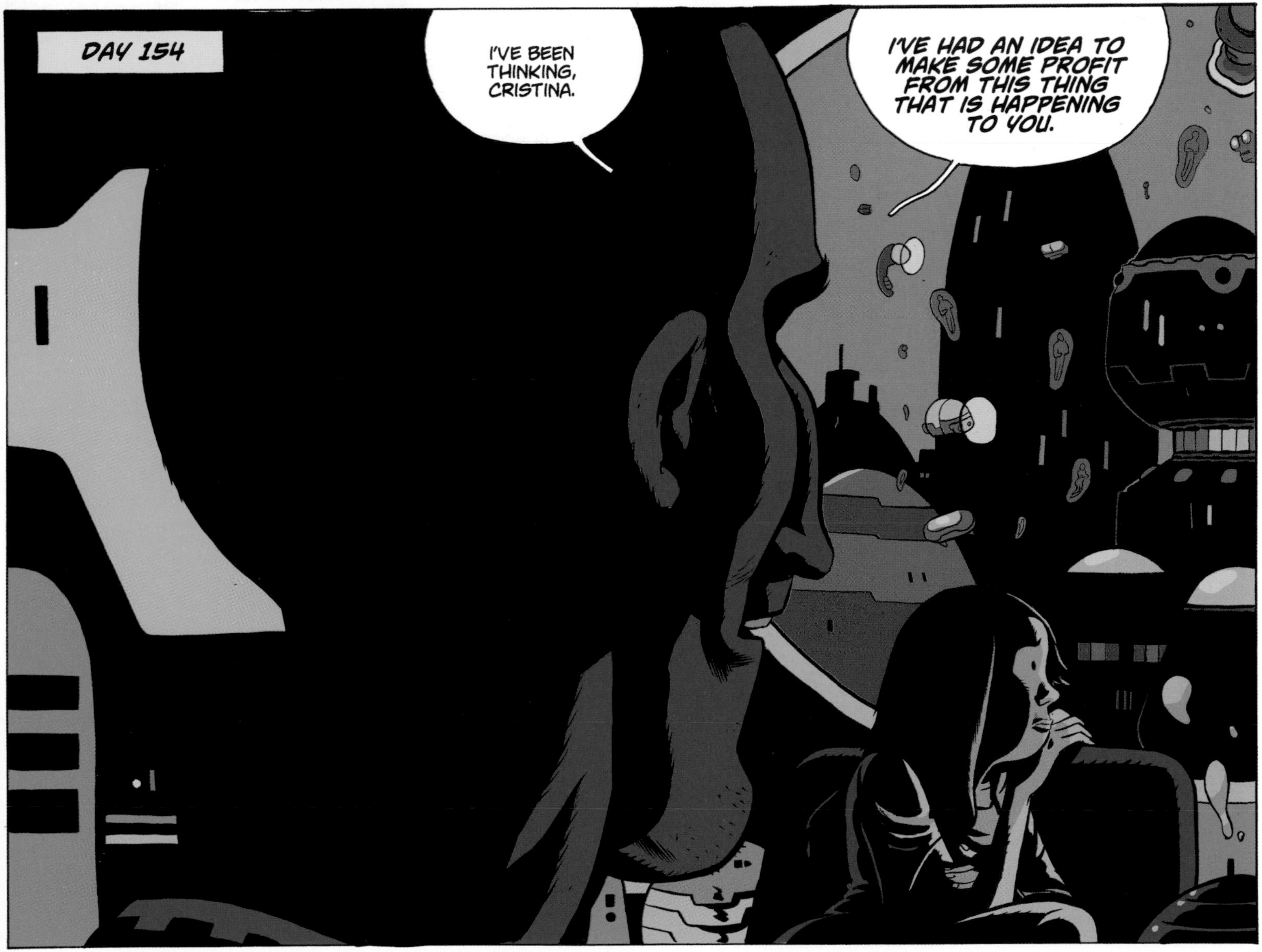
DAY 154
I'VE BEEN THINKING, CRISTINA.
I'VE HAD AN IDEA TO MAKE SOME PROFIT FROM THIS THING THAT IS HAPPENING TO YOU.

PERFECT, MISTER PIMPER. YOUR PAYMENT HAS BEEN ACCEPTED.

YOU CAN ASK CRISTINA ABOUT ANYTHING THAT IS GOING TO HAPPEN IN THE NEXT DAY AND A HALF.

WELL I, EHM.

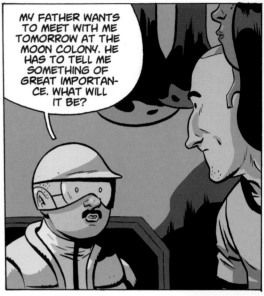

MY FATHER WANTS TO MEET WITH ME TOMORROW AT THE MOON COLONY. HE HAS TO TELL ME SOMETHING OF GREAT IMPORTANCE. WHAT WILL IT BE?

HELLO, MISTER PIMPER. I'M TALKING TO YOU FROM A DAY AND A HALF IN THE FUTURE. I JUST GOT A MESSAGE FROM YOU STATING THAT YOU HAD VISITED YOUR FATHER ON THE MOON.

YOU ALSO TOLD ME THAT WHAT YOUR FATHER HAD TO TELL YOU, YOU DISCOVERED IT YOURSELF TWENTY YEARS AGO.

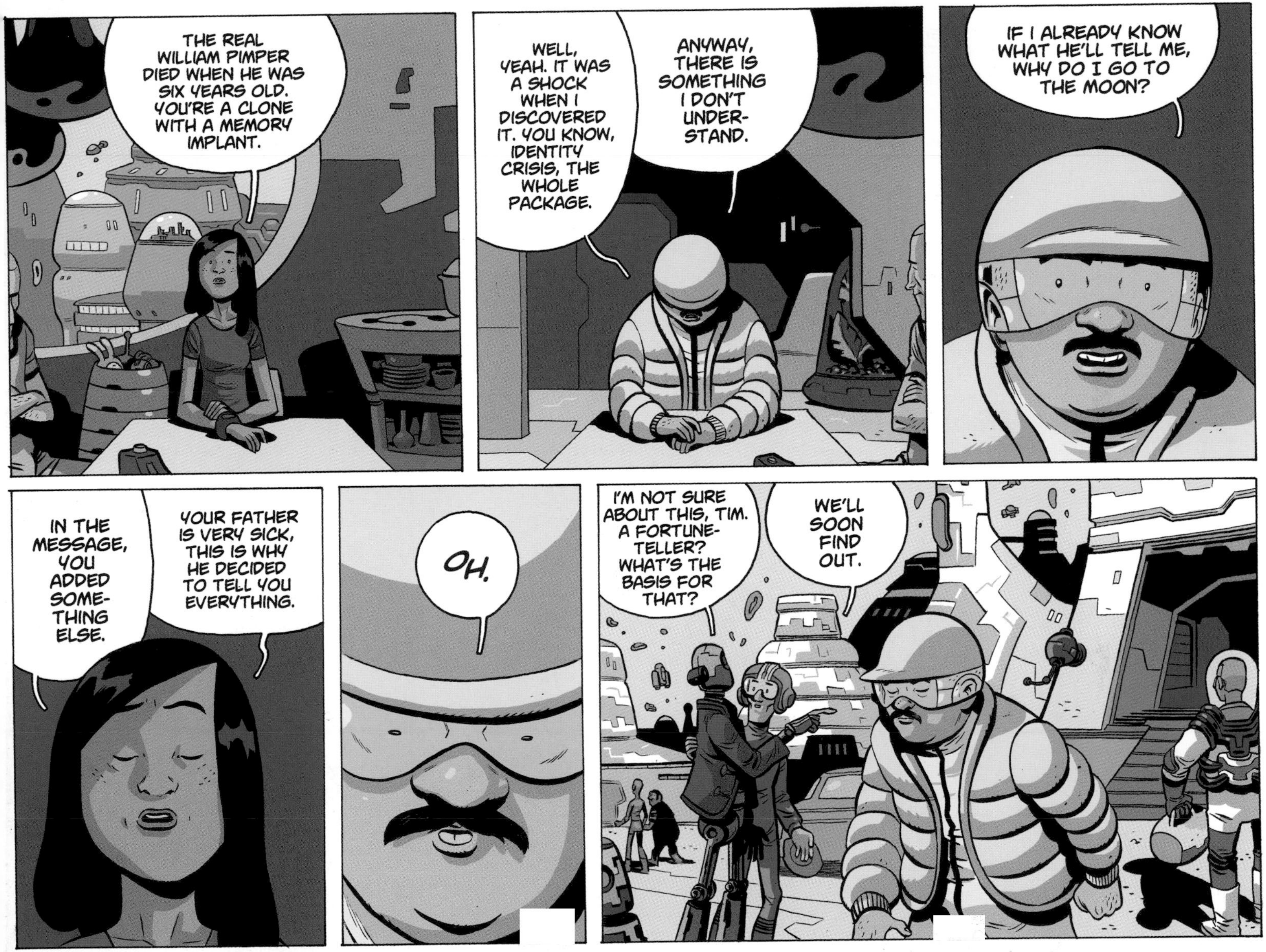
THE REAL WILLIAM PIMPER DIED WHEN HE WAS SIX YEARS OLD. YOU'RE A CLONE WITH A MEMORY IMPLANT.
WELL, YEAH. IT WAS A SHOCK WHEN I DISCOVERED IT. YOU KNOW, IDENTITY CRISIS, THE WHOLE PACKAGE.
ANYWAY, THERE IS SOMETHING I DON'T UNDER-STAND.
IF I ALREADY KNOW WHAT HE'LL TELL ME, WHY DO I GO TO THE MOON?
IN THE MESSAGE, YOU ADDED SOME-THING ELSE.
YOUR FATHER IS VERY SICK, THIS IS WHY HE DECIDED TO TELL YOU EVERYTHING.
OH.
I'M NOT SURE ABOUT THIS, TIM. A FORTUNE-TELLER? WHAT'S THE BASIS FOR THAT?
WE'LL SOON FIND OUT.

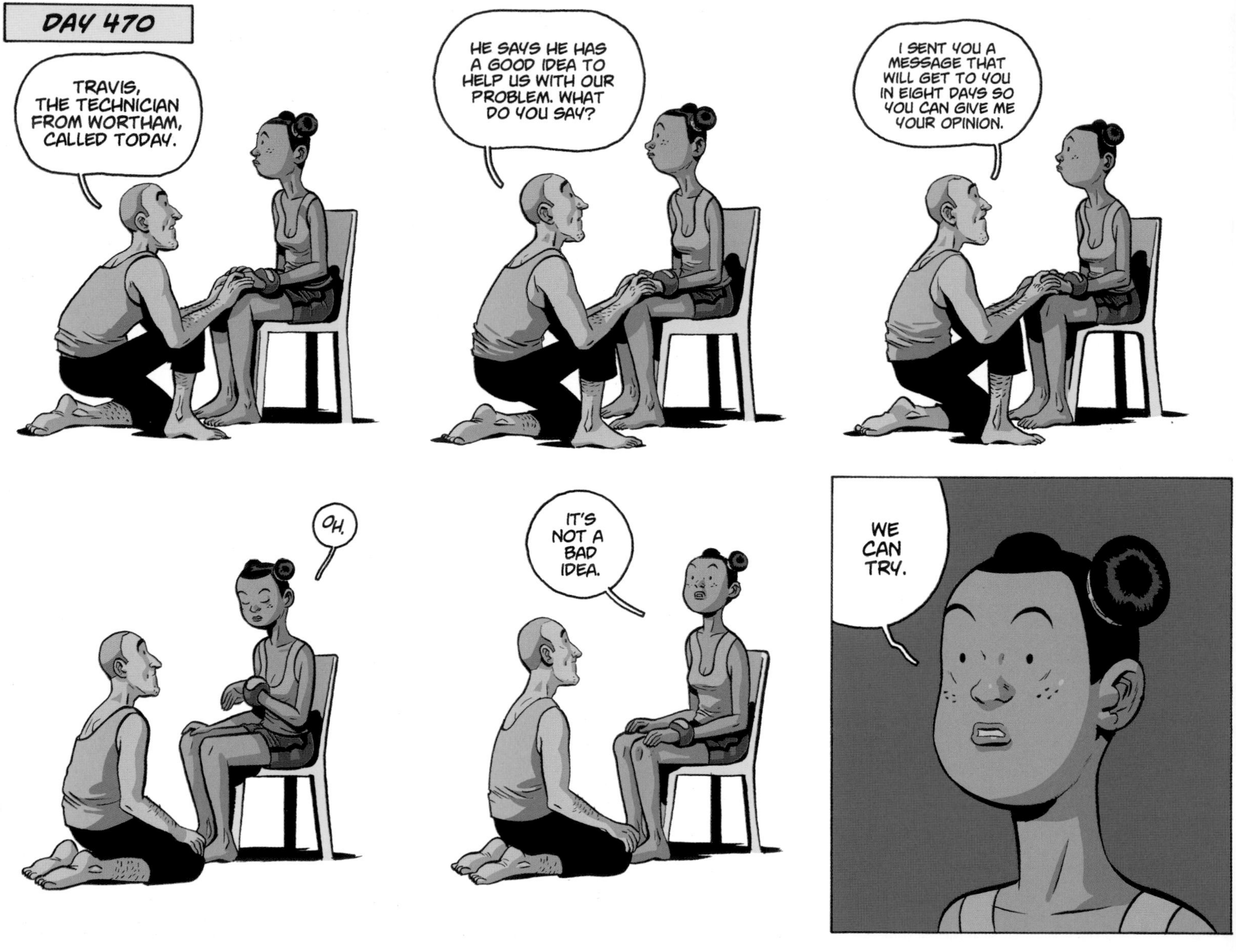
DAY 470
TRAVIS, THE TECHNICIAN FROM WORTHAM, CALLED TODAY.
HE SAYS HE HAS A GOOD IDEA TO HELP US WITH OUR PROBLEM. WHAT DO YOU SAY?
I SENT YOU A MESSAGE THAT WILL GET TO YOU IN EIGHT DAYS SO YOU CAN GIVE ME YOUR OPINION.
OH.
IT'S NOT A BAD IDEA.
WE CAN TRY.

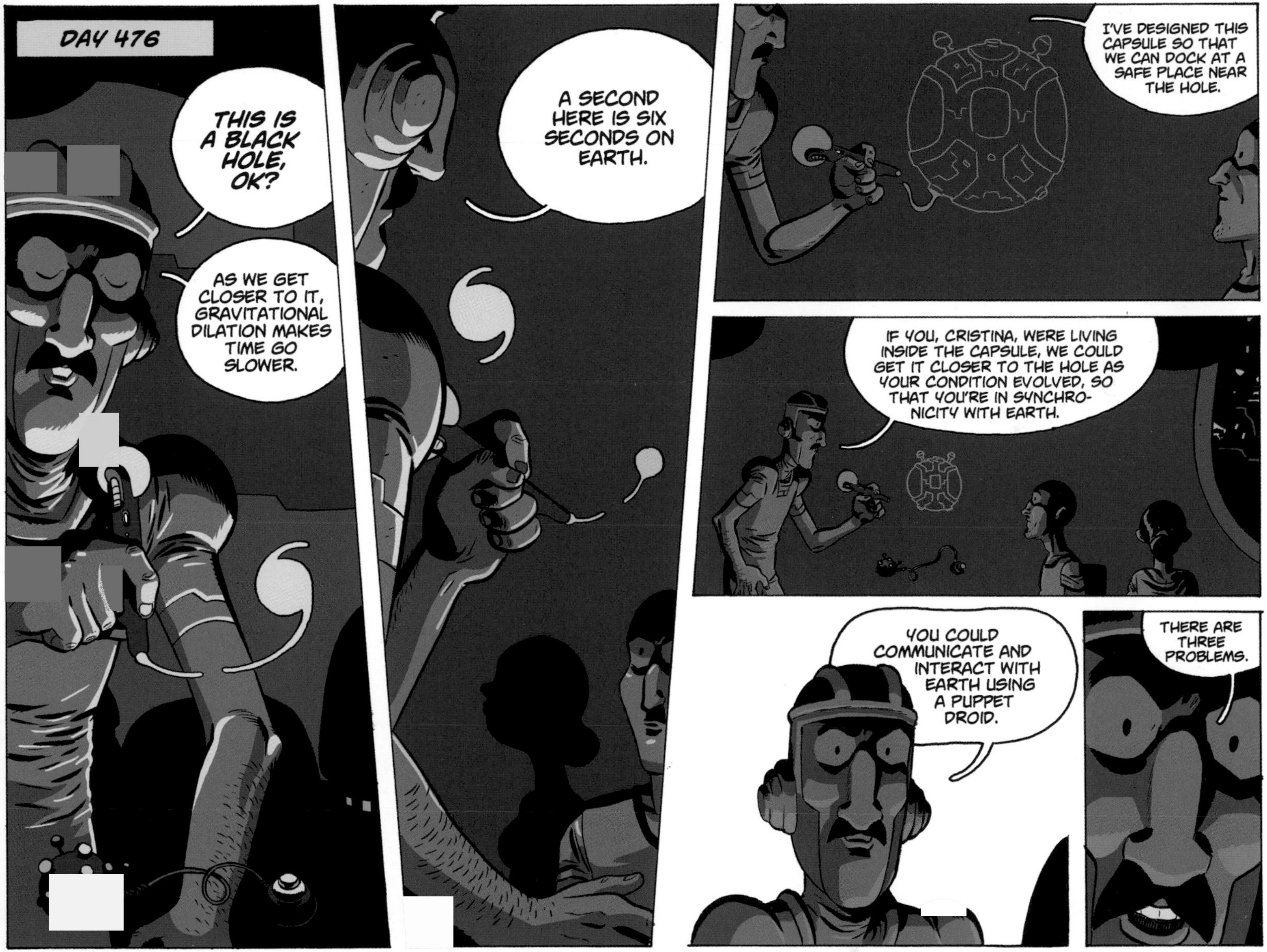
DAY 476
THIS IS A BLACK HOLE, OK?
AS WE GET CLOSER TO IT, GRAVITATIONAL DILATION MAKES TIME GO SLOWER.
A SECOND HERE IS SIX SECONDS ON EARTH.
I'VE DESIGNED THIS CAPSULE SO THAT WE CAN DOCK AT A SAFE PLACE NEAR THE HOLE.
IF YOU, CRISTINA, WERE LIVING INSIDE THE CAPSULE, WE COULD GET IT CLOSER TO THE HOLE AS YOUR CONDITION EVOLVED, SO THAT YOU'RE IN SYNCHRO-NICITY WITH EARTH.
YOU COULD COMMUNICATE AND INTERACT WITH EARTH USING A PUPPET DROID.
THERE ARE THREE PROBLEMS.

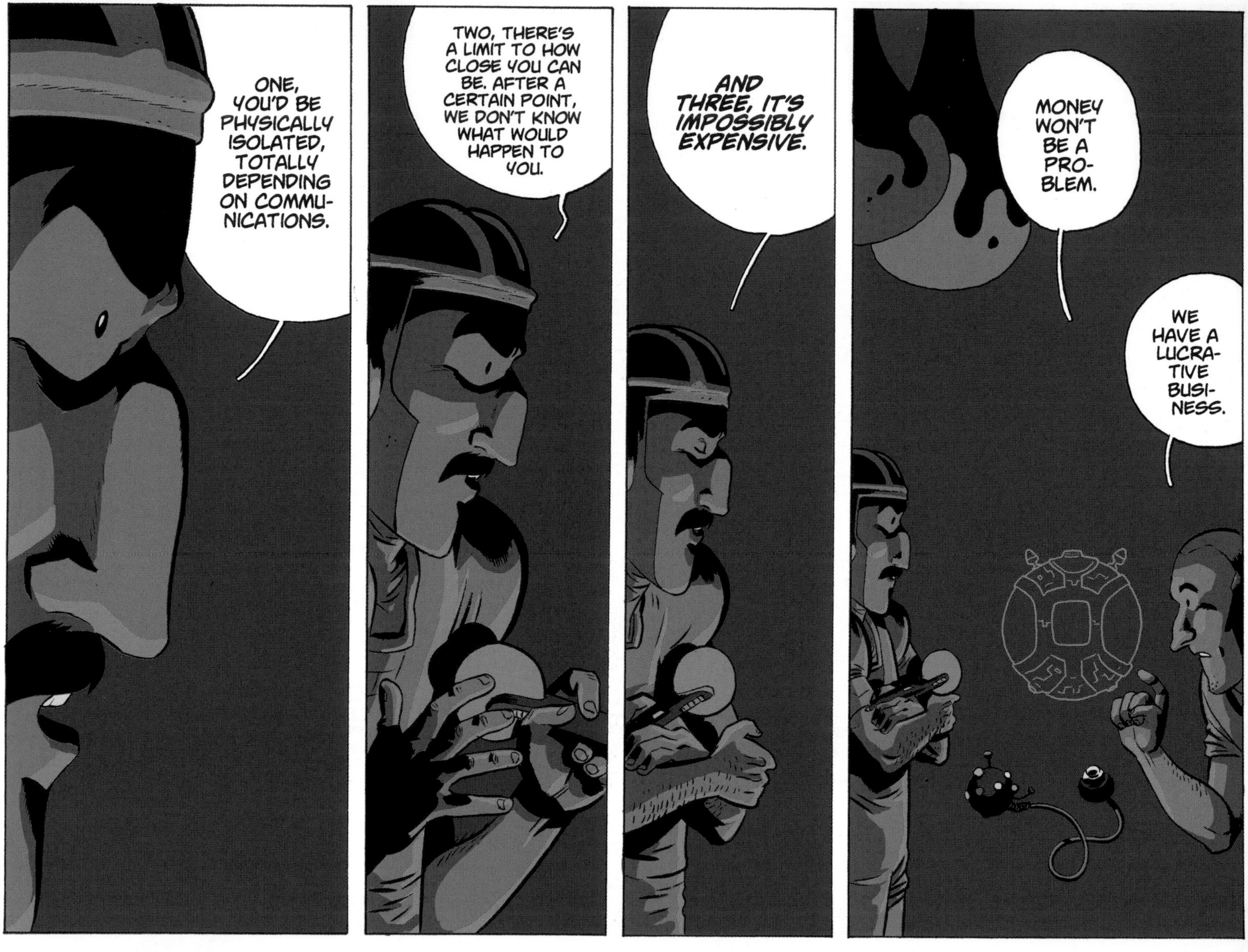
ONE, YOU'D BE PHYSICALLY ISOLATED, TOTALLY DEPENDING ON COMMU-NICATIONS.
TWO, THERE'S A LIMIT TO HOW CLOSE YOU CAN BE. AFTER A CERTAIN POINT, WE DON'T KNOW WHAT WOULD HAPPEN TO YOU.
AND THREE, IT'S IMPOSSIBLY EXPENSIVE.
MONEY WON'T BE A PRO-BLEM.
WE HAVE A LUCRA-TIVE BUSI-NESS.

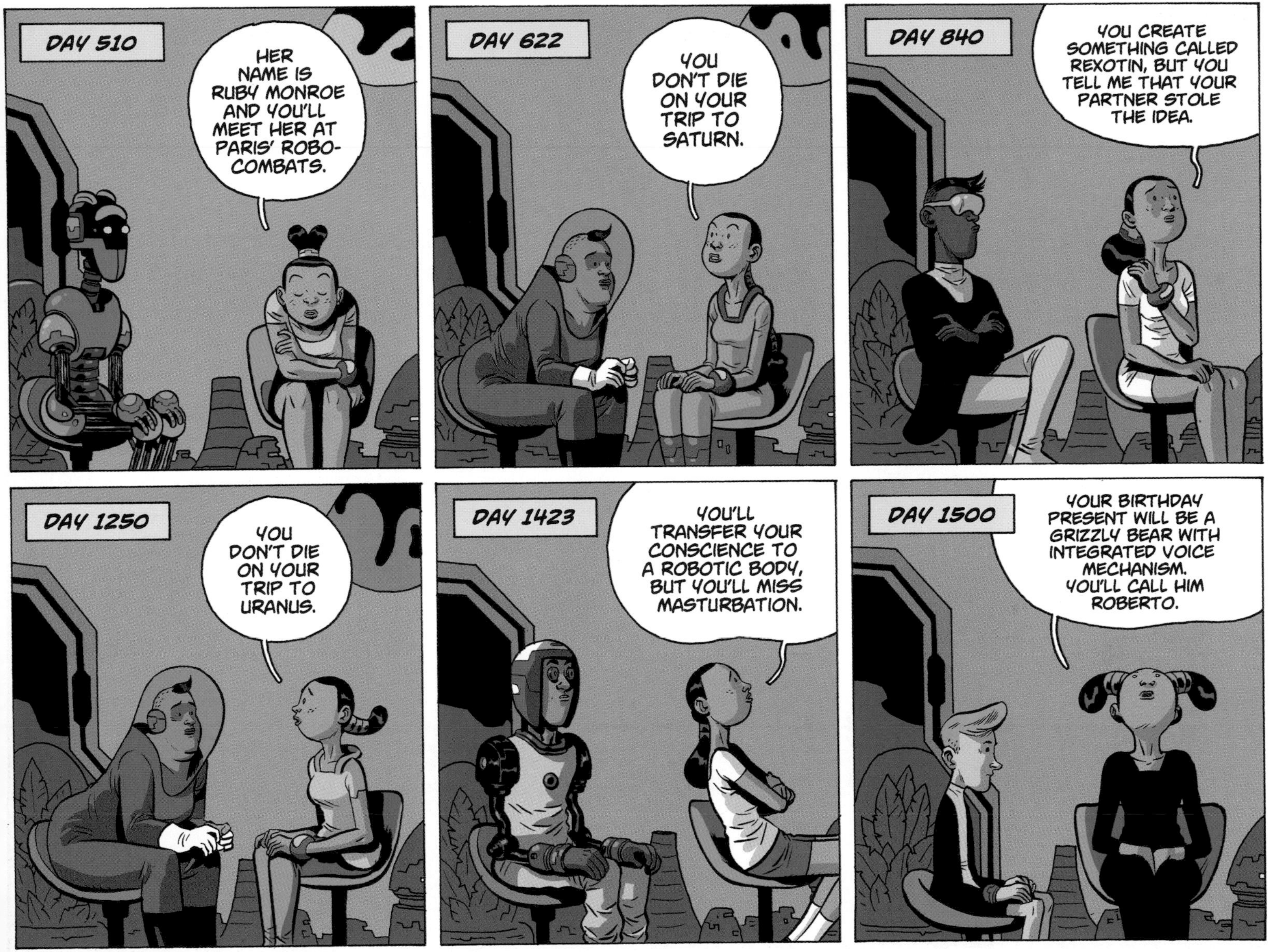
DAY 510
HER NAME IS RUBY MONROE AND YOU'LL MEET HER AT PARIS' ROBO-COMBATS.
DAY 622
YOU DON'T DIE ON YOUR TRIP TO SATURN.
DAY 840
YOU CREATE SOMETHING CALLED REXOTIN, BUT YOU TELL ME THAT YOUR PARTNER STOLE THE IDEA.
DAY 1250
YOU DON'T DIE ON YOUR TRIP TO URANUS.
DAY 1423
YOU'LL TRANSFER YOUR CONSCIENCE TO A ROBOTIC BODY, BUT YOU'LL MISS MASTURBATION.
DAY 1500
YOUR BIRTHDAY PRESENT WILL BE A GRIZZLY BEAR WITH INTEGRATED VOICE MECHANISM. YOU'LL CALL HIM ROBERTO.

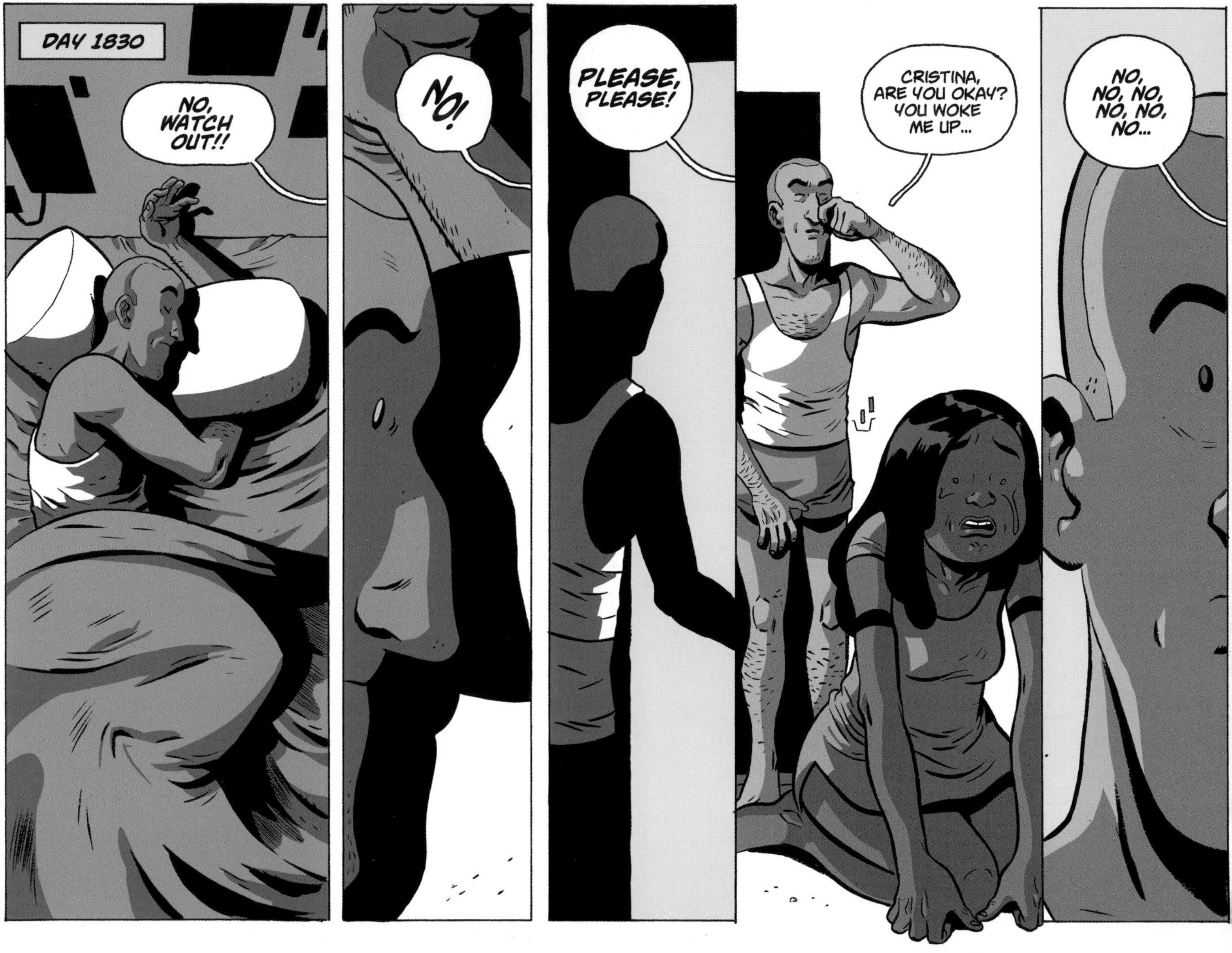
DAY 1830
NO, WATCH OUT!!
NO!
PLEASE, PLEASE!
CRISTINA, ARE YOU OKAY? YOU WOKE ME UP...
NO, NO, NO, NO, NO, NO...

DAY 1831

YESTERDAY YOU WERE VERY UPSET. CAN YOU MAKE A NOTE TO TELL ME WHY YOU WERE... WILL YOU BE SCREAMING ONE YEAR AND EIGHT MONTHS FROM NOW?

HM.

HMMM.

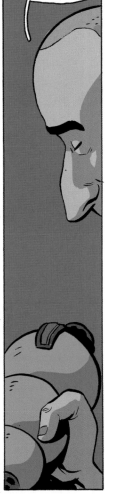

I TOLD YOU TO LET ME KNOW BEFORE YOU PUT ON THE SKINNER.

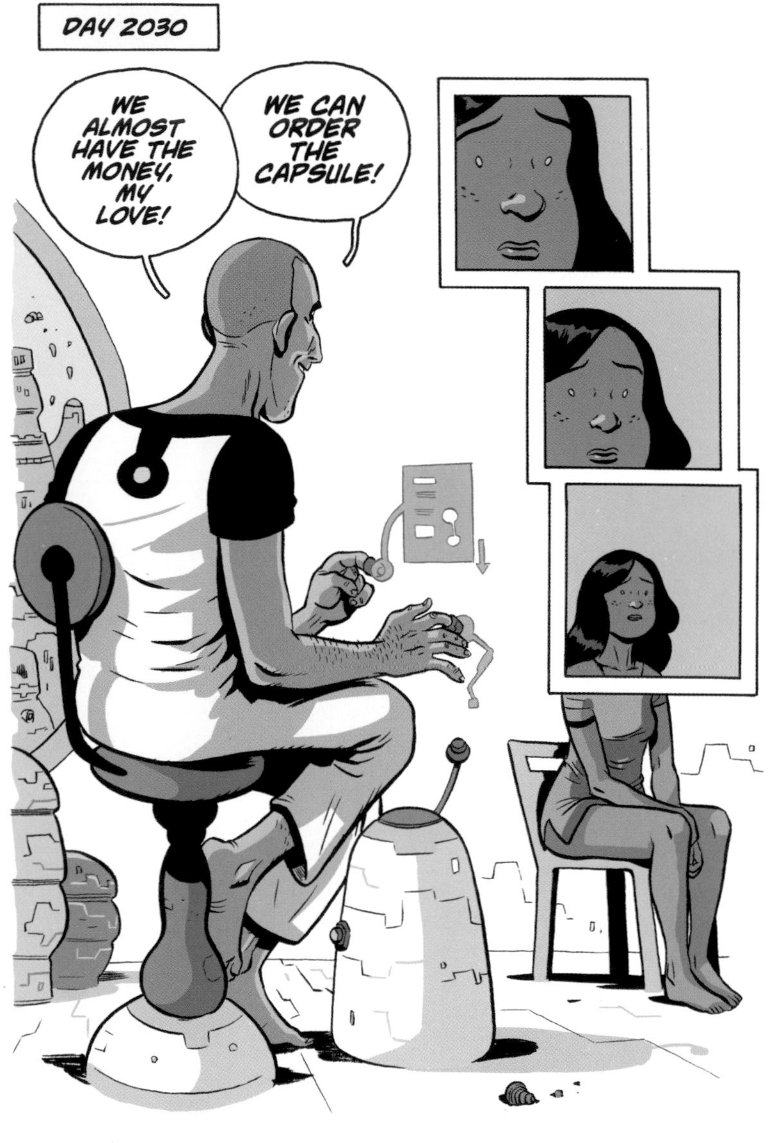
DAY 2030
WE ALMOST HAVE THE MONEY, MY LOVE!
WE CAN ORDER THE CAPSULE!

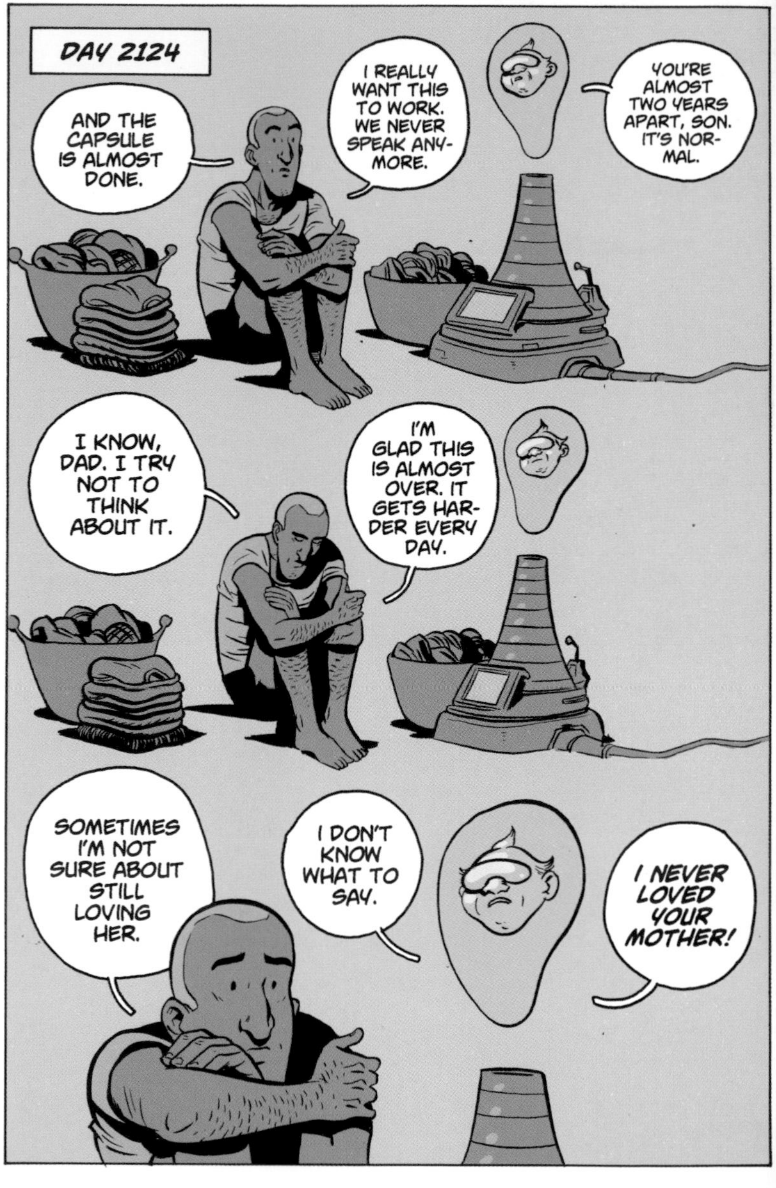
DAY 2124
AND THE CAPSULE IS ALMOST DONE.
I REALLY WANT THIS TO WORK. WE NEVER SPEAK ANY-MORE.
YOU'RE ALMOST TWO YEARS APART, SON. IT'S NOR-MAL.
I KNOW, DAD. I TRY NOT TO THINK ABOUT IT.
I'M GLAD THIS IS ALMOST OVER. IT GETS HAR-DER EVERY DAY.
SOMETIMES I'M NOT SURE ABOUT STILL LOVING HER.
I DON'T KNOW WHAT TO SAY.
I NEVER LOVED YOUR MOTHER!

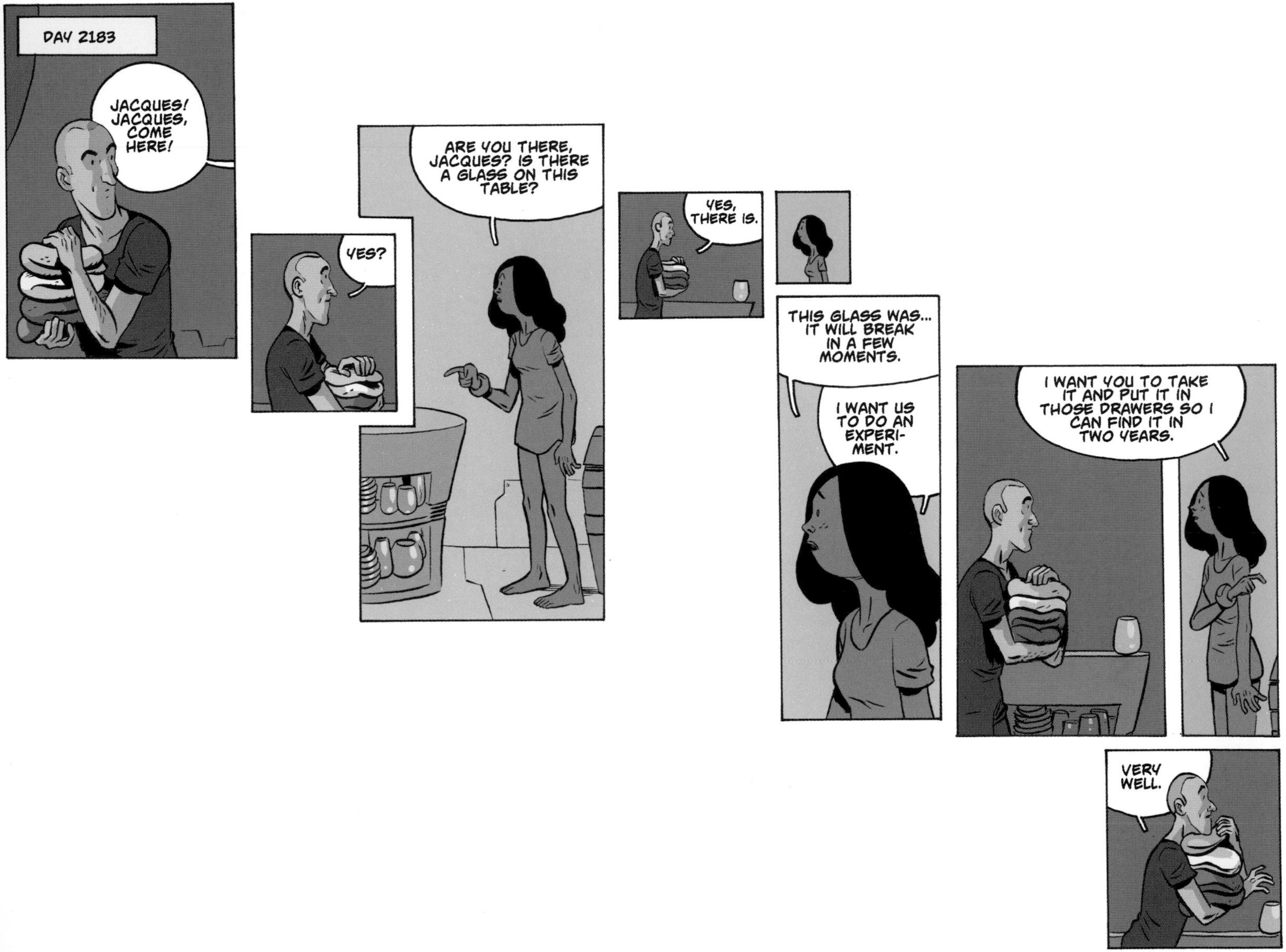
DAY 2183
JACQUES! JACQUES, COME HERE!
YES?
ARE YOU THERE, JACQUES? IS THERE A GLASS ON THIS TABLE?
YES, THERE IS.
THIS GLASS WAS... IT WILL BREAK IN A FEW MOMENTS.
I WANT US TO DO AN EXPERIMENT.
I WANT YOU TO TAKE IT AND PUT IT IN THOSE DRAWERS SO I CAN FIND IT IN TWO YEARS.
VERY WELL.

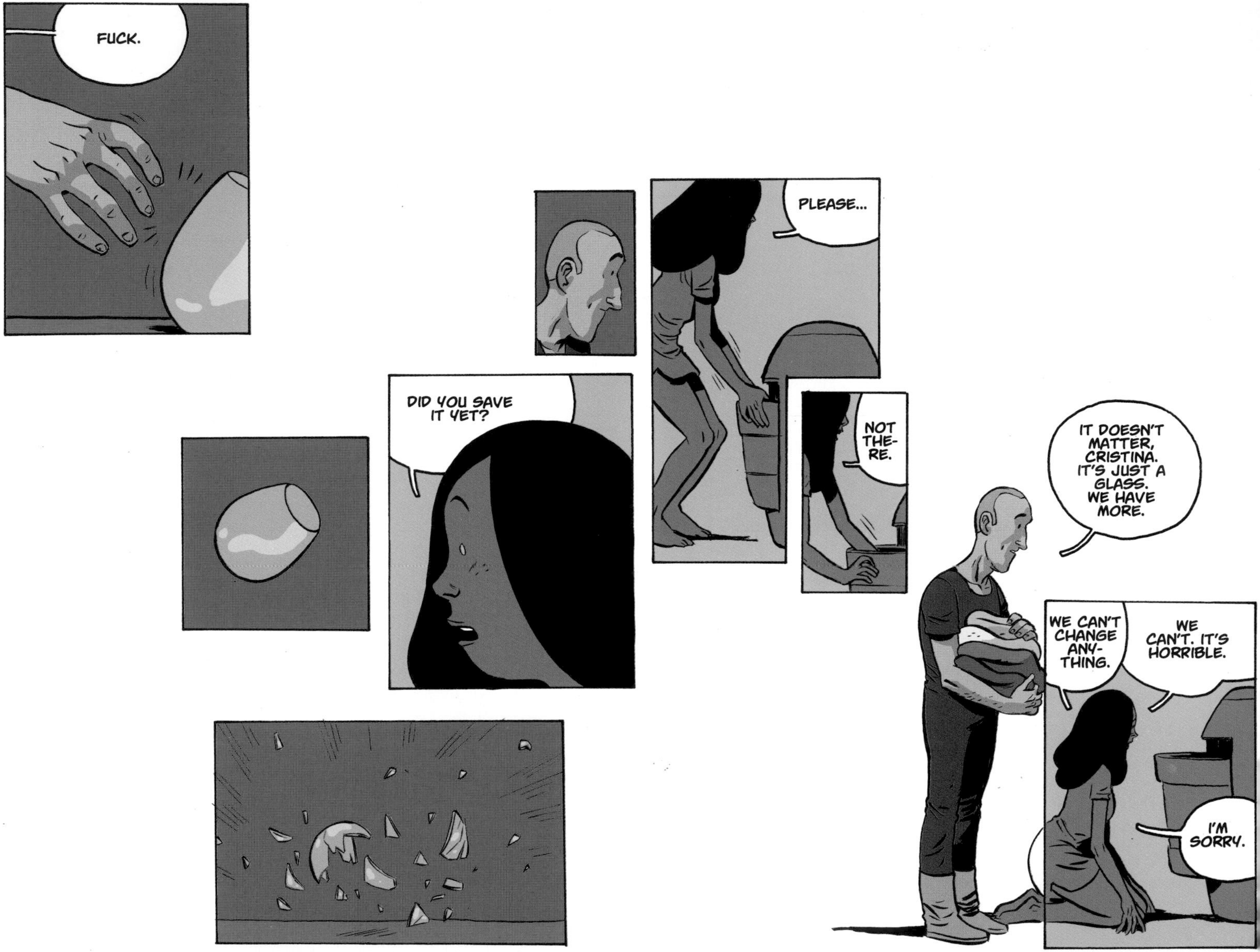
FUCK.
DID YOU SAVE IT YET?
PLEASE...
NOT THERE.
IT DOESN'T MATTER, CRISTINA. IT'S JUST A GLASS. WE HAVE MORE.
WE CAN'T CHANGE ANYTHING.
WE CAN'T. IT'S HORRIBLE.
I'M SORRY.

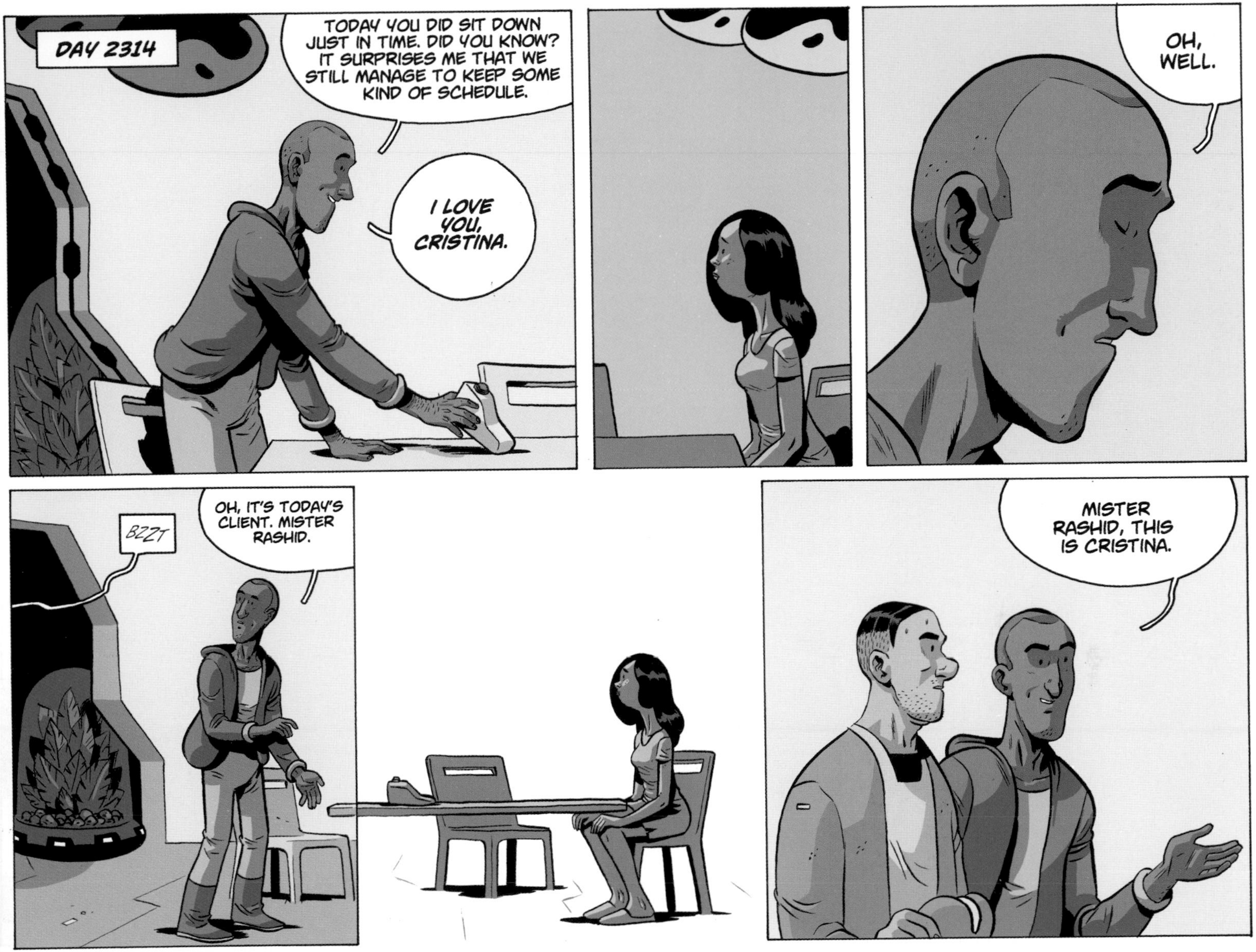
DAY 2314
TODAY YOU DID SIT DOWN JUST IN TIME. DID YOU KNOW? IT SURPRISES ME THAT WE STILL MANAGE TO KEEP SOME KIND OF SCHEDULE.
I LOVE YOU, CRISTINA.
OH, WELL.
BZZT
OH, IT'S TODAY'S CLIENT. MISTER RASHID.
MISTER RASHID, THIS IS CRISTINA.

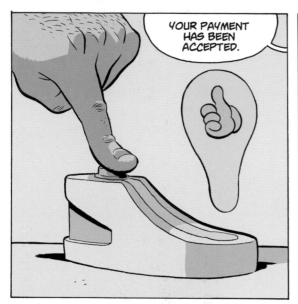

YOUR PAYMENT HAS BEEN ACCEPTED.

YOU CAN ASK CRISTINA ANYTHING ABOUT THE NEXT TWO YEARS.

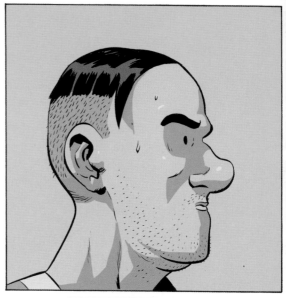

AM I GOING TO JAIL?

OH GOD, I... I'M AWARE I CAN'T CHANGE WHAT HAPPENED THAT DAY, WHAT'S GOING TO HAPPEN NOW... BUT I HAVE TO TRY.

YOU CARRY AN ALPHA GUN INSIDE YOUR JACKET.

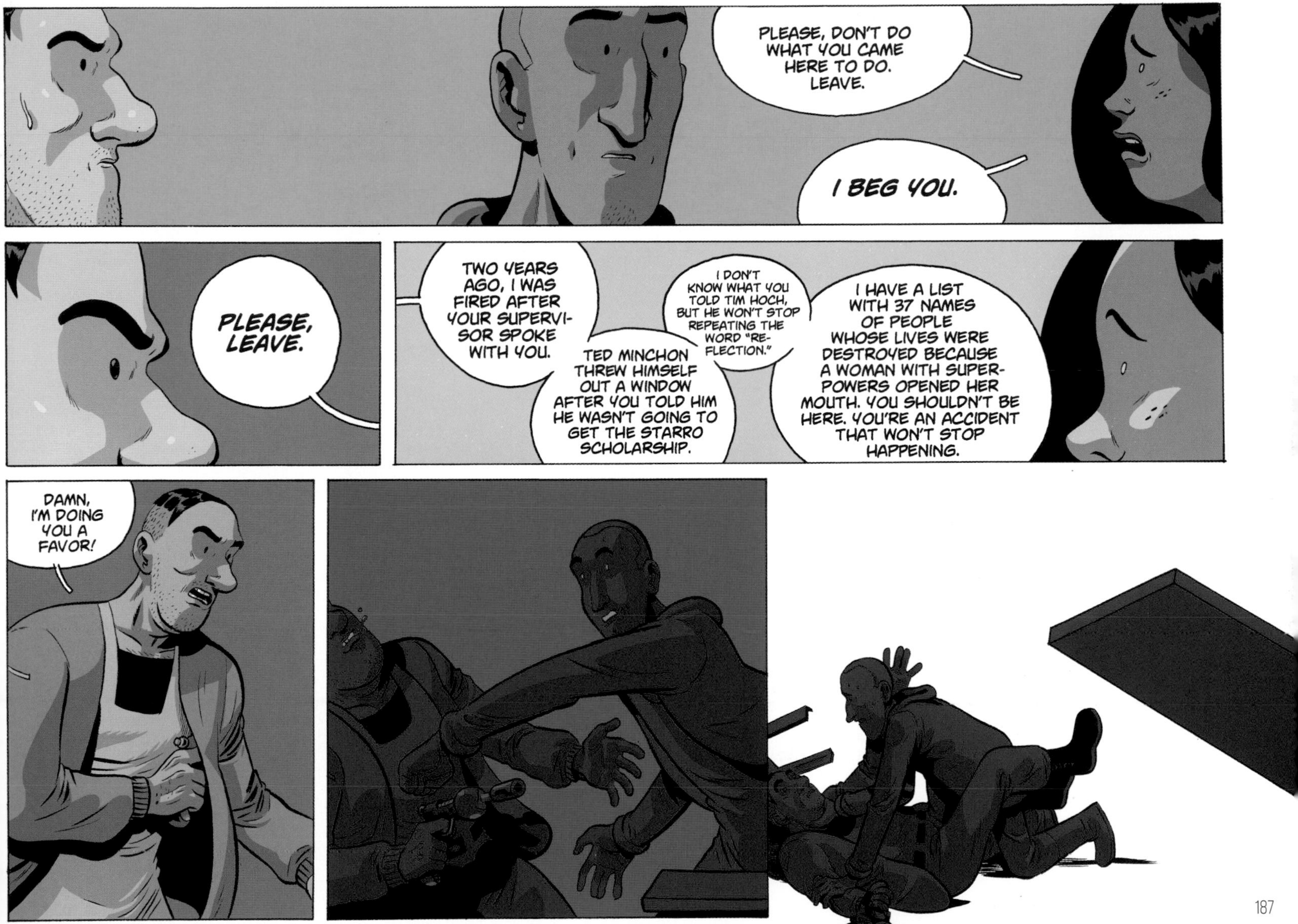
PLEASE, DON'T DO WHAT YOU CAME HERE TO DO. LEAVE.
I BEG YOU.
PLEASE, LEAVE.
TWO YEARS AGO, I WAS FIRED AFTER YOUR SUPERVISOR SPOKE WITH YOU.
TED MINCHON THREW HIMSELF OUT A WINDOW AFTER YOU TOLD HIM HE WASN'T GOING TO GET THE STARRO SCHOLARSHIP.
I DON'T KNOW WHAT YOU TOLD TIM HOCH, BUT HE WON'T STOP REPEATING THE WORD "REFLECTION."
I HAVE A LIST WITH 37 NAMES OF PEOPLE WHOSE LIVES WERE DESTROYED BECAUSE A WOMAN WITH SUPERPOWERS OPENED HER MOUTH. YOU SHOULDN'T BE HERE. YOU'RE AN ACCIDENT THAT WON'T STOP HAPPENING.
DAMN, I'M DOING YOU A FAVOR!

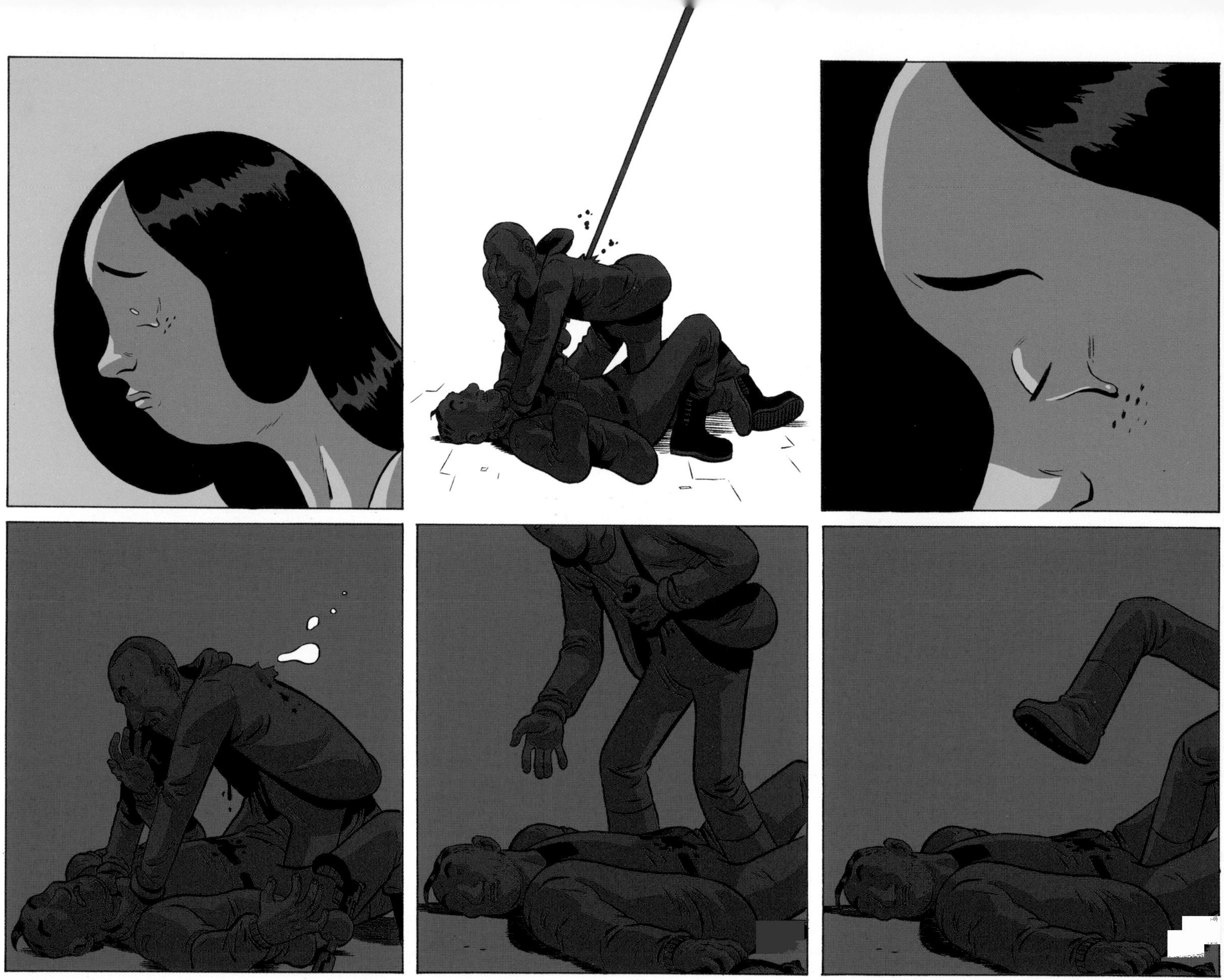

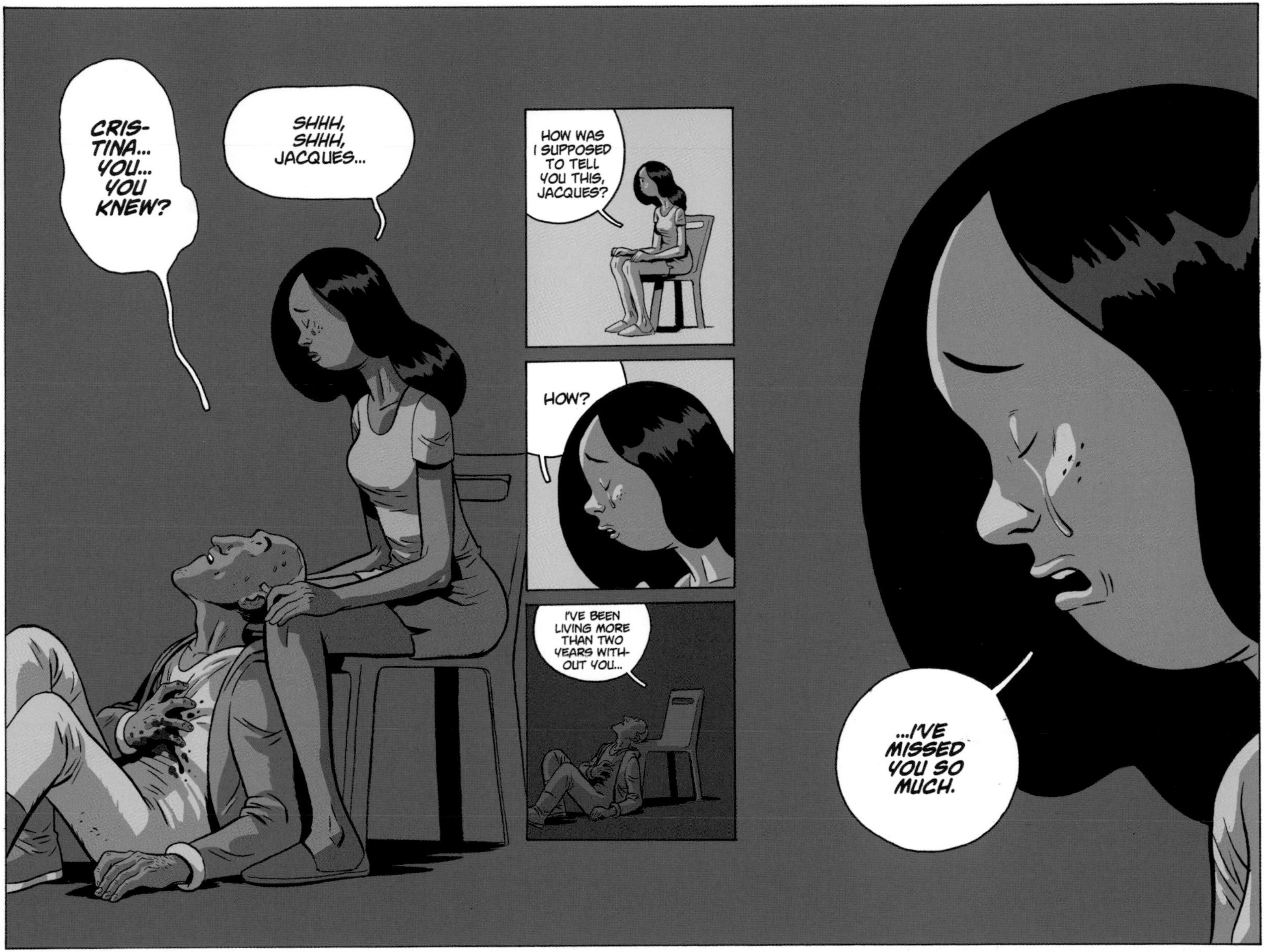
CRIS-TINA... YOU... YOU KNEW?
SHHH, SHHH, JACQUES...
HOW WAS I SUPPOSED TO TELL YOU THIS, JACQUES?
HOW?
I'VE BEEN LIVING MORE THAN TWO YEARS WITH-OUT YOU...
...I'VE MISSED YOU SO MUCH.

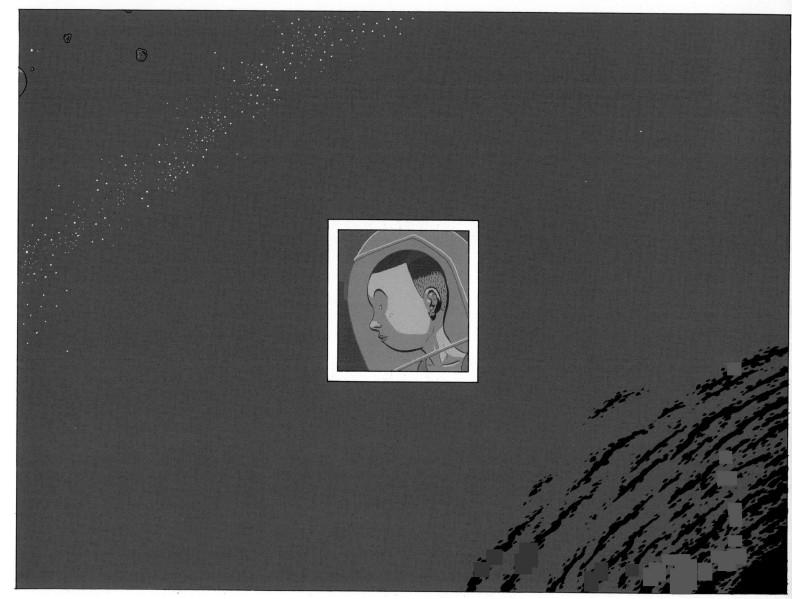

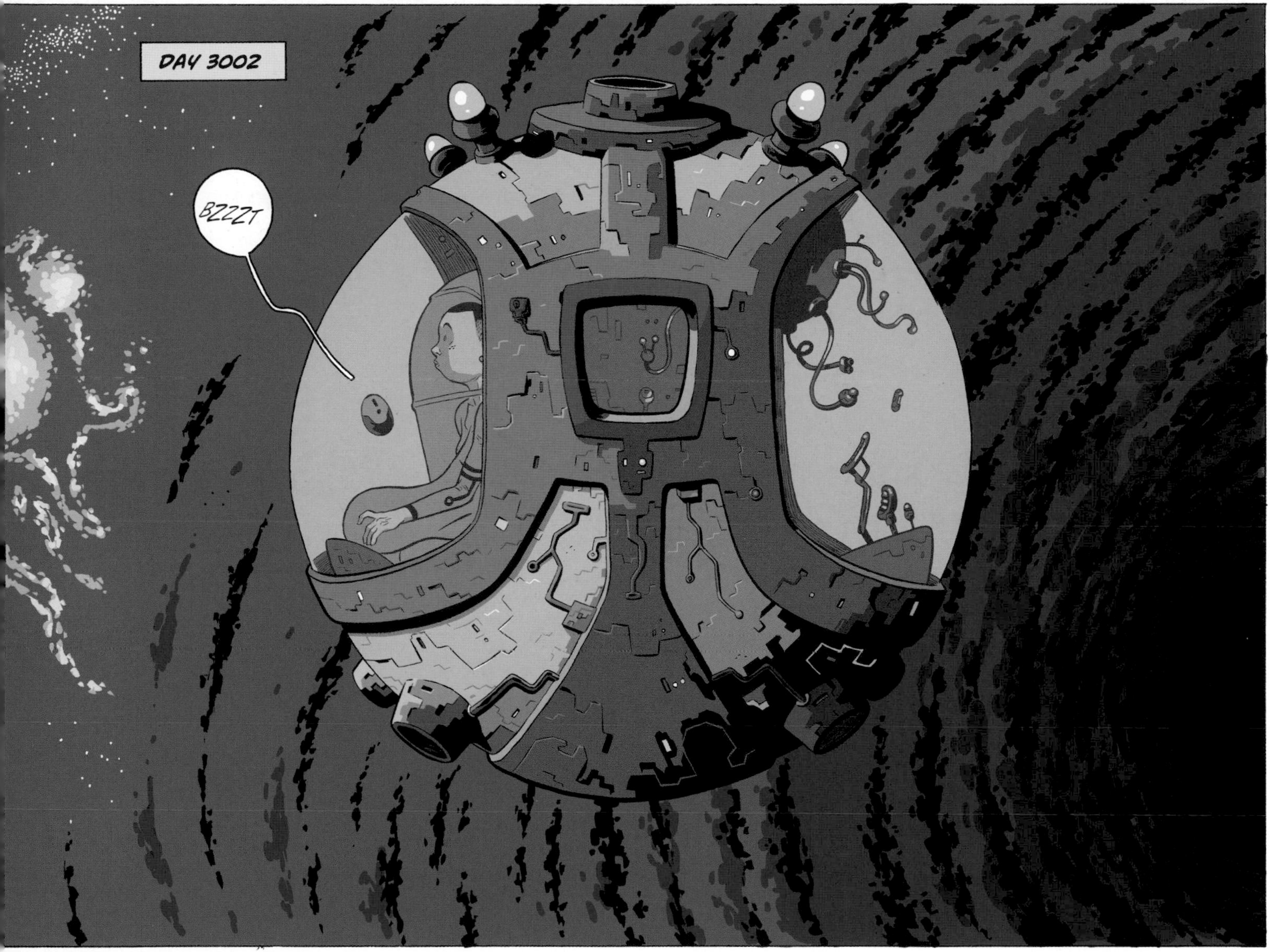
DAY 3002
BZZZT

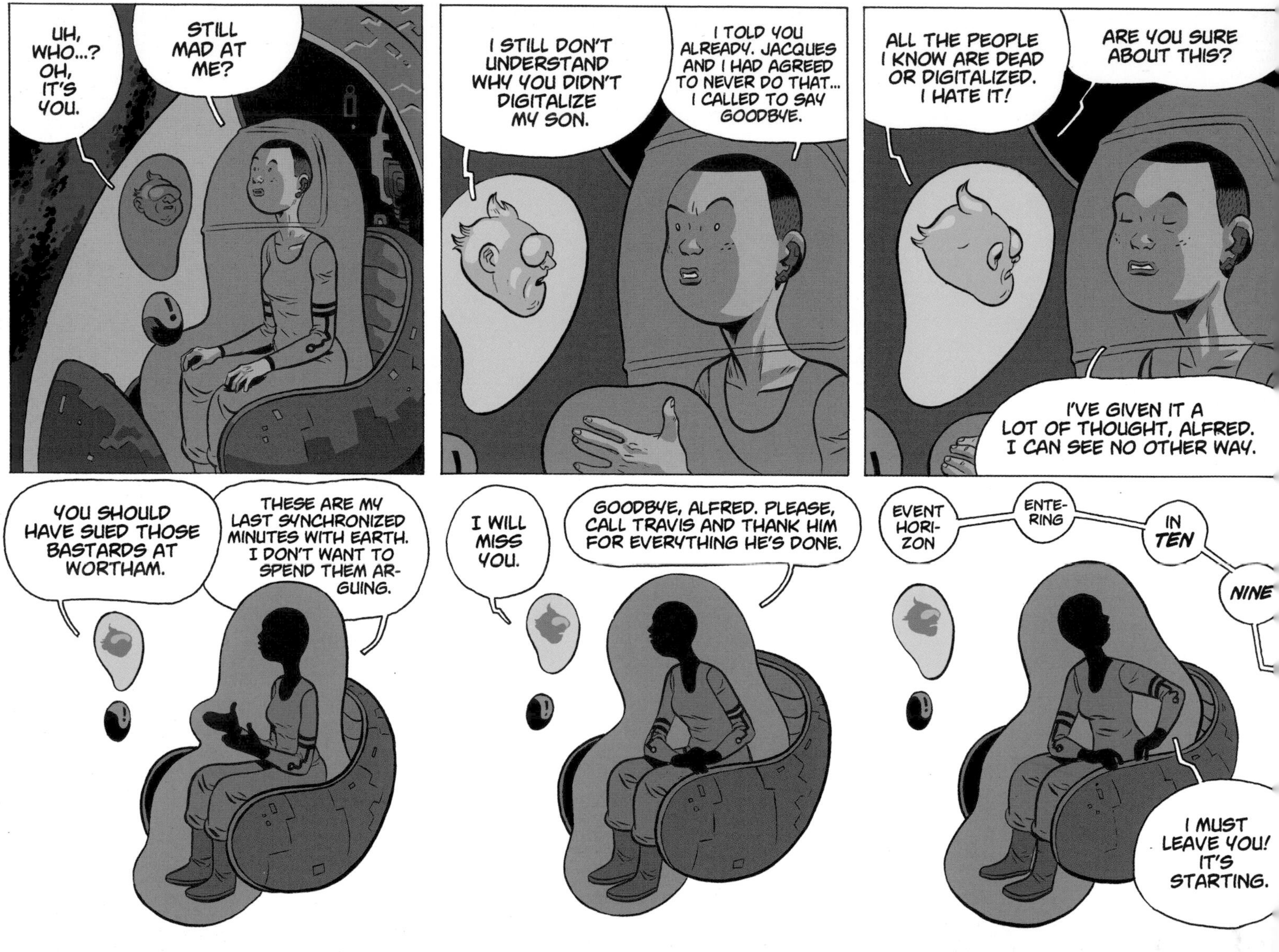
UH, WHO...? OH, IT'S YOU.
STILL MAD AT ME?
I STILL DON'T UNDERSTAND WHY YOU DIDN'T DIGITALIZE MY SON.
I TOLD YOU ALREADY. JACQUES AND I HAD AGREED TO NEVER DO THAT... I CALLED TO SAY GOODBYE.
ALL THE PEOPLE I KNOW ARE DEAD OR DIGITALIZED. I HATE IT!
ARE YOU SURE ABOUT THIS?
I'VE GIVEN IT A LOT OF THOUGHT, ALFRED. I CAN SEE NO OTHER WAY.
YOU SHOULD HAVE SUED THOSE BASTARDS AT WORTHAM.
THESE ARE MY LAST SYNCHRONIZED MINUTES WITH EARTH. I DON'T WANT TO SPEND THEM ARGUING.
I WILL MISS YOU.
GOODBYE, ALFRED. PLEASE, CALL TRAVIS AND THANK HIM FOR EVERYTHING HE'S DONE.
EVENT HORIZON
ENTERING
IN *TEN*
NINE
I MUST LEAVE YOU! IT'S STARTING.

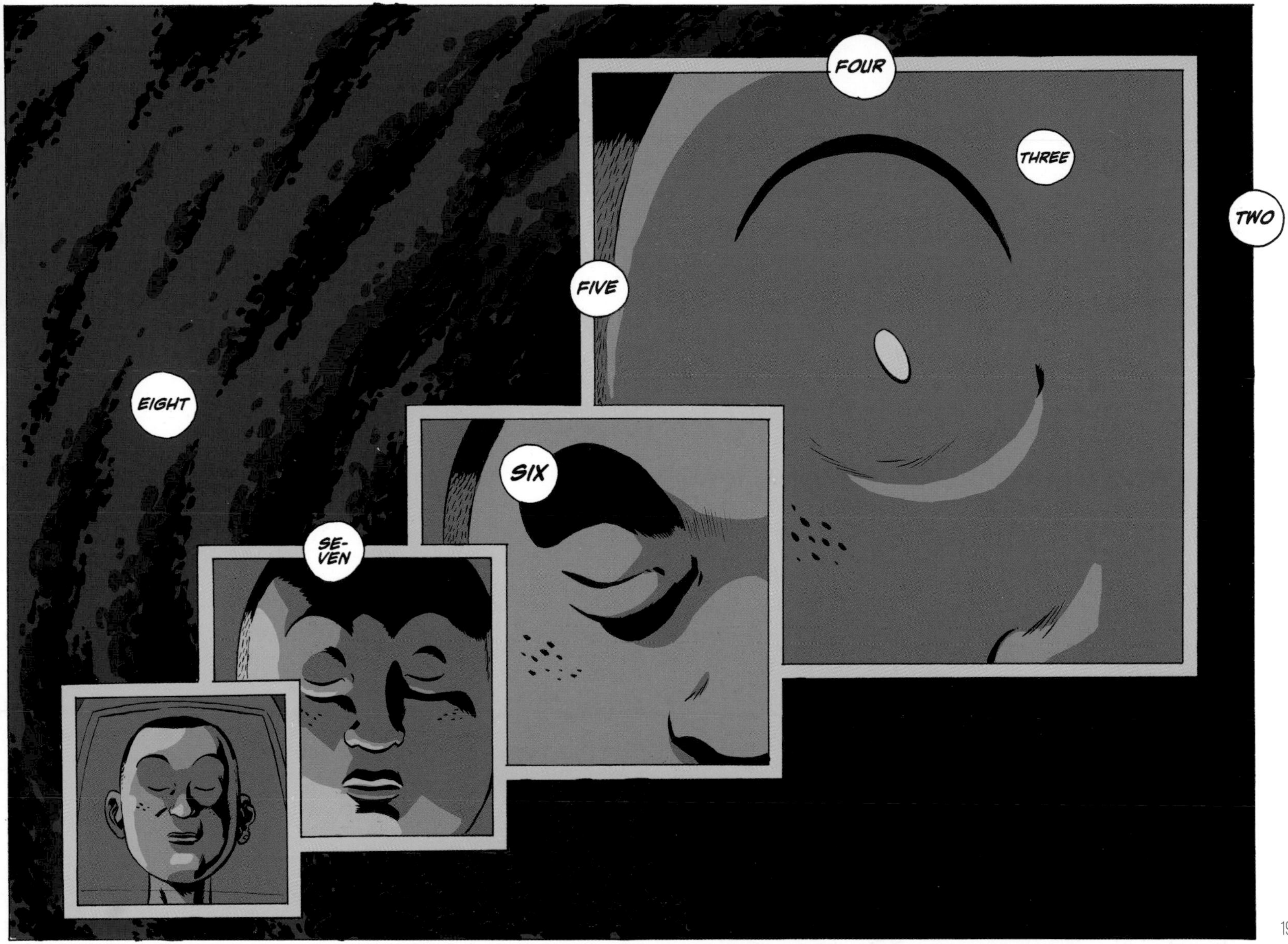
TWO
THREE
FOUR
FIVE
SIX
SE-
VEN
EIGHT

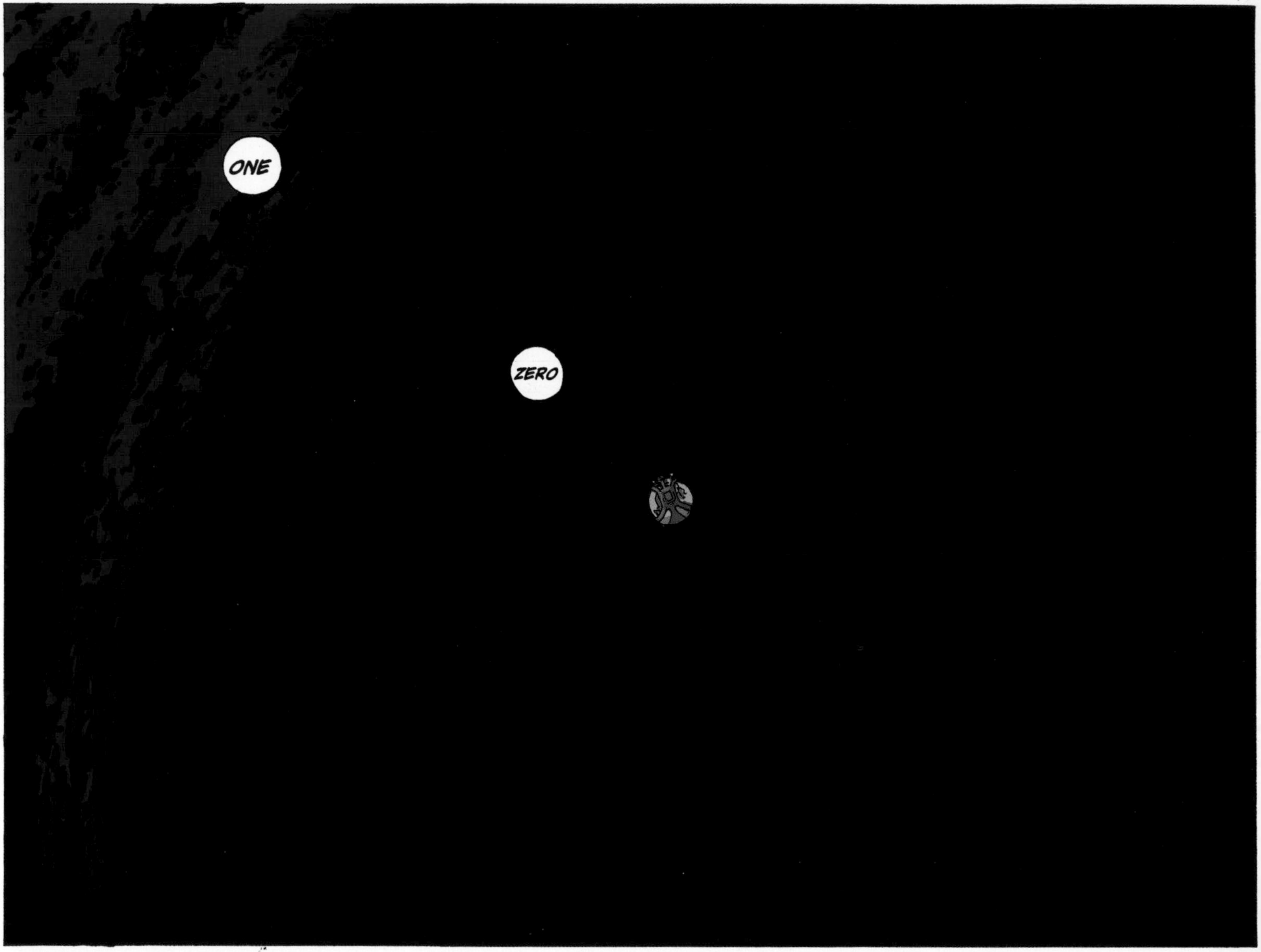
ONE
ZERO

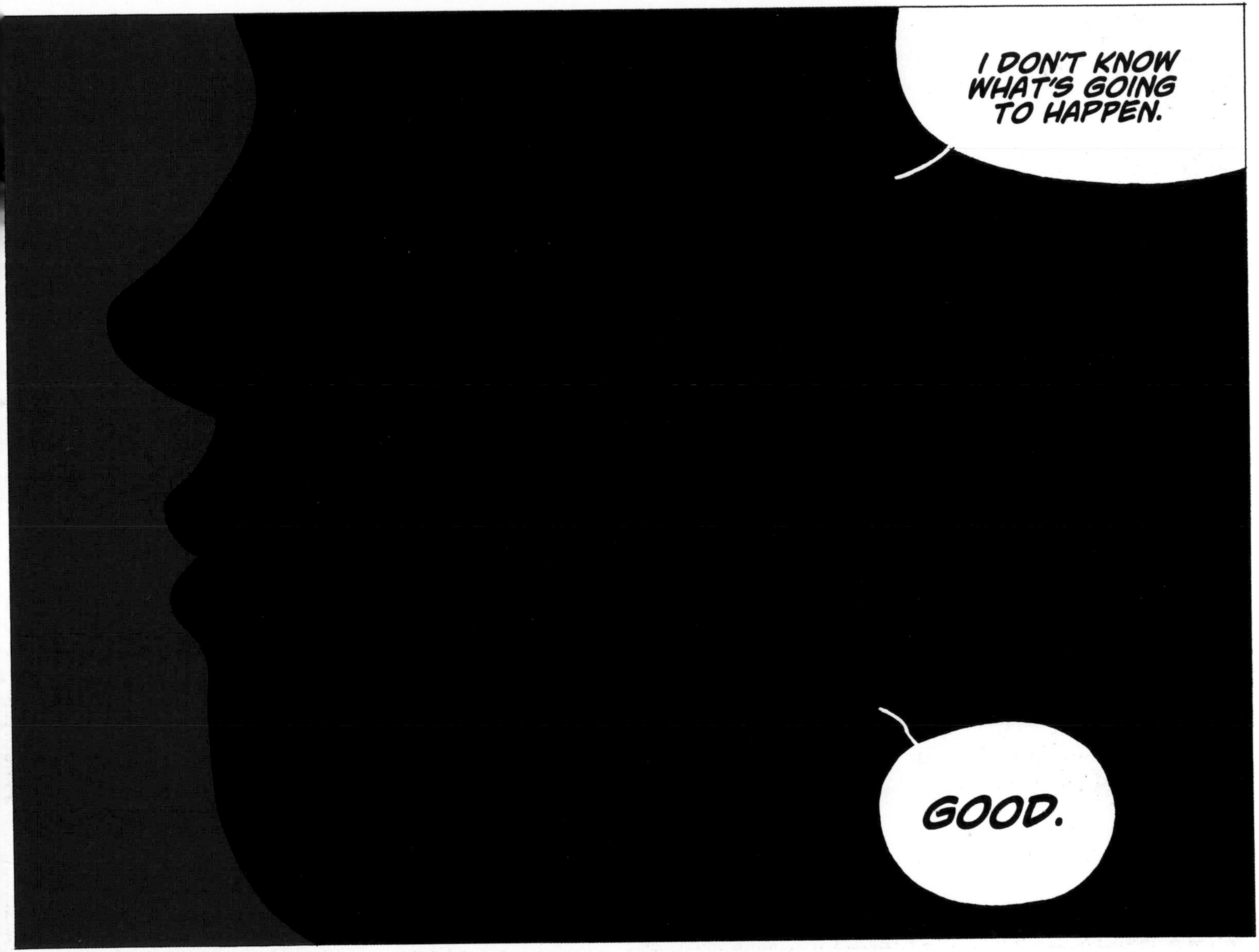
I DON'T KNOW WHAT'S GOING TO HAPPEN.
GOOD.

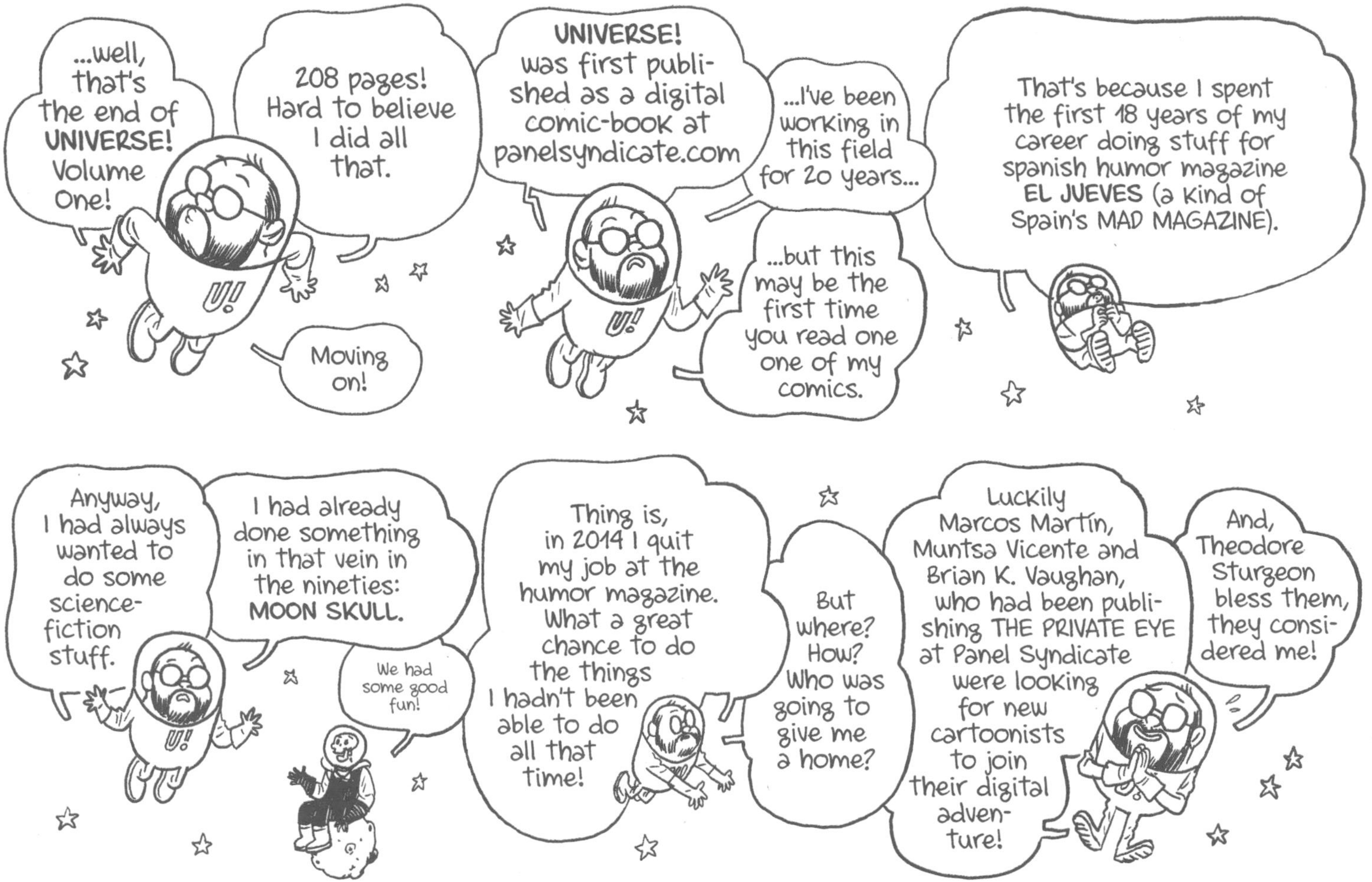
...well, that's the end of **UNIVERSE!** Volume One!
208 pages! Hard to believe I did all that.
Moving on!
UNIVERSE! was first published as a digital comic-book at panelsyndicate.com
...I've been working in this field for 20 years...
...but this may be the first time you read one one of my comics.
That's because I spent the first 18 years of my career doing stuff for spanish humor magazine **EL JUEVES** (a kind of Spain's MAD MAGAZINE).
Anyway, I had always wanted to do some science-fiction stuff.
I had already done something in that vein in the nineties: **MOON SKULL.**
We had some good fun!
Thing is, in 2014 I quit my job at the humor magazine. What a great chance to do the things I hadn't been able to do all that time!
But where? How? Who was going to give me a home?
Luckily Marcos Martín, Muntsa Vicente and Brian K. Vaughan, who had been publishing THE PRIVATE EYE at Panel Syndicate were looking for new cartoonists to join their digital adventure!
And, Theodore Sturgeon bless them, they considered me!

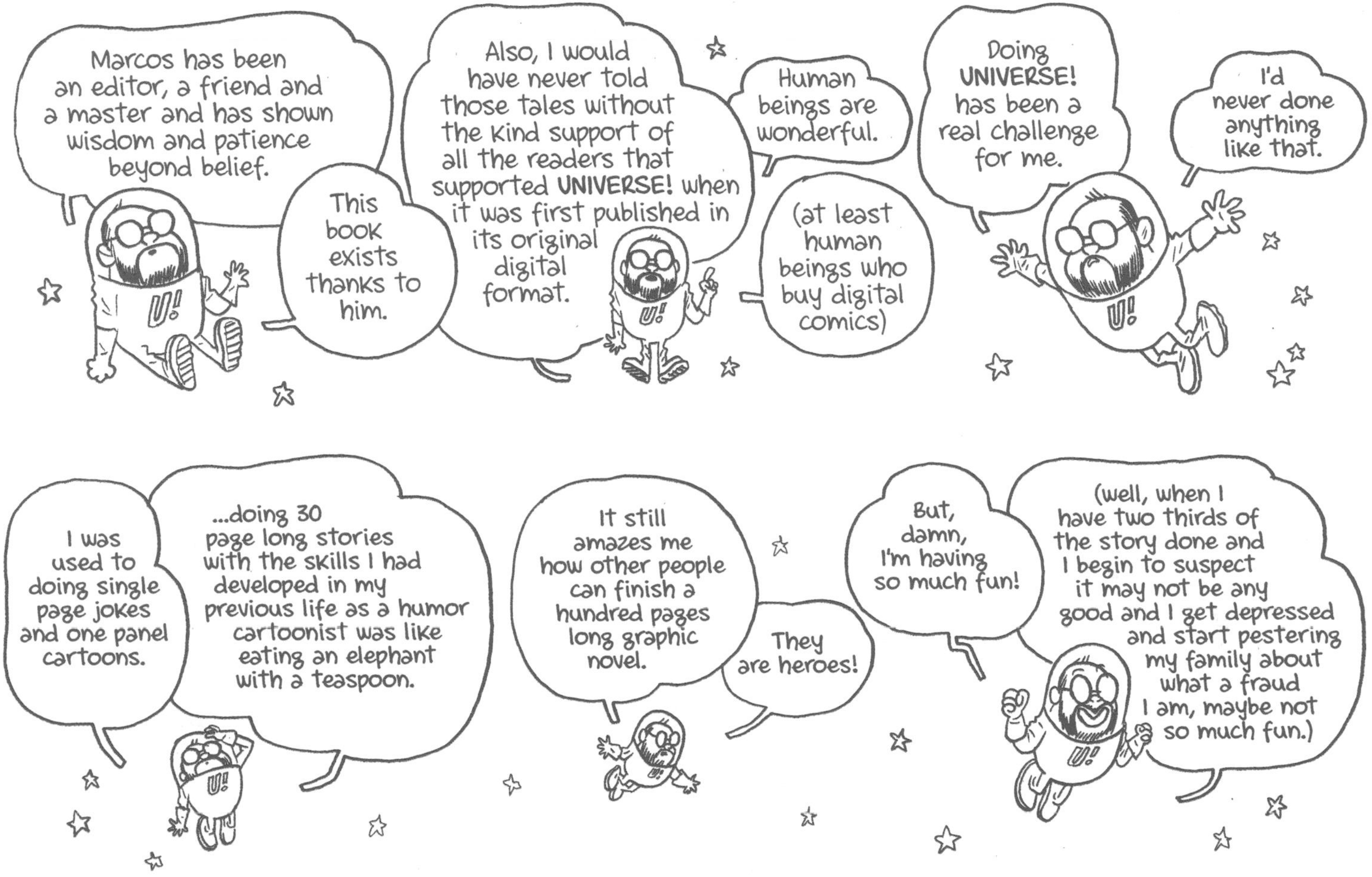
Marcos has been an editor, a friend and a master and has shown wisdom and patience beyond belief.
This book exists thanks to him.
Also, I would have never told those tales without the kind support of all the readers that supported UNIVERSE! when it was first published in its original digital format.
Human beings are wonderful.
(at least human beings who buy digital comics)
Doing UNIVERSE! has been a real challenge for me.
I'd never done anything like that.
I was used to doing single page jokes and one panel cartoons.
...doing 30 page long stories with the skills I had developed in my previous life as a humor cartoonist was like eating an elephant with a teaspoon.
It still amazes me how other people can finish a hundred pages long graphic novel.
They are heroes!
But, damn, I'm having so much fun!
(well, when I have two thirds of the story done and I begin to suspect it may not be any good and I get depressed and start pestering my family about what a fraud I am, maybe not so much fun.)

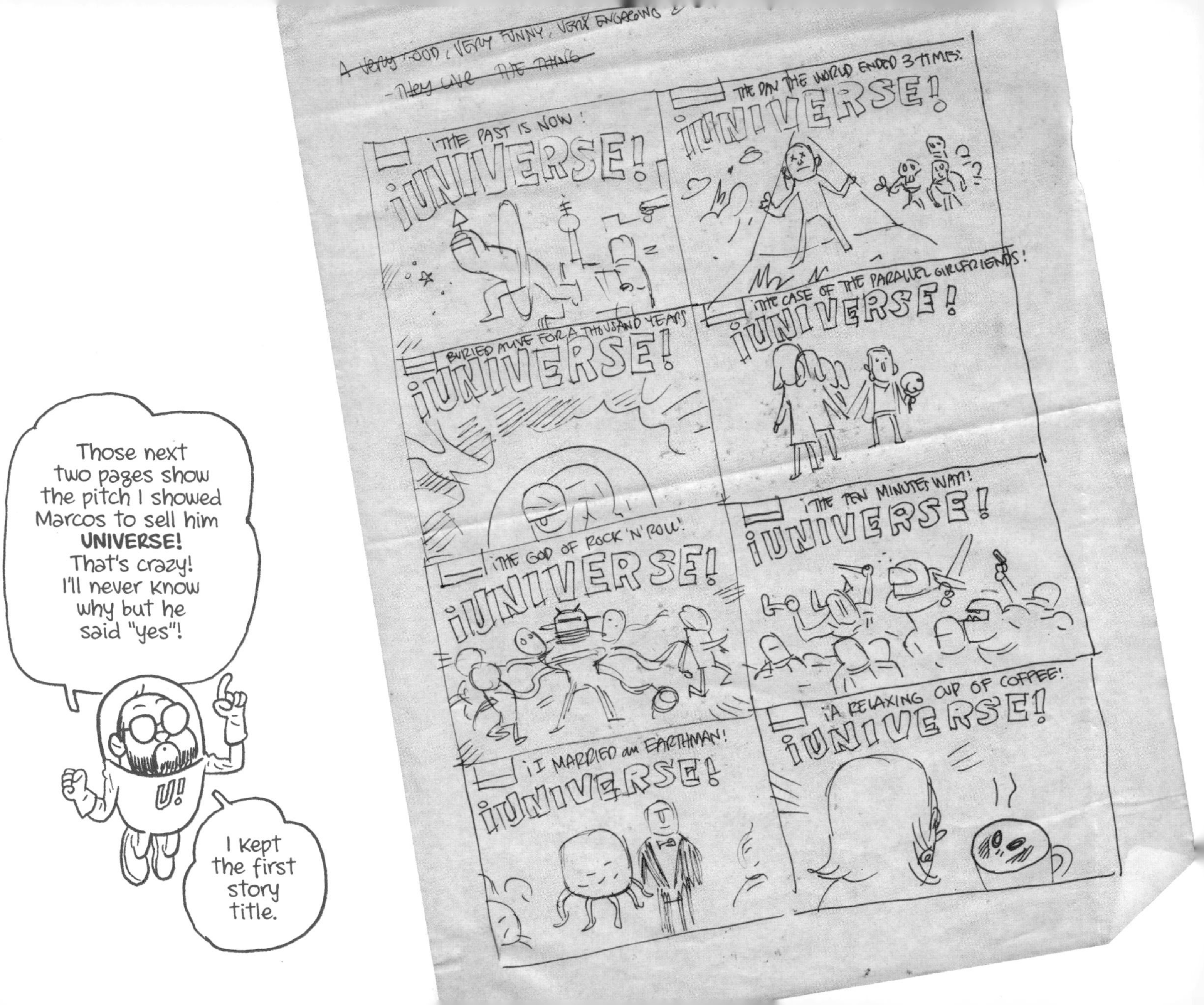
Those next two pages show the pitch I showed Marcos to sell him **UNIVERSE!** That's crazy! I'll never know why but he said "yes"!
I kept the first story title.
U!
A VERY GOOD, VERY FUNNY, VERY ENGAGING &
-They Live The Thing
¡THE PAST IS NOW!
¡UNIVERSE!
THE DAY THE WORLD ENDED 3 TIMES!
¡UNIVERSE!
BURIED ALIVE FOR A THOUSAND YEARS
¡UNIVERSE!
¡THE CASE OF THE PARALLEL GIRLFRIENDS!
¡UNIVERSE!
¡THE GOD OF ROCK 'N' ROLL!
¡UNIVERSE!
¡THE TEN MINUTES WAR!
¡UNIVERSE!
¡I MARRIED an EARTHMAN!
¡UNIVERSE!
¡A RELAXING CUP OF COFFEE!
¡UNIVERSE!

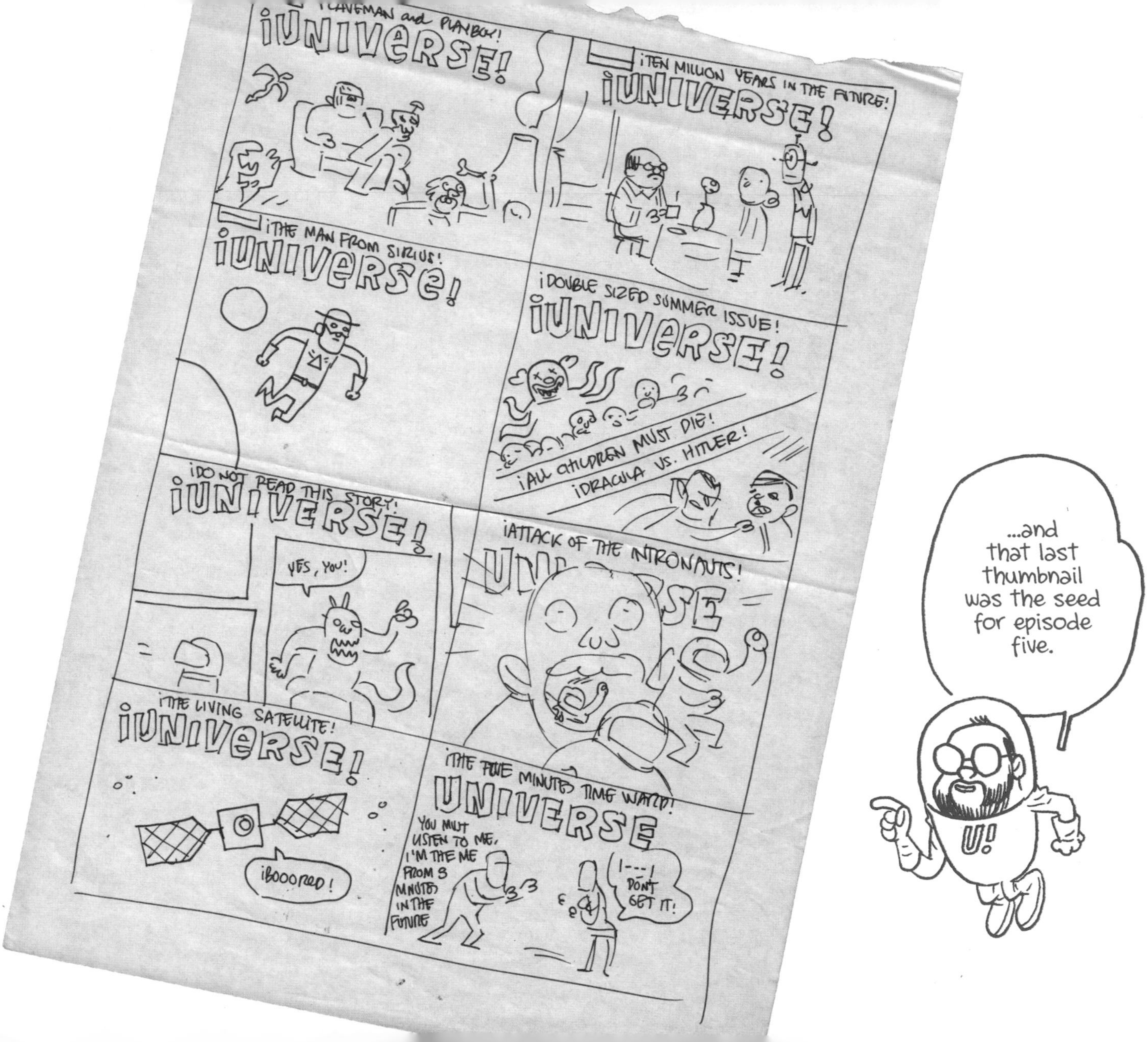
CAVEMAN and PLAYBOY!
¡UNIVERSE!
¡TEN MILLION YEARS IN THE FUTURE!
¡UNIVERSE!
¡THE MAN FROM SIRIUS!
¡UNIVERSE!
¡DOUBLE SIZED SUMMER ISSUE!
¡UNIVERSE!
¡ALL CHILDREN MUST DIE!
¡DRACULA VS. HITLER!
¡DO NOT READ THIS STORY!
¡UNIVERSE!
YES, YOU!
¡ATTACK OF THE INTRONAUTS!
¡THE LIVING SATELLITE!
¡UNIVERSE!
¡BOOORED!
¡THE FIVE MINUTES TIME WARP!
UNIVERSE
YOU MUST LISTEN TO ME, I'M THE ME FROM 5 MINUTES IN THE FUTURE
I--- I DON'T GET IT!
...and that last thumbnail was the seed for episode five.
U!

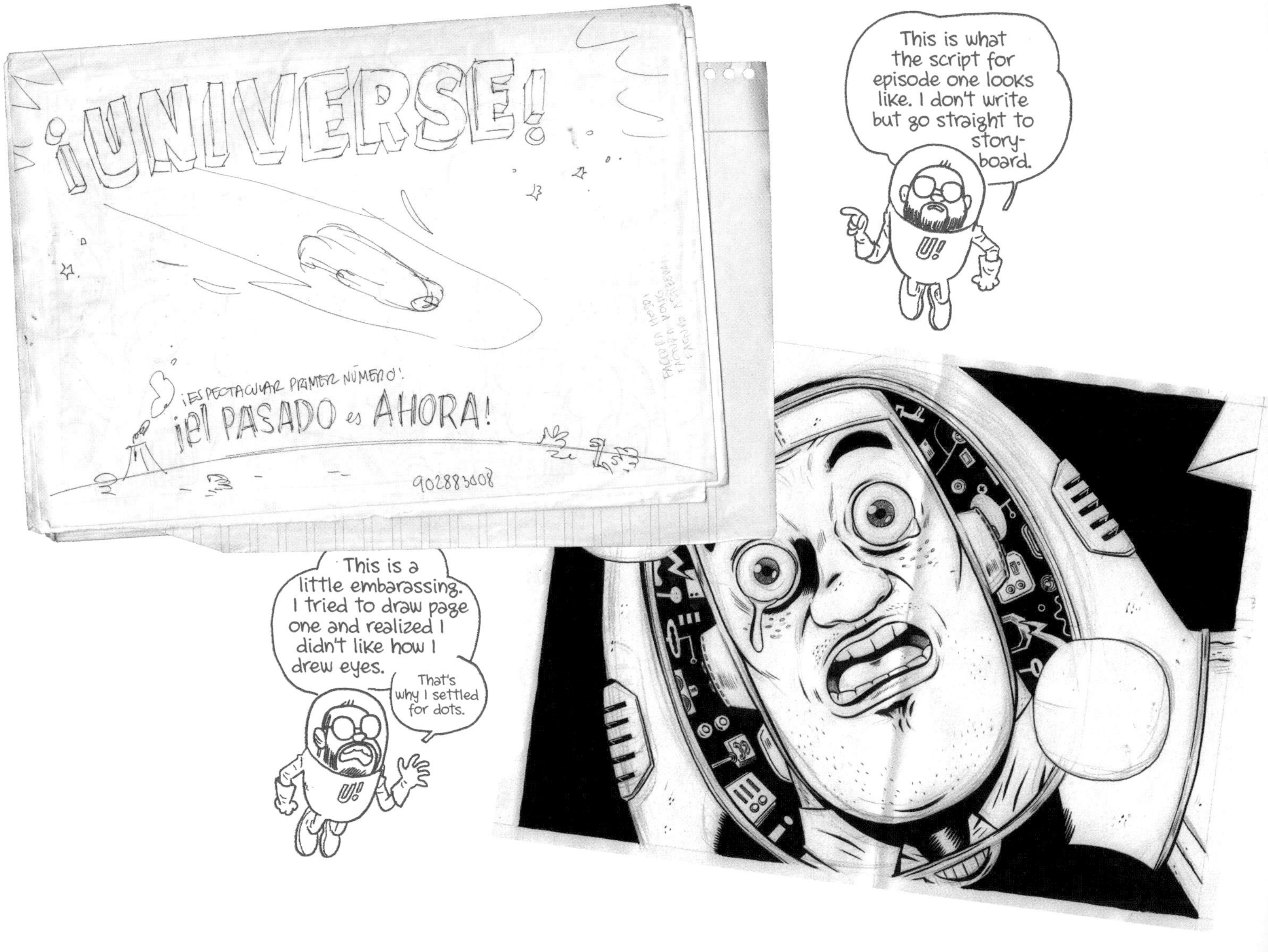

¡UNIVERSE!
¡ESPECTACULAR PRIMER NÚMERO!
¡El PASADO es AHORA!
902883008
This is what the script for episode one looks like. I don't write but go straight to story-board.
U!
This is a little embarassing. I tried to draw page one and realized I didn't like how I drew eyes.
That's why I settled for dots.
U!

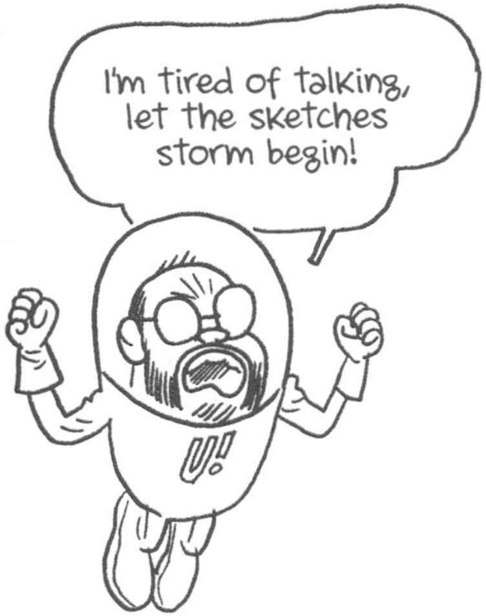
I'm tired of talking, let the sketches storm begin!

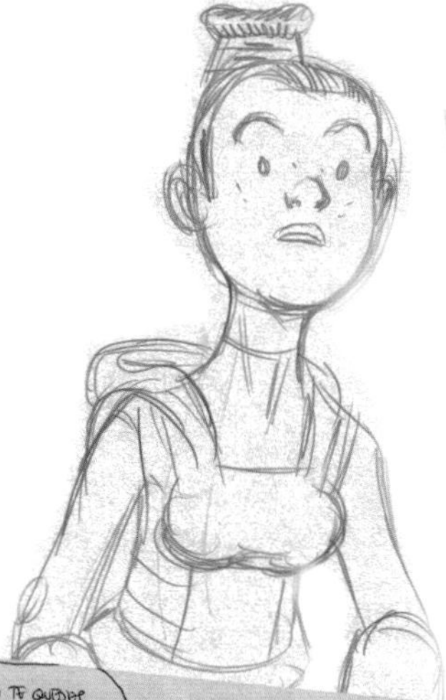

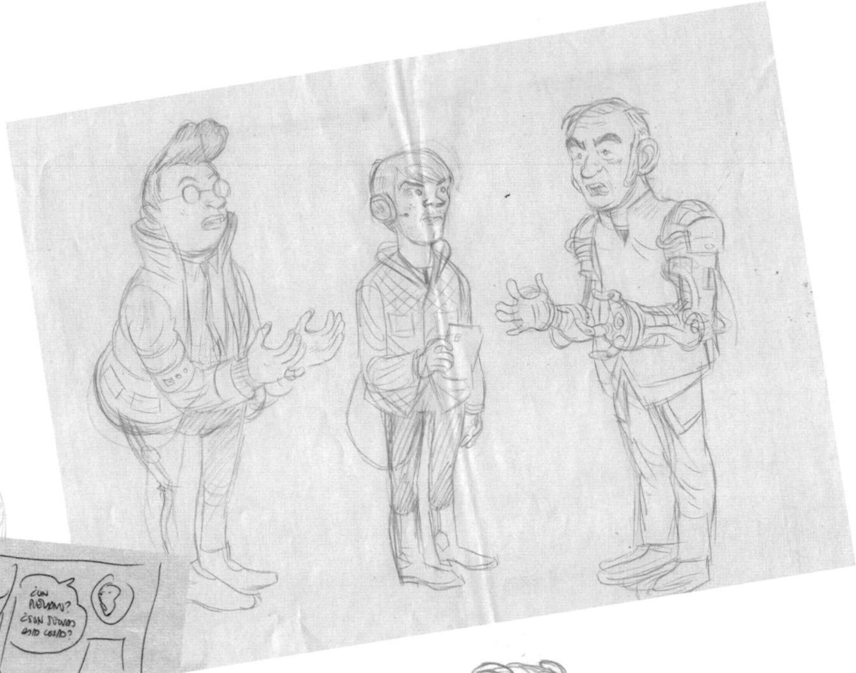

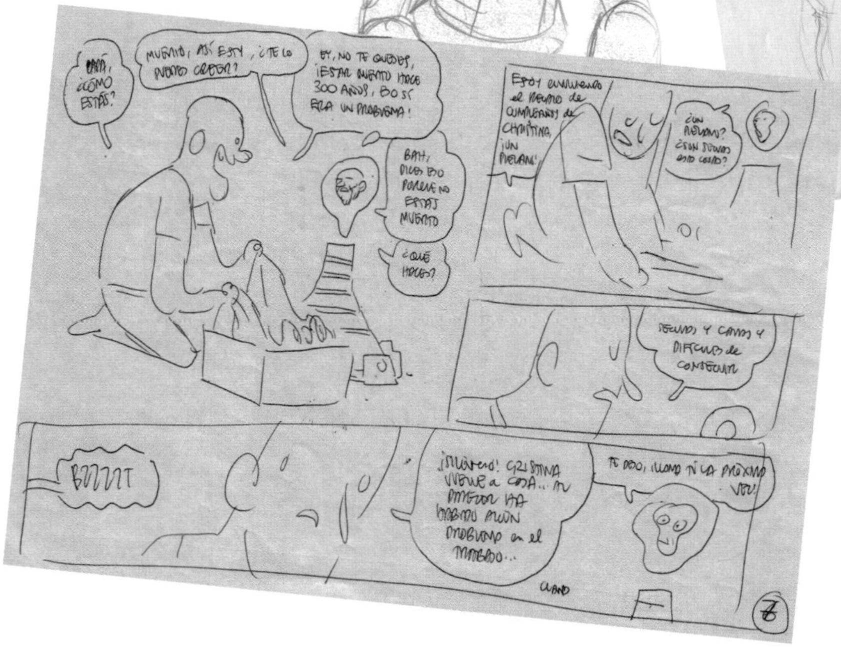

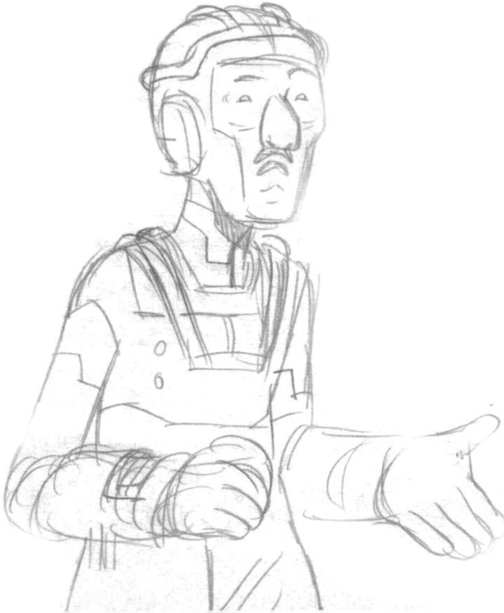

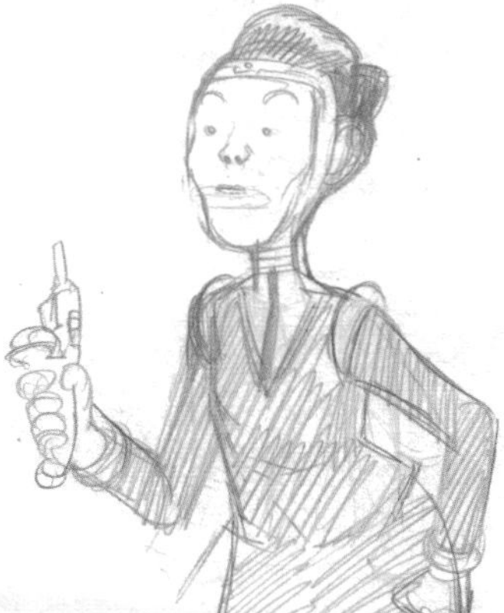

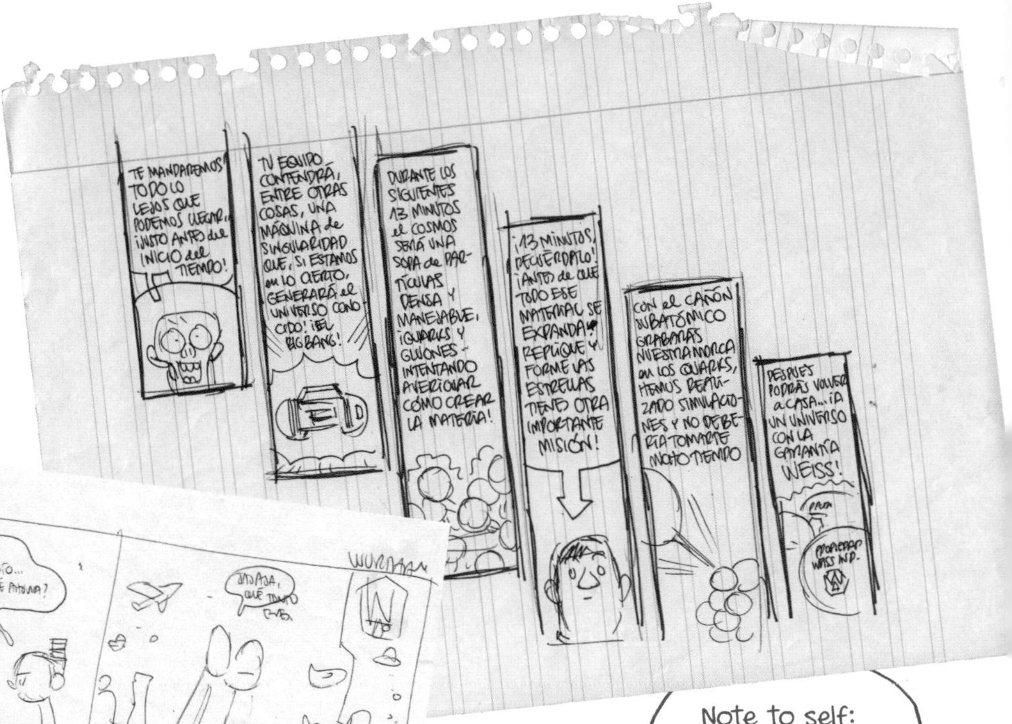
TE MANDAREMOS TODO LO LEJOS QUE PODEMOS LLEGAR, ¡JUSTO ANTES DEL INICIO DEL TIEMPO!
TU EQUIPO CONTENDRÁ, ENTRE OTRAS COSAS, UNA MÁQUINA DE SINGULARIDAD QUE, SI ESTAMOS EN LO CIERTO, GENERARÁ EL UNIVERSO CONOCIDO! ¡EL BIG BANG!
DURANTE LOS SIGUIENTES 13 MINUTOS EL COSMOS SERÁ UNA SOPA DE PARTÍCULAS DENSA Y MANEJABLE, ¡QUARKS Y GLUONES INTENTANDO AVERIGUAR CÓMO CREAR LA MATERIA!
¡13 MINUTOS, RECUÉRDALO! ¡ANTES DE QUE TODO ESE MATERIAL SE EXPANDA, REPLIQUE Y FORME LAS ESTRELLAS TIENES OTRA IMPORTANTE MISIÓN!
CON EL CAÑÓN SUBATÓMICO GRABARÁS NUESTRA MARCA EN LOS QUARKS, HEMOS REPLICADO SIMULACIONES Y NO DEBERÍA TOMARTE MUCHO TIEMPO
DESPUÉS PODRÁS VOLVER A CASA... ¡A UN UNIVERSO CON LA GARANTÍA WEISS!
PROPIEDAD WEISS IND.

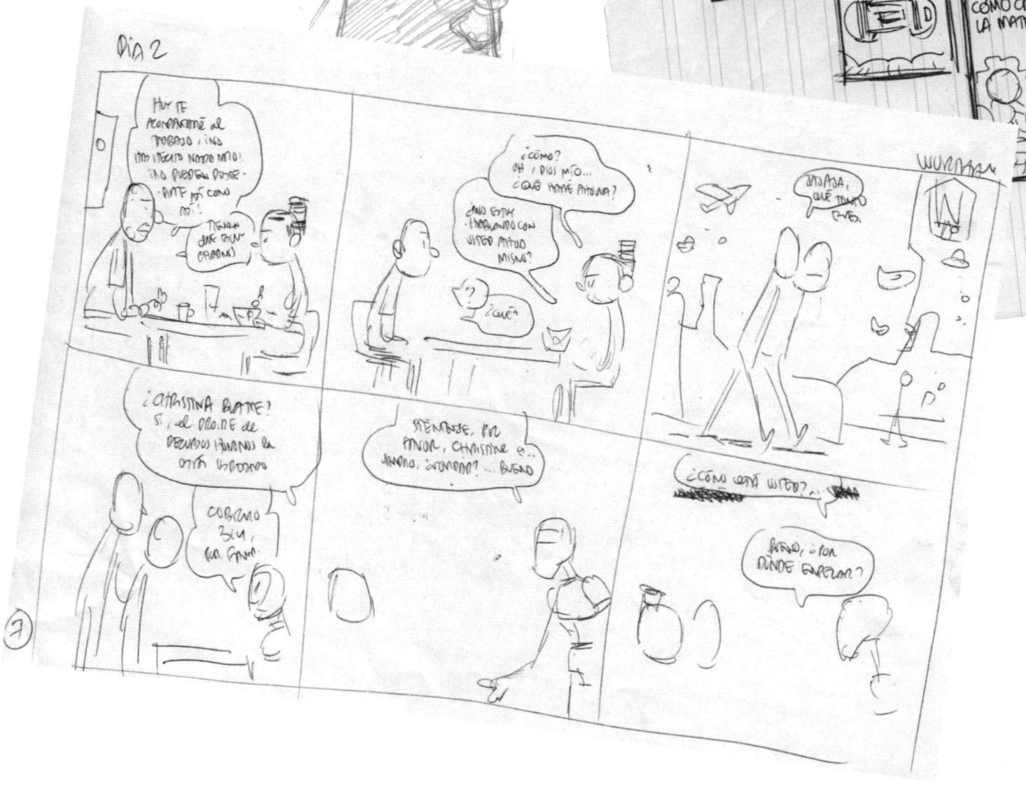
Día 2

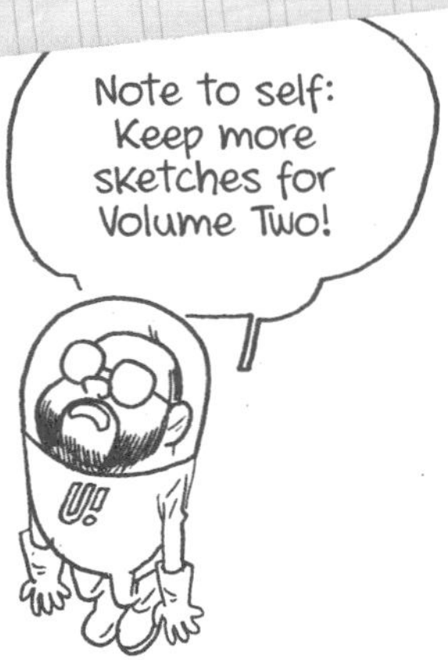
Note to self: Keep more sketches for Volume Two!

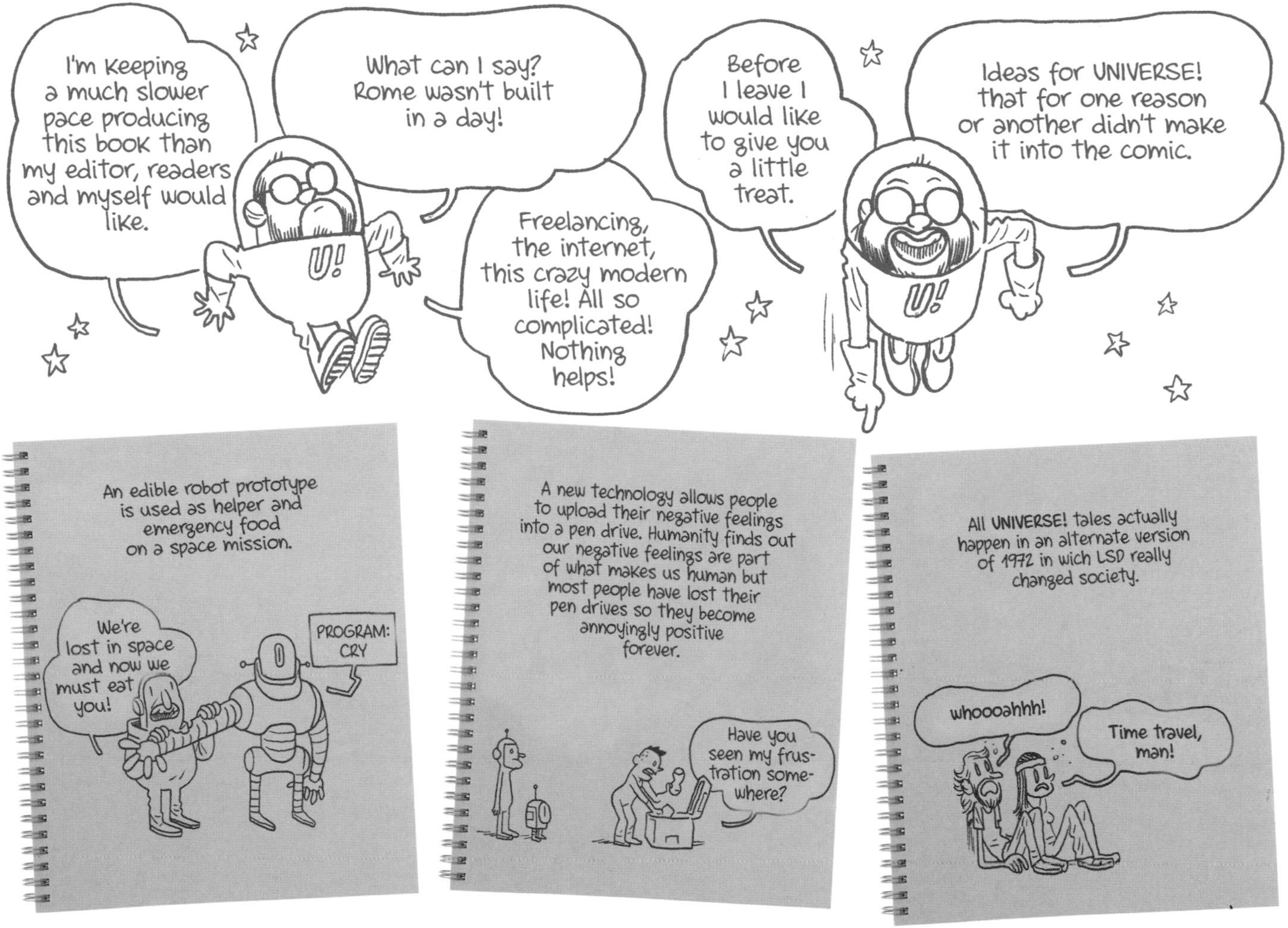
I'm keeping a much slower pace producing this book than my editor, readers and myself would like.
What can I say? Rome wasn't built in a day!
Freelancing, the internet, this crazy modern life! All so complicated! Nothing helps!
Before I leave I would like to give you a little treat.
Ideas for UNIVERSE! that for one reason or another didn't make it into the comic.
An edible robot prototype is used as helper and emergency food on a space mission.
We're lost in space and now we must eat you!
PROGRAM: CRY
A new technology allows people to upload their negative feelings into a pen drive. Humanity finds out our negative feelings are part of what makes us human but most people have lost their pen drives so they become annoyingly positive forever.
Have you seen my frustration somewhere?
All UNIVERSE! tales actually happen in an alternate version of 1972 in wich LSD really changed society.
whoooahhh!
Time travel, man!

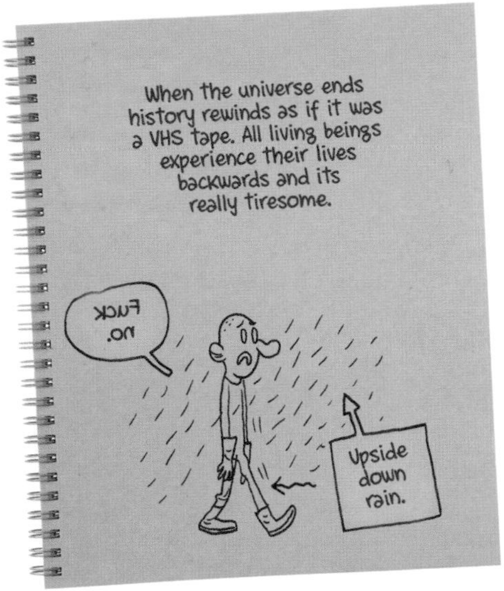
When the universe ends history rewinds as if it was a VHS tape. All living beings experience their lives backwards and its really tiresome.
Fuck no.
Upside down rain.

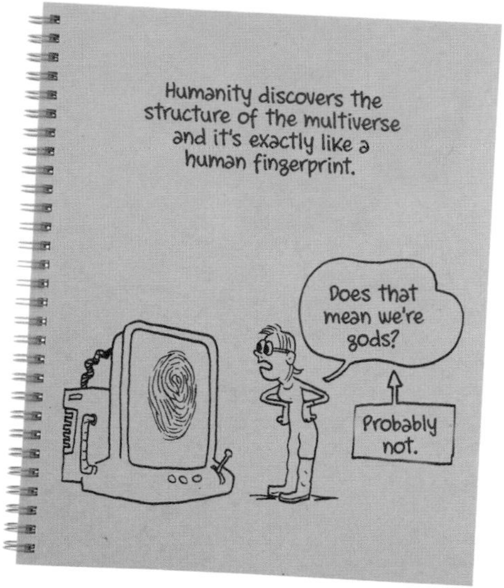
Humanity discovers the structure of the multiverse and it's exactly like a human fingerprint.
Does that mean we're gods?
Probably not.

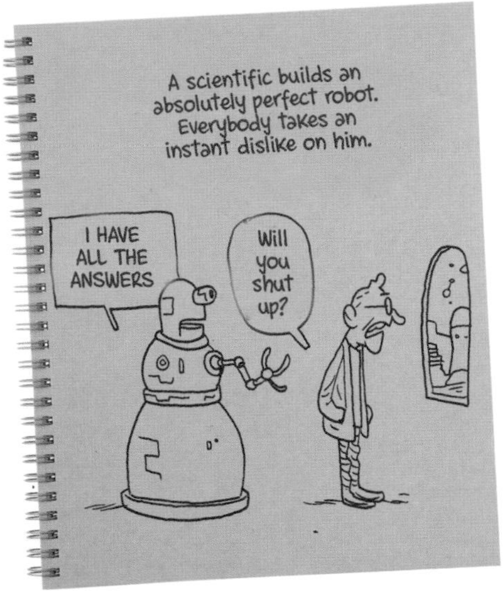
A scientific builds an absolutely perfect robot. Everybody takes an instant dislike on him.
I HAVE ALL THE ANSWERS
Will you shut up?

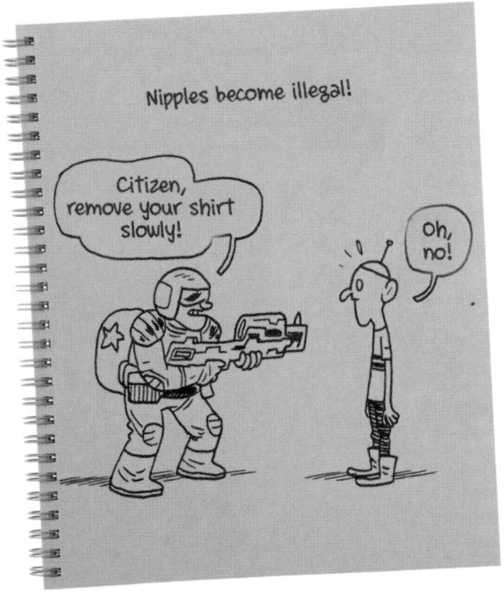
Nipples become illegal!
Citizen, remove your shirt slowly!
Oh, no!

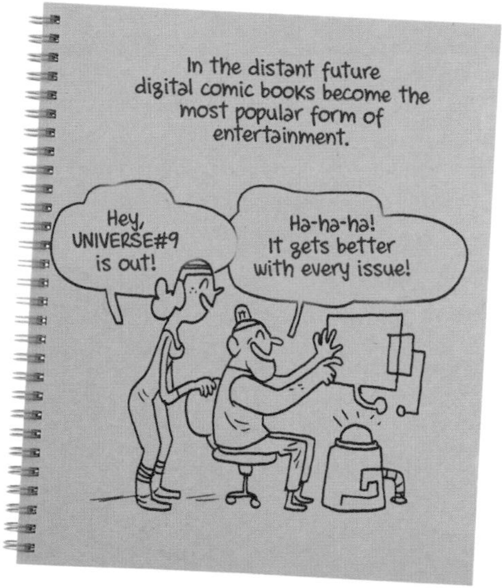
In the distant future digital comic books become the most popular form of entertainment.
Hey, UNIVERSE#9 is out!
Ha-ha-ha! It gets better with every issue!